Underneath

A Merfolk Tale

M. N. Arzú

Cover design by M.N. Arzú.

Published by M.N Arzú, Guatemala, 2016
http://www.mnarzuauthor.com/

Dedicated to…

Mom, who has always believed in the depths of my imagination.

And Erick, for navigating the crazy ideas I bring to him with all the enthusiasm in the world.

*"The pure and simple truth
is rarely pure and never simple"*

Oscar Wilde

1

What the Tide Brought In

Daybreak usually found Neil Thompson walking down the shore.

At this early hour, the deserted Maine beach was his and his alone. At fifty-two, few were the pleasures left to him from childhood, and fewer still the moments he got to enjoy them.

He loved this part of the beach, his own private sanctuary. Thoughts formed and vanished with the surf, a rare quiet downtime on an otherwise busy life. He breathed deeply and walked slowly. Further down the beach, the waves were washing against something large, but the dim early light and seaweed distorted its form. Frowning, Neil wondered if the sea would reclaim it, or if he would find trash polluting his little piece of heaven.

Wind beat on the back of his neck, and he tucked his hands into the pockets of his jeans. He kept walking, leaving footprints that quickly washed away while taking his time to reach the mystery item so generously delivered to his feet.

His heart slammed in his chest.

He was looking at a dead body. Frozen to the spot, he could only stare. Wave after wave crested over the white chest and dark trousers of a male corpse, and all he could think about was how much he truly wished the sea would claim it back.

Neil held onto his breath, trying—and failing—to look away. His stomach felt tight and heavy, his mind navigating some strange mix of morbid curiosity and utter disgust.

A large wave crashed in beside him, drawing him from his thoughts and reminding him that the tide forgave nothing on these ever-changing shores.

A full minute passed, then Neil resigned himself to the grisly duty of dragging the dead man from the ocean's grasp. He would need to call in the authorities on what was becoming anything but a normal day. Quickly, he dialed the number and waited, impatient.

Holding his phone in one hand, he reached for the man's shoulder with the other. Movement met his touch, and he jerked his hand back in shock. Life still clung to this body. The man was still breathing.

"9-1-1, what's your emergency?"

The voice caught him off-guard, and he almost dropped the phone.

"Sir? What's your emergency?"

"Yes! Hello? I'm Neil Thompson, I'm at the beach. I've just found a man here. He was brought in by the tide. I think he's still breathing, but I—I don't know what—" ... *to do.*

The words stuck in his throat.

He'd honestly thought those were trousers. Through the dark seaweed, 100 shades of blue glinted off each scale as the sun rose in the early hour, the sea no longer able to disguise what Neil had ignored before: a tail.

Longer than legs would have been, the tail rolled lazily with the tide, somehow at an odd angle. Instinctively, he took two steps back, almost losing his balance.

Every fiber of his being screamed for him to turn around and *run*, but he was trapped in his *fight or flight* instinct. Gentle waves reached them again and again, as Neil struggled to breathe. Where knees should have been, a deep gash ran horizontally, torn flesh and scales the testimony of some gruesome accident.

Closing his eyes, Neil swallowed bile.

In his ear, the dispatcher kept asking questions, though God only knew about what. He wished yet again that the sea would take back what it had brought in.

"Mr. Thompson, paramedics are on their way, but we need an exact location."

Hysterically, he looked around, a tiny part of his mind deciding this must be a prank. Somewhere, nearby, cameras were recording his reaction and one day soon he would watch this on reality television, laughing at his gullible self. And yet, no matter where he looked, or how much he wished it wasn't, the beach was deserted.

This is real. God, this is real!

"Mr. Thompson? Can you hear me?"

Neil looked down at the man who wasn't a man, coming to grips with myths having crossed into reality, and no one but him was witnessing this bizarre life twist.

"Mr. Thompson!"

10

"Yes!" He snapped out of it. It didn't matter if this was the strangest day of *his* life, he could only guess the man in front of him was having his *worst*.

"I'm here," he reassured, giving his address and a good estimate of how far he'd walked from home. "I'm across from Cluney's, the store. I'll stand by to signal the ambulance; you won't miss me."

"Okay, Mr. Thompson, this is what I need you to do while help is on the way."

The operator listed off tasks: get him safe, check his breathing, check the man's responsiveness to touch. Maybe there was more. Maybe Neil only half understood what the woman was trying to tell him, but he insanely needed to correct his own early statement; *you're not coming to aid a man because there's no man here.*

She was asking too many questions, expecting him to do all kinds of things.

Placing the phone in his shirt pocket on speaker, he mentally went through the instructions from the dispatcher. Finally, taking a deep breath, he fixed his eyes on the lifeless face. Bruises were emerging, starting to turn purple alongside the right temple, the product of one hell of a collision. Neil had to see if he could get a response.

"Hey," Neil whispered, his voice deserting him.

"Hey," he tried again, this time slightly louder. "Well, crap, I don't know what I'm doing." Shutting his eyes tightly, he took a moment to gain control of his racing heart before positioning himself above the head. With trembling hands, he reached beneath the ice-cold armpits.

"Okay, here's the deal. I'll move you out of the sea, and you don't bite me, okay?"

The man was heavy, and with some considerable effort, Neil dragged him free of the water. Part of Neil expected the tail to turn into legs. Part of him expected those eyes to pop open and sharp teeth to gnash at him.

None of that happened.

He took out his phone and returned to the dispatcher. Drowning people swallowed a lot of water, she informed him. Neil had to move his unconscious victim onto his side in case he vomited.

Neil stared at the tail on his victim and almost laughed. This *man* was surely the furthest thing from drowning that one could get. In fact, maybe he should push him right back into the sea.

"Mr. Thompson, do you understand?"

"Yes," he said, absently nodding.

What he understood was, he'd just found a mermaid—mer*man*—yet no one would ever believe something so fantastic could happen to someone so mundane. Turning to look down the road, he strained to hear the ambulance sirens, but all he heard was the sea. He still had time.

Hanging up, he deftly turned his phone camera on and began gathering proof. No one would *ever* be allowed to doubt what he'd just seen.

* * *

To the untrained eye, the hospital Emergency Room was nothing more than a chaotic arrangement of wailing patients, along with doctors and nurses shouting at each other, working their shifts on caffeine alone.

Well, that last part is true, Gwen Gaston thought, the last drops of her coffee still tasting like heaven. She'd been crazy for a fourth cup of liquid energy since two patients ago. From her vantage point on the opposite corner of the ER entrance, Gwen watched gurneys and paramedics come and go, their patients delivered to the capable hands of her colleagues. Being the ER on-call surgeon guaranteed she never got bored, the main reason she'd applied for the position two years ago. She'd been missing the adrenaline from her early days as an emergency doctor, and the intricate puzzles and challenges each ambulance brought to her hands.

Her timer went off, the cue for getting back to work. She threw the empty paper cup into the nearest trashcan and rubbed her hands.

She was overweight and out of shape, and knew she didn't look like the ideal surgeon to handle the turmoil of the ER; half her diet comprised an unhealthy dose of soda and chips to compensate for too-long hours at work, but damn, was she good at what she did. Most days, that included patching people up from the inside out, topped up with six cups of coffee and a good measure of yelling.

The speaker overhead chimed, and a man's voice called a code blue for the trauma room. Gwen's phone buzzed with a simultaneous alert: they needed her to start prepping for emergency surgery. She walked faster.

"Some idiot in a mermaid costume's half drowned down the beach," one of the paramedics told her. His partner looked anything but amused; the guy looked downright scared.

"Okay, he's stabilizing. Can someone get that tail out of the way?" Dr. Bill Shore ordered, sounding calm and collected despite such an odd request.

Gwen entered the trauma room, the smell of the ocean hitting her before she could even look closely at the man. She'd been expecting a half-assed costume made of cheap plastic in pinks and yellows, adorned with shiny fake gems to complete the look. What she wasn't expecting was how real the disguise looked. It was decorated with hundreds of tiny bright scales, complete with thin lateral fins torn everywhere. The length of the tail reached to the floor where people narrowly missed it with their shoes.

"What did you page me for?" she asked, shaking her head at the crazy things she had to put up with. This close, she could see small clusters of scales framed the youthful face and parts of his shoulders, that then disappeared down his back. His ears were pointy, his skin almost translucent.

"We've been having a hard time with his vitals, and I could really use your help figuring out where he's bleeding. We can't seem to keep his blood pressure up."

Gwen's fingers expertly palpated the abdomen, looking for the elusive internal injury. Intrigued at what she felt, she listened with the stethoscope, the bank of monitors keeping pace with his shallow heartbeat and barely-there breathing. Bruises adorned the right side of their patient's head, and she would bet good money his right wrist was broken.

What the hell is this? Her face contorted.

She kept moving down, unable to identify the odd internal sounds. Something was off, she just couldn't put her finger on what it was.

"Someone page Neurology, please," Bill ordered. Jackie, the senior staff nurse, looked in.

"Are they filming something nearby?" she asked, touching the line where normal skin became the tail. "This costume's definitely professional. I can't find where it comes off."

Still listening, Gwen's eyes fixated on the middle of the tail, where she could see sluggish blood pooling onto the gurney. That gash was bleeding real blood.

Bingo!

"It might be painted on the skin," Gwen explained. She stopped listening, seeking where real muscle became part of the disguise. Her hands methodically felt beside and beneath the tail's smoothness, imagining how two legs might fit inside the narrow outfit. Where knees should bend, there was an unexpected pulse. She looked up at Bill, who was busy checking the monitors.

"I need to see what's going on down here," she said, signaling the tail.

"Okay, on three!" Bill said, and they deftly moved their patient onto his side. The back was as meticulously decorated as the tail, the blue scales following the spine in a narrow line, all the way to the back of his neck. The deep gash ran from one side to the other, cutting through several layers of tissue.

"Let's clean this wound," Gwen ordered to their other nurse, Oscar. It unnerved her that she could be fooled by an elaborate Halloween costume. She pressed down on her newly discovered pulse point and saw the tail twitch further down. Blinking, she pressed again, sure she was imagining things.

It twitched again.

"We really need to get this thing off," she heard Bill saying, but he sounded so far away. "Gwen, how bad are his legs?"

"I can't find—" she said, sounding equally distant. The gash hypnotized her, forbidding her even to blink. Some forty percent of the tail had been cut deep, and her surgeon's brain automatically calculated the odds of keeping the limb or amputating it.

For the first time, Gwen saw that tail as part of a body.

"Gwen?"

"It's not a costume," she muttered, bewildered, but only Oscar turned to look. Everyone else kept going at it as if they were treating a human.

"What?" Bill asked, listening to the lungs with his stethoscope.

"It's not a costume," she repeated louder, turning to look at Bill with round eyes. "It's—it's real!"

Only Oscar understood, moving away immediately, his eyes becoming as large as her own.

"What are you talking about?" Bill asked, forgetting his stethoscope.

"The ta—tail is bleeding," she forced herself to explain. "There's a pulse, even a reflex. Bill, I can't find any legs in here."

This time, Jackie moved back. Frowning, Bill moved next to Gwen to take a closer look.

"X-rays," they said at the same time.

Hesitantly, Oscar helped her and Bill to place their patient onto his back. Two seconds later, they cleared the room to evade the momentary radiation.

"I'm sure this is perfectly logical," he told Gwen, looking through the door at the impressive tail that still touched the floor.

"Birth malformation?" she offered, equally locked on their patient's body. "With that length?"

14

"Someone's playing a prank on us," he muttered, entering the room once more. Behind them, only Oscar entered willingly.

"Or maybe he was playing a prank on someone else and it went horribly wrong," she reasoned, looking at the monitors. "You just can't fake these vitals."

By the door, Jackie made the sign of the cross. On the hall outside the room, the paramedics argued with each other about who had been right. This was fast becoming a circus.

"Bill?"

"We're not dealing with a Disney character!" he snapped. She silently agreed: she doubted she'd ever seen a Disney character with abs like those; she chuckled at the stupid thought, barely containing a full-blown hysterical attack.

"Get the labs done," he told Jackie; the poor nurse looked suddenly paler than their patient while she fled the room.

"Get another gurney," Gwen ordered Oscar. "We need to level off that tail."

More people crowded the door, blocking anyone trying to work. The news of what was going on in the trauma room was spreading like wildfire.

"This is getting out of control," Gwen warned Bill; for the first time, chaos was taking over their highly tuned, efficient ER.

"Listen up!" Bill said, walking towards the door. He towered over everyone. "This is not a mermaid, and this is not a freak-show! Get back to work and let us save this man! Now!"

They cleared out of the room in two seconds flat.

"Are you sure?" Oscar asked, bringing the gurney Gwen had asked for into the room.

"Yes," Bill shouted, his impatience showing through. "And whoever suggests otherwise—"

He didn't finish, but the meaning hung in the air. Silently, Oscar helped her get the tail up.

"Here, let's see..." Gwen murmured, clinical eyes looking for a better angle into the wound. They turned their non-mermaid onto his side again, and methodically she assessed the damage.

"He needs the OR," she said aloud—*for his not-tail*, she privately added.

"He's going to need a whole lot more than that when he wakes up and explains what the hell is going on here," Bill murmured under his breath.

She couldn't agree more.

2

Calling

Eighteen hours earlier.

Matthew Brooks slid through the air and entered the swimming pool at a perfect angle. No one would ever outpace him when it came to competitions, because something was perverse in letting humans won a freestyle race against a merman.

He kicked hard with his two legs, fleetingly missing his tail—which would be no match for anyone, Olympic athletes included. It didn't matter he was barely seventeen, and this was nothing more than High School practice with his teammates; Matt took it seriously.

On the sidelines, their coach yelled his grandma could outrun them without even trying.

I'd love to see that happening.

Water flowed through his fingers, propelling him further. He'd taken swimming as a way to outrun his bad temper and his negative thoughts, because swimming without shifting to his fins and scales required a great measure of control. It was hard to be angry when chlorine threatened to suffocate his lungs if he so much as thought to breathe water.

Swimming had been good to him in a way nothing else had. He had nothing to hide under water, nothing to prove, nothing to fear. For the two minutes it took to complete the distance, he wasn't a merman hiding in plain sight. He was just an accomplished swimmer making his team proud.

At 5'10, he was amongst the tallest members of the entire Saaban Academy, the private school his oldest brother had attended gazillion years ago, and where his youngest brother tried to survive high school with a geek label attached.

"Come on ladies! You're swimming like puppies today!"

I know a few mermaids who would make you choke on those words.

Under his skin, red and orange scales rested, occasionally itching their way out when he was stressed out. Suppressing those unwanted shifts was the price he paid for sharing time with his human friends and teammates. In turn, he compensated hiding his scales by wearing red and orange swim suits, something his father found amusing, and his brothers wholeheartedly approved. Tail colors mattered more than anything else in merfolk culture—and certainly in teenage merfolk culture—no matter if his family didn't see other merfolk with any regularity.

Unlike the fiery colors of his true self, his gray eyes and white skin gave people the impression he was shy, maybe soft-spoken even, some sort of a loner who didn't want people around. He didn't deny it had been hard to integrate, and harder still to keep so many secrets without the need to blurt them out, but the Matthew Brooks who swam this Monday at 3:42 p.m. was nothing if not popular and friendly, a little bit intense, but a total badass when it came to his pool, his family, and his kin.

He felt the bubbles rushing out of his nose, and watched the light-blue bottom of the swimming pool in some sort of trance. Swimming became automatic, as the joy of the moment faded in favor of a growing feeling that something was wrong.

He didn't want to shake it. He wanted to understand it.

"Brooks! What the hell are you thinking?!"

Nothing… it's just…

He'd been slowing down to the point half the team had passed him by. He reached the end of the pool and deftly turned around. For a moment, the blue painted lines at the bottom blurred out, and then became so sharp it hurt looking at them. Closing his eyes, he blindly kept swimming with no hope of following a straight line.

Pain exploded in his head. He forgot everything about the practice and became a tight ball, hopelessly sinking, fighting against his natural instinct to shift, with no other option but to hold his breath if he could. He'd seen white stars one second, and then nothing but darkness, along with a horribly ringing filling his ears.

It felt like eternity passed him by at the bottom of his watery cage until his coach reached him and pulled him out. By the time he grasped for air at the edge of the pool, it felt as if he'd swallowed the entire swimming pool down, and then some. He couldn't stop coughing, while the entire swimming team looked at him, dumbfounded. It wasn't as if any of them were ever in danger of drowning in their pool, and certainly not their star freestyle swimmer.

For the first time since he'd met the man four years ago, his coach looked worried.

"Kid, talk to me," he said, his hand on Matt's back.

His coughing fit was abating, his chest still burning. No one moved but him. He'd never experienced pain like that before; in fact, he was sure that once he raised his hand to touch his head, he'd find a bump to go along with the headache.

"Kid?"

"Where's the Squid?" he asked without thinking, still curled up on the floor beside the swimming pool. He closed his gray eyes, shivering dramatically; he couldn't feel the cold, but years of hiding had showed him how to feign it.

"In class, I'd hope," his coach said, helping him sit up while someone handed him a towel. It was no secret *the Squid* was his little brother, Alex. What *was* a secret was their telepathy, muted as it was when they were out of the water, and especially since they were still young.

Squid? he sent into the ether, his headache increasing with the effort. He winced, vaguely feeling the beginnings of nausea, certain Alex hadn't heard him.

"What happened?" his coach asked.

"A migraine?" Matt answered the first thing that came to his mind. He wasn't even sure if it was plausible, it just sounded painful enough to be a legitimate excuse.

"Okay, people. Get back to practice. Mr. Brooks, I'm taking you to the infirmary."

"Right. Just... Call my father, please? He'll know what to do."

* * *

Alexander Brooks remained motionless on the floor of the computer lab. One minute he'd been happily coding, and then he'd gone still, motionless, like a deer caught in the headlights.

Something's coming, was the last thought he'd had before being hit so hard in the head he'd not only seen stars, he'd seen galaxies, a few comets, and maybe even a UFO.

Lying on the floor, he only dared to breathe shallow; anything else felt too painful to sustain. Under his uniform, his green and yellow scales had emerged in patches along his spine, the back of his legs, and parts of his arms. A persisting ringing filled his mind, and he felt an odd emptiness in his stomach.

"Mr. Brooks? What's going on?"

The computer lab was a dark place, illuminated by twelve monitors and nothing else. Filled with people whose main interest lied in the abstract and mysterious cloud, Alex's classmates knew more about someone in Iceland than the person next seat. For Alex, who couldn't share much about himself and his hopes for the future in a city under the ocean, this was heaven.

Unlike his brother who loved the irony of belonging to the swimming team, Alex's chosen hiding strategy was behind a monitor. At fifteen, he was the youngest—and the shortest—kid in the AP computer sciences class, where all the seniors mostly ignore him. They also had a healthy dose of respect for his brother Matt, ensuring they would never pick on him.

He had a love-hate relationship with this class: on one hand, this was the only time at school where he could get into cyberspace and do some hacking with no one being the wiser. His teacher was an excellent coder, and he'd learned a few unexpected tricks from her. She kept a close eye on his progress, suspecting his illicit intentions without a problem. His heaven came with heavy control, he knew, finding it amusing that even his human activities came attached to secrecy.

In one year, he would graduate high school. Five more and he would be out of college. And when he hit twenty-eight—the unusual adult age for merfolk—he could go to *The* City, the place where merfolk lived, his true heritage and birthright. He lived for that day, even if right now living was one painful hell.

Lights came up, and Alex heard chairs scraping and people murmuring around him.

"Is he dead?"

No, just wishing I was…

He groaned as he meticulously shifted every scale into skin, the ringing intensifying and fading in waves. Disoriented and in pain, he had absolutely no idea what had happened, besides *maybe* someone playing one horrendous practical joke on him. Merfolk reflexes were *fast,* though, so he should have seen it coming.

"—xander?" his teacher asked, and by the way she said it, he had the impression she'd been calling him a few times already.

"Alexander?" she repeated, kneeling beside him, worried.

That's not good… A worried human was a curious human. He couldn't be absolutely sure he'd gotten rid of all of his scales, and people always found it odd that they were so cold to their touch, so he avoided hands as much as he could.

20

"I'm okay…" he lied, still on the floor, still unwilling to move beyond halfway opening his green eyes. "Just give me a minute."

"Gill went for the school nurse, but maybe we should call an ambu—"

He sat up before she had finished that sentence, the world wavering for a moment. "Just call my dad," Alex said, deadly serious. "He'll know what to do."

* * *

"Are you sure you're okay, sir?"

Julian Brooks couldn't accept the offered glass of water, knowing full well his hands would shake enough to drop it. With his broad complexion and his 6'1 stature, falling down would sure make a commotion hard to hide. His assistant gazed at him in concern, several papers and folders on the floor while he leaned on his desk, barely meeting her eyes. To her, he must have looked as if he'd been having a stroke. It felt as if he'd had one, too.

Julian swallowed and tried to smile.

"It's okay, Sarah, whatever it was, it's over now."

Disbelief was written on her face. The irony was not lost to him; he could lie about his age, his family, his purpose in life, and most certainly about his non-human status, but try to tell a woman he wasn't sick, and all his skills evaporated.

"Your health is nothing to play with, Mr. Brooks," she scolded, the way she would her own children. Out on her desk, the phone rang. Being the Executive Assistant to the CEO of Brooks Inc. was a never-ending job. "I'm going to clear your schedule so you can have yourself checked," she stated. He had to love the power of senior assistants and obediently nodded, even if that made the ringing in his ears worse. In his pocket, his cell phone chirped with messages.

Lingering a few seconds more, Sarah left the glass of water on Julian's desk and went out to pick up her phone. Julian closed his eyes; he let go of all pretenses and sat down on his leather chair, his legs finally giving out on him. The only reason he wasn't on the floor right now, was Sarah. There was no way in hell she wouldn't have called an ambulance if he'd fallen all the way down, so he'd stood straight. Beneath his suit, he could feel the tingling sensation of scales on his broad back and shoulders.

He tried to reach for his children, all three of them, and found a wall collapsing against his mind, his headache escalating as each mental brick hit

21

him. His sight unfocused a few times before he got it right, and his hands still trembled when his phone rang. He answered on the second ring.

"We're at the infirmary, but we're fine," came Alex's voice, sounding too loud to Julian's ears.

"What the hell's going on?" came Matt's voice a second later.

Julian wasn't sure, but none of his options were good. His telepathy had been fried for the time being, forcing him to rely on cellphones.

"Dad?" Alex prompted, scared.

"I'm here," Julian said, his hands weak and his stomach queasy, but his mind stayed alert and waiting. Where was his oldest son? *Come on, Chris. Where are you?*

"It happened to you, too?" Alex asked, somehow connecting invisible dots. He could be scarily accurate that way.

"It happened to Chris," Matt answered, with a whole other meaning, picking up the trail Alex had started. All his children were sharp, but Matt didn't shy away from ugly truths. Never had, never would. "Someone knocked him down enough to knock all of us out. He was reaching out for our help, wa— wasn't he?" he whispered, his voice faltering in the last question.

Julian closed his eyes, his heart aching with despair.

"Stay there, I'm coming to get you."

3

Grounded

The fact both Brooks kids had been at the infirmary at the same time, under the same odd circumstances, did not go unnoticed by half the staff at Saavan Academy—and by pretty much the entire school.

That's a problem for later, Julian thought, as both Alex and Matt looked relieved at seeing him, a sickly white pallor on their faces. Alex hugged him, while Matt remained a few steps back, looking grim. Never one for hugs, Julian still reached for his son, placing a hand on Matt's shoulder.

"Let's go home," Matt said, picking up his backpack.

"Mr. Brooks?" the principal said from the other side of the hallway.

"As soon as I sort this out," Julian told Matt, and then Alex. "I'm sure it won't take long."

By the time they were let go, he'd gone through a stern lecture about not letting his sons fake sickness, and had almost signed a vow in blood that he'd take them directly to their doctor if they weren't faking it. Only half an hour had passed; it felt more like an entire day.

"Stupid principal," Alex murmured as he got in the car. Matt sat in front, his head on the window, his gray eyes vacant. On any other day, their driver would have been behind the wheel. On any other day, Julian wouldn't be here, talking about sensitive subjects.

"I can't reach him," Matt said before Julian started the car.

"Stop trying, then," Julian told him. "You're just hurting yourself. Even if he were nearby, we wouldn't get a clear connection for a few hours."

Matt looked at him without emotion and went back to lean on the window. In the back, Alex had taken the entire seat, looking at the ceiling.

"How could it have been Chris? He's in Nova Scotia this week, isn't he?" Alex asked.

Julian started the car, the throbbing on his head diminishing slightly as he concentrated on getting his family home.

"He left two days ago," Julian answered. "Took one of the boats, said he expected to be home by the end of the week."

"He's in open sea?!" Matt shouted, making Julian wince, his grip tight on the wheel.

"Maybe. Probably, yes."

"Then we have to go! We have to get on a jet and—"

"Calm down, Matt."

"But—!"

"Calm down. I've already mobilized a discreet team," Julian said. "The boat is where it's supposed to be according to its GPS. I'm getting you home and then—"

"—Then you're taking us with you." Matt meant it as a warning; he meant *everything* as a warning, and Julian knew it already.

"—then I see where we stand," Julian answered. "Charging out blindly in search of your brother is not going to help anyone."

Matt glared, ready to argue but not knowing about what.

"He's still a long way from home," Alex said, oblivious to his brother's animosity. "I know he's a good telepath, but I didn't know his range was so large."

"He's been practicing," Julian said, stopping at a red light. Chris was twenty-six, and still had twenty months to get better on his stats to gain his entrance to the City. Julian had no doubt he would excel; if he stopped to think about it, it really was an impressive feat.

"He must have been thinking about us when—whatever it was that happened hit him."

The three winced at the memory.

"We need to help him," Matt said to the window, looking as miserable as Julian felt.

"I'll be reaching for him until I get something back," Julian promised. "Wherever Chris is, we'll find him, okay?"

Matt slouched on his seat and somehow looked small. "Don't make promises you can't keep," was all he said.

* * *

The thing about belonging to this family, Alex had learned, was that everyone wanted to do everything alone. Except for Chris, of course.

Chris was their glue, his contagious enthusiasm and perpetual good humor bringing everyone together, no matter what. It was only natural that if someone was going to disappear, it would be the one piece that could bring the whole castle down.

In Alex's room, time slowed down to a crawl. No one had slept; silently watching night becoming day, their nerves had fried to crisps. It had been eighteen hours since Chris had been knocked out, eighteen long, agonizing hours with Alex's brother lost at sea. Their collective headache had receded but a lingering ache remained, tampering with Alex's telepathy, leaving him angsty. *And if I'm angsty, I don't even want to know what's going on in Matt's mind.*

He didn't kid himself. Even at 100 percent and submerged in water, Alex had no hope to reach all the way to Canada—not even all the way to the next five miles. He doubted even Julian could reach Nova Scotia, but then again, their father liked to keep things to himself occasionally.

Alex's friends kept phoning, asking if he was all right; he ignored them. Until Julian gave them the official story, Alex couldn't say one thing or the other so silence was his only answer; he smiled at seeing that at least he mattered to some people out there. He was just about to put his phone down when an unrelated classmate posted a link. He read the title on the tiny screen. "The World as We Know It Has Changed." But that wasn't what caught his attention. It was the sea.

Wanting to escape reality, he clicked on it.

Two minutes later, he raced through the penthouse in search of his father.

* * *

Submerged in the deepest part of the salt water pool, Julian fought against his mind's limitations and searched for Chris.

His son needed to see his birthright city, had been planning for it since he was ten years old; Chris did nothing without a plan. Or two. Or three. And whatever the plan, he followed it with passion. The hardest physical trial he would face to gain his entrance to the City was swimming to reach it.

Hidden at a three-mile depth, reaching it would be the harshest test any of his sons would ever face—and prove their commitment to their kin.

When Chris had called to say he was taking the long way by boat, Julian had known he'd wanted to practice his deep diving along the way. He'd managed one-and-a-half miles so far, but he'd always done it supervised, with Julian swimming not far behind. Had Chris had an accident in deep waters, Julian would kill him. *We're all prone to make bad decisions, but did you have to choose this to gamble on?* No one answered that.

Julian wanted to do exactly as Matt had said: take a jet to Canada and trace Chris's intended path to New York, but that would waste time. He had to piece together what might have happened and take it from there, because he couldn't risk his other sons by blindly deciding. No matter how hard he tried to make an educated guess, Chris's silence pulled every logical plan into pieces, reminding him eighteen hours had already been lost.

He didn't hear Alex's anguished voice as his youngest shouted at him to get out of the water, but he felt it in his mind, a desperation so deep it had him out in the open in seconds. In his hand, Alex had his phone.

For one eternal second, Julian thought Chris was calling, but nothing could have prepared him to see his son lying on an unknown beach, filmed by an unknown man, being watched by thousands of strangers on the internet.

4

Impossible Choices

The hardest part about calling an emergency Council meeting was that Julian wasn't able to be out there helping to get Chris back.

On his computer, he had gathered the other four members, who were scattered around the world. Grim expressions met his dark blue eyes on the screen, having all just watched the video that encapsulated Julian's worst nightmare. Not long ago, the worst fate merfolk could expect at the hands of humans was death. Now, though...

"Do you know if he survived?" Mireya asked, her sea-green eyes filled with sadness and pity. They all knew what Julian couldn't bear to contemplate. If Chris had not died, then life in captivity promised to be hell.

Julian's eyes stung, but he couldn't afford to lose control.

"Barely. Alexander traced the video to Maine and was able to access the hospital's preliminary records. His injuries are extensive. Without treating him, they don't think he will survive the next hour."

Maybe not even that.

"I'm so sorry, Julian," Mireya said, his longtime friend speaking words he'd never wanted to hear.

"Thank you," he answered without emotion, willing himself to remain numb. "I understand I'm too close to the problem now, but we still need to solve this. Even if he were—weren't my son, we still must decide how to handle this. Do we leave his body or attempt a recovery?"

The three women and one man on the screens nodded, grave faces turning to the problem at hand. He didn't want to accept Chris was gone but had to be realistic. What were the chances Chris could pull through from such injuries?

"The most likely scenario is that Chris's body will be taken for examination," Mireya said to the group. "There's a lot they can gather from that."

"Let the humans wonder at us," Aurel said, frowning. Her short, blond hair undulated as she shook her head. "One more mystery in their hands won't change things. They can search for us all they want, Maine is as far away from the City as it could get."

"Chris might have looked shifted for the most part," Mireya argued. "But we don't know where his internal structure ended. They might know we can shift."

Aurel looked intimidating. "We're not getting the body back. It's too risky for anyone involved. Chris didn't shift to legs, so there's nothing they can conclude about our dual identities."

"I'm far more worried about the images gaining exposure in the mainstream," Lavine interrupted, taking her glasses off and rubbing at the bridge of her nose. "It won't be just a handful of men in white lab coats looking for us now."

"They'll deny it," Aurel said. Her tone betrayed her exasperation. "They have a blurry video and a crazy tale. Those who know the truth will deny it; this is too huge for human society. Whoever sweeps this under the rug is already taking care of our problem."

"What about your cover, Julian?" Drake asked. He was the other man on the Council. "Can Chris be identified? Your children are good at keeping a low profile, but your circles have earned you notoriety."

Julian shook his head. "I don't think his face will be recognized. He was caught as a merman, his face still had distinctive mer-features."

In his mind, he could picture the blurry image of scales still clinging to Chris's shoulders. Their faces changed enough when they were submerged, especially at great depths; it was possible Chris hadn't shifted all the way back.

"Keep an eye on it," Drake warned, his black eyes emphasizing his words. "I'll take care of the hospital surveillance and keep this Council informed."

"Well, that's decided then," Lavine said, conciliatory. "We'll leave this whole thing alone."

Aurel shook her head. "Not so fast. What happens if he survives?"

Julian felt his heart freezing. It physically hurt him to think about that. To think what humans would do to—

"He won't be able to shift into legs until his tail heals," he heard himself saying, his calculating mind unable to stop addressing the situation. "Without proper medical attention, he won't be able to escape for weeks, at the very least." The four members on the screen looked at him with concern.

"Julian," Mireya said quietly. "The risk involved in this kind of operation goes beyond Chris."

The cold in Julian's heart spread to every cell in his body. "It would be proof there are others," she went on. "Proof that we can locate him, free him. The people who have him will jump from wondering at his biology to wondering at our technology level. They'll know for sure we can walk on land, shift. It'll become a nightmare."

This is already a nightmare.

"And that's assuming no one else gets captured," Aurel said. "I don't doubt your son knows what's at stake, Julian, but he's young. Under pressure, would he talk?"

Julian's stomach tightened. He was going to be sick.

"We're getting ahead of ourselves," Lavine said. There was a tremor in her voice. "Chris's survival is almost impossible, as much as it pains me to say it. If he survives and if he's in any position of betraying our world, then we can have this conversation. Right now, it's just unnecessary worry."

"Unnecessary or not, this does bring to the table the fact we're more vulnerable than ever to our human hosts," Drake said. "Chris might be the first they caught in modern times, but he won't be the last. As much as I know we all hate to admit it, we need to call the City. We need protocols beyond *do nothing and hope for the best.*"

Julian wanted to agree. He truly, honestly wanted to have this discussion, not because Chris was in the middle of it, but because he still had two other under-age children to worry about. One day, it might be either of them in this position and he couldn't bear this emptiness to choke him again. Yet he couldn't talk, couldn't move; his whole body felt paralyzed. He was about to agree with this Council on doing nothing about Chris. He was about to abandon his own son.

He turned the computer off before emptying his stomach in the trash can.

* * *

Julian didn't bother re-entering the conference a few minutes later. He couldn't keep going down this path, not without a break to sort out his mind and his feelings, and not without time to mourn.

Outside his study, Alex and Matt waited anxiously. He could feel them, the same way he'd been able to feel Chris's vibrant energy every time his son came home or stopped by the office. How Julian yearned to feel that connection again. In his mind, he couldn't stop reaching for it, even if no one answered on the other side.

With a heavy heart, he opened the door, both teens looking expectantly. Alex closed the computer on his lap.

"They—we don't think there's any reasonable expectation Chris will survive."

He could see how their hearts shattered at his words and hated himself for being the bearer of such terrible news.

"He's not dead, though," Matt said through clenched teeth. "Alex just hacked into their security system; we were going through his files."

"His prognosis is not... hopeful," Alex murmured, looking sick.

"He's not dead, damn it!" Matt turned on his brother, taking him by the collar. Alex didn't stop him.

"Matthew," Julian said, placing a stern hand on his son's shoulder. Matt had gotten better with his temper as years had passed, but under pressure, old habits resurfaced. After a tense moment, Matt let his brother go.

"The Council thinks it's far too risky to try to get his body back. And I agree."

Matt's eyes flared. "What?"

"He'll live on in our hear—"

"No, not that," Matt said. "You're going to leave him for dead even when his heart's still beating? How about you tell him that to his face, huh? *Hey Chris, sorry you're not dead yet, but we're going to pretend you are, so we can go on in our merry ways.* Is that what you and those hacks want?"

"It's not what any of us *wants*, Matt. Just—we need to be realistic."

"That's what I'm doing. He's not dead! He's not dead and you're already burying him."

The hole in Julian's heart grew bigger. He felt so hollow. "What do you want, Matt?" Julian asked, trying to convince both his sons and himself this was the right decision. "What can we reasonably expect? If we go, we'll just prove to the world there's more of us, that we have at least as much tech skill as humans do, and that we can camouflage as one of them. Is that what you want?"

"Hell if I care about that! I care about Chris. Shouldn't you?"

It took everything in Julian to remind himself he was arguing with a distressed teenager who cared too much and let on too little. He couldn't lash out the way he'd wanted to at the Council—or at himself.

"I do. I care about all of you. Chris wouldn't want you falling prey to human hands in a misguided attempt to save his body."

"Chris would be the first to bring those doors down in order to free us," Matt whispered in rage.

"Matt—"

"Maybe if we were your blood sons—"

It was Julian's turn to grab Matt by the shoulders, shaking him once. "Don't. Don't ever doubt I wouldn't give my life if it would help Christopher in any way. You *are* my sons, no matter what blood runs in your veins. But I can do nothing about Chris without jeopardizing you, your brother, or the rest of us. Do you understand?"

Matt's eyes had grown large and his whole body tensed. He was scared, Julian knew; he was terrified for Chris's fate. Julian hugged him then, as strong as he could without leaving bruises, and poured as much love as he could into their connection.

"This is killing me, too, Matt," he whispered in his son's ear. "This is killing me, too."

* * *

Alex had been able to hack into the hospital live feed in less than two hours. He was good with computers, but that didn't mean he was good at watching his brother on the monitor while his life ebbed away. Closing his laptop, he walked down the hall, still undecided on what to do.

Taking a deep breath, he knocked quietly on Matt's door, bracing himself to be yelled at. When no response came, he took it as an invitation. Slowly, he opened the door, expecting to find his brother ripping out the insides of his pillow or something. Matt was prone to destructive attacks whenever he was anxious, but Alex couldn't quite remember the last time he'd seen his brother out of control. Maybe two years ago?

Instead, he found Matt lying on his bed, on his back, eyes closed. The silence was so oppressive that Alex almost turned around and left.

"Has he...?" Matt asked, so low Alex strained to hear him.

"What?" he whispered, afraid to break his brother's quiet. For some reason, his laptop weighed a ton.

"Has Chris died? You've been watching, right?" Matt asked, opening his eyes and staring at the ceiling.

"No! Not that they know what they're doing with him, but, no."

If the truth be told, Alex didn't want to keep watching the live feed alone. To see Chris, usually so full of life, lying there, his bandages turning pink and then red… To see his chest rising and falling so lethargically, when last week he'd been there, right there, laughing at some stupid joke Alex had told. To see all that, was unbearable.

He didn't want to watch, but someone had to. He couldn't ask Julian to do it, not after the intense scene a couple of hours ago. And maybe he shouldn't be here either, his laptop in his hands, asking Matt for this.

"Sorry," he said to his brother, ready to leave.

"I keep reaching for him," Matt said, still looking at the ceiling. "I keep thinking I'll feel it if he dies, but who am I kidding? It feels as if he's already gone."

"They think he's in a coma," Alex whispered, trapped in the doorframe, caught between fleeing the horrible truths in his mind and sharing this helplessness with someone.

"Maybe it's for the best," Matt said, sitting up. He was drained, all his anger and fear gone. It was like watching Chris, really, a shell of what was inside. "He won't suffer. Whatever they do to him, he won't suffer."

Alex leaned on the doorframe, claiming it as neutral ground. "I wish we could be there," Alex confessed, the weight of his computer growing with each word. "You know, tell him to not give up. That… maybe if he knew we wanted him here, he wouldn't… leave."

"Come here," Matt said, his face softening, as it had when Alex first arrived at the house five years ago, feeling lost and abandoned. Alex sat beside his brother, the comforting weight of Matt's arm over his shoulders reminding him he didn't have to go through this alone. None of them did.

"We'll watch him together," Matt said, taking the laptop from Alex's hands, fingers now numbed from holding it for so long. He'd always understood Alex far more than anyone else. "Maybe, if we keep watching him, he won't leave us."

* * *

32

The whole house felt dark and heavy as Julian searched for his sons.

It felt as if he was walking through a nightmare, the hall going to swallow him whole if he stood still. He went to Alex's room first and found it empty. He passed Chris's room on the way to Matt's. Chris had always been the one in the middle, a natural mediator if ever there had been one. He knocked and wasn't surprised when his youngest answered instead of Matt.

"Come in."

Taking a deep breath, he opened the door. Sitting side by side on the bed and against the wall, neither looked up from Alex's laptop.

"May I sit down?" He didn't know how to start this conversation but knew he needed them to look at him. Alex looked up, and his hand went immediately to close the lid. Matt stopped him. "You may," Matt said. He sounded curt, clearly still not giving an inch on his silent declaration of war, while his eyes stayed glued to the monitor.

"I know how hard this is, but we need to plan ahead." His words got no reaction out of Matt, but Alex looked down at the floor. "I'm going to hold a press conference tomorrow. I'm going to declare Chris missing in what we think is a boat accident. Once enough time's passed, we'll have a memorial. This way, you don't have to pretend things are all right."

Alex lost a tear or two before wiping them with his hand. Matt, though, stayed stoic, looking at whatever he was looking at, but his hands had balled into fists, clutching the sheets beneath him.

"If you want to stay here, it's fine. You don't have to go to school. If you want to go somewhere else, that's fine, too. Wherever you want to go, I'll get you there."

"Maine," Matt said without missing a beat.

"What?" Julian asked, knowing he'd heard that wrong. Alex turned to look at Matt so fast, it was clear they had both heard him wrong.

"Anywhere I want to go, you said; that's Maine."

"Matthew—"

"I want to be near him, okay? This—" he said, turning the laptop around, showing Julian an overview video of what he recognized a second later was Chris's hospital room. "This is not enough for me."

Julian didn't know what to be more upset about: the sight of Chris, unconscious and surrounded by so many people, or the idea of losing Matt to the same fate.

"Anywhere but there," he said. The words were out before Julian even realized how full of anger and fear they were. Matt was up and going out so fast, Julian couldn't stop him.

"You can't help him!" Julian said, his heart barely able to keep up with this.

"I don't care," Matt answered, opening the door. "You can't stop me. I'll walk if I have to." He left, slamming the door on his way out.

"Let him go…" Alex whispered, still on the bed. "He knows, Dad. He knows he can't do it alone, but he also knows he can't stay here."

"What about you?"

Don't say Maine, please, don't say Maine.

"I'll stay right here. Someone has to keep watching," he said with resignation, taking the laptop back from where it had landed.

"Alex. No. The Council is monitoring the situation. You don't have to keep watching—"

"Yes, I have to."

Gently, Julian closed the laptop. "Alex."

He didn't fight him when he took the computer away.

"Matt's right," Alex whispered, looking at some point on the wall. "Chris is not dead and we're already burying him." Hugging his knees, Alex became a tight ball.

Getting closer, Julian hugged Alex. Where Matt needed his space, Alex needed to be reassured that those who loved him were still there. And if he thought about it, Julian needed to be reassured of that as well.

5

Viral

"Kate, you're not going to believe this!" Jeff said with the incredulity he reserved only for outstanding internet trash. His job at *Veritas Co.* entitled watching videos all over the net, looking for an interesting scoop the digital news company could exploit.

Her job, meanwhile, was actual, solid journalism, the kind that required a gut, a brain, and networking skills. She had more contacts than the CIA, and that hadn't happened while sitting at her desk watching dancing cat videos, thank you very much. Even if she didn't particularly respect Jeff's work, she liked the guy well enough. Plus, who didn't need a good laugh once in a while?

Following him to his desk all the way down the end of the hall, she couldn't contain a grimace; the amount of kids' stuff on her colleague's desk was appalling. It was even worse than last time. She'd asked him once if he was saving it all for his nephews, and he'd looked at her as if she'd shot him.

Collectors' items, she remembered being corrected. Expensive collectors' items, too. It was scary the things men who never wanted to grow up could afford to buy with their salaries. He lent her his seat while he stood behind her. On his large screen, a lot of windows were open, but the one at the top was the main event. The video title was simple. *The World as We Know It Has Changed.* She snorted, her eyes going to the view count: 480,293. The comment section seemed lively, too. For a video uploaded a little over six hours ago, that was quite an impressive feat.

"If this is some religious nut—"

"Shhhh... Just watch!"

He pressed *play*. An unfocused view of the ocean opened on the video along with the sounds of waves crashing and someone breathing heavily. Dawn was just about to break on the horizon, the poor light making everything look murky.

"I know this is going to be hard to believe, and I'm not sure I believe it myself, but I've just found a merman on the beach."

Now she laughed for real. Jeff hushed her, serious as hell.

On the semi-dark screen, a man lay on the beach, looking rather dead. Pale skin, short dark hair, and what may or may not have been pointy ears flashed before their eyes. The shaky camera didn't help matters, but it quickly went from the man's chest to his actual, large tail.

Water and scales reflected the coming sunrise, and the video was becoming clearer with the increasing light. She had to admit the artwork on his skin looked impressive.

"I've just called 9-1-1, and I'm waiting on the ambulance, but before he's taken away, I needed to prove to the world this—this—my God, what does this even mean?"

Kate rolled her eyes. "Come on, Jeff. Why would a merman drown in the first place? Isn't that like an oxymoron?"

On the video, the guy seemed to read her mind. "I have no idea what's wrong with him, but it seems like he hit something pretty hard. And, if you can see here," the camera made a blurry zoom and then refocused. "Here, you can see something's split his tail. I'm guessing a boat propeller."

Torn flesh and scales were not a pretty sight, and something about it struck her as uncomfortably real. In the distance, sirens could be heard.

"I'm not sure what's going to happen now. I-I'm not even sure if they will take my phone away… I'm uploading this now." The video ended with another hasty shot of the ocean.

"Look," Jeff started. "It's a pretty elaborate hoax, but don't you think it's worth following? A lot of people are going to believe it's true and—"

"Jeff, come on. A lot of videos go viral all the time. Sure, it's a great hoax, but—"

"Ken's already said we should look into it."

"What?"

Their boss was a practical man, and usually, his sharp mind found news under every rock. But this? "Ken asked you to look into this? Good luck."

"Um," Jeff said. "Not exactly. He said *we*, as in you and me?"

She stared at him, knowing she was imagining things.

"Look," Jeff continued. "He said this kind of thing needs a fresh angle. To get the upper hand on those pranksters."

She arched an eyebrow, clearly not buying this.

"He might have said we kind of needed the traffic. Look, this kind of stuff gets people onto our site, and that generates revenue, and—" He seemed unable to stop.

"I know what *needs traffic* means, Jeff. I just can't believe—no, you know what? I actually can. Fine. Let's *look into it* now, so I can go back to real work tomorrow."

"So you're not going to chop my head off?"

"Don't tempt me. Do we know who uploaded it?"

"We can know in about an hour," Jeff said, getting excited. God knew the guy's talents were usually wasted at this place.

"Do it. Can you get me a copy?"

"Sure."

"Thanks."

Jeff started typing, while Kate went back to her office, already checking her phone's contact list. She had eight names under video production, but only one under video manipulation.

"Liam? This is Kate. I've got a video I'd like you to watch..." The sooner she got what her boss wanted, the sooner she could look into something real. "Maybe you can tell me what's wrong with it?"

* * *

"Name's Neil Thompson," Jeff said exactly an hour later, reading from his tablet. "Lives in Maine, work history's spotty. Has been trying to get a half dozen companies off the ground, but nothing's caught on."

"Sounds like the kind of guy who's desperate for attention."

Here's the motive, Kate mused.

"Divorced, no kids, lived in various states until he went back to his hometown."

"What kind of companies? Anything to do with special effects?" *And here comes the smoking gun,* she thought.

"Nope. Nothing like that. He doesn't seem to have the technical skills to pull this off."

"Then we widen the circle," she said without losing the trail. "See which of his friends does. What's the exact address again?"

"Close by some beach in Maine, close enough to go for a run in the early morning," he pointed out.

"Yeah, it's not his claim that he lives near water that interests me. He said he called 9-1-1 and that an ambulance was on its way. Let's see what the hospitals in the area have to say about drowning victims they've taken lately."

* * *

The first four hospitals proved to be dead-ends, and then the fifth had *really* been a dead-end, as in a *no comment* dead-end. But—and this was a big but—if there was a *no comment*, then there was something that could be commented on. In her line of work, *no comment* was an engraved invitation to *come and look at my secrets*.

In front of her, a floor to ceiling whiteboard covered the wall, Kate's neat handwriting detailing what she knew. *Neil Thompson – Video* had been scribbled at the top. From that, she'd started a timeline, while the video replayed on her phone.

Under *Facts*, she'd written the hour, a summary of what was said, and what she could see in the footage. She'd added a reminder to follow up the 9-1-1 dispatcher logs. On a column beside it, Thompson's information simply begged her to take the next plane to Maine and track him down. That was always her favorite part—the hunt.

What I want to know was followed by *What I need to know*.

Want and *need* were two warrior forces; early in her career, Kate had learned to let go of the first to get to the bottom of the second. The news came in all shapes and sizes, but great news always came in complicated messes.

A scoop on a mermaid hoax didn't seem like much, true, but she was a professional and she'd treat this story like any other. Facts, logic, hard work; that's how it went. She stared at the whiteboard and took a pace back.

Want was strangely empty. *Need* had only one sentence: hospital *no comment*—on what?

"Kate," Jeff said from the doorway; he looked all serious now. "They've taken down the video."

"You're kidding me," she said, forgetting the *no comment*. "We're no longer following it, then?" she asked, a little too excited.

"It's starting to pop-up everywhere, so there's no way to contain it now. I thought you should know. The conspiracy's growing."

She rolled her eyes inwardly. So much for *taken down*.

"Right," she said, capping her marker again. "Have you had any luck contacting Neil Thompson?"

"None. But... I called my friend Sam, and he said they're tracking this down, too. The video will show up on the 10:00 p.m. cycle on their *Weird Stuff* section. So, it's going national."

Great... She would never understand people's fascination for hoaxes.

Who knows, maybe I'll have fun. Maybe doing a frivolous piece sometimes isn't so bad. As in one every ten years.

"Keep trying Thompson, I'm sure he's just waiting for a fat fish to fall into his lap."

"What are you going to do?"

"Call my contacts. See who's got anything credible on mermaids and why they will never exist. You know, telling the facts about mermaids and why they're a myth."

Jeff laughed, and then went thoughtful. "Hey, Kate? What if it's real?"

"God, I hope not! I have no experts on that."

"I'm serious."

"I'm serio—" she stopped, the look on Jeff's face causing her to pause. The *no comment* came back into her mind. "You seriously think this could be true?"

"I seriously think it's better to be prepared. That video was awfully convincing."

"That video was awfully shot!" she pointed out. "Okay. Okay, okay, I'll play. If this is real, then Thompson would have been the first point of contact. We would have paramedics, the hospital staff, some activity going on up there in Maine, for sure. I don't know—the Navy, maybe?"

"Why would they cover it up?" Jeff asked, his fingers flying on his tablet, taking notes. It wasn't a real question, just the way Kate liked to *soundboard* stuff. He'd ask obvious questions, and she'd answer with the things she needed researching.

"Well, imagine what you could do with a mermaid," she started, backtracking at the look in Jeff's face. "Not that, Jeff! Gross! Okay, yes, that. But, you know. An entire army of those things could either help you or destroy you. Wouldn't you want to be their friend? Or their conqueror?"

"That's nasty."

"That's history. Now, if there is a mermaid, I bet there'd be some unusual activity going on at the hospital."

"Quarantine?"

"Quarantine! Sure, why not. Police officers, maybe even soldiers. Maybe more people would be called? I'm sure I have someone in here who knows someone in there who can tell us if today was an odd day at the hospital." She turned her phone on, fingering names on her list.

"So, how do we prove this thing is real if they're covering it up?"

"You get to those people before the government does."

"They've already pulled the video."

"We don't know who pulled the video. But it doesn't matter. A mermaid gets wheeled into an ER, people will notice. Look further down the internet, see if anyone else has uploaded pictures or whatnot. Lightning might strike twice."

"You got it!"

"Jeff?" she called after her coworker before he left the office. "Don't feel bad if you don't find anything, okay? This is a hoax, so it won't go that far."

6

Conspiracy

So much for *not a mermaid*, Gwen thought, while her patient clung to his life by an increasingly thin thread.

Sixteen hours ago, she'd been happily drinking her coffee on what promised to be a normal day in a long line of normal days. Instead, she'd somehow crossed into The Twilight Zone, had ended up quarantined for the foreseeable future, and perpetually mulled over the problem at hand: how were they supposed to treat a mermaid?

Merman...? Triton?

"We need to call him something," she muttered as she sighed. She hated not knowing the answers, even if this exceeded her field of expertise by light years.

"John Doe doesn't seem to cut it," Bill said from the other side of their patient's bed, the first joke he'd cracked since the x-rays had come back. By now, they'd run so many tests she'd lost count. The problem was, their merman wasn't waking up, didn't look like he was going to soon either, and the threat of him dying on their hands hung like a sword over their heads.

Drugs were out of the question, tying Gwen's hands in unimaginable ways. Infection was more than likely going to start soon, followed by swelling. They weren't even sure what to feed him, not to mention what to do about his blood loss. He was pale but not because the sun never shone on his scaly body: anemia was rearing its ugly head. Their questions grew by the minute.

How did he breathe under water? His lungs weren't human, exactly, but worked the same way. Air went in, not water. He'd had salt-water in his stomach—or at least, in one of the two—so the collective thought was that he'd been in real danger of drowning.

In the MRI scans, the way his spine became a tail had been perplexing, until the results came back on the bone biopsy taken while patching his tail up. It wasn't bone but more akin to cartilage, like a shark's body. Educated guesses flew everywhere about his internal structures, where lungs and a heart made sense, but not when he seemed to miss four other vital organs, not to mention having three new ones, the purposes of which were unclear. Even finding where and how to insert a catheter had been an adventure, with the urinary tract hidden beneath soft scales below the base of the tail, and appearing only with a certain amount of pressure.

Finally, they had risked an IV line after deducing a few facts from lab results, but that was as far as they would take it tonight. Then there was the DNA testing; it was taking its sweet time to come back, but Gwen honestly had no idea where this guy might fit into the evolutionary chain. The fact was, he shouldn't exist.

The intercom came alive. "Doctors, someone's here to see you," their hospital administrator said.

"How about calling him Melvin?" Bill said as they faced the door out of the quarantine area.

"Oh, come on. He'd rather die than be named Melvin," Gwen answered.

"Ariel?"

She didn't dignify that with an answer.

For the past ten hours, CDC had taken over their patient, wearing full protective hazmat suits that covered them from head to toe—which Gwen found both hilarious and depressing. That Bill, the nurses, and half of the ER staff would be on quarantine was a given, it was just a matter of making it official. The man who entered the quarantine area wore normal surgeon scrubs, which in Gwen's mind translated into good news. It meant they weren't treating this as a biological emergency anymore. The man was tall, calm, and in his early forties; he looked rather official.

"I'm Dr. Nathan Forest. I've been assigned to take over your duties concerning our..." He trailed off for a moment, his eyes going to the gurney behind them. "...Concerning our guest," he finished, regaining his attention. Bill smiled tiredly beside Gwen. They'd witnessed just about every reaction under the sun by this point.

"I didn't believe it myself until I saw the x-rays," Bill confessed, giving a firm handshake to the newcomer. "I'm Dr. Bill Shore, this is Dr. Gwen Gaston."

Forest shook their hands with a genuine smile, then turned to look at their patient. His demeanor was serious. "Has anything changed?"

"As far as we can tell, he's still in a coma," Bill explained. "He's unresponsive to external stimuli. Temperature has settled at ninety-three degrees Fahrenheit, about five degrees below normal, so we think that might be his real core temperature. To tell you the truth, Dr. Forest, we're flying blind here. His biochemistry doesn't match ours. The prognosis doesn't look good."

Forest nodded, and Gwen would have sworn his fingers were crazy eager to get close to the merman and touch him. Funny, most people's first instinct was to step away.

"A team of experts is being assembled—" Forest began.

"On mermaids?" she interrupted, disconcerted. Forest blinked, caught off guard.

"Well, no. Not exactly. Experts on anything that might help us explain him."

He finally moved towards their merman, looking at every inch of pale skin and blue scale. Two gurneys had been put together to accommodate the entire tail, which went all the way past the middle of the second gurney. Cleansed of all sea debris, each scale shone under the harsh white lights of the observation room in a different shade of blue, and the thin fins at each side of his hips were spread so doctors didn't tear them further. Wrapped in a thick bandage that hid dozens of stitches from the inside out, he wouldn't be able to flex his tail for weeks, probably a couple of months. She still worried that not enough blood irrigated the lower part of the tail, but no one wanted to discuss the real possibility he could lose it.

The merman's right wrist was immobilized in a cast, and a cut on the side of his head had a couple of butterfly bandages. Whatever had hit him, it left nasty purple patches behind.

I hope you beat the crap out of the other guy, the thought fleetingly crossed Gwen's mind. Bill was giving the latest stats, all numbers she already knew. Little else filled her mind other than their little mermaid at death's door. It was just him and how much she wanted her coffee, really.

"So, what happens now?" Bill asked, tired; all three were taking seats, their guest of honor oblivious to his fate being decided.

"Well, CDC had the authority until this was no longer a biomedical crisis, an hour ago. They'll do a follow-up with all the hospital staff involved, but for all practical purposes, you're off the hook. I'm here to release you."

"You are?" Gwen and Bill asked at the same time.

"CDC's being cautious about our guest, but there's no reason why you shouldn't continue your quarantine at your homes, as a precaution. So I'm releasing you into forced vacations, it seems." Gwen turned to look at Bill's happy face, and then back to Forest's innocent one.

"Why?"

"Why?" he repeated, confused.

"Yes, why? Why are you sending us to quarantine outside these walls without a fuss?"

"We consider that the transmission of an unknown pathogen is unli—"

"I thought you wanted to keep this under wraps? What's preventing us from calling the news while we're out there?" she interrupted, her hands going cold. She hated not knowing what was happening, and she hated, even more, feeling she had no control over anything.

"Videos about what happened this morning are already on the internet, it's just a matter of time before everyone sees it no matter what," he said, shrugging. "We're not denying or confirming anything at this point. We really want to have more information before calling a press conference. Those sharks are smelling blood; they just don't know where to swim just yet."

"Okay, just to make this clear. You're sending us to our homes, but for all intents and purposes, we're free to go and talk to anyone about anything?"

Bill looked at her, clearly saying *shut up*. Forest just looked amused.

"It's your life that will become a circus, Dr. Gaston. You're very welcome to it. As I said, our position is not to talk until we have something concrete to say. *We found a merman, thank you for coming*, is not going to cut it. It would be better if you waited for a time and place where we could make a coordinated release, but this is merely a suggestion."

In other words, you're free to sound like a lunatic because we won't provide any real proof to your claims. She sighed.

"What about the rest of the staff?" With this battle over, she was merely curious.

"The hospital is more than happy to cooperate in any course of action we deem appropriate. Meanwhile, we're sending everyone back to their normal lives, except for a few who have had prolonged contact. This home quarantine is out of an abundance of caution. I'm sure you can understand." He stressed it as if they were eight-year-olds about to protest. She didn't know how to feel.

"I take it this is good news?" he asked, looking at her and then at Bill.

"When do we leave?" Bill asked, all cheers and joy.

"In about an hour."

"Wait," she said, raising a hand. "What happens to... our guest?"

What was the proper term in this situation? Was he still their patient? Prisoner? Subject? All of the above?

"It's unlikely he will survive, I'm afraid," Forest said, regret coloring his voice. "Would have loved to have a chat with him."

"What if he does? Survive, I mean."

Forest looked at her, those intelligent eyes of his seeing something she could only imagine. Was she being difficult on purpose? Was she trying to pull something? What was her game, exactly? She wasn't even sure herself.

"Look, I don't know the procedure here," she said. "I'm not exactly opposed to keeping this whole situation secret, but I'd like some clarity. He's our patient, after all, right Bill?"

Bill looked at her as if she'd slapped him. It was obvious Gwen would not like what he had to say. Forest looked thoughtful for a few seconds.

"If he survives..." he started slowly, his eyes slightly unfocused. "All the answers we want—we need, are inside his mind. Communication is our first priority, then we'll take it from there. Honestly, Dr. Gaston, we have no idea what we're dealing with here."

"I want to help," she heard herself saying.

"You have already done a great deal—" Forest started.

"I want to see this thing through. I already know what's going on, and I'm certainly capable of helping you out. You'll be crazy not to accept me."

Tension filled the air between them, nothing betraying Forest's thoughts.

"Let me think about it, Dr. Gaston. Dr. Shore," he said to Bill. "I'll have your discharge papers ready in no time." And with that, Forest left. It wasn't until she was alone half an hour later that Gwen realized she'd never asked who Forest worked for.

* * *

Somewhere, out there, someone knew what had happened to their triton.

Nathan Forest winced internally at the term. Until six hours ago, he'd never even heard about tritons, one of the definitions for male mermaids. Part of his team called their half-human, half-fish a merman, and the other part a mer*maid*. Someone had suggested *siren*.

If we can't even decide on what he is...

He let the thought go; there were bigger troubles to handle, and solving problems was Forest's most valued skill. He had a knack for finding what people wanted and getting what *he* wanted in return, which had made him an invaluable asset to the United Nations Peace Corps, and had later led him to work on other UN projects. He also had a knack for handling sensitive topics, which usually meant he was dispatched all over the world to deal with conflicts before they got out of hand. He was a problem solver assigned a curious case just because he'd been in the area.

No one had believed this was an honest-to-God merman, but once the CDC got involved, then Washington got notified, and the World Health Organization had also been thrown into the mix, claiming the UN's attention. And so, there he was.

In front of him, four doctors argued among themselves. He ignored them. On the screen in front of him, a set of full body scan results presented a rather intriguing puzzle. He might be a strange diplomat by profession, but he was first and foremost a biochemist, one who loved biological puzzles—as long as he could put them together.

How on Earth did evolution end up with you? he thought.

Right now, though, he was far more interested in what forensics was telling him. The hit on their merman's head had been done with a large object, like a bat, by a man strong enough to crack a wrist and almost crack a skull. Mr. Merman here had had little time to defend himself in a fight that had been a lost cause from the start. And he had been hit on land, evidently, or at least, in the air. He hadn't been attacked underwater.

He'd been taken by surprise, Nathan concluded. Unconscious, he had fallen under a boat—maybe even been thrown overboard—where the propeller had cut deep into his tail. It couldn't have been too far from the coast since predators would have taken advantage otherwise.

The timing of the attack was proving to be difficult to pinpoint; it was anywhere between twelve to sixteen hours before he was found on the beach, and that was assuming a lot about their newfound friend's biochemistry.

This all brought Nathan to their biggest mystery yet: why did the merman breathe air? Or rather, how did he survive in the open sea? If mermaids were like dolphins, needing to emerge in order to breathe, they would have been discovered and captured way before the twenty-first century. No, something was seriously wrong with the picture here; a mermaid who couldn't breathe underwater was like a human who couldn't survive at room temperature.

"You seem awfully mesmerized by your screen," Dr. Gaston said, looking better now that she'd had a shower, breakfast, and coffee.

"Are we sure he can't breathe underwater?" he asked her.

"Seems highly unlikely," she answered with a raised brow, somehow making him feel like a first-year student. They'd run a dozen tests on his lungs, all conclusive on his needs for air.

"He's still stable but not improving." She handed him the latest reports.

"It will have to do," he said, reading the first two pages.

"Do for what?"

"We need to relocate him."

"What? No. He's not going to sur—"

"This hospital is not the place for him. It's not safe, not for him or for us. It's just a matter of time before the media descends here, followed by the nutjobs. We need to move him. He's survived the first twenty-four hours, and he might have survived another twenty-four in the ocean before that. You asked me what happens if he survives. This happens, Doctor. He gets relocated."

7

All in the Details

"I found out what's wrong with your video," Liam said for a greeting.

He was Kate's chosen expert on video manipulation and grinned up from the video chat window in the corner of her screen. He looked excited with that maniac glee in his eyes he got when he hadn't slept.

"You mean besides the fact it's one gigantic special effect?" Kate asked with half a smile. Her boss had come to her office to make sure she was working on it, because that video was well on its way to three million views.

We have to be ten steps ahead of the competition, Kate. This is important. Maybe not Pulitzer Prize-winning important, but it's one sure way to get your next check.

Despite what she thought, she always gave her best to assignments. Liam shared his screen, showing brightly-contrasted stills from the merman's body. With the magic of photo manipulation, he could turn night into day.

"It's top-notch work, that much I can tell you. I could find no flaw in the tail design. Even the cut in the tail was meticulously done. I checked some anatomy articles, thinking a tail wound so big would have been bleeding all over the place, even with the water washing it away."

The screenshot changed to a zoom of the half-chopped tail. A couple of other tears were visible.

"So, that's what's wrong? There's not enough blood?"

"No. Well, not exactly. If he'd been cut right there on the spot, yes, it should have been. But if you assume he was in the water for some time, the cold would have helped in reducing the bleeding. Or that's what I understood, anyway."

"It's not conclusive," she said, narrowing her eyes at the evidence. Liam grinned, his eyes practically shining.

"They messed up in the most spectacular way," he said. She raised her eyes, hopeful. This was the detail she needed to be over with this story and move on.

"As I went over every inch of footage, I finally found this…" he trailed off, a new still showing where the torso became tail. He zoomed on it several frames, and then stopped, anticipation practically oozing from the screen. She frowned.

"Okay, but I don't see what's wrong with the tail…" she said after a few seconds of scrutinizing.

"Ha! There's nothing wrong with that. Look beyond it." He pointed out with an arrow, making a red circle in the top part of the picture. What she'd thought were scales shining in the sunlight was something else for Liam.

"I give up, what I'm looking at?"

"A watch."

She blinked.

"Well, a metal wrist watch. You see, the angle is all wrong for it to be a continuation of the tail, but it fits if you think of this as his arms, and this as his wrist. That thing reflecting sunshine is metal. See how it doesn't match with the reflection in the scales?"

She didn't. If she tilted her head, she could see why the angle seemed off, but… "A watch?"

"It happens. Actors forget they're wearing them, or the wrong earrings, or what have you. Everyone is so obsessed with details they overlook what they see every day. Plus, it hardly shows in the shot, I doubt they noticed they had gotten it on camera."

"Boy, that's embarrassing!"

"And, it's the only thing wrong with the damn thing. I've been glued to this video since you gave it to me yesterday. I swear I see tiny scales everywhere."

"Liam, I owe you one."

"You'll get my usual fee note tomorrow morning." She didn't even wait for Liam to hang up as she scrambled to the door.

"Jeff!" she yelled as she went out of her office. "Tell me you found Mr. Thompson! I have a screenshot here that will trash his video to hell!"

* * *

Thirty minutes earlier, Kate had been thrilled at Liam's discovery. Now, sitting in front of her boss's computer, she was speechless. And so was her boss.

50

"There are eleven videos shot at the hospital," Jeff was explaining. "But only three have any real value. They show him arriving, then leaving the ER trauma room, and then being moved to the OR. All the others have glimpses of white skin and a few scales, but nothing really important or focused."

On the computer screen, the latest video showed doctors and nurses trying to move two assembled gurneys through the hall. It went on for a whole minute with the staff trying to figure out how to move as one with such a large extension. Most of the patient was covered, but the tips of the tail and his pointy ears could still be seen, along with two pale arms.

"Who took this?" Kate asked.

"A patient, most likely," her boss said. "Any hospital staff would be looking at jail time if they so much as thought about recording a patient."

She replayed the video and then paused it.

"There's no watch," she murmured.

"What?" her boss asked.

"There's a watch. In the original video, where he's lying on the beach, he's wearing a watch."

"For real?"

"Well, it's hard to see. Guess they corrected the mistake."

"Someone is going to great lengths to legitimatize this thing," Ken said, thoughtfully. "My money is on an advertising campaign. Kate, call your contacts in the industry, see who that might be."

"Ad campaign?" Jeff asked, dumbfounded.

"That, or you have a real merman in your hands—who wears watches! Which sounds more likely?" Ken pointed out. "In any case, they're naming the hospital. Kate, I want you there by noon today. Get reactions, get interviews. Let's see why this hospital agreed to be part of this thing or if they're planning to sue someone."

"On it, sir."

* * *

Hunting down a man who didn't even try to hide was no fun. Knocking on the door of a middle-class house in a middle-class neighborhood was not what Kate had hoped for when she'd woken up that morning. It was 4:05 p.m. and she had to be at the hospital in an hour, even if she had little hope about what the administration would say.

And yet, why would they have a *no comment* policy on a non-event that happened yesterday? The hospital didn't need that publicity, but maybe her boss was right. Maybe they wanted to sue. God knew America loved to sue.

She rang the bell for the fourth time. Patience eluded her today, mainly because she'd been dreaming about tails and scales last night, and had woken up with a vague feeling she was missing something. Now she could add a watch to the mix. She knocked again. "Mr. Thompson? I know you're in there! I swear I'm not going to bite! I just need to ask you something."

Movement. *Finally!* Her eyes opened and she waited in silence, lest she scare her prey.

"Who are you?" came through the door, muffled.

"I'm Kate Banes, Mr. Thompson. I've been following your video online and—"

The door opened with such speed, she moved a step back.

"How do you know that's me?!" Thompson demanded.

"Ah, well. It's not hard."

"No. No, no, no, no. You gotta leave."

"Ah, I'm sure this is a shock to you, but let me tell you—"

"No, they're going to be here any minute now and they can't think I have anything to do with you."

"Who?"

"The reporters. I'm getting an interview."

"What?"

"I contacted a few stations yesterday when I saw the video gaining so much interest. I thought, well, now people know the truth, I gotta expand on it."

"You contact—you what?"

All logic defied what this man was doing. Was he actively hunting for someone to prove his hoax?

"One made a very generous offer but asked me to take the video down. They're re-editing it, cleaning it up, and adding my interview."

"You've got to be kidding me."

"So, Ms. Banes, I'm going to have to ask you to leave."

"Just—just tell me something. I promise I won't print it or anything. Is it an ad campaign?"

"What?"

"The video. This whole thing. I mean, I jumped into a plane all the way from New York not three hours ago, and my boss has bet good money this is an ad campaign. Just tell me yes or no, I don't need to know anything else."

Thompson stared at her, clearly not understanding a word.

"We are talking about your merman video, right?" she asked, the blank look on the man's face unnerving her.

"What ad camp—oh. Oh! You think I made this up?" Now he was angry. She put her hands in front of her as a peace gesture.

"Not with bad intentions. It's quite clever, actually."

"I found him. I was walking down the beach yesterday as I always do and I found him, okay? I have no idea where he is right now, what's going on, or even why he was there. But I found him, damn it! And if you insist on—"

"Hey! Hey! I saw the watch, okay. You don't have to pretend with me."

That stopped his little tirade right in the middle. He went from being red to being white.

"What?" he croaked, apparently even his saliva deserting his throat.

"It's on the video. It's really hard to catch, but it's there. Your actor screwed up. He wore a watch, and I guess the editor didn't see it."

Thompson shook his head. "I swear, it's true," he whispered, all his rage gone. "I found him, he had a tail, and he was—he was beaten. And the tail was cut, right here," he said, showing somewhere above his knees. "You could see the bruises on his head."

"Come on. I won't say anything. You can have your little fun, do your interview. I just want to go home tonight and not dream about fish. That's all I want, honest."

"I saw the watch, I won't deny that. I saw it when the paramedics came. We all tried to find a way to take the tail off, but he was so cold. They put that neck thing on, and then the three of us put him on the stretcher. I honestly thought he was going to be heavier," he said, remembering with a frown. "They got him into the ambulance, closed the doors, and drove away. I have no idea why he was wearing a watch."

"And that's it?"

He looked past her, and she turned to look as well. A TV crew was parking in front of the house.

"That's it. Now, if you excuse me, the world needs to know what's going on."

* * *

"And what did the hospital say?" Jeff asked over the computer, while she munched on chocolate chip cookies, her number one comfort food. She was barely settling in at her hotel after a frustrating non-interview with the hospital administration an hour earlier.

"Same thing, *no comment*. But, I did get some info from one of my contacts. Turns out emergency services did receive a call for a drowning by the beach. The timing puts it right at sunrise."

"So this guy Thompson did call 9-1-1 as he said," Jeff added, his eyes shining with the possibilities.

"And paramedics were dispatched. There's a lot of activity going on, but it's a big hospital. The other TV networks haven't shown up, but once Thompson's interview hits the airwaves, well... Can you send me the links to the other videos? I want to see if I can match them to actual people working there. I'm going back to get that story one way or another."

"You got it."

* * *

The best part about being a reporter was all the free passes Kate got by showing her credentials. The worst part about being one was how people with something to hide clamped down on her.

Knowing how to play her cards was a skill that did not come easily, but then again, anything worth it required effort, didn't it? She knew the ER staff wouldn't be allowed to talk to a reporter, so she'd come here incognito, hoping the staff members were far more cooperative than any *no comment* administrator. She'd arrived at the hospital two hours earlier, claiming something was tainted in her lobster roll the night before; that was followed by two hours of waiting to talk to someone and thanking all the gods out there that she wasn't in a real emergency. Jeff had helped her compile a few staff faces from the hospital videos, and her eager eyes kept matching the photos to the staff. She still couldn't find anyone.

Getting up, she went to the desk.

"Yes?" a nurse asked curtly, clearly unimpressed by Kate's smile.

"I'm so sorry to bother you, but my cousin said she knows one of the doctors working here, and maybe he might see me?"

The nurse sighed, hating the idea. Kate smiled sheepishly. "I usually don't do this."

"You don't say."

"But is there any chance Dr. Bill Shore could see me?"

That stopped the nurse in her tracks, her eyes slightly widening. "I'm afraid he's already gone home," the nurse answered.

"How about Dr. Gwen Gaston?"

"She's also—"

The nurse stopped, now looking at Kate suspiciously. "How many friends does your cousin have here?"

"A few," Kate lied smoothly. "She sent me a few names in case some of them weren't working and—"

"Listen, sweetheart. Sit down, shut up, and wait. Someone will be with you."

Kate's smile dwindled. The nurse didn't wait for her to leave. She departed herself, instead. Kate went back to her plastic chair, her thoughts regrouping and looking for another strategy. Maybe getting hold of their addresses and paying them a visit later?

"Miss?" a large man in his sixties asked her, wearing gray clothes and a tag that read *Johnny*. A janitor.

"Yes?"

"I heard… were you looking for those people?"

"Yes…"

"Because you're sick?"

Something about the way Johnny said it gave her pause. "Maybe…"

"'Cause, if you're looking for something or someone else who was here yesterday morning, I might have something for you."

"I'm listening."

"But, you see… if it gets out that someone from here showed someone from not here some—"

"Off the record," she said hastily, inclining forward so far on her chair that she was in serious danger of falling down. The man smiled.

"Now, since I'm going to show you something nice here, I'd like something nice in return."

"I'm sure we can work something out," she said with a smile, mentally preparing herself for another shaky video showing a white skin and pointy ears.

It wouldn't be worth a thing–not with so many videos circling the net already—but one could never be certain.

Still smiling, Johnny reached for his pocket and produced something small and shiny.

"He was wearing a watch," he whispered, all serious now, a sports watch in his hand. "He was wearing *this* watch. It's the only thing he was wearing, really. They took it off while trying to figure out how to detach the tail. When Dr. Shore threw everyone out, they forgot about it."

He handed it to her. "Though you gotta wonder, miss, why would a merman be wearing a watch?"

"Because the whole thing's fake," she answered, feeling the watch's smooth surface. She didn't know much about watches but this one looked expensive. Besides the clock, it had six little buttons around the face, and two separate white squares that looked like date displays, except one read 0, and the other read 2931. A diver's watch? she wondered. Turning it around, she was met with an engraved phrase.

Deep breaths. Julian.

The janitor reached for the watch. Kate pulled it closer to herself. Johnny smiled again, this time with a predatory look.

"I want ten thousand dollars for it."

You could get ten times more on e-bay, she fleetingly thought with a smile. Instead, she went with a smooth line.

"Done. I'll get you the money, and you don't show it to anyone."

She handed her card, he gave her his contact information, and then she took off. Sure, her boss would blow a fuse, but ten thousand dollars was a bargain for figuring this out escalating hoax.

* * *

"You want me to authorize *how* much money?" Ken's voice rose to a crescendo. Saying he was not amused by Kate's generous gesture would be an understatement. But damn it, she was a reporter who got stories, not a haggler who got low prices, for Pete's sake!

"To get the watch—"

"—from a janitor!"

Kate moved the phone away from her ear.

"From a janitor who talked to me before all the other networks. Jeff is tracking down the doctors," she said, mentally counting to 100.

"I don't get it. I seriously don't. I sent you to follow a hoax—one you didn't even want to investigate in the first place—and you come back with *real events* at the hospital? What the hell is real about this whole thing, Kate?"

"Come on, Chief. There's more to this than some ad campaign. It looked real enough to the ER staff. Whoever wore that merman suit, was in serious trouble."

"Says your expert ER janitor?"

"And how come all of the people involved are gone?"

"Shift change?"

"And the *no comment* comment?"

"Privacy? Has it occurred to you the guy in the mermaid suit might sue them if they make fun of him on the six o'clock news?"

"Look, I know that, Ken. But isn't it a little bit too coincidental? The watch proves this is a hoax, which we already knew. What I want to know is why is it getting so hard to find this man? No one—and I mean no one—is saying anything."

"What are you thinking, exactly?"

"I don't know. But something serious is going on and the only way to find out what is to track the watch's owner. If it belongs to the actor, maybe he'll want to give us the exclusive. So I need that money."

Silence met her words, the kind that said she'd won but Ken was still chewing on it. "Fine. If he was at the ER, he might still be in the hospital. For ten grand, you better find him, Kate."

8

Classified

Nathan Forest signed the last form, his pale blue eyes speed-reading through the specifications of their new quarters. It was close to midnight, but the place was swarming with people getting ready to receive their patient at first hour tomorrow. Maybe even earlier.

In his newly established office, photographs of killer whales and dolphins decorated the walls, the ORCAS logo painted on the glass door displaying their full name: The Oceanic Research, Conservancy, & Atmospheric Society. He had no use for the Atmospheric part, but everything else seemed to match his needs.

The staff at this fine ORCAS facility had been replaced by the US Army, leaving just a handful of civilians around, mostly marine life experts moving heaven and earth to accommodate the several dozen requirements their special guest needed. And they had the biggest grins Nathan had ever seen in his life. Despite the dozen non-disclosure agreements they had signed, these people were excited, and something at the back of his mind warned him to keep a tight leash on them.

That brought Nathan to his other immediate problem: security. Although the Army had taken over ORCAS in the last hour, the place was still a civilian research facility, not a secret military compound in the middle of the Nevada desert. Even with ORCAS's twelve other facilities along the Maine coast, it would not take much time for people to find out where the merman had been moved to, or for someone to leak the information for fame, money, or both. A knock on the open door got his attention. Nathan turned, expecting to see doctors and their ubiquitous lab coats, but instead found a man in a uniform, and two soldiers flanking him.

From the moment Nathan had received the first phone call about the merman, to this point where the military were coming to his door to check on things, only twenty-three hours had passed.

"Come in," he said, leaning on his desk and leaving his tablet beside him.

"Dr. Nathan Forest?" the man in the uniform asked, while his armed security team waited outside, either side of the doorway. He gave Nathan barely a glance, quickly assessing his skills.

Nathan did the same, and didn't like what he saw. From the slim build to the eyeglasses, the impeccable uniform and the polished shoes, this man meant trouble.

"Yes?" he said, extending his hand.

"I'm Major Jonathan White, Military Intelligence. We're getting ready to receive your patient," he said, shaking hands with Nathan; it was a firm grip as expected. "How are things going at your end?"

"Nothing that twelve different disciplines can't figure out," Nathan said, offering a chair. They both sat at the same time. "As I'm sure you've been informed, the UN is prepared to take a first contact approach with this man's species. A peaceful contact."

White nodded once. "The United States of America wants nothing but that, and we're prepared to follow your guidance in the following days. We're more than happy to be hosts to this historical event." Tension filled the air. It always did when a *but* was inevitable.

"We're only requiring that the security detail is overseen by us, including clearances and special permissions, and that all information regarding the patient's health or any communication gained be shared with us. We think it's only reasonable if you insist on a civilian installation and civilian staff." Nathan leaned back on his seat.

"Well, if you can find an available medical and research facility which can also accommodate underwater scanning equipment in short notice, I'm all ears."

White sat perfectly straight in his chair, his eyeglasses perfectly balanced on his symmetrical thin face. The fact that he blinked was the only indication that gave him away as a human being.

"There's one more reason you're moving him here," White said, with a smidge of respect. "He was found in Maine and you're not going to move him further away—just in case his friends might come looking for him. We're hoping for the same thing."

Touché.

It was reasonable to believe a colony of merfolk would be relatively close to the coast; that would allow this merman to make it to the beach without being eaten by predators in the open sea. That other merfolk would come looking for him was a long shot, but taking Mr. Merman to Area 51 where no one would ever find him had never been an option.

"And what if they do come looking?"

"We're just interested in collecting information, Dr. Forest, not shooting the only living contact we have with them. We want to make it as easy as possible for them to come out and talk. An underwater civilization can be our greatest ally or our strongest enemy."

"You do realize that chances are they're barely a hunting and gathering society, right? That we're dealing with nothing more than water-breathing cavemen."

This time, White smirked. "We're fairly certain that whatever they are is going to surprise us. I don't think you're aware of how unique your patient is, doctor, so let me enlighten you." White reached into his suit and handed Nathan a small yellow envelope marked *for your eyes only*.

"I'll see myself out and start overseeing the installation of much-needed safety measures around here. It's been a pleasure, doctor. I'm sure we'll be in contact."

They shook hands again and White and his security detail disappeared. Impatiently, Nathan opened the envelope and found a white sheet folded in four. It was the merman's DNA results, the key to where in the evolutionary chain this species had started.

"Son of a—" he said, looking at the empty door. With the bombshell written on that paper, it was no wonder White was there. Marked in bold letters at the bottom of the page, the DNA results read: *not from Earth*.

* * *

Gathering intelligence was the easy part of Major Jonathan White's job. He enjoyed having the pieces displayed in front of him, forming a tree of interconnected people and events. He was excellent at analyzing the uncertain paths and half-told lies of the targets he studied, knowing that even the unlikeliest crumbs of information could lead straight to the truth. And there had never been anything unlikelier than a half-drowned merman on a Maine beach, with alien DNA.

The décor in his office comprised several octopus images, though he hadn't noticed it at first. The sea creatures' camouflage was so good they were almost invisible. It was only fitting that his office would be a reminder that nothing, was ever, what it seemed.

"Sir?" a young technician asked, his eyes comically magnified by his glasses.

"Any results?" White asked, for a moment forgetting about life's ironies.

"We've finished running the face scan, but nothing showed up, sir."

"It was a long shot. Thank you."

Facial recognition had been a long shot, but half the legends out there referred to merfolk as being able to shift their tails into legs. His entire Intelligence department had been reading up on mermaid myths for the past twenty-four hours, an assignment no one had seen coming. Sure, it sounded absurd to believe legends could be real, but wasn't he already dealing with the impossible?

And just because you're not in the database, doesn't mean you haven't been walking around.

They'd also searched for fingerprints, just to find smooth fingers holding no identity traits. Not giving up, Jonathan had turned to dental records. Their merman had nicely shaped teeth, human looking. He had no cavities, but most importantly, no obvious dental work either. John Doe was proving impossible to identify, but then again, White had no concrete proof the man had ever been on land, let alone been part of society long enough to have dental work and records.

Someone knows you, White thought. The question here was, did that someone walk the earth or swim the oceans—or both?

* * *

Gwen had to give it to Forest: the man was organized. Like a general, he'd mobilized his troops, set up camp, and ordered all the factions around with an authority no one questioned. He did what was needed and that was all she cared about.

Leaving the hospital had been a rather uneventful ride. Rumors a reporter had been asking questions earlier had not been welcome news, but Gwen still had no idea what Forest wanted to do. The hospital had started receiving calls from concerned citizens asking about a mermaid video, and she would bet other news people had been calling as well, looking for a comment.

As curious as she was, that was no longer her problem. She was barely standing at 4:00 a.m. on adrenaline and coffee alone, while Mr. Merman had been successfully transferred to his shiny new room. It had been a rather interesting problem to move him around since the length of his tail made the double gurney too long for most corners. *For all the trouble you cause, you sure look peaceful.* It was easy to believe he was only sleeping, and she had to admit he'd held on to life remarkably well.

She left her patient's side and made her way to the observation deck in search of one more cup of coffee. She found it, along with Forest. "Well, what do you think?" he asked, for once ungluing his face from his tablet. He looked as tired as she felt.

"I wish my hospital was as well equipped," she answered, wondering when her life had turned so bizarre that she'd become a merman's primary doctor. The Oceanic Research, Conservancy, & Atmospheric Society logo painted on one wall reminded her where she wasn't.

"Oh, the facility was already well suited for our particular needs, but let's not forget a lot of people have a lot of questions."

"A lot of people with a lot of money."

"Indeed. You can't get this kind of speed with public funding. Thank God the UN is not cheap."

"You're not afraid you'll get a lot of leaks?"

"This isn't a cloak and dagger mission," Forest answered with a smile. "We're still unsure how to address this, but everyone wants to wait to see if he pulls through."

She filled her cup and watched her patient from the deck.

"What are we calling him?"

"Merman?"

"No, I mean. An actual name. And please don't say Ariel."

"Right... How about Ray?" he proposed.

"For marine rays?"

"Sure, why not. It's short, relatable, and easy to write. Everything you might need in a press conference."

"You have a lot of practice in those?"

"No. Nor in dealing with merfolk, yet here we are."

"'Merfolk' will be the official word?"

Forest shrugged. "Until he says otherwise. By the way, I'm meeting with your colleagues to introduce them to him—to Ray. Would you mind staying to answer their questions?"

"What, like now?"

Before he had a chance to respond, a couple of doctors came in, excitedly talking. They were followed by another group of three, then two more.

"How many people did you call here?" she asked Forest, her coffee forgotten.

"As many as it takes to keep him alive," he answered, reviewing something on his tablet for the 100th time. "I think this is your audience, now?"

She sighed inwardly. This was his show, but for the time being, she was the one with the most experience in the room. She wished Bill hadn't deserted her, the bastard.

"Doctors," Forest addressed the room. Everybody shut up. "You've all received the latest data, your position on this team, and what is expected of your skills. Let me be clear on something else: He is not a creature. He is not a *thing*. He is not your own little pet project. You will regard him as you would any other patient. We have many questions, but a lack of respect will not be tolerated."

The energy in the room changed, somehow. It went from juvenile excitement to serious curiosity. Professional minds overtook eager speculation. She even felt herself standing a little straighter.

"Doctor."

She took a moment to realize he was talking to her so she could address the room. *Oh, gee, give the grand speech and then throw me to the wolves, won't you?*

"I've been running on caffeine for the last 24 hours, but I've been with our patient since he was brought in. You've read all we've got so far, so I think it's best if I answer any questions you might have."

Seven hands went up, hilariously resembling first-year students. Twenty minutes later, she was so engrossed in all the medical discussions that the last question of the batch caught her unguarded.

"What did it feel like?" an Asian woman asked, her eyes strangely magnified by her glasses.

"What did what feel like?"

"Well, seeing him… the tail… I mean, when you realized in the ER that it wasn't a suit. Sorry, it wasn't on the reports, obviously, but… I'd really like to know."

Gwen opened her mouth and then closed it. She saw herself taking that last cup of coffee, the sound of the ambulance arriving at the ER entrance, a day as any other. She distinctively remembered expecting that tail to be made of pink and yellow plastic. She smiled.

64

"We thought it was a very elaborate disguise. How couldn't we? I was looking for internal bleeding until I realize the wound was on the tail. And as much as I tried, I couldn't find legs."

They all laughed.

"But another part of me just stared," Gwen continued. "And to tell you the truth, I think I'm still staring." The group nodded in approval. Some even smiled. By the corner, Forest cleared his throat.

"If you would like, you can take your first look at our guest."

"Ray," Gwen said, curious faces turning to look at her and then back to Forest. "We should start calling him Ray."

"Of course. Until he can tell us his name—and assuming we can pronounce it—we're going to call him Ray if that's okay with everybody."

In her mind, she saw a *Get Well Soon!* balloon decorating the corner, and made a mental note to get Ray something, not because he would see it, but because everyone else would.

* * *

The best thing about working for the UN had to be the worldwide connections. It was the only reason Dr. Safi Higgs had been flown from a conference in abnormal neuroscience in his hometown in Kenya to a tiny research facility in Maine, one that doubled as a merman's quarantine area and base to his friend Nathan Forest.

"So, did you read everything on the plane?" Nathan asked after their greeting at the ORCAS cafeteria.

"It was a long trip, but you have a pretty long list of tests done. I'm impressed with what I've seen so far. You would think with so little brain activity he wouldn't even be able to breathe. Maybe it's a different kind of coma—a hibernation-healing process."

Like every single scientist in this place, Higgs had a million theories about how the merman's body worked, and a million tests he wanted to run.

"I'm calling a retest on the DNA results," Nathan said, nursing his coffee.

"Come on, Nate. The biochemist in you has to see the beauty of this evolutionary solution," Higgs said with a smile, sipping his chocolate. "The only way it makes sense is if he didn't evolve on Earth."

"I know. I'm asking for it anyways. You can't go to the leaders of the world with this kind of information, just to find out someone messed up down the line."

"It's going to come back the same," Higgs said, taking a closer look at his friend. "Nathan, when was the last time you slept?"

"Yesterday? Maybe two days ago," Nate answered, looking at his watch. "It doesn't matter. I'm sure that the high commands of at least three countries already know. I just have to make it official."

"After you sleep, I hope. I've been on planes since you called me two days ago, and I look better than you do. That's not a compliment."

Nathan laughed, tired. "I just need—you know, to solve this problem. It's one thing to believe he's a sub-species, a sub-technological race representing a manageable threat. It's an entirely different game if he didn't come from underneath the ocean but from far above the skies."

Higgs sipped his chocolate, sweet and almost white with milk, just the way he liked it. "Hmm... well, start with what we do know: he's been living on Earth—antibodies prove that. What if he's been here all his life—"

"—but his parents are the ones who first came to our blue marble? How exactly do merfolk build spaceships, to begin with?"

"Maybe they got a ride? Say, they were bioengineered for this specific world. Surely, it makes more sense to conquer the depths of the oceans than the peaks of mountains? What if they were some sort of experiment, left behind and they went into hiding?"

Nathan shook his head. "They're too good at hiding. They're at least intelligent enough to know how to avoid us."

"Come on. We've discovered five percent of the oceans. Is not like we're making it hard for them. In any case, either he knows about his home planet, or he's clueless."

"Maybe. Maybe he knows, maybe he doesn't. Too many things bother me about him. From his DNA to his choice of beach, to his goddamn lungs. He can't be the only one, Higgs, but where do we look for the rest of them?"

Higgs chuckled, raising his cup in salute to his friend's problems.

"Well, Nathan, I can honestly tell you one thing. I'm so glad I'm not the one who has to bring this to your bosses."

...Or to the world.

* * *

Gwen needed fresh air. It was one thing to have treated Ray in the ER, with the adrenaline rush she'd gotten out of working on uncharted territory while patching up his tail. Now, everyone was talking a mile per hour, theories and hypotheses being thrown out every two minutes, everyone going crazy about this or that, while Ray just lay there.

She had no way to help him physically—no one did—but at the very least, she wanted people to stop seeing him as a science project.

And this is after Forest's grand speech… This is bad, Ray. Everyone wants a piece of you.

It took a few turns and some distance, but she could finally find a place to think in peace. Not twenty feet to her right, some guys were installing fancy equipment on the building; cameras. And right next to them, Forest talked to someone else, a tall guy, probably the crew's boss. She ignored him.

She ignored him, the crew, the building, and the entire world.

Maybe I shouldn't be here.

In front of her, nothing but green grass met her eyes. It was around 7:00 a.m., with people mingling in the parking lot further away, oblivious to the drama unfolding on sublevel 1.

Nothing prevented her from leaving. Nothing prevented her from calling CNN, BBC, anyone. She could see it clearly, the entire lawn filled with camera crews from around the world. Would that make Ray safe? If everyone had their eyes on him, would that be better or worse?

"Dr. Gaston!" Forest's words scared the hell out of her, making her curse out loud.

"What do you want?" she asked, feeling as if she'd been caught trying to escape.

"Well, I'd like you to meet Dr. Safi Higgs. He's the neuroscientist supervising Ray's progress. compare notes?"

"Call me Higgs," the black man said with a wide smile.

"Gwen," she automatically said, shaking his hand. "I'd love to compare notes with someone sane," she added. For some reason, they thought she was joking. Trying to let go of her worries, she looked to the crew still working on the cameras.

"Upgrading to fancy security?"

"Something like that," Nathan said. "Those are thermal cameras. Ray's core temperature runs a little colder than ours. I want to see if anyone else has the same unique problem."

She looked at his serious face and finally accepted he wasn't kidding. "You honestly think they can have legs?"

"I honestly think we know very little about Ray."

"Okay… Okay, it's your money and time." She turned to look at Higgs, then back to Nathan. "Why are you telling us? Shouldn't security details be confidential or something?"

"Why? We're all part of this, Dr. Gaston. I need everyone's attention everywhere. If I tell you to keep your attention on suspicious activity, you will forget it in two minutes. But, if you know exactly what I'm looking for—"

"—people with legs?"

"—people who look out of place because they're not used to legs, actually. Well, cold people, anyway. It'll be easier to remember."

"Mm… You want us to go shaking hands with creepy-looking people who may or may not be from an undersea civilization. Got it."

Higgs laughed hard, while Nathan smiled. "She has a point, Nate."

"Has it occurred to any of you that we might be in way over our heads?" she asked sincerely, looking at the building she'd come from.

"No," Nathan said without a second thought. "I wouldn't be able to do my job if it did."

"How practical."

"Well, thank you. Practical is the name of the game," he said.

"I've just got here. Too soon to tell," Higgs said. "If you'll excuse me, I'll get acquainted with the rest of the team. Go to sleep," he admonished Nathan before walking back to the building.

Nathan's phone chirped, and taking it out, he looked down at his trusty device. She wondered what would happen if she snatched it and ran with it.

"Something important?" she asked instead.

"I've requested a list of unusual sea events from New York to Nova Scotia for the past month, with an emphasis on the past week. Unfortunately, the list is rather long."

"Not practical."

"Not at all," he grinned, turning the screen off. "I'm sure someone will find the right way to filter this." He sighed, then looked at her for a moment. "I'm glad you're both here," he said, the comment throwing her off balance.

"You are? You have far more experienced surgeons with way better credentials. I mean, I bet Higgs there is a world-renowned neurologist. I bet everyone in there is a world-renowned something."

"Don't sell yourself short, Doctor. You kept Ray alive when everyone else was afraid of even touching him. And I have a hunch you'll keep him alive in more ways than the literal sense if he ever wakes up. Now, if you'll excuse me, I have a date with my bed."

She stared at him, and then at his retreating back. As compliments went, that was probably one of the best she'd ever gotten.

9

Unfocused

...In other news, the search for billionaire Julian Brook's son, Christopher Brooks, is now on its second day. Coast Guard patrols from Maine to Nova Scotia have been looking for any clues of what might have happened to the twenty-six-year-old sailing alone on a route he knew fairly well, according to his father. Authorities remain silent as to what causes might have led to the disappearance of such an experienced sailor, especially when weather conditions were favorable for the entire wee—

Matt changed the channel, just to find his brother's face plastered all over the screen again. Exasperated, he changed to a movie station and left whatever was playing as background noise. He needed to finish packing. Since Julian had given the press conference yesterday, Matt had endured a barricade of questions from complete strangers in search of an exclusive—questions that made him want to punch the wall.

He'd stayed for the press conference because Chris's cover demanded that his two brothers and father appeared on TV. Now it was over, his only problem was how to escape their house without the press following. It was so ironic both he and Chris were prisoners of human curiosity at its worst. Someone knocked on the door, but he didn't bother answering. It never stopped people from entering, anyway.

"Matt," Alex said, and for the first time, he thought his little brother looked thinner. "They moved him."

The whole world stopped. Every hour, every minute he expected Alex or Julian to tell him Chris had passed away—two nice-sounding words no one ever wanted to hear—but he was not ready to lose Chris's whereabouts.

"Where?"

"Some ocean research organization. They have several places, often in different states. I'm trying to follow the trail, but thought you should know before you leave."

Matt could count on Alex's support on anything short of killing someone, but he couldn't wait. He couldn't stay here, not with Julian talking to "authorities" all the time, feigning he thought Chris was lost at sea. They should be planning how to break Chris free, not playing with public relations, and certainly not accepting that there was no hope for his brother.

He pushed one last pair of jeans into his backpack. He had enough cash to last a couple of weeks if he was careful. He didn't know if Julian would track him down or if he'd block his credit cards, so for now, cash had to be it. It also meant leaving his phone. He could blind himself to telepaths, but not to telephone towers.

"Okay. Thanks for telling me. I'll call when I get there." He closed the backpack and looked around to make sure he wasn't leaving anything he needed.

"Where are you going to go? Maine's not exactly one small town, you know?"

"Like I care. Up there's way closer than down here. Do the math."

"You leaving is not going to help things. Julian's worried about us, about the Council, about the fallout of involving the Coast Guard. Things are a freaking house of cards right now!"

"Maybe if he was looking into how to save Chris—"

"Stop it!" Alex said, with uncharacteristic rage. "Just stop. Don't think Julian doesn't want to go with you. Or that I want to stay here, okay? You don't love him more than we do, you don't have to keep telling us how much we don't care. You going actually makes everything harder!"

No, seeing Chris in every corner of this house makes everything harder. He didn't say it. If Alex and Julian could stay here and do nothing, that was their problem. Matt had his own.

"Then I guess I'm a selfish bastard."

He picked up his backpack, his cap, his sunglasses, and left the room. Two hours later, he was on a bus to Maine, trying to convince himself this was the only choice he had, the only thing he could do.

* * *

Julian hung up his phone at the same time Alex walked into the living room. Chris would have known what to say to calm Alex's anxious thoughts, but Julian was coming up blank. He just didn't have the emotional stamina to keep it together beyond not falling apart.

"Matt left," Alex said, claiming the couch for himself. Seeing him lying with his legs dangling by the couch's arm, it was easy to picture his tail, so full of greens and yellows, still a bit short for someone Alex's age. Matt teased him mercilessly for it, but the youngest merman still had a few years to grow.

"I know," Julian answered. "There was no point stopping him."

"Aren't you worried he's going to do something stupid?"

Julian chuckled, an odd sound under the circumstances. "Matt is many things, but stupid is not one of them. He just has to deal with this his own way."

"It doesn't mean his own way won't involve doing stupid things," Alex insisted, an arm over his eyes.

"I don't know how much Matt's told you about his life before coming here," Julian said, taking a seat beside Alex's head. "But he's had to make tough decisions before. He's always chosen well."

"He never talks about the past," Alex said, removing his arm. Deep, dark eyes full of curiosity met Julian's blue ones. "I mean, you can ask Chris anything, he'll give you so much information you'll want to throw up. Matt—he just scowls and says it's none of my business. Which, you know, since you and Chris have known him since he came, it's kind of unfair."

Julian ruffled Alex's hair, a gesture he hadn't done in a couple of years.

"He had it rough. And unfortunately, he learned that the only one he could trust was himself. He's grown out of it for the most part, but I can't blame him for reacting this way."

"And it doesn't help matters that it's Chris. Bet he wouldn't have done this if it had been me," Alex said.

Julian put his hand on Alex's shoulder, looking down at his son. "Trust me, he would have. Except Chris would have tried to talk some sense into him and stop him, while you know him so well you didn't even try. He needed to go, and you didn't question it."

"I did try," Alex protested. "Okay, I didn't try too hard, but... I worry." Alex mumbled. "It's different with Chris. Chris is all about making peace and having a good time. Chris is—"

Alex choked, unable to keep talking for a few moments. "Dad... what are we going to do without him?" Desperation poured out of each word.

"What do you think Chris would want us to do?"

Alex tried to blink his tears away and failed. "Make peace and have a good time..." he answered, wiping his face with the back of his hand. He sat up and leaned on Julian's shoulder. "I wish... I wish he would just let go. Matt said this is better because he's not suffering, but…" Alex trailed off. *But we can't let go, either.* Julian hugged him, sideways, and they stayed in silence for a few minutes.

"Dad?" Alex asked tentatively.

"Yes?"

"What happens… I mean… Three days ago we thought he wouldn't survive past the first day, but…"

"You shouldn't keep hacking into it," he scolded without any feeling.

"Yes, but… What if he actually… wakes up?"

"Then we'll ask him what he wants us to do," Julian said, this time meaning it. "And we'll take it from there."

* * *

"He's not going after you, you know?" Alex said, holding his phone between his ear and his shoulder while he typed on the computer.

"Says he…" Matt countered, the reception on his payphone making him sound like a robot.

"Buy another phone," Alex said, most of his attention on the code he had on his screen. "He's not happy with you gone, but he won't stop you."

"He said that?"

"He said you made good choices. He trusts your seventeen-year-old judgment."

Silence met his words. It was prolonged enough that Alex stopped typing. "Matt?"

"So, do you know where Chris is, or not?" his brother asked, his voice still distorted.

"I have the general area. They haven't updated where exactly he is, but medical reports are flying all over the place."

"He's still alive," Matt breathed, and Alex nodded, forgetting this was a phone conversation. "How is he?"

"I have no idea. We'd need a doctor for that. Everything I can get my virtual hands on is in medical jargon," Alex answered, frustrated.

"Okay… Okay, shoot. Give me the address of this general area."

"On one condition," Alex said, calling a window with a map of the ORCAS's many buildings.

"Squid…" Matt warned. Alex rolled his eyes.

"Promise me you won't do anything stupid."

"Didn't you just say you trusted me?"

"I said Julian trusts you. I know better."

"Give me the address…" Matt said between clenched teeth.

"Give me your promise," Alex said, not backing down. "I only have one brother left, and I'm not going to lose you, too."

Silence again.

"I promise you that by the time this is over, you'll still have one brother… maybe even two."

Alex smiled despite himself. "Okay. But Matt? Be careful."

"Always."

* * *

"Mr. Brooks, what are you doing here?" Sarah asked, her voice warning him of her disapproval.

"The truth, Sarah? I needed to get out of the house," Julian admitted. She'd been his senior assistant for almost fifteen years now, and he had the strange feeling she'd adopted him as her surrogate son, notwithstanding the fact he was old enough to have met her great-grandparents.

Her eyes softened. "There are a million places you can go, sir. The office is hardly the place to hide."

"I'm not hiding here. I just needed a few things," he said, reaching for a framed picture of his three sons, all grinning at the camera. The photo didn't show it, but they had all been shifted into their tails.

"I hope you know everyone in here is praying for your son's safe return," Sarah said, her words heartfelt.

"I know. Thank you. I really shoul—"

He felt the muscles in his legs cramp, a terrible tingling sensation spreading all the way to his lower back. He sat down abruptly, feeling his skin trying to shift into scales from the back of his neck all the way down to his toes. Beneath his jacket, he was losing the battle, and he could see faint scarlet scales peeking at the back of his hand. The wretched void where Chris used to be in his heart suddenly came to life in one burning burst that scorched Julian's soul.

No. Please, Chris, don't. Not like this.

"Mr. Brooks?"

A sharp pain hit him in his mind and his legs, making it harder to remain in human form.

"Julian?" Sarah asked, her first-name calling a sure sign she was worried. "Julian, are you okay?"

Nausea hit him as he both tried to reach the mental thread that had gone empty for so long and recoiled from the onslaught of sensations that weren't his. He was terrified he was feeling his son's final moments, but he would not let Chris go through death without him there, no matter if it was killing Julian's soul to do it.

Stinging and burning came in waves, but instead of decreasing, they were coming closer and closer, until Julian finally realized what was happening: his son wasn't dying. Chris was waking up to a sea of confusion and pain, lashing out without control, his body screaming for help, in agony. It was both the brightest and darkest moment in his life.

Chris! Chris! he sent to his son, trying to get his attention. *Focus! Hear my voice!*

There were no words, just a jungle of emotions, of fear and confusion and exhaustion colliding into chaos.

Chris, I'm here!

Chris didn't answer with words, but rather with awareness. In a moment of lucidity, he gripped Julian's mental bond with all his strength. And then he was gone.

10

Wide Awake

Chris was lost.

In the absolute darkness surrounding him, he searched for his watch, the only light in this underwater world, and couldn't figure out why he wasn't wearing it. Looking up and down made absolutely no difference, the pressure of the ocean becoming a relentless cage.

Julian's going to kill me, he thought briefly, his breaths deep and even, just as his guardian had taught him. Unlike human divers, he was in no danger of running out of oxygen, but being lost a mile deep in the ocean was not a good thing. He had to pick a direction and swim. If the pressure increased, he was going down. If it decreased, then he was going up, the way to sunshine, to his boat and the outside world.

He moved his tail—except he couldn't. Even though he was blind to his surroundings, Chris looked down, confused what had caught him. He tried again, harder, and felt a faint sting. He winced. If he was swimming with jellyfish, he was in for a world of pain.

Calm down, he coached himself. Jellyfish could be a deadly encounter, but he'd checked the area before diving. He'd rather face sharks, honestly, but now was not the time to think about that. The sting became persistent, and he tried to reach down to scratch it. His shoulders were restrained, however, and his hands barely reached, unseeing, into nothing but emptiness. Whatever was stinging cut deeper, burning its way through the middle of his tail, while his back cramped. His head felt heavy, and he had the terrible sensation of being swallowed whole by something. He forgot all about taking deep breaths and thought of all the possible reasons why he couldn't swim away. None was pretty.

From somewhere, sound came. It made absolutely no sense at this depth, so he went still, trying to decipher it.

Whales wouldn't sound like that… A submarine?

It sounded like voices. Far away and distorted, but... still voices, regardless. Darkness gained clarity ahead of him, light coming from an unknown source. He wanted to escape, to flee these incomprehensible events, back into the safety of the deep, but he couldn't. Whatever was happening, it had him paralyzed, chained by invisible ties to an invisible—bed.

Dizziness overtook him as his entire perception changed, from being upright to being horizontal. He was lying on a bed—he could feel the mattress below his body—and the more he tried to understand, the more his head hurt.

"—*don't let the tail*—"

"—*one get Forest*—"

"—*pressure is going up*—"

Too many voices exploded in his ears. He reached for something, anything that would make sense, an anchor to hold on to.

"Take deep breaths," a woman's voice whispered in his right ear. He recoiled, his thoughts turning to Julian as he felt himself sinking into confusion and despair, his whole body burning.

There was not enough air—and not enough reality. Darkness gave way to sudden bright lights that made him shut his eyes, and he felt hands touching him everywhere, chaining him. No matter how hard he tried to shake them off, they always came back, until they grabbed the sides of his head, grounding him.

"Deep... breaths..." the voice kept saying, as he realized this nightmare was inescapable.

"Deep... breaths..." He moved barely inches in any direction, and even more hands pinned him down. "Come on... deep... breaths..." the voice coached, a tinge of frustration coloring it. "Forget everything, take deep breaths."

Her voice was hypnotic, luring him into following her lead, into falling into the rhythm she was setting for him. She willed his mind to concentrate in the same way the hands willed his body to remain still. Everything hurt. Not in the way that made him wince after diving a mile deep, not in the way a good workout left his muscles sore but wanting more.

This hurt was bone deep, gripping. This hurt went beyond anything he'd ever experienced, and no matter what he tried to do, he couldn't get away from it. So he took her words to heart and matched her breathing in the best way he could, praying he'd be able to forget everything but breathing.

"That's it... you're doing... great... deep... breaths..."

He fixated on that idea and didn't even realize when he slipped back into unconsciousness.

78

* * *

"He's stable," Higgs informed Nathan as he exited the elevator into sub-level 1. "You just missed one hell of a show. He woke up—but he's unconscious again."

"Did he say anything?"

Higgs shook his head. "Not exactly."

Nathan stopped in his tracks, facing his friend. "'Not exactly'?"

Higgs sighed. "Let me give you the facts first. He had a crisis about two hours ago that we could barely get him out of. Honestly? I thought this was only the beginning of the end. But, we noticed an increase in brain activity shortly afterward."

Nathan nodded. "I got the heads up, that's why I came back."

"Fifteen minutes ago, he actually woke. For less than two minutes, so don't get your hopes up."

"He should be dead for all the good we've done him, Higgs, so I'm damn well going to get my hopes up. So, what happened?"

"He started moving. First his tail, barely a contraction. We thought it might be a reflex, but his hands followed. And then he went from zero to 100 in two seconds, making everyone scramble. We tried our best to stop him moving, but he still managed to rip a dozen stitches from his tail, and his wrist is going to need a new cast. He's in the OR right now, getting patched up again."

Nathan closed his eyes for a moment. They hadn't really prepared for Ray to wake up so suddenly, and certainly not so violently.

"So, what is this business of *not exactly*?"

"Gwen started talking to him," Higgs explained, and Nathan had to make a mental sweep to match Gwen with Dr. Gaston. "She told him to take deep breaths so he'd calm down. And he did."

They both looked at each other.

"He understood her," Nathan whispered, shocked.

"Maybe he understood English. Maybe not. It was very chaotic. He might have understood she was trying to calm him down and decided to match his breathing with hers, but it doesn't mean he understood her words. Or it might all have been just a coincidence. Look, Nathan, he was losing consciousness anyway. We might think he understood, but maybe it's just wishful thinking on our part."

Nathan took a deep breath, the ramifications multiplying by the second. "He's no longer in a coma. So many people are going to flip... What do you think, Higgs? Where are we with him?"

"We have to run more tests, but the prognosis has just turned in his favor. Keep in mind, Nate, we've no idea if there's any brain damage."

"I want to see the video. And I want to talk with Gwen."

* * *

"Do you think he understood you?" Forest asked, eagerly. Around the conference room, three other men and one woman stared at Gwen with varying degrees of disapproval.

"I don't know. We never made eye-contact. The lights were so bright in his eyes he shut them and never looked at me."

"But he did match your breathing."

"Yes, but only for a few seconds."

"Dr. Forest, with all due respect," one of the other men said. "There were twelve people in that room, and we have of what was happening. No one thinks he understood what was going on but Dr. Gaston here."

"What does your gut instinct tell you?" Forest asked Gwen, his piercing eyes not letting her off the hook. He wanted to believe her, he did, and that scared the hell out of her. She looked at the other doctors. Without conclusive proof, she shouldn't be saying anything.

"Dr. Gaston, what does your instinct tell you?" he repeated, bringing her back to his eyes.

She saw Ray's tail barely moving. She distinctively remembered thinking *my God, he's still fighting.* Everyone stopped whatever they were doing as the heartbeat monitor accelerated, Ray's hand shooting up as if he were grabbing a flying bird. He was so fast.

Then everyone was on him, all shouting about the need to immobilize. He was going to hurt himself in the worst possible way if he didn't calm down. In a normal setting, he'd have been sedated, except nothing about this *was* normal. They couldn't risk sedating him because they had no idea what the drugs would do to him. It was bad enough he was waking from a coma as if from a terrible dream, but she knew—she absolutely knew—he was waking to a real-life nightmare for him.

80

With drugs out of the question, she did the next best thing short of knocking him out with a bat; she talked to him.

"You don't understand, he had absolutely no idea of what was happening." She looked at Forest but in her mind all she could see was Ray's terrified face. "I talked to him," she continued. "He recoiled. Everyone was shouting and restraining him, I can't even imagine what was going on in his mind. I've seen plenty of people waking up in the ER, or waking up from surgery after accidents—it's never pretty. Not knowing what's happening and why there's so much pain has to be the worst kind of hell."

Her mind filled with the sounds of the ER, with the alarms, the shouts, the chaos, and tried to imagine how all that had sounded for Ray.

"I talked to him, and I knew I wasn't getting through, even when I gripped his head. I knew it. And then... something clicked in his mind. He went very still. It was deliberate—he still had strength in him. He was gripping the gurney's rail even though it must've hurt like hell since he'd already broken the cast. I don't know if he understood me, Dr. Forest, but I can tell you he understood fighting was not getting him anywhere. He willed himself to relax before he lost the battle. That's what I can tell you without a doubt. Everything else, it's just speculation."

The tension in the room went down considerably. It was one thing to imply he was intelligent—something they all agreed on—but an entire other universe to imply Ray understood English. The thought hurt her brain.

"Thank you, doctor," Forest said. He addressed the group. "I want protocols in one hour on my desk, as to how we're going to take this further. Access will be limited. I'll need a trauma psychologist, a linguist—anyone to facilitate communication between him and us. And get me a physical therapist. The next time he wakes up, make sure you know if he's understanding you or not," he said to Gwen.

"You mean if he's not waking in hell and a dozen humans are not cutting him up?"

Forest didn't smile. In fact, he stood and left the room without another word while she fumed at his demands. She wasn't here to obey Forest's every practical choice. She was here to care for Ray—and defend him from vultures.

I'll give you 'understanding', she thought as she walked back to her patient.

* * *

Major White watched the merman's awakening video without blinking. Those ninety-three seconds held one of the key elements that would define this encounter. Communication.

Did you understand her words or just her meaning?

Or nothing at all?

This was turning out to be a far more dangerous game than anticipated. Where were the other pieces, though? White wasn't fooling himself. He wasn't watching a helpless mythological creature clawing its way to life; he was watching an alien entity who'd been living under the radar, from an unknown civilization of equally unknown capabilities.

What do you know about us? Why were you on our beach?

White leaned on his seat, slowly exhaling. Part of him respected this merman's will to live—admired it, actually—and part of him swiftly planned how to use a fully conscious Ray to bait his friends. *And if you already speak our language, you're just making this easier.*

It was just a matter of waiting now. It always was.

* * *

"You're still seriously considering throwing him into the closest swimming pool?" Gwen asked as she devoured the salad in front of her. The cafeteria was deserted at 3:00 a.m. except for a couple of Japanese researchers, animatedly talking in one corner.

Jet lag is a bitch.

Forest had invited her to a late dinner or early breakfast—however one wanted to define a 3:00 a.m. meal—in order to clear the air between them. And she had to admit, it had worked. She didn't want to punch him anymore.

"When could we move him into any body of water? I know there are water-resistant materials to wrap his tail…"

She paused mid-eat, her fork midway to her mouth. "I'd say, you could move him when he's given his consent to be moved."

Nathan smiled. "Okay, let's just say for the sake of argument?"

She chewed on her meal the same as she chewed on the problem. "Do you honestly think his lungs would change?"

"You saw the skin on his back after he woke up. Some of it changed to scales. So, if his skin did…"

"That's a whole different level of 'changiness'," she said. "He was half-drowned when we got him into the ER. If he can do this, it would have to be with him conscious."

Forest took a sip of his coffee, thoughtful. "I've been thinking about this a lot—"

"—you don't say—"

"—Breathing should be an automatic response. He's underwater, his lungs automatically change in reaction to water. He's in air, they change back. But here he drifts after major trauma, dragged by the currents until he finds land. His respiratory system accommodates the change, but then waves keep submerging him and bringing him to the surface, making the system change back and forth, back and forth, until it finally crashes."

"Leaving us with a half-drowned merman, with a tail and human lungs. Hmm..." she said, rounding up the last of her vegetables. "Interesting."

"Practical."

"I'm still not letting you throw him into a fish tank," she said, pointing at him with her fork, food dangling from its prongs. "He's barely making any progress in the *awake* department for you to try to force his body into some auto-response that may or may not be there."

Forest smiled, raising one hand in a peace gesture. "Wouldn't dream of it. But just the possibility they could be walking among us..."

He had that barely-there, dreamy look he sometimes got when he was talking about Ray and his species at large. She wondered if Forest had a thing for mermaids to begin with. With her salad gone, she leaned on her chair and seriously looked at Forest. "We need food."

His eyes went to her empty plate.

"Not for me," she said, deadpan. "For Ray. How are we going to approach his diet when he wakes up? 'Cause, I don't think tuna and sardines are appropriate."

"Oh, that's taken care of. Once he's well enough to eat, his diet has already been planned out by some nutritionists in Germany. Truly inspired stuff, if I may say. We've also been narrowing down our candidates for physical therapy. There's a guy in California I'm trying to get in touch with."

She looked at him, hoping her eyes were half as piercing as his when he wanted an answer. "What else have you planned out for Ray?"

"Would world domination be too much?" he asked, sipping his coffee with an innocent face. She rolled her eyes. "So far, I'm just happy with keeping him alive," he answered.

She smiled, knowing the feeling all too well.

"How about you, doctor?" Forest asked. "Are you ready for him waking up for real?"

No. Hell no. Why do you even keep me around, for Pete's sake?!

She decided to go with a more diplomatic approach. "I keep reading the guidelines your shrinks gave us—"

"—They're pretty straightforward," Forest said proudly. "And limiting the number of people around him when he wakes would maximize the opportunity of him bonding with either you or Higgs."

She snorted. "You're getting way ahead of the game, Forest. Look, most people wake up in a hospital knowing we're there to help them and we have drugs to keep them nice and comfortable. Ray won't have either. Me explaining he's been in an accident and now he's in a safe place is going to mean zero to him, and that's assuming he understands me."

My God, we're his worst nightmare. Did merfolk even know what a hospital was? Why there'd be so much pain? That it wasn't their fault?

"Well, Dr. Gaston, we can't do anything about doping him, but sooner or later, he's going to believe us when we say he's safe. That's our job."

"But what if—"

"Whatever happens, we'll deal with it."

She glared at him, wishing she were as confident as he seemed. She wished she were as confident about *anything* related to Ray, honestly.

I'm so going to mess this up. I just know it.

11

White Lies

"I've been driving around this goddamn city for the last three hours; can't you get me an exact location?" Matt demanded on the phone.

Alex listened but kept massaging his temples. Not only had Matt gotten himself a new phone so he could yell at his little brother at 7:32 a.m., he'd also gotten a used car and a bad attitude.

"I'm as invested in finding our brother as you are, Matt. Ever since Chris woke up, the entire security system sky-rocketed. It's going to take time."

"Damn it!" Matt shouted, and Alex wasn't sure if that was directed at him, at Chris's captors, or at some random person crossing Matt's path. Julian had been the only one to actually feel Chris waking the day prior, but both Alex and Matt had felt something akin to a nudge, a strange sense of something filling the void where Chris's presence usually was. It was all they needed to have hope again.

"Look," Alex said. "It's just a matter of time. Julian is working on this as well, and the Council has way better resources than yours truly."

"The Council's going to rule out helping Chris. You know how it is; silence and nothing else."

"Don't you think it was easier to say *we won't do anything* when Chris was in a coma and almost dead than it is now he's woken up? For one thing, Chris is almost of age to go to the City, which means he knows way more than you or I do, about it. They won't want Chris babbling out."

"I know that," Matt said. "But he might as well be killed by our own lovely Council to keep him from talking."

"Not gonna happen. Julian would never allow it."

"The same way he'd never allow his eldest son to die at the hands of humans three days ago?"

"That was different and you know it. There was no tactical reason to retrieve Chris's body besides closure for us. We're past that."

"Unless humans finish the job first… Listen, now he's awake, we have the responsibility of getting him out. Not the Council. Us. Which may or may not include Julian."

Alex was honestly trying to cut his brother some slack, but it was getting harder by the second.

"Matt. Let's not jump to conclusions. We don't even know where Chris is or if he's even able to shift right now."

"Get the hell out of the way!" Matt shouted so loud, Alex dropped his phone. His headache increased with each word Matt uttered. "Find out his location."

The line went dead.

"Yes, ma'am," Alex said, into the silence.

Leaning on the doorframe, Julian watched. "Your brother didn't take it well, then." It wasn't a question, but Alex shook his head.

"I can't keep lying to him forever, Dad. He'll figure out where Chris is one way or another."

Alex closed his laptop, the building with Chris's exact location disappearing on his screen. He hated lying to Matt but loathed the idea of Matt crashing through those doors alone even more.

"We both know how much Matt hates to wait, especially for authority figures," Julian said, resigned. "At least now he has something to do while the Council decides on our best option."

"I can't believe they're not letting you vote."

"I respect them. I didn't deal with the situation well enough when Chris was in a coma, so I'm in no position to balance my options objectively now his life's in danger."

Julian turned to go.

"Dad? What if they vote 'no'?"

Julian stopped, and barely turned his head to answer. "Then things are going to get interesting."

* * *

"We're taking a break," Drake said over the phone, sounding as exhausted as Julian felt. The Council had been trying to decide how to handle the crisis for the past twelve hours, almost as long as it had been since Julian had heard from his son.

"Let me guess, you're in a tie."

"There's a reason why we're five," Drake pointed out, sourly. Drake had been against Julian staying out of the Council's voting, but—of course—Julian insisted. If he was going to do something stupid to save his son, he didn't want anyone else going down that rabbit hole with him. His oldest friend sighed deeply.

"You know we all want your son out. Even Aurel with her million neurotic reasons agrees. It's how to go about it without bringing all of us down that's not working out."

"I know. Whatever you vote, I won't blame you. I know how serious the consequences are."

He heard Drake exhaled, obviously relieved their friendship wasn't in jeopardy.

"Things would be easier if this were happening to us..." Drake murmured. "We knew the risks when we abandoned the City, but not these kids. They had no say in being on the surface, dealing with all this crap."

It was a sore point dividing everyone who'd given up the City for the right to be up here: children. No one could survive the trip in or out of the City before reaching adulthood, so most people agreed children needed to be born inside the City, not outside. The problem was, family planning was harshly regulated inside the walls, but there was no one to enforce those rules up here. It was up to the Council members to take care of every orphaned child left behind, and although Julian wouldn't trade his role as father to his three sons, he did regret the situations that had led them to him.

"Listen," Drake said, changing the subject. "I'm sending you everything I've got on the people treating Christopher. If we vote to intervene in any capacity, it's better we're all informed on who we're dealing with."

"Right. Last time I checked, the command chain seemed to have solidified under one Nathan Forest. Alex has been digging into his files but we haven't found much."

"I don't think the US government will let the UN have this for too long, to tell you the truth. There's a Major White we should keep an eye on. I'll send you what I have. Right now, about forty people have been given clearance in one way or another. Almost all of them civilian."

Julian frowned. "That's a lot of people."

"Tell me about it. I'm not sure if they're making our job easier or harder, but at least it won't be so problematic to get someone into their inner circle if this becomes a long-term operation."

Those last words froze Julian's mind. "Lo—long-term?"

On the other side, a heavy silence took place. The kind that meant *I shouldn't have said that.*

"There are three options here, my friend: We do nothing. We do everything. Or we wait. I can assure you we have already discarded doing nothing. The *everything* option is too wide, that's why this meeting has taken half a day without anything to show but a collective headache and finger-pointing. I honestly think we're going to settle with waiting before moving forward."

Julian went as far as opening his mouth to object that waiting was the same as doing nothing for all practical reasons, that Chris deserved so much better than being left behind. And then he remembered; he didn't have any voice in this decision.

"I understand," he said, as calmly as he could.

"Julian," Drake warned, picking on his friend's stormy thoughts. "Don't do anything stupid without telling me first."

Julian barked a laugh. That was such a Drake thing to say. "I know. If this becomes a long-term operation, I'm glad to have you for logistics."

Drake sighed. "We're going to resume the meeting now. If that head of yours comes up with any ideas on how to get your son out, tell me. I hate not having you here…"

The line went silent for a moment, then Julian's phone chirped with an e-mail notification. The files on the people surrounding Chris were many and fairly detailed given so short a time, but Julian skipped them all until he found the one he was most interested in: Nathan Forest.

What do you want, Mr. Forest, that will give me my son back?

* * *

"We're asking the City what they want us to do," Mireya said as if each word was cutting her throat. Three hours had passed since Drake's call, and Julian could only imagine how talks had deteriorated if all the members had voted on calling the City.

88

None of them was fond of the prospect of calling, and much less fond of this mess. "I'm sorry, Julian, we just couldn't decide what consequences to expect from either leaving Chris there or attempting a rescue."

"Or showing ourselves," Julian said quietly, tense at the idea of yet more waiting. Matt wasn't the only one who hated doing that, not by a long shot.

"We've been monitoring Chris, as you know. He still hasn't regained proper consciousness, but we'll coach him—"

"I'll be with him. No matter what the Council or the City decides, I'll be the one to deliver the news to him, and I'll be the one to guide him through this. I hope you can respect at least that much."

"Julian. He's a ward of the Council. All orphaned children are. He's as much our responsibility as yours. Don't think any of us is taking this lightly. It could have been my daughters. It could still be my daughters any given day. Whatever we decide, Chris has already changed our plans for the future in a drastic way, no one can deny that. And no one is blaming him." She paused. "That does bring me to something we haven't discussed yet."

"What?"

"What happened to Chris, to begin with? We've gone through all the humans' files on Chris and found a very interesting report detailing how Chris got his injuries. Someone hit him while he was out of the water. They hit him while he was in mer-form, in the open sea. Most likely when he reached the boat and was getting ready to shift back into legs."

"Which means someone probably already knows he's my son."

"Maybe. Be on the lookout for any threats. Drake's already tracing several media plans on the beach video. He's afraid things are going to explode sooner rather than later."

"Explode? How?"

"One of the big networks is planning to run a special on Sunday piecing together everything that's surfaced on the internet so far."

"If it's a special, all they have are conjectures. If they had something real, it'd be breaking news."

"We know. We're more worried about the special running alongside Chris's search news. His disappearance is big enough for curious minds to make a connection."

Julian exhaled, his mind stretched in too many directions to see the big picture. "You want me to call the search off."

"Actually... I have a better idea."

12

Loose Ends

Gwen lowered herself down to Ray's line of sight as slowly as she could. They'd been giving him a sponge bath and moved him onto his side when she'd noticed his eyes were open. He wasn't moving, but he was blinking every few seconds, his breathing even. She'd said a few greetings but hadn't gotten his attention at all.

He's in some sort of shock, she thought, standing directly in front of him, looking straight into his deep blue eyes.

"Hey…" she tried again, gently softening her voice. "I'm Gwen. You're safe here. You were in an accident."

He closed his eyes and didn't open them again.

She let out a deep sigh. *What are we going to do with you, Ray?*

* * *

Sound came and went. In the darkness where Chris drifted, time stood still. Hunger and pain resided far away. Sometimes, he wondered if he was supposed to be doing something or not, but most of the time, he just wanted to sleep.

Chris?

He opened his eyes, although it was useless in this place. He knew that name, didn't he?

Chris, I'm here…

Reaching for it required too much effort. Recognizing it was out of the question. He just wanted to sleep.

Damn it! Answer me! I'm not leaving you, brother, not ever!

And so, he slept.

*　*　*

"You HAVE to come here!" Matt shouted over the phone, making Alex wince and Julian pray for patience. Again. "Something's wrong with him!"

"Calm down, Matt."

"He's awake but he's not there. Julian—"

"Calm down, Matt."

"But—"

"*Calm* down. You're right for being anxious, but just please, calm down."

"This better be good…"

Even if 500 miles separated them, Julian could perfectly picture his middle son's impatient face. If there was anyone who needed to keep busy or keep worrying, that was Matt. *This is the reason why I didn't want you to find your brother just yet.*

"It's expected that things like this will happen. Chris just went through some serious trauma."

"They say that his vitals and brain activity are improving," Alex spoke, his eyes on his computer as if he was somehow going to misunderstand the information." They're expecting him to gain consciousness any moment now."

"The more reason for you to come here!" Matt exploded, somehow the good news passing him right by. "You HAVE to see—"

"We're getting ready to leave."

"What?" Matt said in disbelief. "You're—you're actually coming?"

Alex glared at the phone. Julian did the same, fervently hoping Matt could somehow interpret their silence.

"We're leaving for Maine in a few hours, but Christopher Brooks's disappearance is not something I can leave unattended. You cannot have the news cycling the merman story and Chris's search effort one after the other. Someone is going to make it click. Mireya's come up with a clever idea on how to deal with this identity problem."

They both looked at the phone expectantly. Matt might not like the Council in principle, but he had a healthy respect for Mireya, who had found him first and brought him to Julian.

"How long is it going to take?" Matt asked, for the first time in a civil tone.

"We're aiming to get it done in a few hours and fly to you tonight," Julian said, mentally playing Mireya's plan in his mind. "We'll be there before you know it. You stay there," Julian added, knowing nothing short of a hurricane would move Matt from Maine in any case. "Chris is going to wake up soon, for real, and he's going to need to know we're there."

"I'm not sure I'm close enough. I barely got—I don't know, something. Like he was dreaming but he wasn't. I'm telling you, there's something wrong with him."

Alex looked at Julian with concern.

"Give him time," he said to the phone, looking at Alex so his two sons could be appeased. "He's going to reach for you the moment he knows you're nearby. I need you to be prepared, okay? Long distance telepathy feels... different. Try to imagine your brother sitting beside you. As long as you can keep a mental image, you'll be making things easier for him. And Matt, don't keep him awake."

"What? Isn't the whole point to help him stay awake?"

"No. Don't be scared if he fades out of your connection. Call us if anything happens, but you can do this, okay?"

Silence prolonged itself long enough that he thought he had lost the call.

"Okay... Just... hurry."

* * *

Alex anxiously reached the study. Half of his brain was on Chris and half on Matt. The remaining percentage of his brain power was trying to keep the fear of discovery at bay. He'd just seen the merman special announced on TV, a reminder that if this thing backfired, he could lose his life as he knew it.

But that's on Sunday, he told himself. *We still have two whole days to resolve things.*

"Come in," Julian said once Alex knocked, taking a deep breath and squaring his shoulders. He wasn't worried about showing his fears to Julian, but on his father's computer, Mireya was waiting. She hardly ever visited New York, preferring her South America region, so Alex had only seen her four or five times in the flesh. Council meetings were Julian's affairs, and for the most part, Alex couldn't care less about them. But Chris did, a lot. His brother had told him about Mireya's daughters, just as adopted as they were. It was weird, Alex thought, how the Council members didn't have kids of their own and he wondered if there was a story behind it.

Maybe it's a requirement.

In any case, Mireya's eldest daughter, Diana, was supposed to do the trip to the City with Chris, even if it meant she had to wait a whole year. It was best for the two of them to go together, and both Julian and Mireya had insisted on it. Chris was supposed to start training with her six months before the actual trip, sometime in the next year. Alex wondered, with a bitter taste, if his brother was still going to be able to make it. Not because he could still be a prisoner, but because the injury in his tail was serious enough to be a problem.

"We're finalizing the last details, so we need you to get up to speed," Julian said with a small smile, looking less on edge for the first time in ages.

Or maybe he's just exhausted.

"Alexander," Mireya said, with an accent Alex couldn't place but that melted his heart. Her big emerald eyes and black hair seemed to shine on the screen, her smile honest and appraising. She was beautiful, and he blushed at the thought. "We're going to get this situation resolved," she stated, in the same practical tone that Julian used in board meetings.

Alex nodded silently, feeling like an idiot.

"Drake's just sent a message," Julian said, checking his phone. "He can have everything in place in an hour."

"That's enough time for us to iron the story and find any weak spots," Mireya said with approval. "Now, Alexander, I hope you're a good liar."

He nodded enthusiastically. Julian just chuckled. "I'm afraid he is," his father admitted, making Alex proud for all of two seconds before flinching.

"I didn't mean it like that," Alex explained, blushing now in embarrassment.

"Oh darling, we all mean it like that. You don't spend 300 years hiding without being a good liar, wouldn't you agree, Julian?"

It was Alex's turn to look at his father with renewed interest. Julian seldom talked about his life from before Brooks Inc. had been founded, a fact that drove all three boys mad with curiosity. Mireya was from *before*, though. She'd been on the Council longer than Julian, but how much time that meant, they could only guess. Now Alex had a good starting point.

Julian barely arched an eyebrow at his son, a silent declaration of *not now*.

"What do I have to do?" Alex asked, eager to prove his worth as a liar or anything else.

"Well, Alexander, as all good liars know, the best lies are the ones with a little truth mixed in. We're about to announce we've just found your brother."

13

Timing is Everything

The man behind the counter was close to tears. Kate tried not to stare, but it was hard to hide her bewilderment at seeing a man in his fifties holding the watch as if he were cradling a baby.

"I never thought I would see one of these. Not one of *these*."

She rolled her eyes inwardly. She would never understand what the fascination was with men and sports, men and cars, and men and their hobbies. Although as hobbies went, Mr. Hans here had a very lucrative one: sports articles. Or rather, luxury sports articles. And that included sports watches.

"Lionel recommended you, said I shouldn't be surprised if you got a little... sentimental."

Or just mental...

Mr. Hans nodded, blinking his tears away. "I worked for Brooks Inc. for twenty years. Everything I know, everything I own, is because of what I learned with them. This, Ms. Banes, is not something a stranger should have."

"I know. I intend on giving it back to its rightful owner, but I've been having trouble finding him."

Big trouble, in fact. In her long list of contacts, Kate hadn't found a sports watch expert, but she did have a couple of jewelers and tons of sports experts. The sports contact had told her it was definitely a divers' watch, and an expensive one. As in *half a million dollars expensive*, but he had no more info on it. She'd almost hired a security guard to carry that thing around since then.

The jewelers had told her they only dealt with standard luxury watches, but they'd sent her to another guy, a specialist in high-profile sports items. In turn, he had sent her to Lionel, who had told her he'd never seen this type of watch before but knew someone who specialized in all kinds of weird rich stuff. And that got her here, two days later, with an engraved half-a-million-dollars watch and a man close to tears. Even if it hadn't belonged to a presumed merman, that watch had one hell of a story.

"So, what can you tell me about it? I couldn't even trace who made it."

Mr. Hans smiled at that. "That's because it's not commercial. Brooks Inc. manufactures plenty of sea artifacts, as you well know, but not many people are aware they fabricate sportswear. Highly professional."

"Highly expensive."

"Yes, but not in the way you might think. This is a Trident watch. What makes it expensive is the technology behind it. From the materials to its calibration, this thing is poetry on your wrist. But, and this is what *really* makes it expensive: a Trident watch cannot be bought. They're given to high-ranking scientists: marine biologists, oceanographers, and the like."

"All water related?"

"For the most part. I've known of athletes getting one as well, but it's mostly smart people."

Why would you want a half a million watch that tells you how deep you go without ever using it?

"How does a scientist earn one?" she asked instead.

"You must have discovered or developed some exceptional thing related to their industries to earn one. They contact you, not the other way around. It's considered one of the highest honors in the field, but you've probably never heard about a ceremony."

"Really?"

"They don't make it public."

She looked incredulous and he nodded with a knowing smile.

"Now, I've seen those *award* watches, if you'd like. They are state of the art machines that not only can withstand the pressure of the ocean, they can withstand a lot of everyday wear and tear. The face never scratches, for example. They have the patent for twenty-three components inside this machine."

"Huh. Something tells me I'll never look at my watch the same way again after this…"

Mr. Hans smiled. Kate tried to hide her own thirty-five-dollar watch as best as she could.

"As I said, it's the high-tech and design that makes it so expensive. The materials are unique."

"The patents, I bet."

"Indeed."

"So, do you know who owns it?"

Mr. Hans nodded, and Kate's heart did a somersault. He turned it, the inscription clear.

Deep breaths. Julian.

"Very few people get these watches, as I've told you unless they're accomplished athletes or scientists. But there's also a smaller group: friends and family."

"Of the board members?"

"Maybe." He turned the watch back. "The watch itself, as you can see, has what a common divers' watch has. But see how there are two depth meters? Those are specifically made for this elite group. They can mark how deep they went. I had never seen one like this. Julian is, most likely, Julian Brooks."

"*The* Julian Brooks?"

Mr. Hans nodded slowly, frowning. "I'd like to run some tests because this is off." He pointed out to the meters. One read 0, the other read 2931. "This one marks at what depth you are, so zero since you're out of the water. This one marks the depth you achieved."

"So, 2931 feet?"

"No. 2931 meters. That's almost two miles deep."

"Whoa, someone likes diving."

"Someone's got a malfunctioning watch, more likely. The world record for deep diving is 332 meters or about a thousand feet."

"What if he was on a submarine?"

Mr. Hans shook his head. "It's too deep even for submarines, as far as I know. Plus, it wouldn't give this reading on a submarine."

"So, you're saying this is a defective watch?"

"Or a fake."

* * *

"Julian Brooks?" Kate's boss said, a note of skepticism warning Kate it had better be good.

"Everything matches. Christopher Brooks is missing. So, okay, I can't match his face to the merman's face because those videos are crap and there's no clear shot , but have you seen pictures of Christopher Brooks? He's got the body of a swimmer!"

"I've also noticed he has two very long human legs."

"Look, all I'm saying is the man on that video fits. And granted, I haven't found any photograph of him wearing his watch, but it's just a matter of time before Jeff finds one."

"So, let me get this straight: Julian Brooks gave an engraved half-million watch to his eldest son, who happens to moonlight as a merman on the beaches of Maine?"

"You wanted to know who's faking being a merman. That's Christopher Brooks."

"Correction. You might have Christopher Brooks's watch that showed up at a hospital from the hands of a janitor. The only people who can confirm this watch's ownership are Christopher Brooks or his prestigious father, who just happens to have a media blackout while his son's search is going on."

"It's connected. Come on, boss, you have to see it."

He leaned back on his chair, thoughtful.

"If Christopher Brooks is faking being a merman, this thing is huge. It went beyond being a hoax to involving emergency and hospital personnel, not to mention a two-country sea search. You might be right in pursuing this, Kate. This is a hoax to cover up a rich kid's prank gone wrong."

"Do you think Julian Brooks knows where his son is?"

"Maybe. Try to independently verify who owns that watch. Go downstairs to ask Paul what he knows about the Christopher Brooks search efforts. See if you can make the link."

"I have a better idea: I'll talk with Mr. Brooks himself."

Her boss stared. "I'll believe it when I see it. The man has other things to worry about."

"You just watch me, Ken. I'll get to the bottom of this."

* * *

Three hours later, Kate was adding names to her ever-growing list of FACTS and munching on a late Friday lunch, when Jeff barged in without knocking.

"You have to watch this," he said, fumbling with the control and turning on the TV by the corner.

"...but authorities are pleased with the outcome. Julian Brooks has thanked each and every member of the search party, promising he won't forget their generous time and effort on searching for his son..."

"What?" Kate said, incredulous. "They've declared Christopher Brooks dead?"

"No."

"...at this point, it is still unclear what kind of diving accident the eldest Brooks boy was involved in, but after four days of drifting in the ocean, it's nothing short of a miracle he survived."

On the screen, a Brooks Inc. blue and white helicopter was shown, a man in an orange suit jumping into the ocean to get another man out. They looked tiny and blurry like all sea rescues.

"Stayed tuned for Mr. Brooks' press conference in a few minutes. In other survival news, the Prime Minister—"

Jeff muted the screen. "They found him about an hour ago. It's barely hitting the waves."

"Wait, no. No. He's the merman..." she said, trying to fit this whole thing into a coherent line once again.

Jeff shrugged. "Maybe the merman stole his watch. We don't know what happened to Christopher Brooks, after all. Maybe—Maybe he found the merman diving and it didn't go well!" Jeff rubbed his hands, his eyes sparkling as if he'd found treasure.

She shook her head. "Where did the Coast Guard find him?"

Jeff frowned. "How would I know?"

She huffed. *This isn't happening.* She stared at her mighty wall of truth in all its tri-color glory and saw no flaw. Even if Christopher wasn't faking being a merman, even if this was something else, she had stumbled into a mystery far greater than that.

"Here it comes," Jeff said, unmuting the TV.

"As you can see," the news anchor said on a tiny screen, while the large one focused on half a dozen men taking the stage and the podium. "We're just about to hear from Julian Brooks. One can only imagine what he must be feeling now his son is back."

Among the men, a teenage boy looked out of place. Alexander Brooks wore a suit, like his father, but it was rather obvious he wasn't digging the attention.

Not fond of cameras, are you?

Julian Brooks took the microphone after a few seconds, and everyone went quiet.

"Thank you all for coming. This will be brief. My son was found today at 3:20 p.m. by one of the teams working the Nova Scotia area. His condition has been downgraded from critical to serious, but he's understandably overwhelmed by everything that has happened to him these past four days. All we know for certain is that a diving accident cut him off from his boat. Matthew, my second son, is with him now, and Alexander and I will be going after this.

"My deepest thanks go out to everyone who spared a few moments of their lives to think about Christopher and wishing us well. To the search and rescue parties, I have no way of ever repaying you what you've given me back.

"I understand this news might be of further interest to you, the media, and I'll be happy to update you as progress is made. But for now, I ask you for your patience and discretion towards these hard days that are coming for me and my family. Thank you."

Twenty hands went into the air, while questions were shouted. Julian looked unfazed, but Alexander came to his side, half hugging him, half standing with his head down. He barely made it to his father's shoulder.

"We're just happy Chris is back," the teen said to an unheard question on the screen. "Whatever he's going to need, we'll be here for him now."

The way his eyes shone with unshed tears looked so heartbroken, as did the way Julian protectively walked with him away from the sharks. This whole thing had clearly been meant as a back off.

She turned around and under *Things I WANT to know* she wrote a comment. *Where's Christopher Brooks? For REAL?*

"Well, as you have seen, Julian Brooks is thankful for having his son back. Details are likely to emerge as we continue to cover this story. Experts believe there's no reason for a castaway not to make a full recovery with the proper care."

She turned the TV off. What had just happened? This was completely throwing the scent off of Christopher's trail. Maybe.

"Did you happen to find Christopher Brooks's photograph with the watch?" she asked, hopeful. Jeff shook his head.

"Worse. I did find the competition's schedule for this Sunday's six o'clock news. They're running a special on what's going on with the viral merman video. They're calling it *Truth From the Depth* or something like that."

"Crap. Crap, crap, crap, crap. Well, we knew it was just a matter of time before they aired the interview with Thompson."

"So, what are we going to do?"

"Well, I have to confirm the watch belongs to Christopher Brooks. We can't do anything about what they run on the six o'clock, though."

100

"Think people are going to buy it?"

"That a real merman washed up on a beach and has been kept secret for the past four days? Yeah. People love conspiracies, Jeff. They see a bright light in the sky and suddenly that means aliens are coming. But, we knew this was going to happen one way or another, that's why we're trying to find the truth first. Our friends are going to look like idiots when we expose the real hoax behind all of this."

All I need is to make the connection. Where did I lose you, Christopher?

Jeff looked at her, fidgeting.

"Are you sure this couldn't be real?"

She stopped staring at her wall. "You mean, that Christopher Brooks is actually a merman and his father doesn't know and was looking for him throughout all the Atlantic? Gee, Jeff, I'm sorry, no. I don't believe it can be real."

"But you saw the tail… he couldn't have fitted two legs in that suit."

"Crappy video, Jeff. Crappy witnesses, crappy fake watch. Look, it's all a complicated mess, but someone, out there, knows the truth. And I intend to have an interview with him. I don't know how, though... So, if you excuse me…"

"Don't you have a contact for that?" Jeff joked as she walked away. She just waved her hand in a goodbye, and got on the elevator, thinking.

How does his rescue change things? The question stuck in her head, and after a minute she smiled. This meant Julian Brooks wasn't untouchable anymore. He wasn't a grieving parent now; he was a celebrating one. Suddenly, getting close to him had become a much, much easier affair.

Fine, Mr. Brooks. Let's see if you can handle what I'm about to throw at you.

14

Point of Contact

Someone touched his back. Awareness filled Chris's mind as he slowly woke up from somewhere deep. His body felt immovably heavy. Had he been partying yesterday? Or maybe he'd been playing all night long with his brothers…? Maybe Julian had taken him into the next phase of his training, something that always wiped him out.

The sweet smell of body lotion invaded his nostrils, together with another smell he couldn't identify. Too clean, too… sterile.

The hand that touched him moved to his shoulder in small circles, firm and warm and calming. He was on his side, some part of his brain informed him, along with the fact his right arm was falling asleep.

Finally, Chris moved slightly, maybe to get his arm out from beneath him, maybe to get a look at whoever touched him, maybe just to bury his head in his pillow so that awful smell would stop, but the truth was, once he moved, it took everything in him not to scream.

His tail was on fire. Eyes too heavy a moment ago went wide open as he swallowed his scream and his hands flew down to get the hell away from that pain. He didn't get too far.

The first thing he noticed beside the fact he was burning with searing pain, was how bright the whole room was. The hand that had been soothing him stayed on his shoulder, firm but caring, as the shock of waking in agony gave way to the shock of waking up somewhere he didn't belong. It must have been only two seconds, really, but in his mind, he saw all the clues of what had happened falling like dominoes, hitting his head. His eyes adjusted to the light, shapes becoming machines, walls, floor, ceiling, windows. The smell clicked then. This was a hospital. He was in a hospital. He was in a hospital in merform.

His first instinct was to recoil, which reminded his altered brain he was seriously injured. He remembered that, from the darkness… He'd been injured, and he'd been terrified. He'd been hurt, and he'd been in the water, a bad combination no matter if he'd had legs or a tail. That was as far as his memory went, his present far more troubling at the moment.

Straps kept him in place, and a nearby beeping skyrocketed along with his heartbeat, a coincidence he absently found peculiar until he realized it was his heartbeat. He was being monitored. He was being caged. He was going to die.

"Hey… hey, it's okay, you're safe here."

No. No, I'm not. I'm going to be cut open, every cell of my body shipped to a lab somewhere. I'm not going—

"You were in an accident."

—to ever see the City. I'm never going to make it—

"I'm Gwen. I'm your doctor. It's okay, just take deep breaths."

—Julian is going to kill me!

"Ray… Ray! You're hyperventilating. Here, look at me, look at me."

He did. His captor wore blue hospital clothes, her hair hidden beneath a blue hospital cap. She looked like those surgeons in medical shows. She was going to cut him open. He recoiled violently, the straps straining, the whole gurney threatening to crash.

"I swear if you rip those stitches one more time, mister, you're not going to like it."

He froze, too scared to think logically, but knowing a warning voice when he heard one.

"You were in an accident," she repeated, placing her hands on the gurney and lowering until they were at eye-level. She was breathing almost as hard as he was, both caught in the uncertainty of how the other would react. "You're safe here. Do you understand?"

No. She knows what I am. The secret's out. My life is over.

They stayed still, neither able to look away. Except… except his throat was parched. No matter how hard he tried to suppress it, his throat constricted into an upcoming coughing fit. When the first cough raked his body, there was no going back. He coughed and coughed until he couldn't breathe. Tormented by every movement, he closed his eyes and hugged himself as best he could. Hands moved him, or the gurney moved, or both, but when he found himself half sitting up and facing a straw, he latched onto it for dear life. It was sweet water, and he gulped it as if there was no tomorrow.

She took the straw out of his reach. "Slowly. You're going to have another coughing fit if you don't watch it."

He didn't care. As soon as that thing was in range, he started drinking like a camel again.

"You were found on a beach, you know, and brought to my hospital. That was five days ago. You've been drifting through a coma since then."

He stopped drinking. *For days? Days?*

She took the almost empty cup and looked at him seriously. "We're not going to hurt you but you're seriously injured."

The burning in his tail took center stage again now his adrenaline was ebbing. He looked down at his predicament; whatever he was expecting to see, this was worse, so much worse. His scales, always so vibrant and shiny, were dull and dry. Both side fins were a mess of torn threads that would take months to look whole again. He felt naked in more ways than the literal one and felt himself blush in embarrassment. It was one thing to be with other merfolk swimming in the open sea, or with his family at home, but here, under the harsh lights of a hospital room, he was deeply aware all he had on his body were wires and tubes.

"We've been worried about nerve damage, although the coloring seems right."

He ignored her. She had no idea how much color he'd lost, but she also had a point. A thick cast covered the upper section of his tail.

Ever so slowly, he passed through the pain and moved the tips of his tail, the same way a man would assure himself he could still feel his feet. Up and down, open and close. Awkward was an understatement. Tails were not meant for beds or land in the general sense. His body protested every single movement, and he clenched his teeth as he proved to himself he hadn't lost his ability to dive. He grimaced as he made a cursory exploration of his entire body. Muscles he didn't remember having made themselves known now. Maybe he could go back to that coma again?

Now, to the hard part. Internally, he surveyed his ability to shift. Most injuries could be minimized by shifting the cells into a better position, but the depth of the cut was too much. The pain was so intense it didn't allow him to concentrate until he had to give it up entirely. There was no way he could shift into legs without passing out or losing his tail. Probably both.

"That's good," she said, and Chris realized for the first time he'd been having an audience while the most agonizing seconds of his life passed by. "You have full sensation and mobility, right?"

He looked at her then, really looked at this middle-aged woman who fully knew what he was. He understood with cold certainty that he was a prisoner to human scientists. He had nowhere to go, nowhere to hide, no one to help him. The only thing he could do—the only thing his parents and Julian and his brothers had been told to do in this hellish event—was to remain silent.

"What? What's wrong?" she asked, reading all too well how he clamped down, how his entire body went from rigid to deflated, how he looked at his lap and nothing else. He was surrendering; he just couldn't say it.

"Ray? What's wrong?"

Ray? He didn't look at her, puzzled as he was.

He had to adjust to his circumstances, he had to understand what life had dealt to him. His eyes stung, and it had nothing to do with the raw cut on his beloved tail. Her hand came back, and he didn't fight her. He had no energy to fight no one. He had no energy to even weep.

* * *

"I screwed up," Dr. Gaston was saying as she entered the observation deck, taking off her cap and gloves off. From here, a dozen scientists looked down, taking notes and talking among themselves in animated conversations, none of them in English.

By the corner, Nathan also looked down at their guest. Gwen had asked for the restraints to be removed now that Ray was awake and in no danger of accidentally hurting himself, so their merman had curled up as best as he could and had fallen asleep after an hour or so.

"I must have said something, done something for him to clamp down. I can't believe he's not talking."

"Oh?" Nathan said, turning to look at her disheveled hair and reddening face. "He is talking, just not with words," he explained, getting out of the room and taking her with him.

"What?"

"People in general place too much value on words, and we certainly need him to start speaking in order to get the answers we want. But his body language is telling enough to start a conversation. He said a lot of interesting things if you were willing to pay attention."

"Like what? *Gimme that cup back? Look at my tail?* What are you talking about?"

106

He opened the door to his small office and waited for her to sit down before leaning on his desk, facing her.

"You're right on both accounts, actually. *Gimme that cup back* was loud and clear, and worked perfectly well. You did give him the cup back."

She glared at him as if he was a moron. In fact, half the time Dr. Gaston looked at him was exactly like that.

"*Look at my tail* was loaded with subtexts," he continued. "While you're understandably invested in the mechanics of muscles and blood vessels working properly after surgery, he wasn't happy with what he saw. He was relieved—once he realized what was at stake—that he still had mobility, but he wasn't happy. He places a lot of importance on how that tail looks, even if we don't fully understand the context of that importance."

"What are you saying? That he's a narcissist?"

He laughed. Leave it to Gaston to come up with the most atrocious conclusions.

"That he has vanity as well as a nudity awareness that shouldn't exist."

Her eyes bulged at that little surprise. "What nudity awareness?"

"He was acutely aware of how naked he was. That's part of why he curled up the moment he could."

"But—but he's a merman! He swims naked, for crying out loud!"

"So do I, from time to time, but it doesn't mean I'm comfortable to ditch my clothes around strangers. Neither does he."

She opened her mouth to argue—she always did—so he raised his hand to appease. "Don't ask me to explain it, that's what his body language said. The mysteries that surround Ray just grow every day."

"Maybe you're just reading him wrong. He's not human, in case you haven't figured that out already."

"Isn't he?"

This time, she didn't even bother to answer.

"He understood you perfectly well. He has a good idea of where he is and what that means. He's been here before, Doctor. Not *here* here, at ORCAS, but he's lived in human society. Complex things like language, cultural conventions, or even a hospital are not lost to him."

"You're insane. If Ray knew all of this he'd start explaining. He would start talking!"

"He should, but not if he thinks that's against his interests. It's not your fault we're the enemy. It's not personal, Doctor. He's not going to talk to anyone."

"What are you saying, then? That he's silent because… because…?"

"He's choosing not to speak out of a sense of duty. Maybe to himself, maybe to his family, maybe to his entire civilization. He's a soldier behind enemy lines."

She stared at him, processing. He'd been watching Ray for more than two hours, and while all these details were glaringly obvious to his trained mind, he had also seen her trying to establish a conversation in so many different ways, all attempts failing miserably. Ray had ignored her as best he'd been able, which was hard to do when faced with Dr. Gaston.

Higgs is going to have a field day with the whole thing, Nathan fleetingly mused.

"If you're right, then I've been doing this wrong…" Gwen slowly said, an idea forming. She suddenly got up and headed out.

"Where are you going?"

"Where do you think? To cover him up! Next time he wakes, I'm not going to mess it up!"

* * *

"Estimated time of arrival, twenty-two minutes, Sir," the pilot informed Julian while the stewardess took his untouched dinner away. Outside the window, nothing but a black sky and endless stars met his blue eyes. Everything was so peaceful up there that he often wondered if wings would have been a better deal than the tail.

"Anything else I can help you with, sir?" the stewardess asked politely. A long time ago, he'd learned he preferred older, married women to work for him, so he wouldn't have to deal with so many unwanted advances. Margaret was no exception, and although she'd been working for him for the past ten years, she'd never crossed the line into personal questions, idle chatter, or anything remotely unprofessional.

"No, thank you. That will be all."

With Alex asleep in the seat behind, he closed his eyes and did what he'd been doing for the past few hours without any success. He contacted Chris. Long range telepathy could be done by a number of techniques, his favorite being visualizing every person as a color. The closer, the brighter. His mind found Alex's green light immediately, and a few moments later, even Matt's muted red color came through in the distance. He couldn't see Chris's blue, and after a while, Julian changed mental tactics. His sons weren't colors any more, they were pieces of himself.

The hole his son's coma had left had been steadily closing up since the day before until Julian had gotten a clear certainty Chris had fully woken earlier that afternoon. It was hard to describe, really, and for the first time in a long time he wondered if blood children had a stronger link to their parents or if it didn't really matter. It still felt as if someone had ripped a piece of his soul, blood ties notwithstanding. He sighed in frustration; he needed a more active approach, an image that would let him move, figuratively. Relaxing body and mind, he imagined himself diving into a dark ocean, reaching with his arms into the void for his eldest son.

Chris?

Aimlessly, he immersed himself in waters where Alex's and Matt's presences were rich, almost solid, but nothing else came to attention. Finally, faintly, he brushed Chris' mind—a whisper to follow even deeper, a direction Julian took gladly.

Chris... I'm here...

Part of Julian was bracing for the onslaught of chaotic emotions his son's mind had sent him in the last two contacts, and another part of him dreaded not getting anything at all. It was one thing when Chris was in a coma, all but gone from this world. It was an entirely different kind of hell to know his son was awake and aware at the hands of curious minds and sharp scalpels.

Julian...

The murmured word barely had any strength, and it occurred to the oldest Brooks that Chris might think him a dream. Julian felt at a loss for what to say. Everything seemed so inadequate. He couldn't promise everything was going to be okay and honestly had no idea how to get his son out of this mess, regardless of what the City wanted. So he said the only thing he knew for certain.

Hey... You're not alone, Chris. He sensed his son's awareness increasing. It wasn't frenzied and it wasn't a reaction. This was Chris, finding his way to Julian. They were too far apart to sustain the link for more than a couple of minutes, but he took anything he could.

You're here... You're really here...

Chris's bewildered words tore at Julian's heart. *Where else would we be? Matt is getting as close to you as he can, you should hear from him soon. And the Squid will set up camp so we can trace you as soon as we get to the hotel.*

Don't call him Squid, Chris said, tired, an inside joke that never got old. *Listen... They... I'm not talking to them; I'm not giving anything but I'm—I'm scared.*

Julian imagined Chris, all smiles, and strong arms ready to hug his unsuspecting brothers, and mentally embraced him. He had no idea if Chris knew what he was doing or not, but it was the best he could manage.

It's okay... It's okay. I'm so proud of you, do you hear me? I don't know how long it's going to take to get you out, so do whatever it takes to survive, okay?

Even if it means talking to them? Letting them know?

Do whatever you need, son. No one is going to hold it against you. One way or another, we're getting you out.

Julian, if I don't—if I don't make it, you will tell my parents I tried, right? That I never gave up on them?

In Julian's memories, Chris was ten years old, crying silently under the cold, full moon, while the yacht waved in the middle of the Pacific. Unlike Matt's and Alex's, Chris's parents were waiting for him in the City, leaving him in Julian's care when no other option was available. Chris had been with him longer than he'd known his own family, but that didn't mean he loved them any less.

Julian sincerely hoped Chris's parents hadn't felt their son almost dying twice. No way could he explain to them how he'd lost their only child to this hell. Or maybe it was for the best. Maybe it would give Chris another reason to fight his way out.

You're going to tell them yourself.

They're coming, Julian. I can hear them. They're coming...

Desperation bled out of Julian's heart, desperation that had him thinking about ripping those doors apart and carrying his son out to safety. If only it could happen that easily.

We're coming, too. Do you hear me? We're coming, too.

15

The Price of Silence

Chris wanted to do two things. He could fall asleep, giving in to the bone-deep exhaustion of his body, or he could stay wide awake, aware of what these people wanted to do with him. Somehow, he seemed to be stuck in the middle: he was awake, but barely aware.

Curled up as he was, his eyes focused on the machines on the walls, little lights turning green or yellow or red, beeping and clicking and keeping sync with his own battered body. He had a blanket now, he fleetingly realized, and he clutched it as he tried to ignore the slow burning in his tail. Behind him, he heard movement. People had been coming and going since the woman had left, all quietly walking around him but not engaging him, maybe sensing his discomfort, maybe unauthorized to talk at all.

Where was he? Was he somewhere deep underground? Was he at some Navy base, with military eyes on his back? Was he at a quarantine sublevel, swallowed by the government to never see sunlight again?

Stop it! He ordered himself, tightening his muscles in a vain attempt to protect his body, closing his eyes to forget where he was. Julian said it might take time. *Julian knows where you are. He'll be here soon. He'll know—*

"Hey…" a man said with a cordial voice, not too close, and certainly not afraid. Chris ignored it. "I'm Higgs, your doctor for this shift."

There was a slight accent somewhere in there, one Chris couldn't place. He had sailed to many places, and had met people from many countries, but this accent had been softened by years of living abroad. Maybe in the UK?

"I'm going to make a deal with you," Higgs said, walking around as if he was a wolf looking at his prey for a weak spot. "I won't lie about what's going on, and you won't lie to me about what's going on with you. If it hurts, you tell me. If it's okay, you let me know, too."

That got Chris's attention. As reasonable as the deal seemed, Chris couldn't trust it, couldn't trust them, couldn't trust his own mind, really, not when he was so afraid and so unfocused at the same time. So he resolved to do nothing. *Keep your eyes closed, don't move, and he might leave.*

"Can you follow the light?"

No.

"Can you grip my hand?"

No.

"Can you say *A*?"

I can bite you…

Chris hugged himself tighter, keeping his eyes close and his blanket closer. The other doctor—Gin? Glen? Gwen!—had already tried this before… He frowned. How long prior had that been? Had he fallen asleep?

Knowing how much time was passing suddenly became a necessity, and that thought brought one terrible question up front. Where was his watch? The heartbeat monitor accelerated, telling the whole world he'd just rushed into a panic attack. So much could be traced with that watch. Had he lost it at sea? Did they have it? Were they—

"Whoa there, there's nothing to be afraid of here, son."

A hand—a big one—wrapped itself over his shoulder, and Chris automatically recoiled, thoughts about his watch spiraling into a dark void in the face of imminent danger.

"It's okay, it's okay. Take it easy… You've survived the worst, you know?"

This time, Chris did open his eyes, wounded and accusatory. This is beyond worst, he wanted to say, his sight focusing on a black man with the whitest teeth he'd ever seen. Unlike Gwen, he wasn't wearing a mask, just an honest face, and a whitening beard.

"You drifted for a few hours in the ocean before making it onto the beach," Higgs started telling him, a variation of what Gwen had told him earlier—however long ago 'earlier' had been. "I was minding my own business when a friend called me with tales of a merman. And three days later, I'm trying to evaluate how much nerve and muscle damage this accident of yours caused, but all I can tell is that you really don't like to talk."

Higgs chuckled. "Maybe we should have named you Ariel, after all. You both ended up in the human world without your voices."

Against all his self-promises, Chris glared at him. His new doctor winked. "I'm glad we had this conversation. Try to get some rest," and with that, Higgs's warm hand left, along with the man himself. The light dimmed a few moments later, bathing the whole room in a dark bluish tint. Tired as he was,

Chris fought sleep, too aware of people around him, of a dozen eyes on his skin.

It looks like the bottom of a lake, he thought, fleetingly, half remembering a night long ago, playing hide and seek with his brothers, an exercise in both telepathy and shielding. He blinked. It almost looked as if Matt was coming swimming toward him, from the darkest corner of the room. He smiled. The walls disappeared, dissolving into the deep waters of an unknown lake in an unknown land, and Chris was whole again, lying at the bottom, just hiding from his little brothers.

Unable to tell dream from reality, Chris watched Matt swam right past, calling his name as if Chris was going to give himself up.

Keep looking, little fish… Keep looking.

* * *

"Goddamn it!"

Matt hit the steering wheel so hard he thought he'd crack it. Cursing even louder, he cradled his injured hand and seethed at the injustice of it all.

He was too young to have any say in how to rescue his brother, too young to master long-range telepathy, too young to be taken seriously, too young to do anything. And he'd been so sure, so goddamn sure he was getting closer to Chris.

He'd been scouting all thirteen of the ORCAS buildings Alex had pinpointed, and this one, the smallest and most secluded, was the one Chris had been moved to. Even if he couldn't really contact Chris, he felt his presence there, as muted and colorless as it might be. The real problem was Matt's own mind, untrained in long-range telepathy. It was a relative term, actually, because *long* meant different things to different merfolk. Julian hadn't trained them in this mental discipline until they were older because he said telepathy was too disruptive in an environment where no one else was using it. The mind would hit walls all over the place instead of a smooth sailing, just to meet another telepathic mind and go right through it.

That was fine by Matt. He didn't need to be picking apart his brothers' thoughts, or chatting the world away. He liked his solitude and peace of mind, and that included keeping his thoughts to himself. So, although *long range* meant a few hundred miles for Julian and Chris, it meant only about half a mile for Matt. And it wasn't like at school or at home, where they'd talk about random stuff. No, this time, it felt as if Chris had dissolved into thin air, and Matt was trying to put him back together before transmitting any thoughts.

Beside him, his phone lit up with an incoming call. He'd set it to silent so his concentration wouldn't be shattered, and sparing a glance at the caller ID, he ignored Alex in favor of looking at the building ahead.

The ORCAS facility was far enough away for it to be a telepathy problem, but it connected to the sea on the other side, a potential way out for his brother. Matt needed to do a reconnaissance mission, but even under the cloak of the night, he didn't feel safe enough to abandon his car. Alex had warned him the security had increased, and although he couldn't see it from here, Matt didn't doubt the Squid.

His cell phone illuminated again, this time, the call coming from Julian. It was uncanny, really, how his adoptive father knew when he was going to do something risky.

"Yes?" he asked curtly, still hurt at Julian for leaving Chris behind.

"We're here."

"Has the Squid set up camp yet?" Matt asked, wincing as he grabbed the wheel; his wrist was loudly protesting the movement. Rationally, he knew there was nothing he could accomplish by staying there, but his heart wanted to be there, close enough, where he could at least feel Chris's presence.

"He's working on it. Come home, Matt. We need to regroup."

Julian had said the only thing that would get Matt out of there: the promise of action. Turning around, he gave one last glimpse to the building through the rearview mirror. *I'll be back tomorrow, brother. I swear.*

* * *

"Drake, I'm so glad you're here," Julian said, hugging his longtime friend briefly. The last time he'd seen Drake in the flesh had been four years ago. Maybe a little more. The Council members tried to stay separated for security reasons, but neither man could care any less about those reasons right now.

Once, a few centuries ago, they'd swum together into the human world and never looked back. In a way, Drake was the reassurance they had made the right decision and that leaving the City had never been a mistake.

"I came as fast as I could," Drake said, taking a quick glimpse around. Alex was cemented to the computer screen in the living room, headphones separating him from real life, still in pajamas despite it already being noon.

"Where's Matthew?" Drake asked while Julian walked him to the kitchen.

"Out. As close as he can get to ORCAS. He's trying to talk with Chris."

Drake winced. "He's not gonna like that long-range chat. Not with Chris injured. Are you sure he's being careful?"

"I trust him."

Drake sighed, passing a hand over his black hair. "How bad is it for Chris?"

"He hasn't woken up since yesterday. I contacted him then, briefly. He's scared, of course, but overall, he's holding it tight. He's refusing to talk and betray our secrets, but I told him he could do whatever he had to."

Drake nodded, understanding. "The City hasn't contacted us back, unsurprisingly. They're going to take their time, as they always do."

His friend's words stung, but it wasn't something Julian hadn't thought himself. Drake turned to the cupboards in search of a glass.

"I don't think the City knows what to do," Julian agreed. "Or how to go about it. It's been centuries since we ceased trying to make any real contact with humans. I don't think there's a plan in motion anymore."

Drake looked at him, hesitant. "You might be wrong on that one."

"What? What have they told you?"

His friend filled the glass with water, thoughtfully.

"Remember when we left 300 years ago? That no one wanted to do that?"

Julian seldom thought about the City, and hardly ever about his life there. He'd been so sure there was so much to see on the surface that nothing had convinced him to stay. Few and far apart were those who departed, but almost all of them had returned with cautionary tales to never go up to the surface.

Mireya had left the City and had never returned. He remembered that clearly.

"And then everybody wanted to leave?" Julian shot back, with a smile.

In the three thousand years of the City's history, there had been three grand migrations. The first one was when they'd arrived on the planet and the City was still on the surface; it had ended in disaster, everyone coming back home and submerging deeper than humans would ever find them. The second wave, about a thousand years later, had been a smaller movement of individuals seeking news from the surface. Almost everyone had returned, then. And the last one, 124 years ago, had seen about 400 individuals abandoning the tight rules and never changing landscapes of their City, in search of freedom, sunlight, and adventure.

Hardly anyone returned to the City from that last wave, and worse, most of them had taken their destinies into their own hands and had disappeared from everyone's radar. Julian's three sons' parents had been part of that wave, all orphaned children descended from the third wave migrators, as a matter of fact, hard to find when the Council didn't even know of their existence.

"Ever since the last migration wave, more and more people are considering leaving the City for good," Drake said in a grave tone. "We might be looking at a fourth migration wave sometime in the next twenty years. Depending on how humans react to Chris and what measures they take to look for us deep in the ocean, they might decide to wait longer or go for it at once."

Julian sighed, grabbing a glass for himself. "We left so we could avoid their politics, and here we are, playing right back into their hands."

"Someone has to look out for all migrants, right? Who better than us, the ones who braved the surface first, never to return?" Drake reminded him, almost making a toast of it with his half-empty glass. "I've been getting concerned calls from other merfolk. They think the Council can be compromised if humans find out about you. Everyone's getting ready to disappear as deep as they can in the human world."

"I'm guessing we should be doing the same," Julian said with a heavy heart. Every few decades he had to start over, of course, but it always surprised him how fast those changes would come and how short human lives were.

"Probably," Drake agreed, looking at the much younger generation in the living room. "Your ward has grown up," he mentioned with a glimmer in his eyes. Drake's youngest adoptive daughter had left for the City fifteen years ago, and he had asked the Council to stop assigning wards to him for a time. It was hard to lose his children where he wouldn't follow, he had once confessed to Julian; at that stage, Chris had barely been assigned to the Brooks family.

Julian had disliked the City, but Drake had right down despised it. It had been Drake's friends who'd planted the idea to leave in Julian's mind; they were the ones who had left first. He fleetingly wondered what had happened to them, to Sheela and Amstel and the others. Had the human world swallowed them whole like the City liked to preach? He shook his mind.

"I never got to thank you for faking Chris's rescue," Julian said, filling his glass and changing the subject.

"Anything for my favorite nephew. Speaking of that, this media problem is not ours alone. The humans don't know what to do. There's an ambitious plan to make this pass as a Hollywood campaign, but it's just getting out of the UN's hands."

It never ceased to amaze Julian how resourceful Drake was. Both Julian and Aurel were tasked with keeping their assets and cash handy, while Mireya and Lavine had their hands on technological development. Drake was their Chief Master Planner, as Julian affectionately called him because his tasks usually involved solving all their problems. Communication was his main business, and many merfolk worked for him directly, especially the occasional lonely mermaid or merman who ventured out of the City for the first time. It was those newcomers who kept Drake informed of what was going on inside the City.

"What do you think humans will do?" Julian asked, concerned.

"Call in the experts, and then make a mess of it. Christopher's existence poses all sorts of problems, but they're far more concerned with their lack of answers."

"I know."

Drake looked him in the eye. "Your kid is brave, Julian, but he's going to be dead soon if we don't give him something to say."

"Tell me something I don't know already."

16

Communication Skills

Nathan's work was anything but boring. In the space of forty-eight hours, he'd coordinated along with Major White dozens of security clearances, sorted out lab equipment, travel arrangements, hotels, transport, meals, and a host of logistics not suited for the faint of heart. While Ray slept all day, 200 people had been cleared, relocated, briefed, and sent to their new jobs. For all his misgivings about having US military so close, he had to give it to White: the man was highly efficient both with resources and personnel.

Now, as the day turned to night, the last task on his agenda was reporting. The UN had formally appointed eight members in a Special Committee to deal with their merman situation. In fact, these eight people had become his new bosses and Ray's keepers at the highest level. Although White reported directly to the Pentagon, he did join him in these meetings as a security advisor. Nathan was expected to deliver reports twice a day on any advances concerning their guest, especially any breakthroughs on understanding his biology. And boy did he have a breakthrough tonight.

"What exactly supports your theory that this being can turn its tail into legs?" the leader of the UN Committee—one Ms. Goransson—asked. What the Swedish woman lacked in stature, she more than made up for with her sharp mind and perceptive eyes. Forest liked her as an ally, yet dreaded her as his enemy. In the small, windowless room, a dozen monitors hung on the wall. Each of the eight members of the Committee connected to a monitor, and a ninth person joined them tonight. His name was Colonel Sawyer. The military liked their answers fast, and there was no faster way than this meeting.

"The *Mermaid Problem,*" he said, the nine screens in front of him showing universal blank stares. Beside him, Major White looked clearly amused.

"The *Mermaid Problem,*" Nathan repeated. "That's the question of how merfolk reproduce, though it's also often applied to how human men and mermaids would be able to reproduce since her tail would be a considerable inconvenience to a man."

Ms. Goransson pressed her lips together, unamused.

Nathan clicked a button, projecting onto a screen a colorized section of their merman's tail, indicating two small sacs.

"Ray's scans show his reproductive organs hidden below scales and muscle, a little lower than what we would think of as hips. Where you would expect a man's genitals to be. The problem is there are no organs or channels that aid in reproductive actions. His genitals seem to be locked."

Half the men readjusted themselves in their chairs, while the only woman frowned.

"What if he's not a he? Could he be the female of his species?"

"We would still have the same delivery problem, Ma'am. If he can somehow change his tail into legs, it would explain how they can reproduce with each other. We have theorized that maybe we're dealing with an immature subject who hasn't finished developing. Or maybe he just has an abnormal deformity that has left him sterile, for lack of a better term."

"But you don't believe that."

Nathan shook his head.

"There's something else, actually. Something we discovered two days ago when he woke up for the first time."

On the screen, he switched from showing the MRI results to two images of Ray's back, marked *before* and *after*.

"As you can see, there were fewer scales on his back before he woke up. This section of his skin became scales, most likely triggered by stress. We know at least a part of his body is capable of shifting from one type of cell to another. This will also clear the mystery of why he has lungs similar to ours, unable to breathe underwater. If he can somehow change his lung function to suit his needs, it would make sense that once he reached land, he started breathing in a human fashion."

Goransson wrote something down, then turned serious eyes to Nathan. "What are we doing to prove this theory?"

"We're studying his bone structure, trying to trigger the same effect in the sample we took. It's too early to tell, but we think we're onto something."

A couple of men wrote on a slip of paper and passed it on to their off-screen assistants. On the last screen on the right, Colonel Sawyer looked grim, poised for a fight.

"So, as of right now, we can't really know what he's capable of by science alone," Sawyer said.

"No, sir."

"You are aware, Doctor, that the implications of a shapeshifting species hiding in our oceans are far-reaching," Sawyer continued.

"I am aware of that, yes."

"Have there been any rescue attempts?" another member asked. Nathan shook his head.

"We're monitoring the entire East Coast for any kind of anomalies. Nothing has caught our attention."

"To tell you the truth, Doctor," the Colonel came again, his voice grating on Nathan's nerves. "I am far more interested in these DNA results your labs are still trying to confirm. What's to say his species is not invading ours?"

"We have many theories—"

"—and no assurances your siren will cooperate with any investigation. In fact, Doctor, he's been awake for the past two days—"

"—briefly—"

"—without saying a word, or showing any intention of communication in the most basic ways. Meanwhile, the United States proposes a coalition among the present members of this Committee in order to do an exhaustive and comprehensive search of our oceans for any hidden alien technology and possible threat. He's not the only one out there."

Nathan's mind zig-zagged through the hundreds of obstacles to this underwater crusade but said nothing. If the military wanted to play watchdog, no reasoning would win this argument.

Major White remained enigmatically silent. Sawyer was more than enough to lead this attack, it seemed.

"We're also requesting that all dealings with this creature be transferred to us," Sawyer demanded, a glimmer of triumph in his eyes.

"No." Nathan didn't care what this man wanted, he had bigger problems to deal with, mainly keeping Ray alive so their only point of contact didn't vanish into the classified abyss that was the Pentagon. The members on the screens remained silent, waiting to see how Nathan was going to play this one out.

"With all due respect, Doctor, you're an advisor to this Committee, not a member of it," Sawyer said, dismissively.

"Contact with Ray's species is our first and utmost priority. The harder you make it—the deeper you bury and silence him—the less likely that's going to happen. We don't know his intentions or his species' intentions, but us reacting like he's the enemy is not going to win us any allies. Ray remains under United Nations responsibility, as a guest, in a non-threatening environment."

If Sawyer had been able to kill him with a look, Nathan would have been dust by this point.

"I'm afraid Dr. Forest has good reasons," Goransson said, her eyes betraying nothing. "If his species is advanced enough to live in an unknown city, underwater and undetected, we gain far more by treating him with kindness than by dissecting him in the closest lab."

"He's a security risk to the planet!"

It wasn't a stretch to imagine what was going through Sawyer's mind. *You bunch of bleeding heart idiots; you're going to get us all killed.*

"He has committed no crime," she countered, not rising to the bait. "Since his arrival, he's threatened no one, broken no laws, or instigated any crimes. I concede to you and this Committee that his silence is worrisome but understandable."

"If I may," Major White interceded for the first time. "We can advise this Committee on security risks and give an assessment of what to do if our guest's silence persists. It might be just a misunderstanding, after all. We have much to learn."

Something about the way White said that didn't sit well with Nathan. White's interests were not aligned with Ray's own.

"Please do, Major. Dr. Forest, do keep us informed about... Ray's progress," Goransson said, for the first time calling him by name. "The entire world has a vested interest in his wellbeing."

"Yes, Ma'am."

Happy for the meeting to be dismissed on such a high note, Nathan gathered his things ready to leave the virtual meeting. Except—the next unlisted topic was of great interest.

"Now, let's hear what we're going to do about this media problem."

* * *

The first thing Matt noticed was the increased security. He was back at ORCAS under the cover of darkness, closer than ever, hoping to catch his brother awake. He'd parked as close as he could, and munched on fast food as he watched everyone coming and going into the building. The security had been increased tenfold since the day before, and he was seeing a lot fewer lab coats and far more military guys patrolling.

In the past hour, he'd counted at least eight soldiers doing patrols in twos on the outer perimeter, and another six closer to the entrance. Getting Chris out by the front door had just become a highly improbable option.

"We have to get you out of there," he murmured with equal parts of anger and fear.

Matt?

The intrusion in his mind felt cold, almost like liquid sliding down his spine and tingling in the back of his legs in all the wrong ways. He spat half his soda into the windshield and grabbed his chest as if it was going to burst. For one agonizing second, he was sure he was feeling his brother's heart beating as if it was his own.

It hurt. He gasped for air and reached for the wheel with half a mind to drive the hell out of range and get out of his brother's mind. He'd wanted so much to hear his brother, that the irony of how much he didn't want it anymore burned a part of his soul.

Hey... Sorry little bro... Let me give you some space.

"God, Chris! Don't!" Guilt colored his face, and he cursed himself for being so weak and scaring so easily. "It's okay, I'm okay, it's just..."

Overwhelming.

Matt nodded, taking deep breaths, letting go of the wheel. His heart was his own again, and he concentrated on that.

Chris, you heard me. I can't believe you heard me. I can't believe I can hear you, he managed to say, desperate to hang onto his brother, no matter how uncomfortable it was turning out to be.

That's why Julian doesn't want you learning it until you can get a hang of it properly, Chris answered, reading his discomfort without a problem.

Don't worry about me! I just need a minute. I'm sorry I wasn't ready... Taking a deep breath, Matt tried to slowly slide back into the mental connection. A few seconds went by in silence until he managed to properly collect his thoughts.

Chris... Are you... Matt didn't know how to end that question. *Are you okay* seemed so clichéd, and stupid under these circumstances. *Are you scared* felt too personal and intrusive. Chris seemed to smile through it all, somehow. Matt felt it, poised somewhere between his heart and his soul, that contagious good vibe his brother always spread, even in the bleakest of situations.

I'm okay...

A strange pressure set at the front of his head, but Matt dismissed it. His back felt stiff, somehow, and his legs became uncomfortably numb. Slowly, the newly-shifted scales at the back of his hands and arms went back to being skin.

What time is it?

Close to midnight. Saturday.

Matt's heart beat a little too fast, his body a little too tense.

You were thinking about soldiers, Chris said at length, though it was more like a question. Matt closed his eyes and came to terms with the fact that long-range telepathy required a great deal of actual mind-reading. It made the whole thing uncomfortable because he couldn't shield his thoughts like it naturally occurred with close-range telepathy.

Matt… it's okay if you want to go.

"The hell I will. Just… stop caring about my thoughts, okay? I'm here for you." If he talked out loud, it was easier to keep his mental distance.

Hmm…

Chris started to fade, and Matt had the disturbing notion he was doing it on purpose.

"There are soldiers all around this place. They weren't here before. You're at some sort of ocean research center, that's why I can get this close," he hurried in answering. Then he fell quiet. Funny how he'd spent the better part of four days trying to talk to his brother, and now he'd finally managed the connection, he was stalling.

I'm okay Matt… I'm… tired all the time… and thirsty. You wouldn't believe how thirsty I am. I think Gwen is starting to figure out she can bribe me with that green cup of hers.

Matt frowned. "Gwen?"

The doctor. Well, the one who is here right now. She talks and talks and talks.

"Sounds annoying."

Not at all. She makes me feel as if I weren't in merform and she's just talking to a guy. Nothing out of the ordinary.

Matt grinned. "That's only because she doesn't know you're a Brooks."

Chris laughed hard, and in the process, he got Matt's mind swept away. He saw what Chris saw, his fingers sticking out of a dark blue cast that protected his fractured right wrist. Matt moved out of Chris's mind immediately, physically moving back in his car seat, refocusing on the dashboard.

Sorry…

"No. No. That's okay. It just—it just caught me unguarded."

Julian had warned him that a good long-range connection would make him feel, see and pretty much be inside the other's mind. Matt hadn't expected

124

anything beyond a few thoughts exchanged, and now he'd gotten a good taste of the whole experience, he had to agree he was way out of his depth.

"How's your hand?"

Itching. Everything hurts…

Matt didn't know what to say. He had a feeling Christ hadn't meant for him to hear that, but honestly, why would anyone expect him to feel anything but crap?

"Hey, Chris? How about you hear what I'm hearing for a change, huh?" Matt turned the dial on the radio all the way up, playing one of Chris's favorite songs. It drowned every single sound, including Matt's own thoughts. He listened long after he couldn't feel his brother anymore.

* * *

Major White looked down at their sleeping mystery from the observation room. Keeping him away from prying eyes was starting to become a problem. By this point, every single square inch of the ORCAS facility was being monitored, but the outside was proving more difficult. Blind spots here and there were still being patched up, and with the TV Special due to run that night, the potential for curious and crazy civilians would increase exponentially.

Colonel Sawyer wanted White to get into the medical bay and extract answers from the merman by any means necessary, but that was stupid. Ray would grow impatient as his predicament grew larger; even the UN would tire of his silence, and then, when everybody wanted answers and Ray actually wanted to talk his way out of this mess, White would get his mission accomplished. For now, though, White's only job was to make sure Ray couldn't leave them, and he was damn good at that sort of thing.

"Major," Forest said behind him by way of greeting.

"Doctor."

"I heard my physiotherapist got approved."

"We just finished the background check," White said with a nod. "If everything's fine with him, he should arrive by Tuesday. Good choice, if I may say so."

Forest looked slightly surprised at the compliment, then nodded once. After a moment, they both turned to look down at their reason for being there: Ray.

"He has to start talking soon," White said gravely. "And it has to be something better than which version of The Little Mermaid he prefers."

Forest winced. Doctor Higgs had made a passing remark on his brief interaction with Ray, a remark White hadn't missed. "Thank you for not bringing that up in the meeting," Forest said.

"Unnecessary paranoia just makes my job harder," White said with a pointed look.

"Don't take this wrong, but you're not exactly aiding Colonel Sawyer on his mighty quest to take over Ray's life. What exactly does Sawyer want, anyway?" Forest asked as both men left the observation room.

"Control," White said, without skipping a beat. "Whoever controls Ray, controls how to approach merfolk. The only reason we're allowing the UN to have this operation on US soil is because you're far less threatening than the Pentagon," White stated. "They might be more inclined to show themselves to you than to us. The long game's always been meeting them on our own terms, but some of my bosses still think showing our softer side is a mistake. Sawyer wants the intimidation route."

"No kidding. What about you, Major? What do you think is better?" Forest asked, stopping in the middle of the hall.

"Whatever gets us the best results. If that means the intimidation route or not, is up to Ray."

"Major White?" a Private said as he saluted.

"At ease."

"Something came up, Sir."

"Doctor, if you excuse me," White said, leaving Forest behind.

"You asked us to report anything odd, sir. It might be nothing, but you should watch this."

Six minutes later, White was in the security room, twenty-six cameras covering the halls and entrances of their building, while another eight recorded the surroundings. The technician pressed a few buttons, and a screen showed the front view. About fifteen people were walking outside the ORCAS building, a few sitting on benches along the way. The man pressed another button, changing the screen to thermal readings. All the people looked to be wearing reds and oranges, except for one who wasn't as warm as the rest, a hooded figure standing with his or her back to the camera, sitting on a bench.

"His temperature is below normal parameters, sir," the Private indicated. "But it might be just what he's wearing or where he's been."

White looked intently at the image. "It might be nothing, but… Can we get a better angle? A shot on his face?"

The Private turned the screen back to normal, scouting for another camera. A few seconds later, they had a partial front view. Their visitor moved his head slightly, but it was good enough to get a clean image.

"Is that a teenager?" White asked out loud, both surprised and confused.

What are you playing at?

"It certainly looks like it, sir. What do you want us to do?"

"Let's run his face on the database. See if something comes up. Let's keep an eye on him from afar, but whatever you do, don't spook him."

"Yes, sir."

17

Public Arena

"Hospital authorities are not confirming or denying any of the events depicted in the videos we've just shown, citing privacy requests and an ongoing internal investigation," the reporter said. On the screen, he wore a stiff suit and stood with his microphone firmly in his grip, perfect hair undulating with the breeze. The Sunday Merman Special was halfway through, and all Julian could do was watch.

"But one has to wonder how a merman made it into the ER and then vanished into thin air?"

Julian cringed at the ominous tone. As Aurel had predicted, someone was cleaning up this mess for them, but the media was relentless.

"After the events in the ER, things get fuzzy. We have been able to confirm that the CDC sent a researcher to this hospital, allegedly in a consultation requested by the hospital itself, an event that is not unheard of, but rather unusual."

The screen showed the CDC logo and a stock image of a man in a protective white hazmat suit. If the whole thing wasn't hitting so close to home, it'd be amusing. Sitting beside him, Alex hugged himself. It wasn't hard to picture what had happened to Chris between being found and being recognized as non-human, but seeing an actual timeline of the events that had led his son to captivity was hard to stomach, no matter what.

"Anonymous witnesses have confirmed the body was moved out of the hospital in the early hours on Thursday. This does bring the question that, if the swimmer had been human, the autopsy would have been carried on in the hospital's own morgue."

The scene changed from the morgue entrance to an interview.

"At this point, we can conclude the footage wasn't altered," a bearded man said, the caption at the bottom reading *Harold Short—Video Analyst*. "I can't tell you what they filmed, just that it wasn't altered with special effects. These are honest cellphone videos."

"Can we do make-up that looks that real?" a new woman said, her caption declaring her a Hollywood make-up artist.

"Absolutely yes. But I would love to meet whoever did this. The attention to detail is superb."

"Although they were not authorized to comment on camera, several people involved in the rescue confirmed what Neil Thompson said in our interview," the lead reporter said. "They couldn't find a way to detach the tail. The scales weren't peeling off. No make-up washed off his body."

"We're not talking about a human mixed with a fish," said a scholarly-looking man. "We're talking about a completely new species. Who knows what evolution's been playing with under our oceans? If this is real, then the hospital has the obligation to share their findings. I demand they share anything that will redefine life as we know it."

"A discovery of this nature wouldn't be taken lightly by our government or any government," an elderly woman said, her title proclaiming her the author of a philosophy publication. "Think of what we can learn from another species that shares the same world we do. Do they have a society like ours? Religion? Economy? What can we learn from them? What are they doing right that we need to change?"

"Mermaid stories have been with us for millennia," a young man said, his long hair tied back in a ponytail. His own caption read *Professor in Ancient Mythology.* "And you know what they say, all myths have truth at their core. Can there be real, water-breathing mermaids? I don't know, but this video proves at least our imaginations can still be captured in the same way they were mesmerized four thousand years ago. Mermaids exist, whether in our minds or otherwise, and the attention to this video proves our fascination with the unknown."

"From this point on, it's pure speculation," the reporter came back, walking outside the ER entrance. "Experts in the field have said there are several places to study a merman in Maine, but something of this magnitude would be taken somewhere else, most likely a military base or any number of government labs."

A dramatization started with a dozen people running alongside a quarantine gurney with an obscured figure lying on its top, a tail visible through plastic sheeting. They ran to a dark tunnel and disappeared.

Alex leaned on Julian's shoulder, his knees to his chin, now hugging himself in a tight ball. Julian put his hand on his shoulder. Alex felt so tiny, so vulnerable in this alien human world.

130

"Well, I'm gonna tell you straight up," a middle-aged man in a lab coat said, the caption too fast to read what type of doctor this was. "I wouldn't want to be that guy. We have no way of treating him up front without the risk of killing him. If he was alive by the time he got to the ER, he's probably dead right now."

But you don't know Chris. You don't know how fiercely he fights.

The words cut him deep, regardless, since he had also believed his son to be dead. Chris hadn't woken at all today and his prognosis was cautious, but now something more dangerous than grief rooted in Julian's heart: hope.

"I don't care what science at this point says about biology," another woman said; she was a sociologist somewhere on the West Coast. "There's absolutely no way mermaids could be more than a gathering society. Think of it as us in the Bronze Age, except there's no bronze, because underwater, you have no fire. No way of building the basic blocks of technology that will eventually lead to advanced civilizations as we know them. I'm all for this being true, but I wouldn't expect these merfolk to be more than a curiosity after a while."

Alex snickered, and Julian let go a chuckle.

"This is so stupid," Alex said, releasing his knees. "I hope Matt isn't watching it."

"I doubt your brother would miss any news on Chris, but... yeah."

"This isn't about Chris," Alex protested. "This is about some video of an obvious hoax. Even I don't believe it and I know it's true!"

"I'm not worried about this, either," he said, muting the screen, where interviews with random people on the street was taking place. "I'm more interested in what happens tomorrow. What happens when more witnesses start coming forward?"

"You think someone's really gonna talk?"

"I think we should start thinking about a future where we'll need to go into hiding, just in case."

Alex's eyes enlarged.

"Do you think they'll let us back in the City?"

Julian smiled. "You're too young to survive the trip, and so is Matt. We're stuck here on the surface until—"

"Yeah, yeah—until we're of age, yadda, yadda, yadda. I always thought you were making up the age requirement..."

"I wish. The City might call us back and let this whole thing die, though I doubt everyone would just drop their lives here and go home. It's not a real solution."

"What about Chris?"

"Drake's exploring some ideas, while the City decides what it wants. Infiltrating ORCAS is proving more difficult than we suspected."

Alex sighed. "I hate waiting..." he rose and walked out of the suite's living room, straight to his room, his computer, his codes, and back to watching Chris. Sometimes it scared Julian that the only reason Alex had ended under his roof was because the Squid had hacked into his computer to ask for help. Where would Alex be without his skills?

He took the TV off *mute*, then winced.

"I don't like it," a woman coming out of a supermarket said. "I don't like the idea of these creatures swimming right under us. Look at all the trouble we already have with all those immigrants. Do we really need to start worrying about mermaids taking over our rivers?"

"Trust me," Julian said out loud. "We're not happy about this, either."

"If you have any more information regarding this story, we're setting up a hotline. Every verified tip will be rewarded accordingly."

Julian frowned, memorizing the number. Drake would have it tapped and traced in no time, but having Alex doing something more than just keep watch on his brother would help the teen feel useful and proactive. Besides, it wouldn't hurt to send some fake information into that hotline of theirs, would it?

* * *

Gwen woke up with a start, but she didn't know why.

The doctors' quarters, although private, were nothing more than a glorified office space with a bed in one corner and a collective bathroom down the hall. Until Ray started talking or interacting, she wasn't going anywhere. Not that Forest hadn't offered her quarters with all the other researchers at the closest four-star hotel, he just hadn't insisted when she'd said she'd be fine with a crappy bed for a few more days.

In the silence of Gwen's room, the ringtone of her phone scared the hell out of her. She could sleep through a goddamn earthquake, but God forbid her subconscious mind would let her sleep through the ping of a notification. She picked up her phone, barely registering it was close to 7:00 p.m., and did a double-take on the number of messages on her screen.

"What the hell?" She was wide awake in two seconds, but it took her a moment to start understanding how she'd received 849 messages in the last twenty minutes. She even had freaking voice mails!

Ray's dead, was her first impression, as she started to thumb down through the mass of messages from strangers, family, and friends who were asking if it was true, what was she going to do about it, and how much would she want for an interview to disclose the details? Twenty minutes later—and 400 more messages—Gwen finally pieced together there'd been some sort of interview on the news, showing videos of her at the hospital, working on Ray.

Meanwhile, her brother was busy sending mermaid images, treating the whole thing as a joke, and her mother was scared for Gwen's safety since people on the internet had edited her into a video. Her friends were in various states of disbelief and surprise, asking her if she was going to call the program and was going to be rich. People she'd never met before were angry for her hiding the truth, or for playing a part in this hoax, or for being a pawn for the government, or for any and every reason under the sun. Total crazies wanted her to lead them to Ray, so they could touch him, be his best friend, go to bed with him, or all of the above. It didn't matter how fast she browsed, notifications wouldn't stop.

News stations hassled for statements, for quotes, for a picture of her and the merman. Half wanted this to be real, and half knew it was fake. All were willing to pay a lot of money for whatever proof she could produce.

How the hell did they find me?

She could reasonably guess her social media accounts hadn't been that hard to find after people who knew her started spreading the news, but her phone number? *Who are these people?*

Her heart raced at the onslaught of humanity's curiosity and judgment. When her phone started ringing with an unknown ID, she dropped it on her bed, afraid of what it might do to her if it kept her attention. Closing her eyes at the insanity of the situation, she picked it up, hung up, and turned it off, with the efficiency of three easy swipes. Her eyes went to the phone in her room, and she grabbed it as a safe line.

"Is Ray okay?" she asked when Higgs answered.

"Sure. He's the same as he was when you left here six hours ago, still sleeping. Why?"

"I—I just had a bad dream. Do you know if Forest is around?"

"No, he said something about a meeting. Have you tried his cell?"

She looked at her own evil device and shook her head, realizing a little too late that he couldn't see her. "I will. Thank you."

* * *

In the two hours since the Mermaid Special had aired, things had been tense. Nathan could sense it like the calm before the storm, a headache of epic proportions shaping up on the horizon, out of reach but not out of sight. Granted, beyond a few inquiries by White and the UN, nothing else had come his way. It was just a matter of time.

In front of him, Higgs had the widest grin Nathan had ever seen.

"You're enjoying this too much," Nathan said, while the other doctor bit into his burger.

"Well, it's not every day you see a conspiracy in the making. You're going to deny all of this, while a bunch of consultants all over the world is going to start babbling."

"I'm not sure I could even deny *all of this* no matter how hard I tried. Ray's been seen by too many people. Plus, we've been calling a dozen different experts in a dozen different disciplines to try to make sense of his existence. But… you know what? If I could, I'd definitely keep him hidden. It's just—the idea of leaving Ray's fate to public opinion is nauseating."

"Eat your burger, Nate. You're too thin, and the whole reason why we're out here in this nice place is to clear your mind. You're too deep in this shit, man. Have you been sleeping every sixteen hours or so?"

"We were already bracing for the media sensationalizing this—"

"—eat your damn hamburger—"

"—but to offer a reward? A reward? Seriously?!"

"—I'll take your fries if you're not interested."

Nathan's fingers flew over his food, retreating his plate from preying hands. "I'm eating them," he said defensively. "And it's not like we're withholding this from the public because we're playing men in black."

"No. It's because we have absolutely no clue what's going on, either," Higgs summarized nicely for them both. "Besides, didn't you say PR duties aren't yours?"

134

"Public Relations with the public? No. But try standing in front of the UN Committee to explain what we do know about Ray. That's a whole other level of PR, you know?"

"And they say us surgeons are the ones who always want to cut everyone up. Speaking of which, did Gwen talk to you?"

"About?"

"She called about four hours ago when I was still on my shift. Said she wanted to talk to you."

Nathan frowned and shook his head. He picked up his phone and dialed, going straight to a full voicemail.

"I'm sure it's nothing," Higgs said. "Eat your food."

"Yes, Mom," Nathan said, leaving his phone and looking at his enormous hamburger with a sudden empty stomach. When was the last time he'd had anything but coffee? *Higgs is right, I gotta take better care of myself.*

"You did a great job, Nate. Ray's still here, we're still here. So, you had to spin it a little, and add some colorful details, but everyone loves a good story. That's why you're so good at this job, you know how to keep things interesting for all parties."

Tell that to Ray. That's one party without a voice or vote.

"Speaking of parties, the UN Committee notified me earlier about our new PR representative, Diana Lombardi." Careful to not spill fries and mayonnaise, Nathan handed Higgs his tablet so he could see the file.

"The one who actually talks to the public?" Higgs inquired, viewing the picture of the newest member of the *I know a merman* club.

"Yes."

"Italian?"

"Argentinian, actually."

"She looks pretty," Higgs said with approval, the woman looking straight at the camera; her stunning blue eyes and high cheekbones seemed to belong to a model agency somewhere in France. Nate slid his finger over the screen, moving her picture and showing her credentials. "She's got some serious work under her belt, too."

Higgs called the photo back, looking at it intently.

"Okay, yes," Nate relented. "It certainly helps Ray a hell of a lot more if she looks like this than some fifty-year-old lady, but I'm just grateful this woman knows her business."

"Hm? Oh, yeah. I was just thinking she resembles someone I knew, that's all."

"Really?"

Higgs shrugged. "Can't place her. So, you like her?"

"I don't know just yet. I have a conference meeting with her and the Committee later tonight. See where we stand, what we can safely tell the public. That sort of nightmare. I'll send you her file so you can tell me what you think when we meet for lunch tomorrow."

"So much to do, so little time, huh?"

Nathan grunted. They both went their silent ways while eating for a few minutes, a dangerous downtime to think about too many things. "Higgs? What did you think? When I called you?"

"That you were joking, what else?"

Nathan smiled, nodding.

"I thought the CDC was joking, too. The guy on the other line stuttered so badly I had to ask him to take a deep breath and start again. I thought he was going to say we had a worldwide SARs epidemic in our hands or something."

"Nope. Just a merman washing up in Maine," Higgs said cheerfully, raising his soda in a toast. "You don't hear that every day."

Nathan looked up at the TV and sighed inwardly. "I bet you we're going to hear about it every day for a long time..."

18

Missing Pieces

Kate Banes was onto something, and for the first time since she'd watched the merman video a week ago, it had nothing to do with fish and scales, but with a warm-blooded male. Or even a family of them.

"You know, the more I look into this man's life, the less I think I know him…" she said, privately musing that it sounded like every relationship in her life.

"He's a billionaire, that's what billionaires do," Jeff said, his eyes glued to his monitor, while the crunch-crunch sound of his late breakfast disappearing made her wince.

Brooks Inc. had been in business a little over fifty years. Before that, it had been Riverbank Enterprises for twenty years, and before that was listed as a conglomerate of several small fisheries. The company website was proud of its roots, it proclaimed, since it had started with a group of friends looking out for each other; it had risen to the multinational, multibillions shipping industry it was now known for. But although the average Joe would pin Brooks Inc. as a boat company, the truth was that they had something going on in every corner of their sector. Boats were the most known aspect, but they had research going on in every ocean, investing huge capital in every hydro-technology they could get their hands on.

Pharma and Food industries also came under their umbrella, a given when the ocean was their playground. Some of their engineering patents were being used by NASA and other space agencies, even if their primary design had been in the field of underwater exploration.

Huh… Who would have thought it's easier to go up there with the stars, than down there with the algae?

"The net's going wild with speculation," Jeff said. "I so don't envy the guy behind that hotline. All the wackos in Maine are going to be calling, and then all the wackos in the country are going to go to—HA! There's a *save the merman* campaign going on."

"Really?" she asked, tearing her eyes from her own monitor. "What do they expect? A Free Willy story?"

"This guy could be larger than that... How's the orphan angle going?"

"When you say it like that, it sounds really cheap," she said, stretching on her chair. While Jeff was in social media heaven and tracking how the story was exploding in virtual land, she'd been hard at work. Chasing legal documents, old newspaper articles, and any other public information she could put her hands on was always filled with mind-numbing tasks. She had to admit, though, this preliminary background research was far more interesting and straightforward than she'd first thought when she'd started digging into Mr. Brooks's personal life. Standing, she reached for her green marker and went to her wall-slash-whiteboard, scribbling facts while she elaborated her findings to Jeff.

"He inherited the family company stocks, all sixty-two percent of them, at twenty-one, when his father, one David Brooks, retired and passed it to him—"

"Retired?"

"That's what it says. I can't find anything from that time but I've made a point of calling the legal firm that handled the whole business. His mom died in childbirth, and he had no other siblings. He never married, and keeps his relationships very low key. Then, sixteen years ago—"

"Here comes the orphan angle," Jeff said.

"Quit saying that! Julian adopted Christopher when he was only twenty-two and the boy was nine—no, wait, ten. Then, later on, he adopted Matthew who was eleven... and Alexander five years ago when the boy was also ten. All were abandoned. Social Services is a pain when it comes to getting information about this, and forget about digging into it without hitting concrete walls by Julian Brooks's lawyers."

She double-underlined *abandoned kids* as if that somehow was the connecting link between the Brooks heirs. She had to admit it made for a rather compelling angle—if handled well—and she was surprised she couldn't find much information surrounding the events.

"Do you think I'm too old for him to adopt me?" Jeff said.

"Yes. But how do you think he met them in the first place? There are virtually no interviews with any of them where they talk about this life-changing event. They weren't even in the system and suddenly they bump into a billionaire? It's as if they are here, part of society and New York and the boat industry, but when you try to see further, they just become ghosts."

"Oh! I like that! One of them is a merman, the other is a ghost... What should the other two be? A vampire and a werewolf?"

"Be real, Jeff."

"About a merman?" Jeff said with a smile. "Come on, Kate. Admit you want to come to the dark side and believe this merman is real," he teased her with a huge grin.

"No. No, I just think that there's more to this than just a prank, you know? These kids are never in the tabloids. They don't do drugs, don't date celebrities, get DUIs... anything you would expect a rich teenage boy to do... I can't find it. It's like they're too aware of how to be invisible that they're absurdly good at it."

She had to give it to Julian: he'd taught his kids well—kids who had come from nothing to having everything—ensuring they weren't the blabbing type. *Keep out of trouble* meant keep out of tabloids, and that meant a pleasantly private life.

"No one's invisible," Jeff said between more crunch-crunch sounds. "Here, let me..."

He put his laptop on the desk in front of Gwen and started typing. "This is going to take a while, what else do you have?"

"Media coverage surrounding them's been almost non-existent. Besides last week with Christopher's search news, these guys have been incredibly discreet. All I could find are a few articles here and there. When Christopher turned twenty-one, he made it into some magazine lists about rich gorgeous bachelors along with his father. And guess what? No comment from either of them."

"Hmm..."

"And then, nothing. They're among the most eligible bachelors in the world, and nothing? Why would gossip rags drop their names out of their lists? I mean, it doesn't hurt to look at either of them."

"Hmm..."

"What are you doing?"

"Magic. So, what about other sources? He's a rich guy but not because he's a model."

"That's what I was looking for all weekend," she added, her *Facts* column getting longer by the minute. "I had a few forays into his economic and philanthropic life. And what do you know, that watch expert of mine was right: earning a Triton watch is done quietly and with zero news coverage. I found a few small articles in science columns here and there, all in other countries and foreign languages, which barely commented on it. I looked up those scientists' achievements, but the award explanations went right over my head. These are smart people, Jeff, way smarter than your average science professor."

"Well, if I were to give a watch that costs twice as much as my apartment, I'd sure hope it went to someone with enough brains to save the world."

"You know what the weird thing is?"

"Besides the fact you can wear half a million bucks on your wrist?"

"These watches are a gift from the Brooks family, not from Brooks Inc., which I guess explains the lack of PR. No company in the world would give a half a million prize without having the entire nation watching. Not here in America, not anywhere else in the world. Who gives that kind of thing quietly?"

"Someone with too much money and too much sense of privacy."

"If he wanted privacy, he wouldn't be giving out those watches."

"Aaaaaanddd I'm in!"

"In where?"

"I friended people who know people who know them."

"What?"

"It's called *social* media for a reason. It takes some digging and some creative friendships with public people who know people who know them, but voila!"

For the next hour, Kate looked at vacation photos, party images, and a few candid family activities where one of the kids was pranking the others. They looked like so few families in her line of work ever looked: happy.

She could tell they weren't blood-related, but there was something that made them fit. Maybe in their smiles? Maybe in the way they stood? Maybe in the shapes of their shoulders? The more she stared, the less it made sense.

Of course, they could all be merfolk.

She smiled and then sighed. She could trace the crumbs of their social activities all day long, but knew she'd gain very little about things that mattered, things like Julian Brooks's early teens and childhood, not to mention his father's life.

That was the prize right now. This was the kind of hunt that sang in her veins and kept her awake at night. Sure, there was a nicely put paper trail, but she couldn't find anyone alive today who could corroborate anything. No college sweethearts, no childhood friends. Oh, Julian had friends now, she had found out about that without much problem, but in terms of everything before he took on his company, things had been silent.

140

She narrowed her eyes at her whiteboard. She didn't have enough evidence on anything, yet, just one alarming pattern of too little information on a man who really should be everywhere.

So she copied a few Julian Brooks photos into her computer and closed her browser, just to open her research folder and look into the other images she'd been gathering.

Well, Mr. Brooks, how do I find the real you?

* * *

Gwen parked in the VIP section at ORCAS and took a deep breath. No one out there had recognized her, no one had followed her, and even the guards at the entrance had smiled at her on her way in. Her little escapade to the outside world had gone without incident, and now it was time to get back to her merman.

Smiling at the absurdity of it all, she got out of her car, took her bags, and walked to the main building with a renewed sense of purpose. On her way in, Forest greeted her with a nod of his head while he talked on his phone, then hung up.

"Here, let me help you," he offered, getting a couple of bags from her hands. "Did you happen to watch the merman special yesterday?"

"No, but you could say it found me anyway."

He frowned for a moment before it dawned on him: "You got recognized. How many offers have you gotten?"

He asked it in a good-natured way, but she knew him well enough to know he was fishing for deeper answers. Calmly, she reached into her pocket and got out a shiny new toy. "I had to change my phone. I closed my social media accounts and went off the grid with a few messages to my family. Those reporters won't find me for some time."

It was almost imperceptible, but she thought she saw him relax his shoulders a fraction of an inch. Then he smirked.

"No matter what we do, this is going to blow. The Committee knows it as well as I do."

"The UN Committee? Your bosses?"

"Yes. They've already recruited someone to handle the whole PR side of this, but it's only a matter of days before we actually go to a press conference. Would you like to—"

"Hell, no."

"You don't even know what I was going to suggest," he said, bewildered.

"You're talking about PR, I'm hiding under a rock. With Ray. I'm not giving any press conferences, or talking to the public in any capacity."

"That's not what I was going to say... but now that you mention it, it would be incredibly helpful to have a face who's had direct contact with him."

That made her realize Forest here had never really talked with Ray; he'd just looked at their merman literally from the inside out, but had yet to come to Ray's room and talk to him.

"Why not you?" she asked.

"That's not my area of expertise. I organize people, things, resources... even budgets from time to time. I don't talk to the press."

"I already know you like to give orders, but—" she suddenly stopped. "Crap! I forgot something in the car," she said, going back. He followed suit.

"There's nothing wrong with liking your job, you know?" he said with a smile and a shrug. That she could understand. She'd wanted to be a doctor since she was four, and still felt a rush every time the doors to the OR opened for her.

"What were you going to suggest? If it wasn't me talking to a camera?"

"Oh. Would you like to give me your new number, actually," he said, and she blushed, feeling like an idiot. She already had him on speed dial, and the man had no way to contact her. Not that she went out much, really. These days she was either with Ray, at the cafeteria, or sleeping. She pressed his number and his phone went off in his hand. "There you go," she said, turning to open her car and retrieving the bags from the back seat.

"What do you have in all those bags?" he asked, while they carried her stuff inside.

"Just a little bit of color... You'll see."

* * *

If last Monday, someone had told Alex he was going to be in another state, discussing how to break his merbrother out of human hands, he would have

142

nervously laughed while going pale. Capture had always been a bogeyman, a fear best left in the shadows where no one was looking. It was a reality no one wanted to contemplate, but one the four men at the table were forced to discuss.

"They keep adding more security to the building," Matt said, cutting his pancakes with a vengeance. Having Matt around for breakfast was weird since he came at odd hours and left without anyone being any the wiser. Part of Alex wished Julian would stop him, sternly tell Matt he was risking his life in some stupid attempt to be closer to Chris, and order him to stay sheltered in their hotel suite where no one could hurt him. But the rest of Alex knew better, and only wished he had the mental control to talk to Chris from the parking lot—let alone the hotel suite.

As it was, Alex's only way of seeing what was going on with his oldest brother was via his computer, and he didn't waste a second away from it.

"What are they saying on the net?" Matt asked, stacking three more pancakes on his plate.

"Stupid things. There are forty different hashtags trying to capitalize on the Special, and a lot of talk of *believers* getting trolled and mocked by *non-believers*. People are taking sides and it's not going to end pretty."

"So, basically, people are being people on the net," Drake said over his scrambled eggs, adding a generous amount of salt. "But give it enough time and it's going to spread like wildfire."

"They're going to get bored when nothing else official happens," Alex said, closing the laptop for the moment. He was tired, so damn tired of seeing Chris's life being played like some cheap B movie.

"We'll see," Drake said with a pointed look.

"There might be another problem we haven't considered," Julian said, sipping his coffee. All three stopped eating and looked at him.

"Something I'm not aware of?" Drake asked, his eyes narrowing slightly, his shoulders tense.

"I spoke with Chris earlier this morning. He says he lost his watch."

Drake closed his eyes and exhaled deeply, clearly thinking this was the last drop on an overflowing glass. "Of course," he whispered, leaning on his seat and forgetting his breakfast.

Alex felt his heart constrict. They only wore their diving watches when practicing really deep dives, a detail that had gone under the radar with all the recent chaos, obviously, something unseen but not forgotten. Not if it was coming back to bite them in the butt.

"It could have been lost during the boat incident, right?" Alex pointed out. "His right wrist was broken, the watch could be at the bottom of the Atlantic right now."

Drake looked at him and then at Julian. "Maybe. It's been a week since Chris was hit and left for dead and no one's come forward with it."

"What do you want us to do?" Matt asked, eager to get ahead of any problem.

"Be alert, as always. Alex, I need you to see if there's any mention of that watch anywhere on the net, no matter how small the inquiry. In the best case scenario, we find Chris's attacker and deal with that problem at once. Otherwise, whoever has it can easily trace it back to us. We need to find that watch before it finds us."

19

Connections

"Tell me you have good news," Julian said as Drake entered the suite. Matt was already gone, and so was Alex, disappeared into his digital world.

"I just have plain news," Drake offered with a tired smile. He looked exactly like Julian felt: drained.

"Shoot."

"We've got a good lead into intercepting Chris's medical supplies. If we can switch the IV bags, we can give Chris better medical care."

"That sounds good," Julian said, frowning.

"It has problems and a few loops, so I don't want your hopes up. But, we're working on it."

"Thank you," Julian said. "That's a pretty bold idea."

"Well, it sure is easier than infiltrating ourselves."

For Julian, every single waking hour was divided into three priorities: get Chris out, get someone else in, and keep the secret safe. Sometimes two of them aligned, sometimes, all three went in extremely different directions. Making them converge was the goal of the game, and so far, Julian was losing.

"This isn't all I'm bringing." Drake sat down at Julian's desk, looking grim. "I've got some ideas on Chris's attacker."

The tension in Julian's shoulders got tighter, but he didn't even notice. If there was one more problem to lose sleep over, it was whoever had put Chris in the hospital, to begin with.

"Tracing Nova Scotia's marina has been its own headache," Drake said, opening his small laptop between Julian and himself. "Too many ships, too little to center on. But, we managed to trace Chris's steps. We got receipts, surveillance videos, and his texting between him and his brothers."

"Any leads?"

"A few. We're cross-referencing anyone who knew he was traveling alone. It's an off chance—"

"—but it's a starting point," Julian finished for his friend, the screen coming alive with the marina video of ten days earlier.

Their theory was simple: someone had known a very rich guy was sailing alone for seven days and decided to take advantage of it. To kidnap or to rob him, it was irrelevant. Their best guess was these people had gotten to the ship while Chris had been diving, waited for him, and had gotten a merman coming out of deep waters. They'd panicked, and then had hit Chris with a bat, leaving him for dead in the ocean.

Maybe some details were off—or maybe all of them were—but whoever had hit his son knew exactly what he was. On the screen, the video showed Chris's boat, the *Deep C*, leaving the safety of the pier and sailing in swift waters to meet its destiny. How much Julian wished he could yell at his son through the monitor and warn him to stay. A couple of minutes later, another boat moved, *The Lucky Thirteen*, and Drake stopped the video. "That one has a crew of three. They were supposed to be out for the day, but they took four days to come back. There are four other boats with some iffy thing going on; all were out the same day Chris left, and could have gotten a hold of him in the open sea."

"Okay, that's something."

"Hate to say this, Julian, but it'd be much easier if they'd just come forward with their merman story, so we could wipe them out once and for all," Drake said, half joking, half serious. Whoever these people were, as far as Drake was concerned, they were dead men walking. And Julian felt no remorse about that. No remorse at all.

* * *

No, no, you have the wrong playlist, Chris complained while Matt fumbled with his brother's atrocious taste in music. Chris was nine years older but his music felt ancient.

"I'm not going to listen to this crap," Matt muttered, thumbing through selected songs. "There has to be something we can both listen to without passing out."

Au contraire, I'm taking this opportunity to teach you a lesson in good taste.

Matt randomly hit play, the speakers blasting to the point the whole car vibrated. If this could keep Chris's mind out of his prison and pain, surely Matt

146

could endure a few hours of musical torture. He still remembered his brother dabbling at the piano from time to time, a shared interest Chris used to enjoy together with Julian.

If Matt really concentrated, he could picture a ghostly image of his brother sitting beside him, moving his leg with the song's rhythm, closing his eyes and letting himself go in the moment. Long gone was the awkwardness of sharing one mind or the embarrassment of asking stupid questions. Whatever it took to keep his brother in good spirits, Matt was going to do it.

They listened to four more crappy songs—along with Chris's commentary about the band, the lyrics, the awards, and all the boring details—until something strained their connection.

"What? What's wrong?"

Nothing, Chris said, evasive.

"Chris?"

A long pause followed while the fifth song went by unnoticed.

Some new doctors are here. Just—

Chris vanished in an instant, and Matt panicked.

"Chris?! Chris!" he yelled, his voice drowned by the song he'd forever associate with a void in his soul. Elusive as it was, Matt followed his brother's mental trail. He knew it so well by now, that he slammed into Chris's mind on the other side. His car dissolved and became a gurney, the strange antiseptic smell of the room invading his nose, right before the feeling of an iron rope strangling his tail brought him to tears.

Like a freight train, Chris pushed him out of that room so fast it physically hurt to get back into his own mind. He'd never seen his brother so angry before—or so horrified.

Don't!

The word was loaded with too many implications and warnings. *Don't come to my side, don't suffer with me, don't do this to yourself, don't stay here, don't see this.*

Matt breathed hard, his hands holding his legs while phantom pains clutched at his muscles, Chris's playlist still blaring from the speakers.

"Chris?" Matt whispered, feeling lost, disoriented, and hurt. "Chris, what's going on?"

Silence. Matt swallowed and turned the radio off, needing to get his thoughts in order and follow Chris once more.

They're going to run some test. Chris's voice filled Matt's mind, still on edge, but calmer. *I don't want you here right now, okay?*

"But—"

Just go, get some fresh air. I'm probably just gonna fall asleep anyway.

"No," Matt said, angry.

Matt—

"No! The only thing I can do right now is be here for you, and you're not going to take that away. Let me be here for you, Chris. If you can't be on my side, then I'll be on yours. Just don't—don't leave me out. Don't go through this alone."

Chris never said yes, but he didn't say no, either. Tentatively, Matt took a hold of their connection a few minutes later and went in, ready for the pain and the tiredness that clung to Chris's body. His brother muddled their connection somewhat so Matt didn't get the entire onslaught of sensations and pain. A compromise, Matt guessed, and one he took gladly.

What are they doing? Matt asked as his brother closed his eyes to the three men surrounding him, stopping Matt from seeing anything going on in that room.

Chris, if you think you can just shut me out and—

Sshh... Chris admonished.

Sshh? What the—

Just listen... Chris said, taking a deep breath.

So he did.

* * *

From the observation room, Nathan took his usual spot to look down on Ray and the three enthusiastic Swedish doctors around him. Now that their merman was slowly crawling out of the *critical* condition and into the more desirable *serious* state, sixty people wanted time with him for different purposes. The UN Committee, along with Higgs and Gwen, were prioritizing what Ray could or could not be subjected to, a task Nate also supervised, even if he had minimal input into what got approved or not. Most of the time, requests were shot down because they depended on Ray's full collaboration, a problem when Ray was neither talking nor acknowledging them, but today's special brand of test had been both appropriate and amusing. This was a musical test.

"They're all ready to go," Higgs said with a smile, coming to stand beside Nate. One of the doctors was carefully placing the biggest headphones Nate had ever seen in his life over Ray's ears, to ensure quality and no contamination. Ray would hear whatever they wanted him to hear and nothing else.

"It's a rather clever idea," Nate said with approval. Not only were they testing for musical recognition in Ray's brain patterns, they were also testing for recognition of other languages. Ray understood English without a doubt, but what about anything else? Songs in twenty-three other languages were integrated into the playlist, a subtle ambush if one felt inclined to think about it that way. Plus, was it too much to ask for Ray to have a good time? For once?

A few more minutes went by before the test officially began, the doctors' full attention on the monitors, while Nate and Higgs watched Ray from above. Not even twenty seconds had gone by before their guest winced slightly, his eyes remaining closed.

Higgs chuckled, a grin spreading wide over his face.

"What?" Nathan asked, curious. Higgs wouldn't be smiling if it wasn't something funny, right?

"I bet $200 our merman wouldn't understand the first ten minutes, and if his face is any indication, I think I've just won," his friend said. Turning to look at Nate, he added. "It's whales and dolphins chatting. Not a pretty sound with those headphones, believe me. I checked."

For a full minute, Nate didn't know if to feel outraged at the idea that people were betting on Ray's tests, or curious about why anyone would think a merman could understand another species' language. Humans didn't recognize anything but their own languages, after all.

"What made you so sure?" he asked instead.

Higgs shrugged. "A hunch."

"Really?" Nate asked, clearly not fooled.

Higgs smiled sheepishly. "It really was a hunch, but… I've been with Ray a few days now. If you look closely, when he's pretending he's not here, you see his fingers moving with a beat. Different beats, actually, as if he was singing in his head to different songs. And that's no dolphin beat he's playing."

"What? Why haven't you—"

"Reported it? Because I don't want it on paper," Higgs said seriously, a warning some things were better off the records. "Nothing that can't be proved beyond a doubt, anyway," he amended a moment later, smiling again. "As I said, it's just a hunch."

"Do you have any other… hunches?"

"I'll tell you when they come," his friend said, getting his eyes back on Ray.

Nathan chuckled, his eyes still gazing at their merman. And for a moment there, just a moment, he'd swear the merman had faintly drummed his fingers in one perfect piano scale.

* * *

Watching Ray's brain waves had become an involving activity. Higgs had seen some pretty weird stuff in his career, including people with half-brains fully capable of normal lives, or epileptic patients reporting all matters of unusual events.

The key to the human brain didn't lie in healthy brains, but in the abnormal ones. Knowing what a defective section of the brain didn't do helped to explain what the other parts did.

He didn't have that with Ray. Everything was brand new when it came to their merman, from the brain structure to its biochemistry. All Higgs had were patterns, so he'd started to match those with Ray's cognitive states: was he awake or asleep? Was someone talking to him or was he left alone? Was something different when it was Gwen or himself?

Lately, though, a new kind of pattern had started to emerge when Ray was awake. A complex process that required many higher brain functions Higgs would usually associate with rigorous tasks, like a trapeze artist in a balancing act. Ray was paying a lot of attention to something that wasn't physical, and much less obvious. Maybe it was some sort of meditation to reduce the pain?

"When you look like that I really wish I could read your mind," Nathan said as he came into the lab, and for one moment Higgs saw those patterns and wondered how telepathy would look.

Smiling, he turned to meet his friend. "Nothing you would like to know. You seem in a good mood, considering last night's mermaid special."

"Don't remind me. Are you looking at the music test?" he asked curiously, looking at the three large monitors behind Higgs, which displayed the electroencephalogram results of Ray's brain. The mess of electrical impulses had little to do with how the human brain worked. No matter how much Ray looked like one of them from the torso up, he was an alien being with an evolutionary path that had led to different inner workings.

"No, this is actually from an hour before the test."

"Okay. What are we looking at, then?" Nathan asked.

"This," Higgs said, selecting one of the screens and highlighting a section with a particular, intricate wave. "Gwen talks to him all the time, so we've established some baselines of when he's having social interactions, even if he's not talking back. If you look closely, every now and then, these more active events happen." Higgs highlighted another wave pattern from another monitor. "They last a few minutes, maybe up to fifteen, then disappear. Everything else keeps doing what it does, but... if you compare this with Ray's facial expressions when no one's interacting with him, it almost—almost looks as if he's having a conversation."

Nathan turned to look at his friend. "He's talking to himself?"

"I don't know. Every time I've seen this popping up, you can tell something is catching his attention. Or that he smiles or nods without realizing it."

"Maybe he's just remembering things to help pass the time," Nathan said, frowning.

"Maybe he's just about to have a psychotic breakdown," Higgs added, smiling. "Something's going on with that man's brain that's beyond what we can explain at this moment. All I'm saying is, he looks as if he's having a conversation."

"Well, if it turns up that he can do telekinesis and telepathy, do me a favor and keep it to yourself. Between his alleged shapeshifting and underwater breathing... Wait for the military to do something about it."

Higgs's smile dwindled. "I like Ray, Nate. I really do. But you can't get attached to him this way. He's going to end up in some lab somewhere, especially if he doesn't start talking soon. He needs to go home, Nate, because he won't have many friends left otherwise."

"I know," Nathan said with a tired smile, one that said *it's already too late for that*. "Anyway, I was looking for you to share the physiotherapist's file. His name is Andrew Summers, he's starting tomorrow morning, and I want you and Gwen to be with Ray when they meet."

"Sure, no problem."

"And whatever Andrew says, we can't let Gwen gut him."

Higgs raised his eyebrows in question.

"Just a feeling," Nathan explained, handing Higgs a folder. "You think I'm attached? Wait to see her disagreeing with her patient's care."

Higgs laughed, forgetting about strange brain patterns and concentrating on the newest team addition. *Well, Mr. Summers, I sure hope you're ready for one hell of a ride.*

20

New Arrivals

Andrew Summers was nervous as hell—but he hid it well. Years of working with wild animals had taught him to manage his fear and embrace his wonderment, a useful skill when one was about to meet an honest-to-God merman.

"Do you have any questions?" Dr. Higgs asked as Andrew was getting ready, adjusting the blue cap one last time over his blond hair. He'd read the reports and watched the videos—both the internet and the ORCAS ones—and he'd met with several people already, to discuss the test results. What he needed now was to talk with his patient, and that was something he had to do face-to-face.

"What's his mental state now?"

"Oh, that one's easy," Dr. Higgs said, the tall, lanky man showing a strange mix of optimism and honesty. "He's miserable."

Andrew looked at him with bulging eyes. "What?"

"He's bored out of his mind," Higgs explained. "Because he refuses to engage lest he breaks some sort of code, he's been alone with his pain for the past week. He doesn't fight us, doesn't do anything but lie still and sleep. We haven't even been able to remove his feeding tube for fear he'll refuse to eat."

Andrew swallowed. Generally speaking, physical therapy made no one happy. Patients were already in a lot of pain to begin with, and although they wanted the end result, they seldom stuck with their plans and worked for it. Depression was high on the list of symptoms, so the therapist's goal was not only to get the body back in shape but keep the mind focused as well.

"You want me to cheer him up." It wasn't a question, more like part of the job description.

He guessed the reason he'd been chosen was because in his early career he'd started out rehabilitating marine animals, usually dolphins and sea lions that found their way to the Californian beach. He still volunteered once a month, so was in a position where he understood both worlds. He had no idea who'd recommended him for this job—even if he was damn good at it—but he was still waiting for someone to say *gotcha!* because mermaids weren't real.

"We want you to give him something to think about," Dr. Higgs said. "There's nothing we've said so far that's gotten him to trust us, but we know his tail matters a great deal. Engage him on his own rehabilitation and we'll have won our first battle."

"I'll do my best."

"Oh, and Andrew? Talk to him as you would any other patient. Use all your technical vocabulary. We're trying to figure out how much he actually understands."

Walking through the corridor felt vaguely surreal. His stomach was tight, his shoulders tense, and his heart beat fast. Taking a few calming breaths, he managed to get his anxiety level under control. Finally, he opened the door into the merman's room, Dr. Higgs right behind. The things he saw first were the *Get Well Soon* balloons crowding the entire opposite wall. Reds, greens, and blues, the wall was decorated with confetti and ribbons, happy suns and rainbows completely at odds with the dark blue walls and medical machinery. It was so unexpected he stopped abruptly enough for Dr. Higgs to collide behind him.

"Ah..." the older man said, knowingly. "Dr. Gaston here thought Ray needed some color," Higgs said with a grin, introducing him to Ray's on-shift doctor. Higgs and she were Ray's primary doctors, although an army of specialists was behind his every breath at every second. He doubted there'd ever been a patient in history with more eyes than their mythical creature.

"Yeah, well, Ray has yet to let me know what he thinks," she said, shaking his hand. "Call me Gwen, please. There's way too much formality everywhere else."

"Andrew Summers, and call me anything but Andy, and we won't have any problems." They both smiled.

"Will do. And, here's the star of the hour, Ray."

The three of them moved toward the overly-large gurney. It was one thing to read about the extension of the tail, and an entirely different thing to see it. Almost six feet long, it was covered in tiny blue scales, reminding him of a piece of art he'd seen somewhere. The gash in the tail had been wrapped in a cast, hidden now under a blue blanket. Lying on his side with his back to them, Ray had coiled himself up as much as he could despite the cast, and all Andrew could read was tension coming off in waves.

154

The therapist in him wondered about the speed at which that tail would propel Ray's body, and with practiced ease he conducted a preliminary evaluation of Ray's muscle structure, taking particular interest in how everything about his posture was screaming *go to hell*. His new patient didn't want to be there—the heart monitor displayed proof enough—and if he'd been a wild animal, Andrew would have braced for a lot of thrashing, and probably bites.

Please, don't bite me.

Slowly, Andrew walked around the gurney, until he was face to face with the merman, who studiously ignored him by looking at some random point on the wall.

"Hi, I'm Andrew," he said, getting a nearby stool and sitting down, taking a few seconds to relax his body. Ray—whose name wasn't even Ray—was way more nervous than he was. "I'm your physiotherapist." No reaction, not even a glare or a flicker of interest. "Listen. Something really bad happened to your body. And although it doesn't look like it right now, sometime soon, it will heal. Now, if it heals right or wrong depends a great deal on what you want, what you do. I'm here to guide you through this. It will hurt, it will take time, and most importantly, will take discipline. But Ray, I promise you, I'll do whatever it takes to make it right."

Ray didn't look at him, but his posture slightly relaxed, his eyes had stopped wandering. He was listening.

"Okay. I'm going to need you to extend your tail for me."

Everyone in that room held their breaths, waiting for Ray's decision. Andrew had had stubborn patients before, but he had absolutely no idea what to expect from Ray, not because he was a merman—although that was a big part—but because for all intents and purposes, he was a prisoner. Ray didn't move. Gwen was about to open her mouth but Andrew stopped her with a look.

"I want you to do me a favor," Andrew said in a neutral tone, appealing to every trick in his bag. "Close your eyes. Imagine, for one moment, that none of this exists. You're not here, it isn't today, life is not crap. You're back at your favorite place in the world, swimming. Moving. There's no pain, there's no rush. I want you to stay there for a while and feel your body relax."

It took a whole minute, but Ray closed his eyes, and gradually he let go of the tension, relaxing his muscles, the heartbeat monitor slowing down. Gwen's grin almost split her face, while Higgs gave him an encouraging thumbs-up.

"Now, you and I know nothing in your life will ever be the same. But you being a cripple doesn't have to be part of your future. I need to see your tail, Ray. I need you to help me understand what needs to be done."

Ray still wouldn't move.

"Take your time, pal. I've got all day and so have you."

Six excruciatingly long minutes later, Ray started to stretch. Gwen almost threw a party right there, even if both Andrew and Ray ignored her as best as they could. Higgs was looking at something in one of the monitors, throwing more thumbs-ups from his position.

"Slowly… I see you're in a lot of pain, there's no hurry. Gwen, help us out, please?"

There were a lot of wires and tubes to be careful with, and so Andrew and Gwen helped his new patient as best as they could until the merman was completely stretched on his back, studiously looking at the ceiling.

"I'm going to touch you now, okay?" Andrew wondered how many people asked him that, or just went ahead and laid their hands on him. In his experience, doctors in the ICU often forgot the intimacy of touching since they did it so often and for so many life-saving reasons.

Ray didn't answer, but also didn't move when Andrew placed his hand on his scales a few seconds later, in an unspoken agreement that it was okay. Sure of where he stood now, Andrew went from the tip of the tail all the way up to the cast, worrying at what his hands felt. So many knots. So much tension had built up in the muscles for the past week that it wasn't even funny. He raised his eyes and whistled. That, finally, intrigued Ray enough to make eye-contact with him.

"You need a lot of work. And man, you're going to thank me for this someday."

* * *

You're getting a massage? For real?

Matt's mental voice sounded as if he thought Chris had finally lost it. And maybe he had. But man, this felt absurdly wonderful.

Andrew was going through every inch of his tail, pressuring, dissolving, and soothing every cramp, every knot, every single thing wrong with it. With the constant throbbing on the back of his tail, he couldn't fully appreciate the relaxation technique—but, for now, he just didn't care.

Julian said it was okay... Chris admitted, almost apologizing for giving in. His adoptive father kept a constant eye on him whenever Chris awoke, and having him advising what to do lifted a huge burden from his shoulders.

I didn't mean it like that, Matt said, offended. *But, you know, the general weirdness of your situation. They get you a massager—*

—A masseur, Chris corrected his brother.

Whatever. You get your own personal trainer, a chatty doctor, freaking balloons, and all that for being a jerk. With all due respect, I should be the one in there. I would give them a run for their money without even trying!

Chris laughed, prompting Andrew to stop.

"Ticklish?" the man asked. Because Chris wouldn't really answer, he just re-accommodated, the muscles on his lower back protesting. "Dr. Higgs, can you help us getting him on his side?"

Until they took the stupid feeding tube out, Chris couldn't be on his stomach. He wished he could tell them he wanted to eat. He wished he could tell them a dozen different things, from being thirsty to thanking them for trying to make this bearable. Matt was right, he was being a jerk and he hated every minute of it. And it wasn't like Julian hadn't given him permission to do anything he needed to, except that for Chris, talking felt too much like betrayal. So he'd made a deal with himself: if it meant survival, it was okay. If it meant discomfort, he could deal with it—silently.

What else did Julian say? Matt asked, curious.

The City hasn't decided yet on what to do about me.

What did you say? This time, Matt was angry.

That I'm fine. These doctors have told me, repeatedly, and in no uncertain terms, they want to help me.

Oh, sure! 'Hey, we landed some three thousand years ago and then we were unable to leave, so we decided to go where you couldn't put your hands on our technology and our people, and we've been hiding ever since. I hope you don't mind, but could you wait a couple of years until I can swim to the City and then come back? It's kind of my long-life dream.' *Sure Chris, they're going to help you.*

I'm not stupid, but this is way better than being dissected, you know? I'm thankful for any small favors I can score in here.

"Okay, let's roll you in one... two... three!"

Moving him required the effort of moving not only his torso and tail but also the cast. Chris couldn't do it himself without some serious tears filling his eyes. After a moment, he felt Andrew's eyes on his back, the same way he'd felt so many eyes on his back already.

"So, let me get this straight: scales here mean stress?"

Chris just sagged. By this point, he could shift everything above his tail back into place, but what was the point? They knew him like this, so he'd stay exactly this way.

"We think so," Gwen said. "He had fewer scales when we found him and more when he woke up the first time last week."

The first time? It was suddenly crystal clear he'd missed a lot more than he'd thought. *How many times have I woken up?*

Well, you started resurfacing five days ago, it was pretty bad… Julian thought you were dying, so I'm so glad you don't remember. Alex and I… we didn't feel more than a nudge. Best nudge ever, by the way.

Wait, how long have I been here?

Nine days… No, wait, eight. You got the shit beat out of you last Monday, but they found you until Tuesday morning, so a week ago. Chris… do you know what happened? Who knocked you down?

Andrew pressed his hands at the nape of Chris's neck at the same time the flashback of getting hit startled him. He felt his shoulder blades shifting into scales, and moved his hands and chin to his chest, unconsciously bracing for impact.

"Whoa there… it's okay. See? No more hands on you."

Chris?

I've just messed up my massage. Chris sighed in frustration, both mentally and out loud. He wanted to do something that would indicate it was okay, that he really, truly wanted those hands back. He had no idea what.

I don't know, he answered, wincing as Andrew withdrew from his side to talk with the other two. *I don't think I can remember, anyway.*

Julian doesn't like it. He and Drake are moving hell and heaven to find out who did this to you. Don't ever tell him I said this, but he's kind of a badass when he gets intense about things.

I know… Matt hadn't seen Julian those first months when his little brother first joined them. How much their guardian would have loved to strangle the life out of Matt's parents if they'd still been alive.

"You swim a lot, don't you?" Andrew asked, getting closer to inspect Chris's back. Chris chuckled, not because Andrew was wrong—he wasn't—but because he was right for all the wrong reasons.

He did not just say that, Matt said in complete disbelief. *These people are morons!*

158

"Okay, Ray. Have you seen your x-rays?" Andrew asked with a spark in his eyes.

What kind of name is Ray? Matt's insistent commentary was funny when Chris didn't have to pay attention—which was usually every single minute he was awake—but Andrew was talking about things that mattered to his survival, so he hushed his brother.

Gwen got the x-rays from somewhere and handed them across. Getting his stool really close, Andrew played with the gurney's control until it started to elevate. Chris winced. If the angle was too elevated, his tail was going to hurt ten times worse.

"It's okay... just a little... there. Now, as you can see, that propeller made a good number on your muscles here. Do you know they're having a nerd contest up there about how to name your muscles?"

Chris just blinked.

"Anyway. Gwen patched you up—"

"—Twice—" she said, leaning on a counter by the wall.

"—isn't she nice? But scar tissue can become a problem, especially on a wound this size. I bet it hurts like hell, too. I'd like to apply electrical stimulation along with an ultrasound. It's too early for some things, but we're right on time for others."

Andrew held the x-rays at the right angle so Chris could see. He'd never seen an x-ray of himself before—or of a merfolk for that matter. He knew how his body worked in the same way the general human population knew how theirs worked, but that had come from diagrams and Julian's teaching, not from bloodwork, MRIs, and God only knew what else he'd been subjected to while unconscious.

"It didn't touch the bone—or cartilage. Do you have a name for it?" Andrew asked, and Chris went as far as opening his mouth before realizing his vow of silence was about to be broken. He closed it and sighed.

"That's okay, we'll find something nice, long, and complicated to name it. So, it didn't touch the structure, but we're getting worried about the area around it. We don't know what a healthy recovery time is, but we're not happy with the discoloration we're seeing."

He went on and on about muscles, and therapies, and compromise, as if Chris had any ideas of quitting. Twenty minutes in, Chris was almost asleep. He couldn't understand it. All he did all day long was sleep or worry the hell out. He'd been so tired these past days it was embarrassing.

"It's okay. We don't have to rush into anything. I'll see you later, okay? Get some rest."

Chris? Matt asked. He'd been quiet all this time and Chris was just about to shut him out anyway.

Hmm?

Maybe not all of them are morons.

* * *

Chris let go of their connection and faded back to sleep.

Now that Matt's mind was completely his again, he needed to get out of the car and walk his anxious energy away. He was far enough that it was hard to distinguish the patrolling soldiers, but the building where his brother lay unconscious was plenty visible from here.

He shut the door of the car and cranked his neck both sides. He wanted to walk ten miles, run another five, and swim to the bottom of the ocean so he could escape this feeling of helplessness. He wanted to get in there and take Chris out, so his brother would wake up in his own bed, with his family around him.

Damn it, Chris! His thought went unnoticed by his brother, but not by someone else.

It pricked his mind, this sensation he was being watched. Matt froze, automatically closing his mind to unwanted ears. Ever so slowly, he turned around, gray eyes searching for something that didn't belong.

Nothing seemed out of place. People, trees, cars. More people. More trees. A bird. His eyes saw everything and nothing, dismissing every passer-by until he finally landed on a promising lead; a guy was sitting on a bench some fifty feet away, no bigger than himself. He wore an oversized green sweater with his face partially hidden in its hood, and faded jeans. His eyes were closed, and earplugs gave the impression he was listening to music and nothing else. He was too young to be one of the researchers, Matt knew.

Although merfolk were a tight knot, it didn't mean they all knew each other. Matt didn't know the exact number, but he'd figured there were about a thousand merfolk on the surface. Who knew how big the City was underwater, how many more of his kind lived secluded, never seeing the sun, never fearing discovery.

160

It didn't matter. Here was a merman listening to his private conversations with his brother. This guy was really stupid, really nosy—

—Or really desperate.

The thought gave him pause. Not so long ago, he'd been desperate, too.

In his mind, he started a one-sided conversation with Chris, as if nothing had changed. It kept the guy concentrating on listening, unaware he was being approached. It must have taken him ten seconds to reach the guy, but Matt felt each and every one of those as hours.

"Hey," Matt said to the other guy, standing some good six feet away. Plenty of room to let him try to escape. "I think you've been meaning to talk to me?"

Yes, I'm talking to you, he added, looking with satisfaction as his last mental words got the startled reaction he was looking for. The hood fell partway, and it was Matt's turn to be startled at how young this kid actually was. Probably as young as the Squid, maybe even younger than fifteen.

"It's okay," Matt managed to say, swallowing his surprise. The kid's blue eyes became guarded, and it was easy for Matt to see his posture changing, calculating how best to flee.

"I'm Matthew," he said, minding his own last name for now. No sense in outing his entire family to a stranger.

The kid didn't move. Beside him, a battered backpack was all he had, his tennis shoes dirty and worn, his clothes clean but more than well-used. He was thin, the same way Alex was thin, and in his dark blue eyes, there was a quiet desperation at being caught, one that permeated his every breath. That look Matt knew; he'd been seeing it in the mirror most of his life before coming to live with Julian and Chris. It was the one saying *I don't belong anywhere, so let me go.*

"I'm going to shake hands with you, and they're not going to be hot like everyone else's. Because we're the same," Matt whispered, getting closer, mindful of their lack of privacy.

Matt extended his hand while slowly walking toward the silent teenager. He knew that for humans, merfolk were perpetually cold, but between them, they felt perfectly fine.

It took a few seconds, but his foundling finally extended one utterly steady hand. His grip was strong, two perfectly even matched temperatures between them—

—until the kid pulled Matt down with enough force to send him to the ground, and the brat ran with all his might, leaving nothing behind but a cursing merman.

21

Best Intentions

Unlike an hour ago when his nerves had threatened to paralyze him, Andrew had no problem dealing with humans. Both Higgs and Nathan were discussing the latest test results on Ray's condition, while the three of them enjoyed a late brunch at the cafeteria, where everyone wore a lab coat or military uniform. The two groups did not mingle.

"So, what do you think?" Nathan asked Andrew as the young physiotherapist added notes on his tablet for his preliminary report. He was used to writing reports and keeping tabs on his patients, but the level of detail these people wanted was exhausting.

"He's in a bad shape. And he shouldn't be on a bed. The scales are dry and starting to crack in some areas, and you should suspend the body lotion, even in his upper torso. You're not dealing with human skin, and nothing is going to substitute for seawater. Also, he needs exercise, and that's not going to happen in that room."

"I like this guy," Higgs said approvingly as he opened a bottle of water.

"What do you suggest?" Nathan asked.

It felt great to know his opinions mattered, even if he'd just landed there.

"ORCAS has everything you need to rehabilitate marine animals, including the pool area. It's large, it's cold, and it's what Ray needs right now."

"What do you think, Higgs?"

The tall doctor chewed his sandwich thoughtfully. "I know what worries Andrew here, and I agree. The problem here is Ray. We've no idea what he'll do. For all we know, he might sink to the bottom of the pool and make it hell for us to get him out."

"Even sinking to the bottom of the pool is better than sinking on his bed," Andrew pointed out. The thing people didn't realize was how dangerous delaying therapy was. And they were in uncharted territory here, so who knew how many trial and errors were waiting for them.

"Gentlemen, we need a compromise," Nathan said in that calm way of his.

"Yes," Higgs agreed. "But it's Ray's compromise we need. And if he's not cooperating, we're back to square one."

Oh, come on!

"Put yourself in his shoes for a minute here," Andrew argued with both men, who stopped eating and looked at him. "The only thing Ray's able to control in that room is who he talks to or not. Everything else, from who touches him to who turns the light on is off limits. You told me he was miserable, but I don't think you realize how deep that misery runs." They both stared at him. "Look, I know I'm the new guy, but Ray was interested in rehabilitation. I'm sure we can get him to cooperate. It's something he can have control over."

Higgs and Nathan looked at each other, then back to Andrew.

"Tell you what, Andrew," Higgs said. "If Ray starts communicating on anything else, I'll take him seriously on his rehabilitation."

Andrew turned to Nathan, looking for an ally. "You contacted me for my expertise, Nathan. He's not going to get well under these conditions."

Nathan looked at Higgs, awaiting a comeback from the other man. When all Higgs did was reach for the salt, Nathan turned back to Andrew.

"Compromise," he said. "Higgs, you get to convince Ray this is for his own good. Andrew, find a way to start Ray's rehabilitation on his bed. And let's find out what Gwen thinks about this, please? Now, if you excuse me, I've another UN meeting to attend."

* * *

Major White had a problem: Colonel Sawyer had decided things were too boring in Washington so he had opted to pay him a visit in Maine.

As in his office.

As in right now.

"You've been withholding important information," Sawyer accused him not two minutes into their conversation. "You caught one of them on camera around here not two days ago."

"The thermal cameras are not conclusive, Sir. The three degrees' Celsius difference with our temperature can have many explanations."

"You have a suspect, Major. And I want him now."

"We've only spotted him once, Colonel. There's not much to tell."

164

"Don't be a disgrace to the Military Intelligence Unit." Tension hung between them, and Sawyer smirked. "I know you, White. You wouldn't be in this position if the High Command didn't trust you, especially if you didn't have the brains for this operation. What do you have on this visitor of yours?"

"As I said, nothing conclusive, sir." White opened a drawer, reluctantly giving the file to Sawyer. Like Dr. Higgs's comment on Ray's understanding of The Little Mermaid, certain details were better kept in the dark until they made sense.

White had spent the better part of the last two days piecing together who'd been sitting on that bench on Sunday morning. The teenager who'd looked at the camera was Scott Hunter, a thirteen-year-old runaway foster kid from Miami, Florida.

"A teenage boy?" Sawyer asked a moment later.

The picture on the Child Protective Services' file showed a hardened teenager. Scott had already been to eleven different foster homes in the last four years, meaning he'd been nine when he'd first entered the system. Nothing about his biological parents was on the record, nothing beyond Scott's stubbornness to remain silent about his original family.

"I told you, he's not a credible suspect, sir."

"Hmm…" Sawyer grunted, reading the file.

The last time Scott had popped up in the system had been three months ago, and then nothing after that as if the earth had swallowed him whole.

Or maybe the ocean did.

So, here was an interesting question: why would a thirteen-year-old merman be left alone in the world?

"Why would he have been here two days ago if he wasn't spying on us?" Sawyer asked, closing the file.

Maybe they're family, White silently answered. He could picture this kid watching random videos on the net until he found the merman one, or maybe he even caught the news in some dark corner of the world. White could straight up ask Ray and be over with the question, but if that was his brother, it could be a disaster of misunderstood motivations.

If Scott was really a merman, how their first meeting went was vital to their future relationship.

"He hasn't shown up on the thermal scanners again, so we don't have a comparison thermal shot," White answered, evading the question. "I've been waiting for him to come again, establish a pattern. But the truth is he's just a kid, Colonel."

"Is he? The truth here, Major, is that we don't know how well these people can hide themselves. He could be pretending to be a teenager for all we know."

"In all honesty, Sir, I find it unlikely a thirteen-year-old boy who's been hopping from foster home to foster home for four years, can be a merman with no one the wiser."

"Interesting question, indeed. Let's get some answers. I want the entire East Coast Intelligence branch tracking Scott Hunter's every move. If he's out there today, I want him found. In the meantime, get a team ready, White. Once he pops up, we're going fishing."

* * *

Julian and Drake had been talking behind closed doors for over an hour. Outside, in the plushy living room with the white leather couches and cream rug, both Matt and Alex tried to bear the waiting as impatiently as they could.

Matt kept walking in circles. Alex kept staring at his screen.

Every two minutes, one of them would curse, and every five minutes or so, one of them would inevitably ask—

"Why are they taking so long?!"

—stupid questions that had no answers.

Exasperated at his own pacing, Matt went to the kitchen, while Alex kept trying to hack into police cameras to follow a boy in a hoody. Breaking into computers was fun, but not when tension hung so dense in the room it clouded everything, including his own judgment. If he wasn't careful, Alex could bring some serious trouble right to their doorstep.

Leaving his laptop aside, he stood and stretched, the penthouse view breathtaking. The sea met his young eyes, beckoning and familiar, a world of possibilities literally waiting for him. The future always put a smile on his face.

"This kid's going to come back," he said to his brother, still looking at the dark ocean, still riding a wave of optimism.

"He's not," Matt answered in a brooding tone, pouring a glass of water. "He thinks it was a mistake to come. He's long gone by now."

"You don't know that."

"The hell I don't. I should've—I should've followed him, run faster, looked longer."

166

"Matt. Hey, it's not your fault. We'll find him. Now we know he exists, we'll find him."

"You don't get it, Alex. If I were him, I wouldn't come back."

Alex sighed in frustration at Matt's negativity crashing his happy thoughts. When Matt got in one of his moods, all he'd get were cryptic and broody answers. "Okay, he won't come back. But now Julian knows, and the Council knows. If he's twelve or thirteen as you think, he'll need guidance to go through his first tail shift, right?"

"You're assuming he even knows that."

"You're assuming he's the one leaving forever," Alex shot back, rubbing his eyes and missing Matt's glare. Alex needed to take a break. Between worrying about Chris and finding the trail to this wandering merkid, he was all burned out.

"You just don't get it because—like Chris—your parents were wonderful people with a crappy fate. Chris still has them, waiting for him all the way down there. Yours told you to find the Council with their dying breath even if they'd no idea where to look for them. Mine? You know what my mom's final words were? *Get lost.*"

Stunned silence filled the room.

"Wha—what?"

"It's okay, she said it all the time," Matt said with a smirk as if those words didn't hold any meaning anymore. Yet Alex knew his brother, knew the bitterness of his tone and the void in his eyes. He looked dangerous, ready to lash out at the least provocation. And then, Matt blinked, maybe coming to the present, maybe realizing Alex had no idea what he was remembering.

"It doesn't matter," Matt said dismissively. He sipped his water and closed the door to his past faster than Alex could protest.

Get lost? Who says that to their kids?

For the first time in his life, Alex understood why Chris hugged them so much.

"I'm sorry," Alex whispered, feeling his chest tightening. Like everything that made him uncomfortable, Matt shrugged it off.

"It's all in the past now, Squid. The thing is, that kid? He was told to get lost as well. And he'll keep getting lost until someone binds him to the floor and makes him listen."

This time, Matt finished the entire glass in one go.

"I'm getting out of here."

"But Julian said not to leave!"

"No, Julian said not to go back to ORCAS. I'm not planning to. Maybe I'll spot this kid on the street. Call me if you find him first on your monitor, okay Squid?"

"Hey! I'm not—" *your secretary.* The words died after Matt's disappearing back, both knowing Alex would call him no matter what.

He sighed, frustrated once more. One day, he was going to be the one getting out everywhere and doing stuff, instead of sitting and telling others where stuff was happening. One day—

The door to the studio opened, and Drake looked at him. "I could really use your help now, Alex. Get your laptop and let's crack some codes."

Alex's mood swung back to elated, and he ran for his computer. Not only would he get a chance to help Drake, his surrogate uncle would never call him Squid.

* * *

Scott Hunter was exceptionally good at one thing: running.

The wind embraced and called to him, becoming one with his soul. The rhythm, the sound, the beat of his heart, it all collided into speed and stamina that carried him anywhere and everywhere, no distance too long, no landscape too difficult.

Sometimes he thought he could run forever.

Now, though—now he couldn't run fast enough. He was short of breath, still feeling the ghost of that guy's hand in his, their temperatures the same. He kept looking backward, feeling eyes in every corner, as if suddenly this stranger had multiplied or told all his friends to be on the lookout for him.

How many were out there?

Scott shuddered, walking as fast as his aching legs were able, putting as much distance between them as he could manage. How long had he run? Ten miles? Twelve? He was too distracted, too disoriented in this unknown town to be able to even guess. Streets looked all the same, one merging into the other with no end in sight. He was panicking, and he knew it.

This had been a stupid idea.

So what if curiosity had filled him to the point he couldn't stop himself from coming here? What if he wanted answers to the questions his own parents had never answered—and would never answer since they were already gone?

He clenched his fists and kept walking. There were no answers in Maine. He did not belong here, with a captive merman and his helpless brothers. He did not belong to these people who had bigger problems of their own, problems that did not include a runaway from sunny Florida, whose parents had forsaken the mysterious City, warning him to never seek others for merfolk meant only trouble.

So ingrained were those words in him that he'd panicked at the first sign of recognition. He was so stupid. He had no plan beyond getting to Maine and seeing if the merman video was real. He'd arrived here six days ago with little cash and big illusions, and absolutely no idea what he was doing. Now, he was running away for no good reason besides that he was good at it. He was exhausted, scared, hungry, but most of all, he was so lost.

He was so tired of being lost.

He collapsed on a bench, his breathing barely under control, his mind reaching for some plan. *Leave*, one side said. *Run and hide and grow up until no one cares how old you are or what you are doing.* That was usually the plan. He hadn't left nine foster homes because it was fun. The idea of discovery terrified him, and stress only led to his scales emerging.

Stay, a tiny voice said, a little whiny and a little hopeful. He'd only gotten wisps of conversation from Matt, Chris, and Julian, glimpses into ideas and places, fleeting emotions too strong for Scott to avoid. These people cared about each other deeply, and although they were going through a major crisis, maybe they could tell him what to do. His first change was coming, and he barely knew what to expect.

His stomach growled, reminding him he had problems of his own. Standing, he spotted a grocery store by the corner and crossed the street. His reflexes were twice as fast as a human's, making shoplifting a rather easy feat. Someday, when he was older, he might even choose to be a magician, impressing people with tricks faster than they could explain. And hey! Maybe he would even add a number where he turned into a merman. That would be something...

That would be *awesome*.

With his mood improved, Scott went right into the store with a smile. The trick was to do it fast. Get in, get out, no one would even remember him. He picked up a couple of things and put them down as if undecided on what to buy. He moved further in, looking for food easy to conceal. Nutritional value had never been a priority in these situations.

Scott looked up at the cashier to make sure he wasn't calling attention, but his eyes went beyond the double glass doors in time to see two black SUVs parking. One wouldn't have meant a thing, but two?

A man stepped out from one of the vehicles, thin and well-dressed, his small glasses and calculating eyes making Scott's skin crawl.

This guy means trouble.

The thought crossed his mind at the same time as he dropped the bag of chips. He'd learned a long time ago to follow his instincts, especially when they screamed *run*. He was tall for his age, and certainly stronger than the average guy, but he'd rather avoid uncomfortable questions and suspicious inquiries.

The doors opened automatically for the man, and Scott moved further down and then to another aisle. From there, he watched his presumed assailant walked slowly to the aisle Scott had vacated. Beyond the doors, Scott's eyes centered on the ominous black cars.

It's just your imagination. Keep moving. Keep moving. Keep—

"Hey," the man said to Scott's back, scaring the hell out of him. "Is it okay if we talk for a moment?"

Scott's heart jumped to his throat as he froze, his mind backpedaling in search of an alternative exit. There was none.

He slightly moved toward the doors, getting ready to run the hell out of there, something the mystery man didn't miss.

"Don't," the man said quietly. "You'll give them reason—"

Scott didn't listen to the rest. He sprinted towards the doors which barely opened enough for him to pass through. He chose left and didn't stop to see how many people were getting out of the SUVs. He didn't see how many were pointing at his back, and he definitely wasn't aware of who shot him.

Later, much later, he would remember he'd run for it and had managed two full blocks before giving up, but he wouldn't remember the sound of the gun going off or even the sting of the dart on his shoulder. All he would really remember was lying on the sidewalk, the numbness of his body, and those thin eyeglasses reflecting the sun.

22

Personal

Whatever illusions Major White had had about Scott Hunter not being related to Ray died as soon as he'd seen the silvery scales adorning the backs of his hands.

By the time White brought the merkid to ORCAS, Colonel Sawyer had already been waiting for them. The Special Assistant to the Pentagon couldn't be happier—or greedier to take over White's command.

Although ORCAS and Ray's security were still his responsibility, Sawyer had swept in and taken over everything Scott related. In truth, too many people wanted to take control of this—from the Army to the Navy, from Homeland Security to freaking NASA. The only reason Nathan Forest still had control over ORCAS was because everyone was fighting with everyone else, and no one was coming out with the upper hand. Yet.

There was no doubt in his mind that if Ray could be sliced into forty-three pieces, they'd all gladly take one and leave. That brought him to his current prisoner: he didn't know where thirteen-year-old Scott Hunter fitted in the whole picture, but he knew without a doubt that they would tear him apart if they could. And Sawyer, with his theatrics and booming voice, was more than ready to make the first cut.

To drive that point home, Sawyer had already ordered one of the main rooms in the south wing to be cleared, leaving only bare walls and one solitary metal chair in the center. Sitting in it with his wrists handcuffed behind him, Scott kept fighting to stay awake, fighting to keep his eyes on Sawyer at every moment. He'd been knocked out by the sedative on his way here not an hour ago and had woken up kicking and gnashing, uncoordinated as it might've been. For a thirteen-year-old, he sure knew how to put up a fight—and how to curse like a sailor.

Sawyer looked down at the kid with disdain, circling him. From the closed door, White kept watch over the procedure. Sawyer was an experienced interrogator, so it wasn't a matter of *if* Scott would break, but rather how fast.

Come on kid, make this easy on yourself, White thought anxiously. Sawyer didn't have to touch the teenager to scare the hell out of him, he only had to press the right buttons, conjure the right evils, and offer the worst nightmares. He had to give it to the kid, though, he didn't look one bit scared.

Breathing heavily, Scott spat on Sawyer, angry eyes following his captor as best as he could. For the past twenty minutes, Sawyer had done nothing but watch. Silence could be a powerful motivator to talk, especially if one thought the subject was weak-minded.

"Go to hell," Scott said, holding his head straight for five seconds before letting it fall back. He closed his eyes at the bright white light in the ceiling, while his strained breathing was all the sound in the room. Outside, armed guards stood, even if no one expected Scott to be able to stand, much less escape.

He's going to fall back asleep, White thought, a part of him relieved.

Minutes went by, while Sawyer relentlessly walked around his prisoner. Scott coughed but otherwise kept quiet, retreating to a world of his own.

"We know what you are," Sawyer finally broke the silence. "We know who you are."

Deliberately, Sawyer moved slowly closer. "We can't touch your precious older brother while everyone's watching, but no one's watching over you, brat. No one knows you exist. We can do anything we want. Cut you up in so many pieces no one will even recognize you."

A pause to let the threat sink like a rock.

"Unless you're more valuable alive, that is. Are you more valuable alive, Scott? Is that even your real name?"

The only indication Scott was listening was his increased breathing.

For someone with such spirit, he seems oddly close to losing it, White noticed, moving away from the door and closer to the kid.

"Or maybe we've got this wrong," Sawyer said, ignoring both Scott's agitation and White's closeness. "Maybe we should just cut your friend up into little pieces and then turn to you for anything we couldn't understand."

Scott's eyes opened with terror, and for a moment, White thought Sawyer had hit the nail on the head. But then, Scott coughed, little red drops staining Sawyer's face. Blood.

"Can't—bre—aaaa—the."

"Get a medic!" White shouted, going behind the boy's back and cutting the plastic handcuffs off. "Calm down, kid, calm down!"

172

The coughing got worse, and for the first time, Sawyer looked worried. It was one thing to scare a teenage boy into confession but an entirely different one to have a prisoner die during an interrogation, even if Sawyer hadn't laid one single finger on the boy's body.

Free of their confinement, Scott's hands flew to his chest—clawed at it, really—his eyes fixating on White's. "Wa—wa—ter," he choked, half a dozen medics flowing into the room.

By the time they managed to stabilize him, two hours had passed, Scott was fighting for his life, Sawyer had all but disappeared, and Major White had one hell of a mess on his hands.

* * *

"And he hasn't said anything at all?" Ms. Goronsson asked Nathan on one of the monitors. The UN Committee was starting to tire of this silence, but at least the Swedish woman reined them in.

"Not verbally. But we had our first breakthrough today. The physiotherapist got him to cooperate in assessing his injuries. It's the first time Ray has interacted willingly with one of us."

He could see approval in half the eyes on the screens. Instead of Colonel Sawyer on the ninth monitor, Diana Lombardi silently watched the exchange between the members and Nathan's report. She was gathering information so she could advise the Committee on dealing with their public relations nightmare.

Thirty minutes later, the meeting came to a close. All screens went dark except for Diana's.

"Dr. Forest, what's your opinion of Ray? I mean, what do you think he's like?" she asked, her American accent impeccable. He wouldn't have known she was from Argentina if he hadn't read it in her file.

"You mean besides stubborn, loyal, and insanely quiet?"

She smiled, nodding. "Exactly that."

"Why? I mean, why would you want to know?"

"We need to humanize Ray—for the public, I mean. Since he's not willing to participate in the narrative, we have to create one for him. A personal story, you know? One that makes sense to human ears."

"You want to invent his background?"

"I want people to like him," she answered with serious eyes. This close on the monitor, Nathan could see her eyes were a strange mix of green and blue. "He has everything to lose, doctor, and we're the only ones between him and an angry mob. He's going to become a political subject, a social subject, a scientific subject. Everyone will want a piece of him, so it's our job to keep him whole. And that can only happen with the right story."

He liked this woman. Heck, Higgs would love her.

"I'm told I'm a man of colorful tales," he half-joked. She nodded, looking at something on her desk.

"Good. Let me gather my notes and come up with some ideas. I should be arriving in Maine tomorrow. We can talk over dinner."

"Sounds like a plan. When do you think we should tell the public about this?"

"Honestly? Never."

He blinked. She smiled. "Soon. The more we delay, the worse it's going to be."

* * *

"Okay, this is the best angle we're gonna get," Drake said, while Alex stopped typing and nodded. Traffic cameras had been hard to get into, then they'd slowly gone through several days of footage, following an elusive hoody with a backpack while navigating an unfamiliar city.

Now that Drake had a shot of just two days ago, Julian took a good look at it. The angry eyes in the screenshot seemed to pierce Julian's soul. The boy kind of reminded him of Matt, but somehow older. A strange mix of a child who'd grown up too fast and too alone, but who knew how to hold himself against the world.

This one is going to be tough.

Finding an abandoned child was always hard work demanding full attention, and this kid couldn't have picked a worse time to show up.

"He looks kind of familiar," Drake said, narrowing his eyes while the face was matched against different databases. "Let's see what our own files find."

The City kept perfect records on all its members, but little could be known about those who had left centuries ago. Drake kept his own records on newcomers, but there was a limit to how accurate and updated he could keep them. Of course, unknown children wouldn't be there, but their database had one more useful tool; partial parental recognition. Based on the few hundreds of surface merfolk, it matched the most likely candidates to be the parents of any given child. Tail colors would be a more accurate way to measure this—not to mention an actual DNA test—but they'd take whatever they could.

"At least Matt's showdown with him wasn't caught in any footage," Julian said with relief.

"None that we could find," Drake said under his breath. "You know, this kid is young enough to be someone's grandchild, we might not even match him to the last migration wave files."

"Got him!" Alex exclaimed excitedly. "He's got a pretty big file with Social Services—um... here: Scott Hunter, thirteen, a Florida runaway. He's been in the system four years, and has a really long list of foster homes."

Drake cursed. "Where are these kids' parents disappearing to? A black hole no one has cared to share with us?"

If Drake had a sensitive spot, that'd be children. He'd seek Mireya and Aurel when he'd found his first abandoned girl, furious and outraged at the irresponsibility of others. It was the Council's upmost interest to keep these children safe, he'd argued because they'd no idea about their heritage, the City, or life as merfolk. They thought that little girl would be the one and only they'd ever find. Two hundred years and eighteen children later, it still came as a shock to find yet another wandering kid.

Muttering about irresponsible adults and the dangers of going off the grid, Drake sat down and started loading the information into his system. It was going to take a few minutes.

"Look, we know he came from somewhere," Julian pointed out. "But right now I'm far more concerned about knowing where he is than where he was. If he has family up here or in the City, that's going to be a headache for later."

Drake sighed, then frowned. "Speaking of later," he said. "We've managed to infiltrate the IV bags supply chain. Chris will get the real deal tonight."

Finally! Julian sighed inwardly. Good news was so rare these days he almost felt like celebrating. Almost.

"Thank you. The more advantages Chris has, the easier it'll be to get him out of there."

"Indeed. If we're lucky, Mireya will get one of her own to infiltrate soon as well, though I'm not comfortable sending anyone to ORCAS right now."

"I don't like it either."

"Well, yeah, since you're not voting on the Council, you don't get to decide the fun parts. She said she should have some news for us in a couple of hours. Heard anything from the City?" his friend asked, typing something.

"Aurel said the City's Council's divided, so they're reaching a compromise as we speak."

"Charming," Drake said with disdain. "Chris will be able to walk before they actually reach an agreement. You know I'm more than willing to break your son out of there than wait for whatever they decide, right?"

"Let's not burn that bridge if we don't have to," Julian said, glancing at Alex, who was studiously ignoring them while looking at his screen.

As much as Julian wanted to say *to hell with the City*, if things got out of hand they still needed a place to go back, or at the very least a place that would have their back. They couldn't win with both the humans and the City hunting them down. If they went against the City's wishes, Julian could always claim he did it for his son. He didn't want to leave his three wards without any means to claim their heritage, or for Drake to be dragged into this mess.

Drake's computer beeped, the system having found a match for Scott's parents.

"No..." Drake whispered, bringing Julian's attention immediately. "Not them..."

"Who?" Julian asked, walking to stand by his friend. The faces on the screen took Julian a century into the past, if not more. He couldn't honestly remember the last time he'd seen them, but that wasn't surprising. They hadn't been his friends. They'd been Drake's.

Amstel and Sheela had already been "loud" citizens by the time Julian had started paying attention to the City's politics. They had left the City at least a decade before Julian and Drake had followed their same path, and he'd known his oldest friend had actively searched for them on the surface, too. Finally, about 200 years ago, he'd found them. In a way, Julian guessed they were Drake's war heroes, the people who had planted the seeds of wanting more, needing more than what the City offered.

In Julian's memories, they were the kind of people too quick to judge and who were never pleased with anything. He'd never really liked them even if he shared plenty of the same ideas, and he'd avoided their company whenever Drake brought them back into their lives.

Then the Surface Council had been formed, with Drake becoming a vital part of it.

They never told Drake they considered him a traitor, but they did cut all ties. It was subtle in the beginning, their friendship straining, until time, ideals, and life itself separated them, to the point Drake hadn't mentioned them in decades.

"When was the last time you saw them?" he asked, mindful of Drake's worry.

"Twenty, maybe thirty years ago. That's why he looks so familiar, he looks so much like Amstel, down to that steely glare."

"Think you can still contact them?"

Drake shook his head. "They never wanted the Council to know where they were, so they made sure I didn't know. But you don't get it Julian, they would've never abandoned their own son. They would've moved heaven and earth to find him, even contact us—contact me. Something's wrong here. So very wrong…"

"Holy shit!" Alex said, and ignoring Julian's stern look of language, he looked at his father as he turned his computer. "I found where Scott went after running away from Matt. It looks like someone in a black car took him about four hours ago."

Right there, on Alex's monitor, Scott collapsed on the pavement and was efficiently taken away by three men in a black car.

Something was wrong, all right. Something was terribly wrong.

23

Vanishing Act

As much as Kate loved hunting down a story, when things came to a standstill, she felt like banging her head against her whiteboard. The elusiveness of Julian Brooks was grating on her nerves. After days of putting her hands on everything and anything about that man, she had a mountain of details and gossip to sort through, even if gut instinct said she was looking in the wrong places.

All she had to show for her efforts on this sunny Wednesday morning was a pile of conjectures and dead ends, not to mention *no comments* and no Brooks interviews. She knew it would take time, lots of it, and that made her restless.

No matter how close she got to talking to him, one of his minions would always steer her away, be it his lawyers or that goddamn assistant of his. It didn't help matters that there were other reporters trying to get a scoop on Christopher Brook's ordeal and rescue, reporters who were clogging the lines, as it were.

None of them were onto the merman angle as far as she could tell, but then, how long was it going to take for someone to make the connection? How long before she lost the advantage—or worse, before Julian Brooks could actually sweep the entire thing under the proverbial rug?

"Still no luck with Brooks?" her boss asked from the door, a slightly smug face relaying *I told you so.*

"The guy's been swallowed up by the sea, I swear! Everyone's giving me crap about privacy and time with his family, but get this: Christopher Brooks is not listed in any hospital or medical facility or anywhere, and I mean *anywhere* in the entire State of Maine. But Julian's still there. His private jet is ready and waiting. I just haven't been able to find where, exactly, he's holing up."

Ken's smug face grew excited.

"I happen to know something about that," he said, taking a sheet of paper out of his pocket. "One of my contacts found him for you."

What? It was hard to swallow that someone had contacts she didn't, true, but she had absolutely no qualms in using the info. She reached for the paper and practically snatched it out of her boss's hand.

"He checked in under another name, and I got as far as confirming his other two sons are there, but no Christopher. I want you out there today, Kate. Get a feel of the situation, then talk to him."

She could almost, almost hug her boss.

"On it!" was all she said, her frustration evaporating. The hunt was back on, and she couldn't be happier.

* * *

Chris woke with a start. He could've sworn someone had been shouting, but the memory was fuzzy, rapidly disappearing under the room's white light.

Strangely, Matt's mind was completely gone, and Julian's was... distant. Still there, still aware of him, but his attention was clearly on something else. Maybe the City, maybe the escape plan. Whatever it was, they would tell him when he needed to know.

Meanwhile, he was too tired of sleeping to want to sleep even more. Gwen had installed one of those creepy cat clocks on the wall in a misguided attempt to cheer things up—and how anyone could find those things appealing was beyond him—but at least the clock was a much-needed measure of time, with the lights on and off a clear indication if it was day or night.

It was 9:35 a.m., and for the longest moment, Chris knew something was different but couldn't place what. He blinked slowly, thinking, until it hit him that the constant tension in his body had diminished. He felt rested. In fact, the pain in his tail was still considerable, but less.

For the first time in ages, he felt he was making progress. His tail looked brighter, his muscles felt stronger, the whole world wasn't out to get him. Even the humming sound of the machines seemed relaxing.

Beside him, Higgs looked up from his tablet and slowly smiled.

"Someone's in a good mood," he commented, leaving his device and getting closer to Chris. "Maybe good enough for you to humor me for once?"

Higgs reached for his pen light and place it right in front of Chris's face. Ten times Higgs had tried to engage him in these simple tests, and ten times

180

Chris had refused. But today—today Chris felt he had a purpose, and it wasn't lying around, passively refusing these people's care.

When he started following the light, Higgs didn't miss a step and went from one test to the next.

"How about headaches? Dizziness? Good," Higgs said when Chris barely shook his head. "I'm not sure if you've noticed, but you've been losing weight, about twenty-five pounds, I'd say. There's been some concern you might refuse to eat if we offer, but I think you're more than ready. So, how about you promise me you'll eat, hmm? Does a hamburger sound good to you?"

Treacherously, his two stomachs growled loud and clear, to the point Chris blushed.

"Point taken. Now, we can't give you a hamburger after ten days of no solids, I'm sure you know, but we can set the goal high so the bland diet isn't so… bland while you're eating it. Motivation is the key to everything," the doctor added with a wink.

Then, Higgs became thoughtful for a moment. "There is something else, since I have your good graces today. Andrew has been pushing to get you underwater."

The beeping of Chris's heart monitor accelerated at the prospect of leaving this bed. He was so sick of being confined that he'd have agreed to jump through hoops if they had asked.

"Gwen thinks there's too much risk of infection, and I tend to agree. But the truth is, you're the only one who knows what's good for you. Ray, do you want to be underwater? And would you behave if we agree to it? No fooling around, no putting in jeopardy your stitches, or your health as a whole?"

He was about to say yes, but the problem with accepting this offer was that he would have to shift his lungs to be able to breathe in the water. Give them one more piece of himself. And they had already taken away so many pieces.

"Think about it, you don't have to answer right away if you have any con—"

Chris reached for Higgs's hand fast enough to give the doctor a fairly good idea of how quick merfolk reflexes were. To hell with worrying about how much humans already knew, he needed to be out of this bed now. Nodding once, he let go of the warm hand, while Higgs was still surprised this even happened. The older man looked down where their hands had briefly touched, blinked, and then looked at Chris.

"Ok—ay. I guess that's a resounding yes. I'll get the logistics started, though it might take the better part of the day to figure everything out. I gotta say, you sure are talkative today—and I'm not complaining." Chuckling, Higgs stood up. "'Must be something in the water', as they say," he said with a laugh, getting his tablet. "I'll be right back," and with that, he headed out of the room.

Frowning, Chris turned to look at the only source of water available right now: the IV bag. The familiar Brooks Inc. logo filled him with warmth instantly. In tiny letters below all the medical inscriptions, it read: 4Ch RIs.

* * *

"I can't find where Scott is," Drake said with a tinge of desperation. They'd been tracking several dozen communications regarding ORCAS and Chris, but nothing panned out on what was happening with Scott.

Tired as they were, it was hard to concentrate on a clear plan of action beyond gathering as much information as they could, but Julian had to admit the speed in which Scott Hunter had been swallowed up by the military scared the hell out of him.

Slightly snoring beside his computer, Alex was oblivious to the world. In the kitchen, Matt prepared his breakfast in the most brooding way. Not being allowed to go to Chris meant Matt had acquired a dark cloud over his head, one that followed him everywhere.

Sensing eyes on him, Matt stopped pouring milk into a bowl and looked up.

"Someone has to tell Chris," his son said with all the seriousness in the world.

"We'll just worry your brother for no good reason," Julian answered, omitting the fact that he was so tired by this point he doubted he could get a clear connection with his son. When had been the last time he'd gotten any meaningful sleep? Three days ago? Four? He'd had nightmares after the Sunday Special, that much he remembered.

"Chris might be able to establish a connection with Scott if they're close enough," Drake said, closing his laptop in defeat. He looked at Julian for confirmation, but both men knew the only reason they couldn't reach Scott themselves was because he was either too far away or unconscious.

"I can't believe those animals would shoot a kid," Drake said in disgust.

182

"At least they didn't shoot him with bullets," Julian said, getting up and walking to the kitchen.

"Small consolation when they'll eagerly cut him open," Matt murmured as they crossed paths.

"We need to get into ORCAS," Drake said, as if they hadn't been trying to figure that out for the past week. "We must be missing something, overlooked some detail…"

"We need to rest," Julian pointed out, serving his tenth cup of coffee. Caffeine didn't work as well on them as it did with humans, but he would welcome any burst of energy he could get.

"What?" Drake said with disbelief.

"Come on. The answer could be staring right at us and we wouldn't even notice."

"They have a thirteen-year-old child at their disposal," Drake said with clenched teeth. "I'm not going to sleep until I know he's safe!"

"Drake, be reasonable—"

"You go to sleep!"

"All I'm saying—"

"You know what? I'm getting out of here."

Picking up his laptop, Drake wouldn't listen to another word. Even Matt had stopped eating at the uncharacteristic exchange.

Drake, come on, Julian tried one last attempt via their telepathic link. *I'm as worried as you are, but—*

Drake shut the door with as much strength as he shoved Julian out of his mind.

Don't do anything stupid! were the last words he sent to his friend, even if he knew they hadn't been heard.

* * *

"And please sign here, ma'am," the woman behind the front desk said with the whitest grin Kate had ever seen. This was the first time she was staying at a five-star hotel—as in a *really expensive* five-star hotel—and she was loving it.

From the personal concierge to the dedicated women's floor, to the complimentary bottle of wine, she wished with all her heart the Brooks investigation would take months.

Signing the last form, she received the key to her room from perfectly-manicured hands. She did her best to shake the unflattering feeling she was completely underdressed. Even the flower pots in the lobby looked fancier than her suit.

Beyond those flower pots, the elevator doors opened, and a man in a black jacket and jeans stormed out, furious enough to turn heads. He wasn't Julian Brooks but seemed familiar. She'd seen him before, she was sure. *Maybe someone from Julian's circle?*

"If you have any questions, please don't hesitate to call us," the woman said, conveying nothing but good vibes and service.

"Oh, I'm sure everything will be perfect," Kate said, ready to start her research. She loved this place, sure, but she loved a good mystery even more.

24

Familiar Faces

For as long as Nathan could remember, trouble had seemed to find him in threes. Good stuff, on the other hand, happened about every once in a while, so by his estimation, he should be seeing something good happening any time now.

Diana Lombardi was bound to arrive in a couple of hours, a welcome ally in this ever-growing logistical nightmare. Every day, new theories and new rumors floated around, to the point that more prominent aquaria had started to be consulted on this story as potentially real. And the longer people talked about it, the riskier it became for someone who was in the know to really *talk* about it.

White had been strangely absent from last night's meeting, probably ordering new security measures and restricting access to everyone in sight. It also meant Nate needed to track him down to grant final clearance to Ms. Lombardi, and while he was waiting for that, he'd also made the arrangements at the hotel where most of the researchers and doctors were staying. Practically half the hotel was theirs by this point, with more than thirty-eight medics and specialists being transported around each day.

If a reporter lands here, we're doomed, Nathan gloomily thought as the elevator doors opened to the hotel's underground parking lot.

He'd parked his rental at the farthest point, and his thoughts turned to Ray and the seeming change of attitude Higgs had reported earlier. Maybe Nathan was right, maybe this was the good thing coming.

He stopped abruptly, thinking he'd seen something in the shadows. No one—and hopefully nothing—seemed to be down here but himself and two dozen cars. Yet something about this place put Nathan on edge; white lights washed every vehicle in stark colors, leaving little room for shadows but plenty of hiding places behind cars and columns alike. He'd never been fond of closed spaces, but after a few seconds, he chalked it off to baseless paranoia.

He kept walking, watchful eyes moving around discreetly, every instinct telling him something was off. When a fist came from his left, he moved just in time to avoid the worst of the hit, but he still lost his balance momentarily, his precious phone landing on the ground.

His attacker lost no time in grabbing his arm, and Nathan used the momentum to hit him back, except his reflexes were no match against the other man's. It didn't matter, because all he really caught from his enemy were furious eyes on an equally furious face, one with faint silvery scales at the sides. Before he had time to register anything else, he was half-spun by a strong arm that swiftly went around his neck. He was efficiently put into a choke-hold less than ten seconds into this fight.

"He's only a child," the man hissed in his ear, disdain and hatred in every word as Nathan struggled to get away.

"Ray?" Nathan asked, the question sounding stupid even to his own ears. Their merman was many things, but *a child* was more than a little stretch.

His attacker went very still, and so did Nathan.

"Your men captured a thirteen-year-old child at midday yesterday."

"What?"

"He sat outside your building. You followed him. You shot at him. And you drove him back. How could you do that to a child?"

Nathan shook his head, limited as he was. He didn't need to deny this. He needed proof he had nothing to do with it. "Would I be here if we had another one of you?"

They both contemplated the answer in the silence of the parking lot; there were twenty cars around, and none were blaring those blasted alarms. And then, as if lightning had struck them both, they spoke simultaneously.

"White."

The merman let him go, and Nathan immediately turned. As tall as Nate himself, his assailant had broader shoulders, and the same black hair and blue eyes as Ray. Part of him felt relief that finally, *finally*, someone had come for Ray. The other part of him wanted to punch the man's face and return the favor.

As much as he wanted that, he still had more pressing matters than a sore pride—or a sore jaw.

"You said he brought him back? Back to ORCAS?"

"Yes. We know something's wrong with him. We've been trying to communicate with Scott since we found out, but nothing's working."

Which means he's either dead or unconscious, and neither is a good answer when you're talking about a thirteen-year-old kid. With growing trepidation, Nathan realized he was not only having an actual conversation with a merman, but he had a spiraling crisis unfolding in his hands.

"If White took—Scott? If he took him back to ORCAS, then I can find exactly where and what happened. Now, I know how bad this looks on us, but I can assure you most of us want things to work out in—"

"I don't care what you want, you're giving me Scott back. Today."

This man was deadly serious. Whatever else was going on—however Nathan was going to resolve this problem—there was only one question left in this conversation.

"How do I contact you?"

The man smirked.

"That one's easy: you're coming with me."

* * *

"He did what?!" Matt asked, his eyes large and round as his excitement went through the roof faster than Julian could say *calm down.* Matt had the same look every teenager assumed when someone had the audacity to go against authority—and won.

Unfortunately, Julian had neither the admiration nor the patience. Not that Drake was answering his mental calls to explain himself, beyond *there's been a change in plans.*

"Are we going to go get Chris now?" Matt continued, his thoughts heading in dangerous directions. "If Drake has their leader, we can make things happen! We can—"

"We can think this through first, something Drake didn't bother to do," Julian said, a monstrous headache building behind his eyes. He wanted to wake and find out the last ten days had been a nightmare.

If only.

"But Drake knows what he's doing! He always knows!"

"Matt—"

"No! You've always told us how Drake always has your back, and he's been pushing to do something about this mess since the beginning! You can't tell me he isn't right!"

187

The hell I can't.

"Drake's not perfect, and doesn't always make the best choices."

"If he's getting Chris out, I'll call that the best choice no matter what."

At some point, Julian had survived Chris's teenage years. He was sure of that. So why was Matt so hard to deal with?

"We don't know how things are going to fall here. Maybe Forest will agree to help us. Maybe he'll set up Drake. What I won't risk is your safety. I want you out in the next hour. I've already arranged with Mireya for you to spend the next few weeks with her in South America—"

"I'm not running away," Matt interrupted, his admiration replaced with hard determination.

"We don't know how they found out about Scott. I'm not going to watch them take you away and tear you apart." The words barely escaped through clenched teeth, and it took everything in him not to shake Matt into common sense.

"I don't want to run away either," Alex said in a tiny voice from his spot on the couch. Julian closed his eyes and held his breath before he would yell at his sons. Nothing worked worse than yelling at teenagers.

"I don't get it," Matt went on, looking hurt of all things. "You left Chris to die at the hands of those people, took days before deciding he was worth the effort and haven't still done a thing to get him out after more than a week. But this goddamn kid shows up and two seconds later Drake is doing what he should have done for Chris in the first place! Who the hell is this kid tha—"

"It's not about Scott. Or about Chris for that matter. The rules of the game have changed, drastically. Chris was an accident. He washed away at the beach and ended up in human hands. It's an entirely different situation with Scott. They hunted him down and took him away. We have no idea what they already know, or what they'll find out. Until we have a firm grip on the situation, I need you to be safe. Do you understand that?"

"Let us help," Matt said, glancing at Alex. "We're not your weakest links, we're your greatest assets. No one's more interested in getting Chris out than his brothers."

One day, Matt would sure as hell make a great lawyer if he ever set his mind on that.

"Matt—"

A knock on the door silenced all three, and for one hellish second, Julian could imagine the penthouse being swarmed by SWAT teams, his sons taken, his life obliterated.

188

Alex moved to open the door, and Julian stopped him with a hand on his shoulder. Swallowing his fears down—and doubling up his decision to send his family away—he opened the door knowing the SWAT team wouldn't knock.

The Concierge stood in front of him, a black envelope on a silver platter held in one hand.

"Excuse me, Sir. This was left for you at the front desk."

Frowning, he thanked the man and took the envelope addressed to *J. Brooks*, liking this less and less as each second passed. No one knew he was here.

"What is it?" Matt asked while Julian read the card in silence.

"It's a—a dinner invitation," he said slowly, his mind going blank for a moment at the prospect of dealing with one too many complications. "It's from whoever stole Chris's watch."

* * *

"I just gotta say it, Kate: that takes balls."

Jeff's voice on her speaker came across loud and clear, and she could almost imagine her co-worker balancing on his chair, his feet up on the desk.

She smiled in front of the full-length mirror, undecided if she should wear her hair up or down for her dinner that night.

"Well, thank you, Jeff. But it's more than just balls. Something's gonna give soon, and I have to be on top of that. Julian Brooks has all the answers, and even if he doesn't say anything, his reaction will speak volumes."

"I thought Ken warned you he won't publish anything if you can't back it up, especially not that Christopher Brooks is a merman."

"He did. And we aren't. I'm just giving Mr. Brooks his watch back," she said innocently, turning on her laptop. She had a list of questions to prioritize and memorize before 7:00 p.m.

"But you don't have the watch."

"Details. The expert will hand it back once I'm at the office next week. At the very least, I'm pointing Julian in the right direction to get it back. I bet you ten dollars he tells me some spectacular tale about how his son lost it."

"No deal. He is going to tell you something. Unless he says his son moonlights as a merman, I'm not interested."

On her laptop, she called up the Brooks folder and opened one of the social media images saved a few days back, recalling the Brooks kids' bios. God, she missed her wall of truth and her multi-colored markers.

"What do you have for me on the social media front?" she asked.

"Well, there are a few rumors here and there. A couple of guys in Germany claiming they're formulating the merman's diet. Something in Japanese about sound testing... but I think I need a real Japanese person to translate that."

"Anything related to Maine?" she asked.

"Actually, yes. There's someone who works at a hotel saying a lot of doctors are staying over there. Says they talk about weird stuff all the time. Very hush-hush."

"A convention in town?"

"Nothing I could find about. Oh! There's one little tidbit: Our very own Neil Thompson has shown up in a couple of conspiracy channels, recounting his story about how he found the merman. To tell you the truth, it's becoming last week's story in the mainstream, but it's picking up a lot of steam in smaller places. So, whatever we're doing, we have to do it now."

"That's exactly the plan, Jeff. Call me if there's anything else interesting going on."

"Are you kidding me? I wish I could be a fly on the wall at that dinner of yours tonight!"

She hung up with a laugh and then looked at the mirror again. "Why, Mr. Brooks, what are you going to tell that the world doesn't already know?"

Whatever it was, she sure as hell hoped she was playing her cards right here. Because once Julian Brooks knew about her, there was no turning back.

* * *

Nathan absent-mindedly rubbed his jaw, his eyes lost in the ocean and in the secrets hidden beneath it. Beside him, his companion talked on his cellphone while barely driving under the speed limit. They were going to reach their destination fast—wherever that destination might be.

"Sorry about that," the merman said, glancing at Nathan, the bruising already forming. Whoever was on the other end of the phone connection got his attention back.

"Yes, I'm on my way. Listen, I might have a better way to get in. I'll let you know once I know more." A pause. "You worry too much. She'll be fine. I—" This time, he scowled at the interruption. "If they vote, you mean. Haven't we been hanging on their every word for the last week?"

This time, the man sighed at whatever discussion he was having. "Fine. We'll wait. I'll call you later."

Who's she, who's voting, why are you waiting, and why does that frustrate you so much? The questions kept coming, but Nathan held his tongue. He wasn't going anywhere anytime soon, plus the free information was invaluable.

"You can call me Drake," he said after hanging up, checking the rearview mirror and accelerating to pass a few slower cars.

"Nathan, but you don't strike me as a man who would punch the wrong guy."

Drake barely let go a ghost of a smile before changing gears. "Should've known it was White," he said, dripping disdain at the name.

"I can't believe he'd shoot a kid," Nathan answered. Clearly, he hadn't known how far White would take it.

Drake shook his head. "Not exactly. We think he drugged him. There was no blood on the footage." He slowed down behind a trailer, and looked in the rearview mirror again, probably checking if they were being followed, Nathan guessed.

"Footage?"

"Traffic cameras are a bitch," Drake answered without humor.

He was shot on the street?

"You said Scott sat outside our building?"

Drake rubbed his forehead, ignoring Nathan's question.

What are you not telling me?

"You seem to know a lot about what's going on at ORCAS," Nathan noted after a minute went by. He was sure he wasn't a prisoner per se, but didn't know what exactly he was to the other man. An ally? An informant? Bait?

"It's my business to know," Drake answered, expertly changing lanes, the ocean view getting lost in the side-view mirror.

"You know you don't have to 'rescue' him, right? I'm sure we both want what's best for him. And Ray."

"And White," Drake added with a pointed look.

"Let me call the United Nations' Committee. We have many resources—"

"Not against the US government. They'll never find him if the Pentagon doesn't want him found. Scott doesn't have much time before we lose the trail."

Drake changed lanes abruptly, eliciting well-deserved honking from three cars. "I'm not worried about Ray," Drake said nonchalantly. "At least not for the moment. Too many people know about him, so he's rather well-watched. He won't disappear. But Scott is at the mercy of anonymity, easy to sweep under the rug if something happens to him." Another abrupt change of lanes, but this time, Drake slowed to take an exit. Nathan frowned. Were they going to the airport?

"What happened to Ray was an accident," the merman continued. "He landed on your hands, and so far, you've worked hard to ensure his safety. We are nervous, but we keep watching. Waiting."

"Voting?"

Not even the slightly tremor betrayed Drake. "I wish. It took us by surprise, that much I can tell you."

"And now this happened with Scott, and it's not an accident," Nathan concluded, while Drake was forced to slow by a red light.
"He was kidnapped." Drake's words sounded ominous, and for the first time, Nathan wondered if Drake was Scott's father.

"Do you have—" another airport sign caught Nate's attention. "Do you have a plan for how to get Scott out? I understand you don't want to wait for official channels, but there's little I can do if we're going against the Pentagon and the US government without the UN's backup."

Drake held the wheel a little too tight, his eyes lost somewhere beyond the road for a moment, seeing possibilities beyond Nathan's reach.

"We need to find out where exactly he is, and in what condition. We can't really plan without that. If he's—if he's dead, there's nothing we can do about it, and we'll concentrate on Ray. If he's alive, he becomes our priority."

If he's dead, I'll kill White.

What choices did Nathan have? If he somehow convinced Drake of showing up at ORCAS or anywhere else, the most likely scenario would be that both Scott and Ray would end up hidden in the farthest hole Washington could find, maybe with Drake as well. Did merfolk really know what they were going against here?

Could he even stop them?

"What exactly do you want me to do?"

Drake took his time answering, while Nathan's phone chirped with notifications he ignored.

"We're missing key information. Now you know Scott's life's at stake, maybe you can find some way out of ORCAS that we're unable to see. At the very least, you can look for him and bring his existence into the light."

That's easier said than done. If this was going to work—whatever *this* ended up being—he'd have to enlist Higgs's help at the very least. Maybe even Gwen's. Everyone else was too risky.

"What about afterward?"

Drake frowned, not following him. "Afterward?"

"You'll take Scott to safety, and I'm guessing Ray too. You'll just... disappear?"

"One problem at a time," Drake murmured, taking one final turn. The third airport sign was a dead giveaway of their destination.

"Are we flying somewhere?"

"No. We're picking up someone."

"And here I thought you only traveled under the sea," Nathan said with a smidge of humor, eliciting a fleeting chuckle from Drake.

"You have no idea."

"I'd love to hear anything you have to say on the subject."

Drake didn't answer Nathan's prodding. He didn't go to the airport either. Not exactly. Slowly, he drove to a private hangar and parked right outside, the tail of a private jet visible.

"I'll always be grateful for all the things you've done for Ray, Dr. Forest. That said, don't make me regret this."

"I won't."

With one nod, Drake left the car, not even bothering turning the engine off. If Nathan was going to escape, he was not going to get a better chance.

Too bad I'm not escaping, he thought without humor. His phone rang a moment later, and Nathan looked up at Drake. Had the merman forgotten about Nathan's cellphone? Forget about the police, he had the means to shut down Maine's entire air traffic if he needed to. Yet Drake kept walking, which meant he didn't notice the ringtone—or didn't care. He headed up to the private jet, without even glancing back once to see if Nathan was following. Taking a chance, Nathan looked at the caller ID, his heart skipping a beat at the name. J White.

"What the hell did you do?" Nathan said by way of greeting, his eyes glued to Drake's retreating form. White's silence felt like a wall of concrete. "Damn it, White! Let me help you!"

Outside, Drake hugged a woman in a business suit, the way fathers hugged their daughters.

"How sure are you Ray's lungs would shift underwater?"

"What?"

What?

"How sure, Forest? If Ray went underwater, would he be able to breathe?"

Still looking at Drake's back, Nathan's eyes went a little lower, to the merman's very human legs. If it worked with the tail, would it work with the lungs too? Everything seemed to convey that merfolk had to breathe underwater, but—he'd never seen it.

"I don't know."

White hung up without letting Nathan even argue one word. He was about to call back, when he realized Drake was walking back to the car, speaking to their new lady companion, one who looked surprisingly familiar.

His heart slamming against his ribs, Nate got out of the vehicle. Looking just as striking as her picture, Diana Lombardi fixed him with a serious stare.

"Let me guess," she said, turning to look at Drake. "There's been a change of plans."

25

Something in the Water

Major White had one hell of a dilemma: everyone thought Scott had meant water as in drinking it, while he was certain Scott meant water as in *breathing* it.

The doctors didn't want to risk it, and Nathan Forest hadn't known the answer.

"You said he's basically suffocating," White said. He didn't even know the name of the man in front—one of Sawyer's minions, undoubtedly—but White was the one holding Scott's life in his hands. He'd never agreed to shoot him precisely because they didn't know how sedatives would work. And Sawyer had just not cared.

The kid hadn't regained consciousness for close to twenty-four hours, and he was already spiking a fever, something Ray had never exhibited, and one more thing they had no idea how to treat.

"He might be suffocating, but it doesn't mean putting him in a tank of water will fix anything. Even if the other subject could breathe underwater, there's no reason to believe this one will. The truth is, we don't know."

The truth was only one person knew—except he wasn't a person.

"I'll get you your answer."

Turning, White walked out of the south wing, moving fast enough to turn heads without actually sprinting through the labyrinth that was ORCAS's hallways. How much he had to tell Ray depended on how much the merman was willing to cooperate.

"Major! I've been looking for you everywhere!" Dr. Higgs said with a grin as if everything in life was a goddamn joke.

"I've been busy with other matters."

"I bet. I can't get a hold of Nathan, and I need either his clearance or yours to move Ray to the pool area."

"Pool area?"

"Yes. You wouldn't believe it, but Ray's actually cooperating for once, and Andrew has been pretty set on getting Ray under—"

"Do it."

"—water…" Higgs trailed off at White's sudden need for agreement. "That was fast."

"You said he's cooperating. Did he say yes to this?"

"*Say* might be a bit of a stretch, as you know. But he did give his consent, rather eagerly."

Something inside White breathed easy at Higgs's words.

"Get things ready as fast as you can. If he's feeling like talking, we gotta take advantage of that."

"Yes, Sir," Higgs said with mock respect, but White didn't care. He kept walking towards the containment area, barely hearing Higgs's murmured *must be something in the water, I tell you…*

Usually, Ray's room was occupied by two or three people. The logic behind that proposed that the fewer who treated him, the easier it would be for Ray to bond and feel comfortable. Most people, including himself, only got to see Ray from the observation deck on the upper level, behind glass. Most people, too, would give their right arm to be there right now.

Most people, of course, didn't have a dying kid in one wing and a merman as their only resource in the other.

The hall to Ray's room felt impossibly long, and once White reached the doors and entered, the area felt bigger than he'd expected, taller somehow, intimidating. In the middle, Andrew Summers talked to the merman, explaining the logistics involved in moving him. Ray laid on his side, his back to the doors. From the observation deck, eight doctors stared down. If White had to spend an entire day here for the whole world to see him, he would certainly go crazy.

Walking with a renewed sense of respect and urgency, he cleared his throat, getting Summers's attention. "I need a minute with your patient," he requested.

"Oh… sure," Andrew said, caught between his instructions of never leaving Ray alone, and being asked to leave by a superior authority. Walking to a corner, he took a tablet device and started working on something, deciding this was a good compromise. It wasn't, but White had no time to argue and went straight over to his target.

Standing in front of the merman, Ray looked straight at him, frowning slightly. This close, the scales where his facial skin met his hairline were distracting, his pointy ears belonging to some creature in a movie, not a being in real life.

"I need an honest answer," White said without preamble. "This test Dr. Higgs wants to run, getting you into the water. Will you breathe safely? Underwater?"

Ray's big blue eyes blinked, his face unreadable. He stared at White almost as if he could read his mind. Maybe Ray knew something was up, or maybe he simply distrusted new humans who wandered into his domain.

Finally, one second before White gave in and elaborated that a merkid needed this answer, Ray nodded once.

"Okay. Can you fall asleep underwater?"

This time, Ray's frown was deeper—and full of suspicion.

"Look, I'm the one who's going to approve this, and you were half-drowned when we found you, so there's reason to be cautious."

This time, Ray's mind looked inward, as if he was trying to remember reaching the beach already in a coma. Slightly, Ray shook his head, seemingly talking to himself and not liking his own conclusions.

It dawned on White that Ray hadn't known he'd arrived half-drowned, and the idea was as confusing as it was alarming. There was a good chance no one really knew what would happen to Scott, so all White would ever get was a good guess.

"Is it safe?" he pressed, snapping Ray out of it. Refocusing on him with narrowed eyes, Ray clearly distrusted him now. Slowly, he nodded again.

The doors opened behind them, a startled Dr. Gaston standing with a chart in her hands.

"What are you doing here?" she asked bluntly.

"Making sure we won't end up drowning a merman," he answered, walking to her.

"I'm not happy about it either, but if Ray wants to go, we'll give it a chance."

"I'll follow every step of the way. If you excuse me, I'm sure you've got lots to arrange."

He walked away from the room and didn't stop until he reached Scott Hunter, where he promptly ordered Sawyer's doctors to get the young merman into the water—then prayed he hadn't made the biggest mistake of his life.

* * *

I drowned?! Chris asked into the ether, perplexed and scared. The more he tried to remember, the blacker his memories became, just as dark as his connection to his family was feeling.

Julian? He yelled in his mind.

I'm here. There have been several things happening, that's all.

His father sounded stressed. Maybe even a little unsure.

A man was here, a minute ago. He said I was half-drowned when they found me. Is it true?

Chris searched for Matt's mind, but nothing but emptiness was on the other side. The cat clock read 2:07 p.m., which meant his brother had been silent the entire morning.

We don't really know what condition you were in when they found you. The important thing is—Julian trailed off, and suddenly all of his attention was on Chris: *How did he look like?*

What?

The man who came to ask you about drowning. What did he look like?

Tall. White. He wore glasses and a suit. He looked a military type, actually. Dad, what's going on? What are you not telling me?

The silence did nothing to calm Chris's mounting fears.

We might have a better way of getting you out sooner than we thought. I just don't want to get your hopes up, okay? It's too early to tell.

"Okay, Ray. You seem to have the entire place going crazy," Gwen said with her enthusiastic smile, effectively taking all attention away from his father. It was for the best, because for the first time since he'd been captured, Chris had the uneasy feeling Julian was hiding something.

* * *

The whole world was on fire.

Even if Scott couldn't see it, he knew he was swimming in a sea of flames, heat burning his every cell, suffocating the air out of his lungs. He swam in all directions, moved and recoiled and sank in despair, refusing to believe there was no escape.

No matter what he did, it felt as if he was weighted down.

"Is he ready yet?" a man said in the darkness, an unknown voice that made no sense yet gave Scott hope. The idea of not being alone stopped his sinking, and although it burned to breathe, he had to find the owner of that voice no matter what.

"Wait... he's coming around... Scott? Scott, can you hear me?"

Yes, he wanted to yell, but nothing seemed to come out of his mouth. Instead, the flames that surrounded him started leaping at his throat.

"Ca—can't..." Scott heard himself saying, but it sounded all wrong. His voice didn't have any strength at all.

Can't...breathe...

"He's as ready as he's ever going to be," the same voice said. Someone lifted and carried him, dissipating the darkness but not the fire. Lights and voices filled this world of strange shapes and sounds, air so hot it scorched his lungs. *Can't breathe, can't breathe, can't breathe.*

He grabbed the arm that carried him with the little strength he had. *Can't breathe!*

"You'll need to shift," the voice said, and for the first time, Scott's eyes cleared enough to make out the form of thin glasses. He recoiled—or rather, tried to, his efforts meeting with indifference. "You need to breathe, okay? You'll need to shift your lungs."

Blessed cold dissipated the heat in his skin, and he was sinking again, but this time, he welcomed it. Voice or not, friend or foe, Scott was able to breathe for the first time since forever, and went back to oblivion with not a care in the world.

26

Power of the Press

Kate turned the shower off and took a deep sigh. The answers she'd get tonight could make or break her career—or they could mean nothing at all. If Julian Brooks got pissed at her, he could very well ruin her life, but... her gut told her she was onto something big, and her gut was rarely wrong.

Ping!

Ping Ping

Pingpingpingpingping

"What the hell?"

Outside the bathroom, her phone was going crazy. Wrapping herself in a towel, she reached for it almost afraid it was going to jump in her hands. Her notification screen was full, going up by the second. She focused enough on one message. *Press conference in five minutes.*

About what? she thought, looking for the elusive remote control. It was barely 3:22 p.m., and a more thorough search on her screen gave her the right station.

She turned it on, right on time to find a group of hospital staff, looking worried and as if they wanted to be anywhere but there.

She called Jeff on autodial. "What the hell is going on?"

"The hospital! Kate, the hospital staff called a press conference."

"About the merman?"

"Hell yes! I barely caught wind of it—"

On the TV, one of the doctors took the podium, a sheet of paper in his hands. He was composed until the microphone gave feedback, squealing as only bad mics could. At least he got everyone's attention.

"Sorry about that. My name is Dr. Bill Shore. I'm here on behalf of the ER staff and other colleagues, but I am not representing, nor am I stating anything on behalf of our hospital, or the hospital's administration. Last week, a man came to our ER. He was not a man."

She had her computer going on before Bill Shore finished confirming the ER video was real. By the time she and her boss had finished restructuring her questions for the interview with Julian Brooks forty minutes later, all hell had broken loose.

* * *

Julian glanced at his phone hoping Drake would at least send a clue of what he was doing; he found nothing on the screen. Looking up, his mirror-self regarded him with a grim face.

"He asked Chris if he would drown?" Mireya inquired on the speaker, sounding every bit as confused as Julian felt.

"Something happened to Scott Hunter. We know sedatives can trigger unwanted shifts, so what if this targeted his lungs?"

"What did Chris say?"

"He was confused. He doesn't remember drowning, and it's certainly not something I've brought up since he woke. Now is not the time to admit I decided to abandon him—"

"Please, Julian. Don't do this to yourself. At the time, it was the smartest move for you, your sons, and the entire merfolk community. Chris will understand when you tell him, but I agree this is not the right moment for that. What do we know about this Major White?"

"He's thorough, gets things done. Drake flagged him as a red obstacle. His security measures have been hard to crack; this is the person Diana has to be the most cautious about."

"I can't believe Drake would break ranks right when my daughter is landing in that snake nest. I'll strangle him if you don't kill him first."

In the mirror, a ghost of a smile appeared on Julian's face. "I can't really fault him, you know? Drake's always been protective of children, especially the ones abandoned on the surface."

"Sure, I admire his dedication, when my children are not in the middle."

"Speaking of our children, Matthew and Alexander are refusing to leave their brother's side, so they might take a bit longer to get to you. I just need to get through this dinner with whoever is hoping to blackmail me, then I'll set my sons straight on what the differences are between being brave and being *stupidly* brave."

202

"Good luck with that. Call me as soon as you can if you know any—"

Whatever Mireya was saying was overridden as Alex barged in. "Dad! Dad, you have to see this!"

By the time the press conference was over, the Council was having yet another emergency meeting, albeit with one member fewer.

* * *

"I'll take it you're one of them?" Nathan asked, slightly off balance with Diana Lombardi behind the wheel. She drove like Drake had, fast and secure, dashing through the city's streets with the firm hand of an experienced driver. They had just left the merman at a mall and were driving back to ORCAS.

"I'm rather one of *us*," Diana answered, signaling Nathan and herself. "Trying to weather this storm without anyone ending up in a cage—or worse. We're in this together, Dr. Forest."

"Nathan, please. First name basis does wonders for teamwork," he added. She smiled fleetingly. "What do you want me to do once we're there?"

"To deactivate those thermal cameras so my cover isn't blown would be nice."

"Of course. I've been thinking… if I confront White, he might be reasonable enough to give up Scott, especially if Scott's sick."

Reaching for a bottle of water, Diana thought about it, frowning. "White is not the one at the top of that particular food chain, and we don't trust Colonel Sawyer. Let's leave talking to him out of the equation for the moment."

Taking a long drink, she slowed, passing through downtown.

"I—I don't mean to sound rude," Nathan started, doing his best to not stare. "Are you actually qualified to deal with—"

"—PR at this level? Yes. My résumé is not a fabrication. We've been trying to find a way to get close to Ray for the past eight days, and this is the first real chance we've had. We're not going to ruin it by sending someone to do a job they're not capable of."

So you do live in the human world. Diana Lombardi had been in charge of several NGO's and World Bank programs. *Young but brilliant* was the recommendation that had nailed her this job. Or maybe there was more to it than just credentials.

Someone had to pay for that private jet, and it wasn't us.

"What are you thinking, Nathan?" she asked after a few minutes had gone by in silence.

"Is Drake your—husband?"

The car barely swirled under her capable hands, but he had caught her by surprise. She blushed as she bit back a laugh. "That is so inappropriate on so many levels," she murmured once they reached another red light. "Drake is more like a—a surrogate uncle. The age difference is considerable. We're but children to them. In fact, we're still considered underage citizens."

"Underage?"

She sighed at Nathan's confusion. "Twenty-eight is our coming of age number. Look, there are a million things I'm sure you want to know. Let's focus on what matters to get Scott and Ray out, okay?"

"Why haven't you approached the UN? Or me? Or any representative who could secure Ray's safe passage?"

"We're approaching you now," she said without taking her eyes off the car in front of them.

"You know what I mean."

She took a long moment to answer, probably deciding how much to relate. "We thought Ray was dying, so there was nothing to do about that."

So you've been in the know since the beginning. That wasn't surprising.

"By the time we realized Ray had a fighting chance, too many people had way too many opinions on how to approach this. We are, quite frankly, stuck on what to do." She chuckled in a tired way. "The UN Committee wants to give a press conference next week about their non-classified findings. We're about to admit we exist to human society. Everyone's nervous."

Nathan's cellphone rang, and he automatically hung up. Higgs had been calling for the past twenty minutes, but he'd have to wait.

"Okay, that's understandable," Nathan said diplomatically. "I'm not downplaying Scott's importance, but once he's safe, I think we have a real shot at getting this right with Ray. Opening communications between our people. For all our shortcomings with Scott, we've done our best to help Ray and to show good faith. That has to count for something."

Lombardi's cellphone rang, and she quickly looked at the screen, frowning.

"There seems to be something happening in the news," she said, the car behind them honking so she'd move forward.

"Well, if it's concerning merfolk, I'm sure we'll find out any minute now."

They shared a knowing smile. Nathan started browsing his phone for anything interesting.

"You're right. About Ray, I mean," Diana said, slowly moving through the lines of cars. "Having him as a starting point seems our best way. He's a smart guy."

"Wait, you know Ray?" Nathan asked, looking up at her. "Personally?"

She sighed. "Yes, I know him. We saw each other from time to time when we were growing up."

"How many of you are out there?"

"I don't know. I'm not old enough to get access to much of our archives. It makes me perfect to come, actually. I can't give up secrets I don't know to begin with."

They sent the equivalent of a teenager to do this job.

"Don't look so surprised, Nathan. I live on the surface, so I'm a liability. They question my loyalty every day, and there's nothing I can do but wait for my birthright at some arbitrary age, one that has nothing to do with my skills or life experiences."

"Right. It sounds tough," he amended, getting back to his phone. And there, in red letters, the breaking news announcement caught his eyes. *Holy shit.* "The hospital staff has just confirmed Ray is real."

27

Still Waters

In his mind, Chris had pictured something akin to an Olympic pool, getting some fifteen feet deep and relaxing while contemplating the world from an untouchable place.

The only thing his imagination had in common with reality was that it involved water.

People in white lab coats inundated his visual field, excitedly talking to each other, getting charts and tablets and phones, while someone came with a huge TV camera. Lights were set, equipment brought in, things moved out of the way, and he could swear he smelled popcorn.

If he had felt like a zoo animal while being watched from all sides by all kinds of people in his room, now he felt like the main attraction at a circus, everyone expecting him to perform tricks for their amusement.

He almost opened his mouth to say he wanted to go back.

Gwen and Higgs kept reassuring him to take it easy, but it was Andrew who understood how chaotic and unrelaxing the whole thing was turning out to be.

"Get everyone out," Andrew told Higgs, while a couple of ORCAS technicians played with the controls of Chris's would-be stretcher. It was designed to carry dolphins or similar mammals from the main pool to shallow, smaller pools on the side, so they could be examined. Up and down, side to side, Chris's stomach felt suddenly empty at the thought of being put in such careless hands.

For the first time since he'd met the man, Higgs wasn't smiling. "You're right, let me talk to them." He turned and looked at the sea of excited scientists, and Chris had a vision of all of those unblinking eyes turning into an angry mob because their show was being canceled. He shuddered.

"On second thoughts," Higgs said, turning to look at Gwen. "Maybe you want to do the honors?"

It was amazing the power a middle aged woman's voice had when it went from concerned to impatient, to downright scary. She had everyone gone but the technicians, the cameraman, and the three of them. The rest had been banished to the observation deck, which was far enough that most opted to go to the video room, where they'd see all the action on TV screens.

Andrew finished attaching the special water electrodes to follow Chris's heart rate and breathing, and finally took a good look at the merman and his tail.

"Okay Ray, we're going to get you onto the stretcher and then into the water. If anything hurts, if anything is remotely wrong, don't be stupid and make sure you tell us. Your safety is first, pal. Okay?"

Chris nodded, getting thumbs-up from his personal trainer, as Matt had called him.

Getting onto the moving stretcher required a lot of finesse and attention to detail. The cast on his tail had been sealed to be waterproof, along with the cast on his right wrist. His side fins were still shredded to long pieces, and Gwen made sure they weren't further damaged.

All in all, from the moment Higgs had told him about getting underwater until now, more than six hours had passed, six hours where Matt had remained absent.

What if something had happened to Matt?

The thought nagged him at every turn, and as Higgs and Andrew rolled him from his gurney to the awfully smelly stretcher, he couldn't help but miss Matt's chatty commentary on the ups and downs of life in captivity.

"Remember, if anything's wrong…" Andrew trailed off with a warning look before finally lowering him down to the tiny pool.

Andrew and Higgs stood either side of the descending stretcher, the water barely reaching above their knees.

You gotta be kidding me, was the last thought Chris had before the water reached him, slowly covering him up as the technicians did their best to maneuver him gently onto the pool's floor.

The water was cold. Perfectly cold to the point he sagged, realizing how tense he'd been through the entire ordeal. From under the water, he adjusted his eyes so he could look clearly, and fully extended his tail as if sunbathing in the Bahamas.

When he breathed in, they breathed out. It was comical, really, how both men had been holding their breath until they saw Chris's chest moving. In reality, he was exhaling the last air bubbles while small gill-like gaps shifted on

208

his back, allowing water to pass through his now shifted lungs. He wondered how long it would take them to figure that out, and then he just let his mind drift. Andrew wanted him to relax, and Higgs and Gwen didn't look like they were going to spoil the moment.

Let them wonder at seeing a real merman breathing water, he thought, closing his eyes. The water helped in relieving the constant throb on his tail. This was where he belonged.

In the distant corners of his mind, he felt Julian exhaling in relief too. Whatever had kept his father so preoccupied, Julian still had a watchful eye on what was going on with Chris.

Movement caught his attention. A *movement of the mind*, as Julian would call it. He imagined himself in the ocean, where Julian's essence was distinctively deep red, like the color of his tail, swimming at the edge of Chris's awareness. For a moment, he thought this other mind was Matt's, but it didn't feel orange and vibrant, the way he pictured his brother's personality. This was sluggish... muted... It didn't swim exactly; it was dragged by the undercurrent of their psychic links.

And then, with a terrible certainty, he knew it was Alex. Young and raw, and inexperienced, so close it could only mean he'd been captured. Blindly, he frantically searched for his little brother, his whole body going rigid, his heart feeling betrayed.

"What the hell, Ray? What's wrong?" Andrew asked while Chris was torn between being here and reaching for Alex.

It's not Alex! Chris, it's not Alex! Julian's voice thundered in Chris's mind, the connection crystal clear now he was underwater. Beside him, Andrew reached for his tail while Higgs reached for his wrist, both telling him not to move. He hadn't noticed he was about to jump out of there in search of this voice, wounded tail and all.

What the hell is going on?

We haven't been able to establish a contact with him, but we know his name is Scott. Scott Hunter. Your doctors don't know about him. We don't know exactly where he is. Maybe you'll have better luck.

It took everything in Chris to stay still and concentrate. He was having no better luck than his father in establishing a connection, but he could definitely feel another merman close by. A kid, to be precise. Only a kid. Minutes passed by in tense silence, until Chris decided to take a more proactive approach.

Hey, Scott... Chris whispered into the darkness, as gently and friendly as he could manage. *Whenever you're ready, I'll be here...*

Nothing happening besides Higgs and Andrew expecting him to do something stupid. Chris was sure his heart rate wasn't doing him any favors.

Finally, a pale light shone at the edges of Chris's mind. *Hey...* he sent again, hopeful and apprehensive at the same time.

When a tiny *hey* answered back, Chris held onto it, knowing full well Scott's life depended on it.

* * *

Behind the glass, Scott Hunter slept underwater. It was as strange as it was a relief. Major White had gambled with kid's life, and it had paid off.

He'd argued with all six doctors about it. God, he'd never argued so hard in his life before. If Scott died, if he as much as had one resultant scar from all this, the fault would be no one's but White's. He'd tracked Scott down. He'd let Sawyer's men shoot at him and then had let Sawyer himself waste precious time, instead of realizing this kid was having one hell of an allergic reaction, or whatever it had been.

He was never going to let this kid out of his sight.

Like Ray in the pools area, Scott had been submerged in as little water as possible, in case he might drown. Unlike Ray, who had pools to move in if he was allowed to, Scott was put inside a fish tank—for all practical purposes, anyway. It had been built for Ray so they could study him properly underwater but hadn't been used yet since pools were considered less claustrophobic and restrictive for their first approach.

It had taken Scott no more than fifteen seconds to start breathing underwater, but White had felt each and every one of those seconds like rocks piling on his shoulders. No one had any idea if the sedative would wear off without any further problem, so all White could do was wait.

Scott stirred, his legs moving reflexively against the glass, then he settled back. They had expected those pale, thin legs to turn into a tail, but all they had gotten were faint scales. On the other side of the tank, two doctors were getting ready to move Scott onto his side, so they could see how the breathing was happening. He wasn't inhaling through his mouth, and no gills had appeared on his throat or any visible part of his body.

The only place they hadn't looked was at his back. Logically, this was the best moment to check. What with Scott's tendencies to thrash and bite and send everyone to hell, this was going to be the only moment they could safely look. Sedating him after this was out of the question. Still, when all was said and done, White couldn't shake the feeling that what they were doing was essentially wrong. Scott was barely a teenager, not a lab rat. No kid should have to go through this.

Carefully, one of the doctors took the shoulder, the other the hip, and positioned Scott on his side, where water barely covered his face. Another doctor was filming everything for posterity, while White watched Scott closely for any reaction.

"Here they are," one of them said enthusiastically, the other pressing his fingers to Scott's back. Scott's reaction was instant; his eyes fluttered and his back slightly arched as if he wanted to escape the hands that held him still.

"Be careful," White warned, imagining it felt like someone sticking their fingers into his nose.

"Let's lower the water a little, so we can take a sample," another doctor suggested. In the pools area, White imagined Ray was having a better time.

You need an ally kid, way more than Ray does.

Once the water dropped a few inches, they pressed a swab on the boy's back, and that made Scott move with enough force to hit his forehead on the glass.

"Hey! Be careful!" White ordered, getting his hands underwater to cradle Scott's head, half out of the water by now. This close, he noticed Scott's lips were moving, not just breathing, but saying something.

Talking in his sleep?

"Hey… it's okay kid."

Scott moved his head, and for a second Jonathan thought it was to get out of his hands, but then he realized Scott was shaking his head willfully.

"I know it's uncomfortable, but we're just making sure you can breathe okay."

A moment went by, and then the shaking again. Scott's eyes half opened and then closed once more.

"You're going to be fine, do you hear me?"

Finally opening his still glazed eyes, Scott frowned. "I'm not talking to you".

The doctors looked at Jonathan in amusement, then let Scott fall on his back. Before the water level was raised to fully cover Scott, White asked a question. "Who were you talking to?"

Looking at White as if he was mad—an impressive feat giving the circumstances—Scott muttered his final words before falling back to sleep. "I'm talking to Chris."

* * *

Gwen kept calling, insistently interrupting Nathan's calls to the UN, and his conversation with Diana. They had parked in front of a Starbucks to re-group and strategize before they both moved to their respective roles.

"I'd better answer this. Maybe something happened to Ray."

"Forest! Where the hell are you?!"

With a mermaid. Trying to salvage a first contact between us and them.

"Dealing with a crisis. Is Ray all right?"

"Happy as a clam. What are you going to do with these people?"

The way she said it made it sound like the end of the world.

"You mean the hospital staff?"

"Yes! Them! I bet you Bill Shore organized it. He was the ER-attending doctor when Ray came in. I patched Ray up, but Bill was the one responsible for his care. You met him that first night, remember? At the hospital?"

He did, vaguely. That first night felt like a year ago. It was astonishing to realize only nine days had passed since Ray had been found. Everything seemed to happen in months rather than days when dealing with merfolk.

"Gwen, there's nothing I can do about a press conference already released."

"But—but aren't they supposed to be in quarantine? Can't you shut them up or something? They can't just tell the truth like that!"

He sighed, thinking the truth was probably going to be distorted substantially before an hour went by.

"We'd look like idiots, and it's not like you can silence the entire ER staff at once. Not with little things like phones and computers around."

"I can say something against it," Gwen started, clearly at a loss of how to feel. "They're going to come for Ray."

"Gwen, calm down. No one is coming for him who isn't already here. The UN Committee is going to release their own press conference, and they're not denying Ray's existence either. If anything, this will fill the gap between finding Ray and what we're doing."

212

"What? *What?* Do you have any idea how many nuts are out there?"

"He's part of something bigger, Gwen. Something larger than us. His discovery, his very existence, is something the world needs to know about."

"Why? So you can feel better about sharing? Well, call me a selfish bitch, but I don't want my merman plastered in all the news outlets of the world so people can tear him apart!"

Diana flinched beside Nathan, obviously privy to the entire conversation.

Nathan shook his head. "It's going to make him safe. It's going to give eyes on him, asking where he is, what's being done to him. You think there aren't people out there who want to cut him up into so many little pieces no one will ever find him? Because I have seen them. I have talked to them. The best thing that can happen to Ray right now is that the whole world knows."

He'd meant those words as much for Gwen as for Diana, but although the mermaid looked thoughtful, Gwen's explosive response was the complete opposite.

"I can't believe you're not going to stop them!" She hung up, leaving Nathan with a sense of foreboding. What if he was wrong?

"At least we know Ray's happy as a clam," Diana said with mock humor, and Nathan chuckled.

"Do you think I should try to stop them?"

"No. You would just look like idiots. The curious thing about the truth, though, is that it doesn't have to be the whole truth. Let me call the UN Committee again, maybe there's something we can do that won't end up putting my dear friend in hotter water."

28

Identity

Gwen was furious.

The last time she'd felt this way was back when the hospital administrator talked to her about a malpractice lawsuit that hadn't been any malpractice at all—the idiot patient had done exactly everything she'd warned him not to do, and then—and then—

My God, I'm seeing red, she told herself, feeling tension creeping up at the back of her neck, crawling its way into her head. She was going to have a heart attack one of these days if she didn't watch it. *The hell with watching it!* She wanted to be mad, and no one, no one was going to stop her.

"Is something wrong?" Dr. Higgs asked with a worried look while the phone in her hands trembled. She'd called Forest the minute she'd found out about the hospital staff—about Bill Shore, the little traitor—and how they had sold out Ray for... for what?

Were they paid? Did they try to reach her and make her complicit?

Did they worry when she disappeared from the social media world, canceled her phone, and pretty much went dark?

Did they think she was dead?

Maybe, a tiny voice said, *they're doing this for you, thinking you've been swallowed by a black hole and have no escape but them bringing your captors into the light.*

Ha!

She was going to find out how much each of those idiots had been paid and then make them choke on their money.

"Gwen? You're getting really, really red," Andrew pointed out, while the news notifications on her phone kept increasing.

"Those *bastards!*" she exploded. Higgs and Andrew turned to look at her as if she was going to explode for real, while Ray remained oblivious under the water.

"What? What did we miss?" Andrew asked, warily looking at Higgs and then at the doors, as if waiting for a mob to enter the room.

She looked at them and then at the pool where Ray was lying, and her anger doubled at the thought of someone selling him off. She opened her mouth to denounce the evils of this world but then thought better of it. Ray didn't need to worry about this—God knew he had enough to worry about already.

She got closer, so she wouldn't have to yell for everyone to hear. "The people at the hospital gave a press conference an hour ago. They're admitting Ray's real."

Andrew and Higgs blinked in unison.

"But we know he's real," Andrew said first, seeing no implications whatsoever to their immediate future.

"Public opinion can be a harsh place to be," Higgs told their youngest colleague.

"Public opinion can kiss my ass for all I care. Don't you see, Andrew? Now you'll have senators, the Congress, the freaking president weighing in on what to do, on what to *publicly* do about Ray. Everyone who's important already knows about him, but they had free hands to do what's right. Now they'll do what is *politically* right. Three guesses why that's a bad idea."

"Okay, okay, I see your point. Don't shoot me," Andrew said, turning to look down at Ray, still restlessly moving as if he knew exactly what they were talking about.

"I very much doubt there's anything we can do about this," Higgs began, reigniting her anger at Forest.

"Don't you start on that as well!" she hissed, trying to not yell and scare Ray even more. "Nathan just told me there's nothing he can do, but I refuse to believe that!"

"What exactly do you want him to do? Gwen, there's no logical way out of this."

"Well, we are on US soil," she reasoned. "The United Nations can only do so much, so we should get him into international waters, hide Ray, wait for him to get well, and let him go."

"Did I mention *logical* way?" Higgs said with a smile.

"Sue me," Gwen said, still seething at the absurdity and cruelty of it all.

"We all want what's best for him," Higgs said. "And maybe this is the best thing for him—"

"Oh, save it. Forest already gave me the grand speech. You know what I think?"

"That you're not buying it?"

216

"That someone out there needs to stop this."

"Who, you?" Higgs asked, now looking concerned.

"No, not me. I'd kill the first moron who remotely suggests Ray is a threat. Someone with finesse. Someone who has Ray's best interests at heart—for real."

"Well, I don't know if there's such a person out there who fits your description," Higgs said in a conciliatory tone. "But don't despair, Dr. Gaston. Ray's still here, still safe, and still hungry. Now, I promised this young man a meal, and I have every intention of keeping my promise."

"You're going to dismiss this just like that?" Gwen asked, feeling the red coming up her face all over again.

"Until there's something I can proactively do, yes. I suggest you do the same. Now, I'm going to see if the kitchen has Ray's meal done already—unless you have a better plan?"

She narrowed her eyes and then realized Higgs was right. Until she had a plan, there was nothing she could do but make sure Ray was safe. She pitied the idiot who crossed that doorway and threatened her patient.

* * *

The diner at the bus station was a busy place. Men, women, and kids all mingled, anxious looks from would-be passengers waiting for their time to board, while happy faces glowed as people met with friends and family with loud greetings and embraces.

For Alex, this place was noisy as hell, and he wished he could be anywhere but here. Anywhere.

"Come on, eat your hamburger," Matt said with little patience, eating his second hot dog without a second glance.

"How can you be so calm when Dad's going to face some unknown enemy at the hotel?"

"He's there. I'm here. I'm hungry. End of the story," Matt said between bites, getting his fries closer to his plate. "It's not that I'm not worried about him, just that worry has never been a reason to stop eating."

Alex had known Matt for the better part of four years. His older brother had weird habits that surfaced from time to time—like his need to always finish his plate—but for the most part, he was a private guy who dealt with tough stuff by quietly brooding in his room.

It hadn't taken Alex long to understand that when Matt closed his door, he really meant it as him putting up a wall. It was cool, Alex thought, that Julian let each of them deal with crises, school, and their secret however they thought was best. It was always strange to think these people—Chris, Matt, and Julian—had not been his family his whole life and that there was a *before* and *after* to being a Brooks.

"Well, I can't eat a thing. I'm going nuts thinking about what's going on, what he'll say, what the other side will say. The possibilities are endless!"

Matt nodded twice and then sipped from his orange juice with ice. The restaurant was hot, and neither of them appreciated so many people so close.

"I mean," Alex continued. "What's the worst that can happen?"

"It's a trap. Julian's ambushed. He ends up dead, or worse, missing."

Alex's eyes grew at Matt's casual admission between his hamburger and his fries.

"Whaaat?" Alex managed to ask, feeling like he was going to be sick.

"Kidding..." Matt answered, deadpan, clearly not kidding at all.

"I'm sure I'm going to regret this, but what's the best that can happen, then?"

"Drake kills them all," Matt said with a smirk, half of his hot dog gone, not a single drop of mustard on the table. He was a pro when it came to eating fast food.

"Be serious!"

"I am! That's kind of what Drake does, you know? He solves the community's problems. Why d'you think he's here, to shake hands and play nice? Drake went after that Forest guy because he saw it as his best option. Not the first, not the last, but the best. You think he wouldn't have killed him if he had actually pulled the trigger on Scott?"

"For real?"

"For real. You're just too young to figure all this shit out."

This was a conversation turning darker and murkier by the second, and he couldn't deal with skeletons in their family's closet right now. Not if they were figurative, much less if they were literal.

"Eat your hamburger," Matt repeated, this time with a warning tone.

"Why? So I have something to throw up?"

"Yes. I mean, not for you to throw up, but for you to have something in your stomach. We have no idea when our next meal is coming, Alex, so you better fill up."

Alex stared at his brother. Between them, they had four thousand dollars in cash, they'd already bought tickets to five destinations, and the Council had sent someone to pick them up here, in about an hour. If Julian was walking into a trap, he and Matt would be able to escape.

It had taken Julian the better part of an hour to convince them to at least be at the ready to escape, away from the hotel and away from anyone who could potentially know who they were. If this night turned out to be a disaster, Alex and Matt would never again use Brooks as their last name.

This is so wrong, Alex thought as he took the hamburger and looked at it as if it was alive and he was about to kill it. *A month ago my biggest problem was not getting caught hacking during class. Now I might never go back to that classroom, see my friends again, swim with Julian and Chris... When was the last time I swam with them? Was it two months ago? Last summer? When was the last time the four of us were together?*

"Alex. Stop worrying yourself sick."

"How can you be so damn calm?" Alex shot back, feeling hysteria rising in his voice. He shut up before half the people in the diner turned curious glances their way, and stared at his uneaten dinner instead.

Matt waited a few moments to see if any nosy adult would come their way. Matt was almost eighteen and looked the part, but Alex was fifteen and barely managed to look as a teenager.

"Because I have bigger shit to think about. Like you. Like what's the worst that can happen to us? Julian's a big guy, he knows how to handle himself, he can call the entire City if he needs to. You and I? That's a whole other story. We have to lie low so we're not caught by association. Yes, the Council is coming for us, and will be here—if we survive the dinner from hell our dear father is attending to. So eat your food, stop whining, and start thinking."

At the back, a little kid started wailing. Alex wholeheartedly agreed. He wanted to wail at the universe for being so cruel.

Matt sighed in front of him, putting his hotdog down and combing his hair with both hands, grease and all.

"Nothing's going to happen. Not really. Drake is not going to abandon Julian, so he's probably lurking at the restaurant right now, making sure his oldest, dearest friend's safe. The blackmailer wants money. If this were a trap, the three of us would already be chained to fish tanks in Area 51. This place? Us being here? It's just to give Julian peace of mind that we've a means to escape. Airplanes were too risky and easy to trace. So, we're going to eat, and we're going to wait for Julian to call us back home. And tomorrow, when you're gloating on pancakes and milkshakes, we'll laugh about this, okay?"

No response.

"Okay?" Matt pressed again, exasperated.

"O—kay," Alex whispered, rapidly blinking a tear or two. He had no idea if Matt was right. After all, there was a real possibility this was his first meal of his new life.

"But what if—"

"God! Talk about something else. That will keep your mind from imploding itself in that thick skull of yours."

"But—"

"No buts. If you're going to open your mouth it's going to be to get food into you, or speak about anything but our current situation. Okay? Okay."

"I—" Alex said, and then thought better of it. "You can be a real jerk, you know?"

"I do. Now eat your fries or I will."

Wordlessly, Alex pushed them towards Matt in a silent declaration of *I don't care*. Matt looked at him, then shook his head, promptly getting all the fries on his plate. "Your loss."

"When did you become so calculating?"

"About six years ago, while I was trying not to die."

Alex instantly blushed. This was from Matt's past, the forbidden topic no one ever brought up without Matt shutting them up. He'd seen Julian backpedal from conversations that had gone down that route. Hell, he'd even seen Chris shutting up in the middle of a sentence. Matt protected his past the same way he protected his family. Tight and firm and with no excuses.

Picking up his hamburger so he wouldn't stare at Matt, Alex slowly started to bite. His stomachs growled in anticipation, but he didn't feel any rush to eat his food.

"Squid?"

"Hmm?"

"How did you find out about Julian? I mean, sure, your parents told you, but it's not like you could pick up the phone and call him."

"Yeah."

"Yeah what?"

"You can pick up a phone and call him. I did. Several times. It's called Senior Assistant."

"What? Sarah intercepted you and never told Julian? You were stomped by Julian's secretary?"

"I never even reached Sarah. This was Sarah's Senior Assistant. She told me she could trace my call and get me to jail. So I traced it back and actually got into Julian's main line. I—I didn't know what to do, exactly. I had to pretend I still had parents before Social Services figured out I was a minor on my own. I thought it was going to be easy, but for a couple of days there, I really thought Julian would never know I existed."

"So, you got Julian on the main line and just blurted it out?"

Alex snorted. "I wish. He was on a business trip. I hacked into his assistant's calendar and checked he was in Argentina, probably visiting Mireya, now that I think about it."

"Ah. Yeah, I remember there was a big commotion at the house. Chris handled it, of course. I was just curious about what was going on and... well... I was kind of jealous. Another kid meant another one of us to pay attention to."

"Oh, poor baby," Alex said with mock sympathy.

Matt glared, then smiled. "What did I know back then? I thought you were going to be another perfect little merman like Chris. And no one can compete against Chris's perfection."

Alex smiled at that. "You don't mean that," he said, for the first time relaxing.

"I guess not. But I did wonder if by having two normal kids, Julian would see how messed up I was. Guess I really didn't believe we were a family back then. I thought he'd taken me because the Council mandated it but had no real feelings for us. Some shit like that."

Alex bit into his hamburger, remembering the night he'd gotten to the Brooks penthouse. He remembered so clearly looking up, up, up at the building. He'd lived on an island before that, and sure, he'd been at ports and places, but to be in New York, forced to live with strangers...

"I didn't know what to expect either. And then—"

"Chris shone his bright light on the doorstep and you were mesmerized," Matt said with a singsong note, both of them laughing at the slightly over-the-top Chris.

"He did make a difference, you know," Alex said, remembering Chris's warm smile. Julian had been on his way back, but that night, Chris and Matt had been the only people he'd met.

"I know. He was relentless in his pursuit of making me part of the family. I'm sure you don't know this, but I ran away from Julian seventeen times, and each and every time Chris was out there, waiting. Seventeen fucking times. He

221

must have been out there every night for months. Waiting for me. Until I finally got it, this was not somewhere I was expected to get lost."

"For real?"

"For real. I have no idea when he stopped waiting for me to escape. But that's what he did. That's why I couldn't believe it when Julian just wanted to leave him there, in humans' hands. After all Chris has done, after everything he represents for this family. I really couldn't believe it. I still can't. I don't think I'll ever forgive Julian for this."

"Really?" Alex asked, his hamburger forgotten.

"I don't know. It's too raw right now. But if someone deserves to be rescued, that's Chris. I don't care if all we get are his fins, anything that belongs to him belongs to us."

Alex thought to argue that Julian had had no choice, but he thought better of it. Matt wasn't going to buy into this just because Alex did. If Matt wanted to stay mad at Julian the rest of his life, there wasn't anything he could do about it—at least not now, in the middle of this diner from hell.

"Eat your hamburger," Matt said again. "You'll need your strength no matter what. I don't think this wait can stretch much longer, not with the humans knowing the merman is real. Maybe not tonight, maybe not tomorrow, but one day real soon, we might find ourselves on the run. So eat your dinner, Alex, you might need it soon."

* * *

I'm talking to Chris.
Talking to Chris.
Chris.

Jonathan White wrote those four words on a notepad, and circled *Chris* some twenty more times. There were five Chris's and two Christopher's in the entire ORCAS compound. One of them was even a woman.

I'm talking to Chris.

It could very well be the ramblings of an ailing mind—a young, drugged mind who could not distinguish between fact and dream.

Talking to Chris.

But the way Scott had looked at him, with that intensity—that certainty that he was, indeed, talking to Chris, set all kinds of alarms in White's mind. He

222

put aside solving the mystery of how he was talking to anyone—this was a being who could look like a human and then breathe underwater, after all—he was far more concerned with the practical implications: *Who does a merboy talk to? And what does he talk about?*

Opening his computer, he accessed the security footage of the pools area, where Ray and his doctors were still in the water. Calling up the video file, he went back in time until he reached the moment the merman had arrived at the pools. Everything looked chaotic, but normal enough given the circumstances, and he smiled when doctor Gaston threw everyone out. He respected people who made things happen like that.

Fifteen minutes after, he found something interesting; out of nowhere, their perfectly relaxed merman tried to jump out of the water as if something had bitten him. After that, he lay still at the bottom, but his pulse remained elevated as if he was waiting for something to happen—or as if upset about something already happening.

Could it be...?

But then, why wouldn't Ray have known about Scott before? And wasn't Scott's early struggle to breathe a far better cry for help than sleeping under the water?

Narrowing his eyes, he looked at Ray's screen. They'd been calling him Ray for so long now it was easy to forget it wasn't his real name. Ray had had a life passing as a human being. He knew the language, the culture, the way of life. He had an identity. For the first time, White had a clue—a flimsy clue, yes, but still a clue—about where to begin.

Forest had started that search from day one, focusing on any instances of strange happenings along the East Coast, all the way to Canada. Military Intelligence was still looking into it, but their priorities had shifted between containing the many leaks inherited in this kind of operation, and dealing with Scott's sudden appearance. Yet no one had found anything because no one really knew what they were looking for.

Accessing the database compiled with a month's worth of news, he typed in *Chris* and hit enter. Nine hundred probable entries appeared, so he settled to reading each and every one.

29

Conflict of Interest

If this dinner didn't mean safeguarding Chris's identity—and his family's identity by extension—Julian would wholeheartedly cancel it. He imagined the sleazeball blackmailer grinning like an idiot, salivating at the enormous sum of money he could take out of Julian's pocket. He didn't care about the money, but he would pay anything to grab the man by the throat and throw him at the wall, just for threatening his family.

He was half an hour early to the hotel's high-end restaurant two floors below the penthouse. Walking out of the elevator felt like walking right into a trap. To collect his thoughts, he walked to the closest window and took a minute to calm himself, his eyes seeking the ocean.

He felt as comfortable wearing a suit as wearing jeans, but nothing would ever compare to the feel of swimming in clear waters, being free.

It had been decades since he'd longed for the sea, centuries since he'd thought about it as home. Even if that wasn't true anymore, if need be, the City would always welcome one of their own back. They might still be the same society he'd run from ages ago, but the truth was, there was no safer place in the world than inside the dome concealing their presence from humans.

His heart ached for comfort and to know his children were safe. Too many decisions hung on whatever happened at this dinner, he was afraid he wouldn't think straight.

I have a plan to get Chris out.

Drake's voice interrupted his pity party, and Julian's eyes unfocused, his mind following his friend's mental presence.

Where were you? he demanded, feeling betrayed yet relieved at the same time. He could do this alone, but knowing Drake had his back meant an added safety net.

I had an idea while I was picking up Diana from the airport. I had to move fast to get everything in place, but I still have too many loose ends. I saw the news, too. The sooner we get your son out, the easier I'll breathe. Now, tell me everything about this blackmailer of yours.

There's nothing to tell, yet, Julian messaged. *I'm early for our meeting, though I've no doubt he's already there.*

Listen, I'm on my way—in about fifteen minutes. Don't start without me.

Instead of looking at the ocean, Julian stared at his own reflection and saw his shoulders relax slightly.

What about your plan, Drake? How feasible is it? he asked.

Well… it has one major problem: it needs a seriously good distraction before we can—

"A penny for your thoughts?" a woman asked. It took Julian a couple of seconds before realizing she was talking to him.

Tall, thin, with long ash blonde hair and a startling blue dress that complemented her pale skin, this woman looked at him with an intensity that didn't bode well. She was after something, every instinct told him, but if it was a favor, a cause, his money, or all of the above, he didn't know.

"It's a breathtaking view," he answered politely.

"I bet you've seen too many sunsets to count?" she said, looking out at the city, the setting sun giving the buildings a pinkish hue. It was breathtaking now he was looking at it.

"Nothing worth anything in life should be counted," he answered with a well-practiced smile, the one he used on board meetings and social events.

"Can I quote you on that?" she said, smiling. Her eyes twinkled.

He chuckled, and then looked at the clock hanging above the restaurant entrance.

"If you'll excuse me, Ms.—?

"Banes. Kate Banes."

"Ms. Banes, I have a meeting to attend."

"I know. We're having dinner together in fifteen minutes, you and I," she said with a bright smile, a little too wide for his liking. He'd been right, she was looking at him as prey, but he'd been wrong about the motives.

"You seem surprised," she said with curiosity, her green eyes seeking a crack in his demeanor. For a blackmailer, she was overdressed. But then again, who said thieves had to wear all black?

"I was expecting a man, to tell you the truth. I'm not used to thinking about charismatic women as part of such a dark world."

She blinked rapidly, clearly not expecting that answer. She paused and thought. "I guess people like you *would* think of it as a dark world."

It takes a special ego to think a blackmailer is one of the good guys, I guess.

226

Tension filled the air. Kate turned to the restaurant, eagerly. He followed behind, half expecting to hear Drake cursing. All he got from his friend was, *ten minutes. Keep your distance from this harpy.*

"You have something that belongs to me," he said in a steely voice once the waiter was gone, ready to get down to business.

"So you don't deny the watch is your son's?"

"There are few watches that would have my inscription on them, as you pointed out on your *invitation*. I'm more curious to know how it came into your possession, to tell you the truth."

"Someone at the hospital spotted it abandoned when your son reached the ER. They took it off. The only thing they could take off, actually."

Someone? If what she said was true, then at least there'd be fewer people in the know. A merman wearing a watch was bound to raise unwanted questions, but if someone had stolen it, fewer people had even seen that watch.

"May I see it?"

"Unfortunately, I don't have it with me right now. My expert is still taking a closer look at it, but I'll have it delivered to you next week."

If there was a real expert involved, it would at least explain why she would know how to trace it back to him.

"What do you want, Ms. Banes? I have a feeling that dinner is too little a reward for finding my son's watch."

He was prepared for a lengthy conversation about prices, along with a promise to return the watch after the money was in the bank. He was also expecting to pay something in seven or eight figures. Maybe there'd be a subtle threat or two since women were always so good at that kind of game. What he wasn't expecting were Kate Banes's next words:

"I want an exclusive interview with you."

What?

"I beg your pardon?" he asked, unable to hide his bewilderment. At the back of his mind, Drake cursed.

"We both know the truth about that watch, that hospital, and your son."

I very much doubt you know the truth about anything, he fleetingly thought, looking at her in a new light. A dangerous new light. An *interview* meant she didn't want to keep this quiet. An interview meant—

"You're with the press."

—that he had much bigger problems.

* * *

The words were heavy in his throat, Kate could tell that much.

Powerful men were used to hiding their intentions well, especially men like Julian Brooks who had years of experience in dealing with all kinds of problems. Right now, she was coming for what he loved the most, his family, and his privacy. Or if she was wrong, then his heirs and his power. Whatever kind of man he was, she was definitely not something he could afford to ignore. And whatever she did, she couldn't afford to make him her enemy.

"We want to know your side of the story, Mr. Brooks. You have two teenage sons to think about, not to mention a corporate empire that reaches all corners of the world, the oceans included."

"We?"

She had to give it to him, he recovered fast.

"An exclusive interview would grant you all the time, all the clarifications you want. You can give all the answers everyone is dying to know."

He hadn't expected this, she could tell. She could see it in the way his eyes moved almost imperceptibly to the left as he regrouped his ideas. He'd been prepared to face something else, but not her, and certainly not a reporter. Now her cards were on the table, she had to seize the moment and get him to agree.

"Your son, Christopher. Is he still alive?" And what better moment for her interview than now?

"Who do you work for?" he asked, refocusing on her with eyes too serious and shoulders too rigid.

"Veritas Co. A digital news medium specializing in unusual angles. We go beyond the obvious, beyond the sensationalist. We want the truth, Mr. Brooks."

"And what is the truth, according to you?"

"We've known Christopher was the merman from day one."

His brow knitted and she had to backpedal a moment, her wall of truth flashing in her mind with all the details of her investigation. "We knew it was him, we just didn't know he was real. We thought your son had been involved in some prank that had gone terribly wrong and you were covering for him. Rich kids, you know?"

"A prank..." Julian said without much humor as if such explanation was beneath him. "I'm sorry, Ms. Banes, but what, exactly, do you think I'm hiding? What are you talking about?"

"Christopher Brooks is the merman the whole nation is talking about on every news channel you can tune into. He was found on a beach a day before

228

you announced that your son went missing, and he showed up wearing your son's watch. A watch that a hospital's janitor gave to me with one incredible tale. The same hospital, Mr. Brooks, that gave an interview not three hours ago about treating a real merman."

"My son was lost at sea and then found. I think he can't be in two places at the same time."

"That's a clever answer. You *rescued* him from the sea, but here's the thing; no one knows where your son is. I mean, do you even know where they're holding Christopher captive?"

The dark clouds gathering instantly in Julian's eyes told her she was going too far, too fast.

"My son had a serious accident at sea. His life was in grave danger and I almost lost him. You don't get to know his whereabouts. You don't get to summon me, sit down in front of me, and implicate my son in this bizarre media fairy tale."

For Kate, those words translated into *do you really want me to tell you what I think about this interview of yours right now?*

"I don't mean to belittle what you're going through. I can only imagine what kind of hell that must be. But if you agree to do this, it will turn the opinion of the world in your favor. Work with us, Mr. Brooks, tell the story. Don't let them take your son and win."

Brooks wasn't buying it. It didn't matter how sincere she was trying to be, this man was not going to be easily swayed. After a whole minute of silence, she couldn't stand it any more. "What are you thinking, Mr. Brooks? Tell me, so I can put your mind at ease."

"No one has taken my son and no one is winning anything. Chris will talk to the press when and if he feels like talking to the press, not when one of you wants to exploit his ordeal for fifteen minutes of fame."

The waiter came to take the table's orders, and for one moment, Kate had to think about ordering something, even if her stomach was tied in ten knots. The whole menu was in French, letters swimming in front of her eyes.

"I'll take one of these," she said, blindly signaling to the waiter, who nodded. Julian Brooks ordered in perfect French, of course.

A million minutes later, the waiter finally left.

"As I was saying," she picked up the interview right away. "We've followed every clue, every crumb along the way. If we could find the truth, you can bet someone else will, too. It's just a matter of time. And we're on your side here. You found a boy who could turn into a merman and then—"

He raised a polite hand in a universal sign of stop. Against all her reporter instincts, she shut her mouth.

"You want to know what I'm thinking?" he asked, clasping his hands on the table and leaning forward. "The amount of damage you can do to my family with your wild conjectures is unspeakable."

"We want to tell this story, your family's story, in the best way possible."

"You found a watch from a man who was already lost at sea by the time someone found this merman of yours. You took it from a janitor, who stole it from an unconscious patient, which I believe makes you an accessory to a crime. And you followed God knows what kind of logic that led you to me."

She couldn't even blink at the sight of those eyes. It wasn't so much what he was saying, but the way he was saying it that had her re-evaluating all her options.

"What are the odds, Ms. Banes, that you connected the dots wrong? And if you're wrong about this and publish it, you would do me, my family, my company, and everyone else implicated in this article, irreparable damage. I can assure you I would do anything in my power to protect my own. And my power, Ms. Banes, is considerable."

Despite her resolved and knowing she was right, she swallowed. Julian Brooks could make or break her life, she already knew that, but she was not going to be intimidated for exposing the truth. She couldn't afford that.

"As I see it, you have a son somewhere in a military base," she said, leaning against the table. "There, scientists are playing with scalpels and syringes, trying to figure out what makes him tick. You have no way of getting him out without blowing your cover, and that of your other two sons, who may or may not be just like their brother. I'm not stupid, Mr. Brooks, even your considerable power has limits, especially when it's pitted against the US government. I want to expose the truth, but I want to do it right. Not with teenagers as collateral damage and ruining your life in all senses of the word."

Julian Brooks stared at her in the same way someone stares at a particularly interesting problem. He didn't know what to do with her, she was sure, because he couldn't silence her and couldn't buy her. If anything, he had to play by her rules, and people in power never liked to play by anyone's rules but their own.

"Let's say for the moment, that I buy this theory of yours, with all of its implications," he said, smirking as if he found this either laughable or distasteful.

That your son is a merman, or that you're a merman? Truth to be told, she had no facts to back up that particular question.

"Okay…"

"Maybe we could be—"

"Friends?"

"Allies. I would never presume your friendship out of thin air."

She narrowed her eyes. "What are you proposing, Mr. Brooks? And why do I feel I'm not going to like it?"

"Think of this as a long-term arrangement."

"You mean I shut up now so you can disappear?"

"If you publish this now, every one of your colleagues would come and trample you. The mess that will come out of it is no good for me, but all you'll have for your efforts is a one-hit wonder and nothing else."

Oh, I'm sure I can live with discovering the story of the century. Heck, of the millennium! Out loud, she kept her face straight. "What do you have in mind?"

"Just for the sake of argument, maybe there are a few facts of which you are unaware. Maybe this story is bigger than you think."

"I'm all for any facts I can verify," she warned.

"Of course, not that it had troubled you until now. But, here's an interesting fact: The United Nations has created a special Committee to oversee anything and everything related to this merman. They will release a press conference in the next twenty-four hours backing up the hospital staff, and updating how things are with their… guest."

She looked startled. *What?*

"What they won't say—what they probably don't even know—is that the Pentagon has found another merman, a thirteen-year-old boy."

Her lips parted slightly with surprise, too many questions stuck in her throat. How did he know? Who had captured this kid? Was he even alive right now? Where were his parents?

"I see you're interested," Brooks said with approval written on his face.

"Can—can you even back this up?"

"I have the moment he was captured on camera."

"How do you know this?"

"I know a lot of things," he said with a charming smile that didn't reach his eyes. "Brooks Inc. extends to the entire world, as you pointed out. Even the oceans. There's more *exclusive content*, I believe you call it, if you're interested."

She swallowed again, but this time, a whole new world of possibilities opened up. Christopher Brooks had been the story for the past two weeks. That this was bigger—*my God, I'm gonna need another wall!*

"If—and this is a big if—you have this proof, why tell me? What do you know about merfolk, Mr. Brooks?"

"Maybe I also want to expose the truth, Ms. Banes. When my son went missing, I cast a wide net and pulled up some surprising things along with the information I was looking for. Maybe you stumbled onto something quite different than what you have put together, and maybe I'm bound by national security to keep my mouth shut. As they say, I can't confirm or deny anything we've just talked about."

What exactly are you admitting here? That your son is a merman? That you know merfolk? That the government knows about merfolk? That—her mind was so full of questions she felt a headache already forming.

"Check your references," Julian Brooks continued. "Who knows? Maybe you can prove the real merman is being held against his will at ORCAS's sixth building, instead of being my son at a private hospital, where all the records in the world will testify he's recuperating from his ordeal at sea."

She swallowed. On her imaginary new wall of truth, she wrote in big red letters: ORCAS SIXTH BUILDING.

"I'm not saying I agree, but let's say I do. I get to keep the watch. As insurance."

Brooks didn't even blink. "Of course. I'm looking forward to reading tomorrow's digital edition of Veritas Co."

He stood up, and she did the same. "Where are you going? Dinner hasn't even started!"

"Oh, I never intended to eat, though I told the waiter to put your tab on me. I do have a son who needs me, and two other teenagers antsy as hell to be here. It's been quite an entertaining evening, Ms. Banes. Make sure you have all your facts straight before deciding what to publish."

He extended a hand, one she didn't want to shake. Once she did, this interview was officially over.

"Mr. Brooks, there are still many oth—"

"Good night, Ms. Banes," he said at the same time the waiter came with her dinner. She grabbed his hand.

"You won't be able to hide this forever," she warned.

"I have nothing to hide," he answered in the same whispery tone. And with that, he walked away, leaving behind a cloud of doubts, and no certainties.

* * *

232

Nathan would never look at the world the same way again. Standing in front of ORCAS Sixth building, he realized his priorities had changed—drastically.

He saw ORCAS the way merfolk did; it was a fortress, a prison detaining a being whose only crime had been to wash up on a beach in Maine. And it also held a child who'd gotten too close and had been caught in the net.

His first priority was to find out where Scott was and in what condition. Diana had told him she didn't trust White's power to free him, because he was not in the chain of command. The problem was, if he went too high in this chain, they would deny any knowledge or involvement. Too low and he would meet a wall of silence. If White wasn't the right one, then probably Sawyer was. Nathan was a big believer in dialogue and communication. The best way to get Scott out was by advocating they had way more to gain by releasing him than by burying him.

As soon as Diana's car had disappeared around the bend, Nathan reached for his phone. He had every single person working at ORCAS on his contact list, and that included a Pentagon number. It took him the better part of ten minutes, but he was finally patched through to Sawyer.

"Doctor. What can the US service do for you?"

"We have a problem, Colonel."

"Oh?"

"You can't detain Scott Hunter."

Nathan had expected the Colonel to deny it. He'd expected a demand to know how he'd found out about this. He'd expected anything other than what he actually heard.

"Scott Hunter is a ward of the state, Doctor. Found abandoned wandering the streets when he was nine, twenty pounds underweight and unable to talk about his parents. He's a failure of the foster system and most certainly a candidate for juvie any day now. They don't seem to treat their own very well." Sawyer's smug voice was all kinds of invitations to insult him, but Nathan couldn't afford to lose his clearance right now.

"They know we have him."

"How?"

"The same way I'm guessing we tracked him; traffic cameras."

"All our suspicions were true…" Sawyer whispered, and Nathan could've sworn he heard dread and the end of the world in that voice. "How did they contact you?"

"In the parking lot. They're getting ready to talk, but they're sure we did something to Scott, that something's wrong. Tell me he's not dead."

Sawyer didn't speak or do anything except breathe heavily, and Nathan's heart went to the floor.

"I can tell you this is significantly above your clearance, doctor. The UN has no business with US operations."

"The last thing we need is to initiate a hostile relationship with these people."

"Why, did they threaten us?"

"No. Of course not. They want to resolve this as quietly as they can, but they're running out of options. People are going to demand answers, and do you honestly want your name to go down in history as the man who killed a thirteen-year-old merkid out of spite?"

"You can tell your new friends they can run all they want, we will find them no matter how deep they dig themselves in."

"Sawyer, we have no idea what we're dealing with."

"That's funny, Forest. Neither do they."

Sawyer hung up without another word, and Nathan felt like banging his head against the wall. It didn't matter what Diana thought, he had to talk to White, see if the man would hear reason.

Before that, though, he had to take down the thermal cameras. Without further delay, he went to the security room, ready to prove to the merfolk that he was trustworthy.

30

Hide & Seek

Well, it's certainly not my fault those fucking idiots shot me!

Chris cringed. Every time Scott cursed, it was like the scrape of nails on a blackboard, making him shudder. Talking to Scott was like talking to Matt when he'd first arrived at their home—except worse.

The kid was a strange mix of his two brothers: young and restless and so, so angry.

How are you feeling now?

Like kicking the hell out of them... Scott murmured, obviously resenting his current condition. One he felt he was—apparently—too smart to have fallen into.

Scott. How are you feeling? Chris stressed again. It had been endearing, even cute to see the little rascal put up a brave front in the face of arguably their worst fear, but two hours of this was wiping out Chris's patience.

I feel funny... my legs tingle a lot, but my hands are numb. The lights are too bright, so I can't open my eyes. I think... I think if I move I'm gonna throw up.

Chris had no idea if that was normal or not, and clearly, no one in this place would know either. Julian had told him to keep an eye on Scott until he could solve his dinner meeting. The thought of that made Chris want to throw up, too, but there was nothing he could do about a watch he'd lost while unconsciously floating in the open sea.

Okay, I don't think they'll be moving you anytime soon. There's nothing you can do but wait this out. Even if they move you or get you out of there, just go with the flow, okay? Don't do anything to aggravate your condition.

You mean, don't do anything stupid. Don't worry, I'm not some idiotic kid who's going to wimp out at the sight of needles.

Chris sighed. Scott knew how to handle himself, sure, but this was a situation adults could barely handle, including himself.

It's okay to be scared, Scott. Just... cooperate and—

Wait. Are you telling me to cooperate? For real? Aren't you a silent deadweight who doesn't do a thing but lie still?

Stunned into silence, Chris heard only the beeping of his accelerated heart rate. The pool time was over, so Higgs and Andrew had already helped him into his gurney, getting him ready to leave the pools area. Beside Chris, Andrew finished taking the wrist protector and frowned at him

"You're acting so weird today," his caregiver murmured, then turned to talk with Gwen.

How—how do you know what I do or not? Chris asked.

Scott's mental voice filled with smugness, the kind that thankfully neither of Chris's brothers had. *I listened in, to you and Matthew.*

What? You're not even old enough to have your own tail!

I'm old enough to do a million things you can't even imagine.

Like avoiding capture, you mean?

That got Scott to shut up fast, which felt great and stupid at the same time.

That was uncalled for, Chris apologized as heartfelt as he could. *Julian didn't teach me how to connect to other mental links until I was twenty-one. Matt barely learned to stretch his range last week.*

That's because Julian's an ass.

On his bed, Chris counted to ten, his fingers reflexively moving into claws as he imagined strangling the kid.

Julian's many things, and right now, he's the only one fighting to get us both out, so I'd recommend you be more respectful of your only hope of rescue.

Silence. Discomfort filled Chris's main stomach as he felt Scott being moved onto his side. The kid was really close to losing the battle with his nausea if they kept doing this. It was maddening to imagine doctors poking and prodding a thirteen-year-old, but he had no choice but to wait. He would stay awake the entire night just to be there whenever Scott wanted to talk.

Twelve excruciating minutes later, Scott was once again on his back, still underwater.

He holds you back, the kid said as if their conversation hadn't been abruptly cut short by men in lab coats. And for the first time Scott wasn't bragging. He was serious, and a serious kid was far more manageable than a bragging one.

How so?

Telepathy is our common way of speaking, yet he keeps you three so—human. You should be able to do long-range telepathy by the time you have a tail. I didn't understand why Matthew had to get so close to you since he's already seventeen. It took me days to understand how far behind you are. You don't even use the proper terms.

In all honesty, all Chris had as a guide was Julian's words. His parents had told him to trust his new guardian, and he did, with all his heart.

I'm sure he has his reasons. Who taught you this?

My parents. They—they wanted me to know everything that was my birthright. Like a muscle, train young and you get more flexible. I should be at your level now... I would be if they were still alive.

Chris closed his eyes. The last time he'd seen his parents he'd been nine. He felt their loss every day along with the hope—the knowledge—that he'd see them again on his twenty-eighth birthday. To lose them forever would have devastated him, maybe beyond repair.

I'm not broken! Scott said with renewed anger, clearly getting at least part of Chris's mental process. *They died, big deal! I'm here! I matter! I know what to do! I'm— I'm—*

—going to be sick? Chris finished for him, feeling Scott's fear at the realization one of his stomachs was turning against him. For all of Scott's telepathic prowess, his own inner mental walls were thin, easily letting Chris feel his body. It dawned on Chris, then, that Scott had probably not spoken to any other merfolk in four years, and now he'd found his kin, now he'd heard mental voices again, the whole thing was so screwed up it wasn't even worth it.

He felt Scott throwing up, and he had to lessen their contact lest he throw up as well. This was a young mind, after all, and for all his bravado, he was still only a kid.

Don't! Don't go! Scott shouted in his mind, making Chris wince and get back at once. Fear pulsed in their connection while Scott's doctors took him out of the now contaminated water. Breathing became difficult again, but at least not life-threatening as before.

It's going to be okay, Scott. Just wait it out, okay? I'm not going anywhere. Not without you.

You're wrong... Scott answered, with less and less energy while Chris gave more into their connection.

About what?

This whole thing? It's worth it.

* * *

Matt knew the exact moment another merman came for them. It was hard to tell when he'd gotten so good with his telepathy, but didn't take a genius to figure out it had been all the practice he'd been getting with Chris.

"He's here," Matt said to Alex, who was halfway through his hamburger, finally seeing the merits of eating.

"Who's here?"

"The Council. I mean, whoever the Council sent. Get your stuff, we're leaving."

Your stuff was one lousy backpack, a cap and whatever was left of his dinner. Alex didn't fight him on this one, and quietly and rapidly took his possessions and stood up.

Outside, Matt looked left and then right, searching for someone looking out of place. And right there, where people walked in all directions, he saw his chauffeur for the night.

"That's not a he," Alex said, having searched and found the same thing. "That's very much not a he," he repeated, probably feeling his heart race in the same way Matt's was.

Mermaids had a strange effect on mermen, Chris had told him a couple of years ago. When it came to the birds and the bees, Matt had asked him why he didn't feel as strongly about girls as his classmates seemed to. *That's because they're human girls. They look close enough to us that we can and do find them attractive, but mermaids... mermaids are our girls if you like. Don't worry, it happens to them, too. They see human guys, and they think they're cute, or even handsome. They see one of us, and they melt right there.*

Funny, because the only thing that seemed to be melting was his brain.

"Oh my God, you have grown up so fast!" this goddess walking among men said, with the sweetest, prettiest, most perfect smile in the whole universe. For one absurdly long moment, Matt almost blurted *marry me*.

"The last time Chris showed me a picture of you two you were still this height," she continued, looking them up and down in appreciation. They were doing exactly the same. "I'm Diana, though you pro...ba...bly—Come on guys, snap out of it. I get it, you don't see many women on your side of the world, but we kinda have to hurry."

Now she was annoyed, and his heart broke into a dozen pieces.

"Is Julian okay?" Alex asked, and Matt felt a million kinds of stupid for letting his hormones take control.

"He is. His dinner turned out to be something entirely different than he expected. Come, let's go. We need to regroup and prepare for a very long night."

She turned around—her gorgeous black hair waving on her back like gentle sea waves—and guided them across the street to a parking lot.

"Entirely different?" Matt asked, blinking and breathing and swallowing once again.

"It turns out a reporter has been following little breadcrumbs leading her to Chris."

"The press knows?" Matt asked, while Alex almost threw up beside him. He grabbed Alex's arm and kept him upright.

"The press as a whole, no. She wanted Julian to give her an interview, give him a chance to answer some questions, speak his mind. You know, tell his side of the story."

"What did he do?" Alex asked in a tiny voice.

"He gave enough evasive answers and enough hints at the truth to make a few dozen versions of the story. She has enough to be a problem, but not enough to bury us beneath damning proof. In any case, if she releases her story, it will mean a lot of trouble for you, Brooksies."

She reached her car, and two minutes later, they were far away from that diner, its dark implications and the future that never would be.

Don't be so confident, Matt, he chided himself. *We can still end up dead, if not worse: in cages.*

"So we're just going back as if nothing's happened?" Alex asked from the back seat.

"Not at all. Drake has a plan needing a big distraction. A *big* one. Hopefully, this reporter will stir things up at ORCAS. Before long, that place will be a madhouse... and we'll be right there, waiting for an entrance."

"What do we have to do? And don't say hide, wait, or stay out of the way," Matt warned.

In the rearview mirror, she looked back at Alex.

"Alexander, would you like to be in a little movie?"

"What?" both brothers asked at the same time.

"We need a push to get things going at ORCAS. So get ready for your close-up."

Matt turned to look at Alex, and shrugging, they both turned to Diana. "Count us in."

* * *

"Major White, have you been watching the news?" Dr. Gaston asked, not bothering with knocking on the door to his office—though strangely respecting his rank.

This is going to be interesting…

On his computer, White had been diligently discarding each and every Chris, Christopher, Christine and Christ article he'd been reading so far, but he still had some 300 to go. And that was assuming Scott Hunter had gotten the name right.

"Doctor. If you mean the hospital's press conference, the UN assures me they're already working on a press release of their own."

"And?" she asked, her hands on her hips.

"And?" he repeated, clueless.

"What are you going to do about it?"

"Oh? I've been busy searching for the needle in the proverbial haystack, actually. But I'm sure the UN Committee is already up to speed."

"To hell with the UN. I want to know what you're doing to keep Ray safe."

He gave her time to lose steam. "I believe knowing that needs a higher security clearance than you have."

She dismissed him with a wave of the hand. "Not the details, I know that. I mean, are you aware of the dangers this will bring us? Because it's just a matter of time before someone else opens their mouth and we'll be surrounded by villagers with torches and pitchforks."

White sighed inwardly. He was good at juggling problems, it was just a matter of finding the right rhythm—or passing the balls to their rightful owners.

"Are you suggesting we move Ray to another area?"

"I don't know what I'm suggesting. That's why they pay you the big bucks. All I want to know is that Ray will be safe. That you have a contingency plan in case something goes wrong."

"I can tell you that be it by land, sea, or air, we're more than prepared to take on any issue that comes our way."

One of Scott's doctors texted. *Problems with the subject. Need expert advice.* That meant leave everything and come now.

"Dr. Gaston, I assure you, little goes on this base that I'm not aware of."

240

She narrowed her eyes as he stood.

"Promise me, Ray's safety comes first. No matter what the Pentagon wants, or what the UN wants. He stays safe."

"I promise you, no merman under my protection would be left without aid. We're not the bad guys, Doctor. We want the same thing."

She murmured something that suspiciously sounded like *I doubt that* on her way out.

How strange, he thought as he walked down to the south side. *Why wouldn't Gaston go to Forest first?* Or stranger still, what if she had but she hadn't liked his answer?

Why, Forest, do you know something I don't?

31

Promises

"Something's wrong," Andrew said to Higgs, as the older doctor turned the lights off in Ray's room, signaling it was 8:00 p.m. Dimmed blue lights illuminated the space, inviting sleep.

Gwen had already taken her place with Ray, leaving Andrew and Higgs free to fill out endless reports on how the whole underwater experiment had gone.

"You noticed it, too, huh?"

"What do you think it is? He was so eager to get into the water and then he was so tense. He still is."

"Does he look like he's talking to someone?"

Andrew paused, frowning. "You mean as if he's talking to himself?"

"No, as if he's talking to someone. Another person, so to speak."

"He looked as if he was arguing five minutes ago," Andrew said, thinking about the way Ray's hands looked poised to strangle someone. "Why, what do you think is going on?"

"I think he got bad news. He's frustrated with something he learned while we were at the pools, but I've no idea what that might be. Maybe he remembered something, or something became clear once he was at the bottom of the pool."

"His tail, maybe? He tried to jump, and he would have done some serious damage to it if we hadn't stopped him."

"Maybe. That's quite reasonable, actually. I just wish he'd talk to us, tell us what's going on. Don't get me wrong, today was monumental when it comes to communication and cooperation. I'm not taking that for granted. But I'd be lying if I said I'm happy with where things are right this moment."

Andrew looked at the monitor where he could watch Gwen serving Ray his first solid food—if that pile of mush could be called solid food—since he'd been taken to ORCAS. On the observation deck, twenty pairs of eyes watched unblinking as the merman took his first bite, perfectly holding the spoon, no less. Would wonders ever cease?

"Do you think the press getting the truth about his existence will jeopardize his life?"

"I don't know. I wonder what Ray would say if he knew. Maybe that's the bad news he got," Higgs murmured, but before Andrew could ask what he meant, the phone in the control room rang. Higgs answered without delay.

"Dr. Higgs here. Yes, one moment. It's for you." Higgs passed him the gray phone.

"Andrew here," he answered, shooting Higgs a questioning expression. Higgs just shrugged.

"Mr. Summers, I need your expert opinion," Major White said, his voice sending a shiver down Andrew's spine. He'd never really liked the guy—found him a bit creepy, in fact—but maybe that animosity stemmed from him never liking the military in general, and soldiers in particular.

"Sure, ask away."

"I'd rather we do this in person."

"Oh?" he said, now really creeped out. "Where do you want us to meet?"

"At the south wing. Can you come right away?"

"I'm processing Ray's stats from this afternoon. Does it have to be now?"

"Yes."

Something about that *yes* set the alarm bells ringing in all their red glory.

"O-kay, I'm on my way."

Hanging up, he turned to Higgs and shrugged. "White wants to talk to me right now, said something about an *expert opinion*."

"Sounds important."

Sounds creepy.

"I'll be right back, but tell me if anything interesting happens with Gwen and Ray, okay? The way things are going, I wouldn't be surprised if he suddenly asked to see the wine menu and ordered dessert."

Higgs chuckled and dismissed him with a waving hand.

It was easy to get lost in the labyrinth of hallways in the ORCAS compound, and he did have to backpedal a couple of times, but after a few minutes of getting the wrong halls, he finally managed to find the south side. Not that he knew it was the south side per se, but the two military guys told him Major White was waiting there.

I hope it's something good, he thought before the guard opened the door and let him in. White was already approaching, a grave look on his face. "This isn't good," Andrew blurted. White pretended he hadn't heard.

"Mr. Summers, thank you for coming."

"It didn't sound like I could refuse," Andrew said, shaking the man's hand. "I mean—"

"We need your help."

"—if this is about Ray and doing something you don't agree with, th—"

"—we found another one of them."

Andrew stopped, mid-sentence. He was prone to babble when a guilty conscience taunted him, or maybe it was just the general unease around authority figures, especially when they summoned him for no reason. Either way, he was surprised at White's admission, before re-processing the last fifteen seconds of this conversation.

"I'm sorry, what?"

"It's a rather complicated story—"

"Wait—someone came for Ray? For real?"

White paused, his face slightly impatient.

"We're not sure, exactly. His name is Scott. Scott Hunter."

He has a first and last name?

For a very long instant, Andrew was sure he was dreaming this whole thing up.

"He got an adverse reaction from a sedative we used to get him here. He's coming out of it, but his legs are cramping really bad. If anyone here knows about muscles and how to treat them without a scalpel, that would be you."

Andrew couldn't process the information fast enough. *Another merman? Sedative?*

Legs?!

White walked with him to another room, passing an empty fish tank. It was big enough to fit Ray into it, and the implication did nothing to ease Andrew's rapidly fraying nerves.

"What did you do to this man?" he asked right before reaching a gurney, where he found someone half the size of what he was expecting, wearing nothing but a hospital gown. He almost, almost turned to punch White in the face. "You captured a kid?"

"I'm not a kid!" the kid said between gritted teeth. Holding his knees in a tight ball, he lay on his side, glaring daggers at both men.

Andrew turned to look at White. "What the hell is going on here?"

"In all honesty, Mr. Summers, he could really use a sympathetic hand."

"Remind me to be very vocal about this after I finish here," Andrew murmured before getting closer to the bed.

"Keep your fucking hands off me," Scott warned, while his legs trembled. Around him, three men took notes and another kept recording. Useless in every sense of the word.

"Right. I'm Andrew," he introduced himself, accustomed to patients with loud mouths, including kids. "Despite the circumstances, you need help, Scott. I'm not saying it's not going to hurt, I'm just saying it's going to get better the sooner we start."

"There's nothing you can fucking do about this shit," Scott said, getting tighter somehow.

For the first time, Andrew wondered if Ray's silence was a blessing in disguise.

"Then you have nothing to lose by letting me see. I won't touch you until you let me," he promised, standing next to Scott, looking at him straight in the eye.

One minute became two, then became three. Finally, Scott took his hands from his knees and turned his face halfway to the pillow.

"Do it fast," he said, angry at Andrew, or maybe at himself.

"Okay, walk me through this. What's wrong?"

"I'm stuck," Scott mumbled, while Andrew's hand slid down Scott's leg. Tiny white and silver scales clustered in some areas, while flawless skin patched the rest. "I'm not ready to change."

"A tail…" Andrew breathed, unable to look away.

"Not if I can stop it." Scott meant that with all his soul, daring Andrew to say something different.

"Why?"

"I won't go through it here, with all these fucking morons taking pictures while the most important change in my life is happening."

Andrew remembered Ray, about to enter the pool, pretty much thinking the same as Scott. *I don't want to be someone's science project and entertainment.*

"Get everyone out of here," he told White, in the exact same way he'd told Higgs.

White turned to look at Scott, maybe considering how serious Scott was— or how much longer he could hold back the shift. Exasperated, Andrew snapped. "If you really meant Scott needed a friendly hand, that's not me. That's you."

246

"Clear the room."

Andrew blinked, seriously considering if he was dreaming.

"We're not leaving this room without Colonel Sawyer's express orders," one of the three doctors said without looking up from his tablet.

A shadow passed over White's face, maybe the physical manifestation of whatever it was that creeped Andrew out about this man.

"Fine. Privates," he said to the guards by the room. "Don't let anyone leave this room without my permission. Mr. Summers, I believe you already know the way to the pools?"

It took Andrew two seconds to understand the changing dynamic of his situation, then he turned and swept Scott up.

"What the hell do you think you're doing?" Scott yelled, pushing Andrew away.

"Taking you out, away from prying eyes, how does that sound?"

He didn't wait for Scott's response—he didn't even dare to look at the outraged faces of the doctors left behind. Dashing past the overly-serious privates, he never glanced back as he walked down the hall. He took a turn right and heard White behind.

"Turn left!"

He did and followed White's directions blindly until they reached the pools area, where Ray had been taken earlier that day. In his arms, Scott was once again a tight ball.

"I'm not going to change," the kid said with tightly closed eyes.

This kid is really going to hold it.

"I'm not going to watch," Andrew promised, finding the deepest part of the largest pool and jumping in, clothes and all.

Scott yelped in surprise, and as soon as he figured he could get away, he kicked with all his might at Andrew's chest, leaving one hell of a bruise.

"I'm not going to watch!" Andrew yelled once he resurfaced, gasping for air. He followed the rapidly moving shape underwater, before turning his back to Scott.

From the edge of the pool, White looked at him askance.

"What?" Andrew asked.

"I meant to use one of the small pools. You do realize it's going to be extremely difficult to get that kid out of this pool, right?"

Andrew turned around and saw nothing. The main pool was designed to contain large mammals, like dolphins or sea lions. Wherever Scott was, it was out of sight. He shrugged.

"I figure he'll come out when he's hungry."

Extending a hand, White helped Andrew get out. Before he took his soaked jeans off, the Major handed him a blue towel from somewhere.

"I can't believe you just let me take Scott like that," Andrew said, turning to look at the still waters. "Aren't they going to court martial you or something?"

"Let me worry about myself, Mr. Summers. It's far more important that Mr. Hunter is healthy and cooperative." Andrew looked at him with skepticism all over his face. "I'll settle with healthy," White amended.

"Why are you helping him? For real?"

White's eyes centered on one corner of the pool, and Andrew followed suit. If he looked intently enough, he could see something there. Maybe Scott. Maybe a play with the shadows.

"I'm sure you've noticed we only have two of them, and only one is willing to talk, however crass that talk is."

"You want to use the kid," Andrew said, that need to punch him coming back with a vengeance.

"Oh, he's already told me more than I could hope for. Make sure he's safe. I'll send personnel to aid you once he wants to come out. Meanwhile, I have some high authorities to deal with and explain this mess to."

Before White was out of the pool area, Andrew reached for the phone on the wall. When Forest didn't pick up in his office, he called his next best option. "Higgs? You're not going to believe this."

* * *

Are you okay? Scott? Scott?!

In the corner of the pool, Scott contemplated with fascination as his legs seamlessly blended together, the colors of his parents slowly turning his scales silver and emerald. Merfolk took the upper color of the tail from their mothers and the bottom from their fathers. In a sense, it was as if they were right there with him.

He couldn't cry underwater but his heart felt heavy with longing.

Scott!

Shut up! He snapped at Chris for ruining this precious time. *It wasn't supposed to be like this,* he explained after a minute. *I was going to be back home—*

248

where home used to be, anyway. It was going to be sunny, it was going to be just me remembering them and seeing my colors emerging just like theirs and—and—

He felt Chris's mental embrace and clung to it for dear life. He wasn't weak, he wasn't a wimpy kid; he'd been taught to do better, to be better than this, but all he wanted was to be anywhere else but here.

It's okay, Scott... We're going to be okay...

You don't know that, he admonished, used to fighting and hating himself for not being able to stop. He'd fought for so long, he didn't know how to stop anymore.

Wisely, Chris chose to change his line of reasoning.

You should try swimming, he said carefully.

Don't be an idiot, Scott answered, sinking into the corner, his eyes following the shy emergence of his lateral fins.

Come on, Andrew won't take you out, so you might as well have some fun...? It wasn't meant as a question, but Chris had no idea how to talk to him. At the very least, he wasn't treating Scott like a mindless, scared child anymore. And frankly, that was all Scott had ever asked; he just wanted respect.

Honestly? Chris went on. *We have no idea when we're getting out, let alone when they'll let you use the pool again. At the very least, enjoy this moment while you can.*

Whatever comeback Scott had brewing died under the weight of Chris's logic. A tiny voice at the back of his head whined it wasn't supposed to be like this. But if he didn't want to be treated like a child, he had to act like an adult. Taking a deep breath, Scott let his tail extend all the way to the tip. He reflexively moved it and hit the back of his head against the wall behind at the sudden rush of speed.

Don't laugh! He glared at Chris's phantom presence, while the older boy choked down his laughter.

Sorry, it's just... I kind of did the same when I first got my tail. Julian tried to tell me to take it easy and I thought I had it all under control.

You could've warned me... Scott said with resentment, and then got ready to try again.

He'd always been a good swimmer, but not even in his wildest dreams had he ever felt the exhilarating freedom of flowing through water as if he were one with it. It barely took five movements to reach the other side. The whole thing was over before he could even begin to grasp the power of his muscles.

Whoa...

That pretty much sums it up, Chris said with laughter.

I'm never getting out of here!

Knock yourself out, kid. For as long as you can.

* * *

While everyone watched Ray take his first quasi-meal in his room, Andrew and Higgs had the spectacular view of the silvery dash zigzagging the entire pool. "He's getting good," Andrew commented, gratefully taking the dry clothes Higgs had brought. Outside the pool area, four privates kept guard. "Can you imagine how fast Ray can go?"

"I'm far more concerned about what Ray might do when he finds out about him," Higgs said, dragging Andrew's attention away from watching Scott effortlessly gliding through the water.

"You think we should tell him?" Andrew asked, putting on a blue t-shirt.

"Not right away, but at some point. We need to know if they're related, at the very least. You said he talked to you, right?"

"Oh yeah, he certainly had absolutely no restraints. He's also a very distrustful kid."

"We'll have to earn his trust, then." Higgs walked to the edge of the pool, squatting. "Scott?"

The little merman turned in the opposite direction and swam to the farthest corner.

That went well.

"Bet you're getting hungry, son. Whenever you're ready, we'll be right back." Standing up, Higgs grabbed Andrew by the arm and turned him towards the door.

"What the hell? We can't leave him alone."

"We'll see him from the video room," Higgs said, quietly. "Giving him space to think things over and calm down might be what's best for everyone. Besides, I need to talk with Nate about this."

Andrew swallowed hard. That meant he was stuck with telling Gwen.

May God have mercy on White.

* * *

Nathan had barely entered his office when Higgs practically ambushed him.

"There you are!" his best friend said with eternal optimism.

"I'm so sorry for not—"

"I'm sure you've enough on your plate right now," he answered with a dismissing hand. "But are you aware we have a new guest swimming around?"

Nathan looked up at his friend, surprised. "White told you?"

"You knew?" Higgs asked, all smiles gone. "And is that a bruise on your jaw?"

"Yes, it doesn't matter. I've just found out about Scott Hunter. Tell me he's not dead, Higgs. Tell me he's not dying, not crippled, not going to be scarred for life."

"Far from it, he's swimming about the main pool, while Andrew keeps an eye on him from the video room. Now, what exactly's going on here?"

Behind Higgs's tall frame, Major White entered, as serious as ever. "I would like to know the answer to that, too. Thermal cameras have been disabled by your command."

For one glorious moment, Nathan imagined knocking down that military face a couple of times. But then again, he couldn't afford to be jailed for the next few days.

"I'm cleaning up your mess, that's what I'm doing," Nathan said instead, with enough animosity to have Higgs scrunch his forehead.

"You've been talking to them," White stated, his tone carefully neutral.

"They're pissed off we'd shoot at a kid."

"Is that how you got that?" Higgs asked, looking at Nathan's jaw, where Drake's punch was already a few shades of purple.

"They thought I'd ordered it, yes."

"They don't know everything that's going on here, then," White answered, surprised.

"They know enough." Nathan imagined Diana Lombardi's clearance and how much more intel merfolk would gather. "We need to give Scott back to them. They know Ray has too many eyes on him for us to vanish him into thin air, but Scott is still a blank to the UN's radar, not to mention the public's."

"I'm afraid he's on the Pentagon's radar, Doctor. They're already planning on moving him in the next twenty-four hours. Maybe sooner."

Nathan felt the air rushing from his lungs, leaving him weak. He leaned against his desk; the possibilities of how merfolk were going to take this—of how they might retaliate in the worst case scenario—were all a headache waiting to happen.

"Why did you have to shoot him? He's a kid, for crying out loud!"

"It wasn't me," White said in that steel way of his. "But I should've stopped it. In any case, doctors, maybe you're not seeing the larger picture here." For the first time, Nathan noticed that the man looked tired, too. "We might have a hostile race gathering information about our species, living under our seas, masquerading as one of us. I thought Scott had been sent to spy on us, disguised as a teenager, not that he was an actual lost boy running from social services. The Pentagon doesn't like the blank spaces Scott's revealed. Whatever's going on, it doesn't make sense."

"Sawyer's already told me they don't take good care of their own."

"You talked to Colonel Sawyer? About this?" Now White looked alarmed.

"Well, I thought you'd shot the kid, leaving me little choice but to go to the next reasonable person to ask for help."

"There's nothing reasonable about Sawyer," White said, heartfelt. "He ordered Scott shot, and he's doing everything in his power to drag him further in. Listen, Forest. If you're in talks with these beings, tell them to come clean. With you, with the UN, with anyone they choose. The Pentagon has too many unanswered questions, and they won't hesitate to use Scott to get your precious merfolk out in the open."

With that, White turned and left, looking like a man on a mission to stop Armageddon.

"So, you disabled the thermal cameras, huh?" Higgs asked after a moment. "Care to elaborate on that?"

32

Falling Pieces

The last time Nathan Forest had looked at the clock, it had been 10:46 p.m. Between the UN calls, the Pentagon calls, and getting Higgs up to speed, his watch suddenly read 2:02 a.m. and he had no idea where the time had gone.

His phone rang once more, bringing him back to Earth. The Head of the UN Committee was calling again, and although he liked Ms. Goransson, he personally wanted to check on Scott first.

"Ma'am?"

"Dr. Forest, I've been receiving troubling news regarding another merman." The sole woman in the UN Committee spoke with enough briskness to make Nathan think he was in deep trouble. Nathan hadn't asked Diana if merfolk did or didn't want the UN to know about Scott, and repeated calls to her had gone straight to voicemail.

"Does the US government have another one?" Ms. Goransson pressed, not too happy about this new development.

"Officially, no."

"Do I need to ask off-the-record?"

"They have one more, a thirteen-year-old kid who ran away from the US foster care system. To tell you the truth, at this point, we have no idea what's going on."

"If the US doesn't confirm they have him, there's nothing this Committee can do. If they can get away with hiding a second subject, it won't be long before they get greedy and want the first one, too. Look for a loophole, Doctor, something to get Ray out of your country. He's not safe there anymore."

"Yes, ma'am, I'll find a way."

* * *

Gwen's salad remained untouched as her eyes followed the dashing silvery tail on the screen. She wasn't hungry anymore.

It was close to 5:00 a.m. and she had just changed shifts with Higgs, leaving Ray in his capable hands. Nothing had been out of place with her colleague, but Andrew had been a different story. By the time he'd finished explaining about Scott, she'd been seeing red again. Before she'd had the chance to go after White, Andrew had redirected her to the pool area. Seeing this kid swimming gave her hope that Ray would get well soon, too. If only she could secure their survival somehow.

Nathan entered the video room where she and Andrew debated what to do.

"Major White says the Pentagon wants to move Scott to another facility," Nathan said, closing his eyes and massaging his temples. "Officially, he doesn't exist, and what does exist about him paints him as a ward of the state. No matter how I look at this problem, this kid's screwed."

"That's because you're looking at it in an official manner. We need to think outside the box on this one," she said. "Ever since Bill told the world Ray's real, I've been saying we need to do something about it. Something drastic."

Nathan smiled as if she was joking. "Forest," she snapped. "I'm talking about breaking Ray free, along with Mr. Little Merman here."

"There's a reason why I'm looking at this in an official capacity, Gaston," he answered, seemingly exhausted. "No one gets shot that way."

"I'm serious," she said.

"Ray cannot swim," he pointed out. "Even if we opened the wide doors into the ocean, he would sink, get an infection, and die a slow, agonizing death."

"Then we don't take him into the ocean. Help me out here," she pleaded. "What's at stake is way higher than the two of us. What about the UN?"

"If the US denies his existence, the UN cannot cry foul. There's absolutely no proof he exists, much less that he's a prisoner."

"Forget about proof for now, can they get him an asylum thing or something? I'm more than happy to shout this to the four winds. You said the UN's going to give a press conference later today confirming Ray's existence. Let them confirm Scott's as well. Let the Pentagon deny all they want, and in the uproar that will follow, we'll sneak our mermen to safety."

Nathan went quiet, thinking through her words. She turned to look at Scott Hunter through the video, reaching one corner and turning, like a caged lion in a zoo. She was ready to go into that pool and jump in just to tell the kid that everything was going to be all right, but Nathan would probably stop her. Besides, the fewer people the Pentagon thought knew about Scott, the better.

"What are we going to do, Nathan?" she asked. She felt so out of her depth in this whole business of world leaders and international politics.

"We don't have the resources to pull this off. But I might know someone who does. If she would answer her damn phone."

Nathan stood up, ready to leave. "You should go back to Ray. Andrew will watch over Scott. I can't promise you anything, Gwen, but start preparing to leave one way or another."

With renewed energy, Gwen walked back to Ray's room. No one was going to mess with her mermen. No one.

* * *

It took Kate a couple of minutes to understand what was different in her hotel room. It was the light. Sunrise had come almost an hour ago, chasing away the darkness from her window, and stating she'd been working all night without even noticing.

On Skype, Jeff yawned loudly, echoing how she felt.

"Whatever this guy is hiding, he's sure good at it," Jeff said a minute later.

They'd been looking into Julian Brooks and Brooks Inc. for hours. Anything suspicious, anything remotely newsworthy, was fair game. Right now, they were hunting for anything just plain weird, and the kids' adoptions were one deep source of suspicious activity.

Calling up her Brooks folder, she opened one of her many Julian Brooks images, this one showed him at a gala in New York. A charity event, maybe? He looked straight at the camera, an almost hidden smile playing about his lips, his blue eyes piercing her soul. For all her research, the man remained a mystery. Where did he come from? Why had he decided to adopt three orphaned kids? And what had he done when he'd discovered his eldest wasn't even human?

What do they want? Clean oceans? World domination?

"I'm telling you, Jeff, something big's coming. He wants this attention of ours elsewhere, so he's going to give us something bigger."

"You seriously think he'll give us that video he talked about? About that thirteen-year-old?"

"Or something equally good," she answered, taking her computer glasses off and rubbing her eyes. She'd replayed Julian Brooks's interview a thousand times in her head by this point. Hell, she'd given her boss a minute-by-minute description of every word, every blink, every subtle insinuation and outstanding clue she'd gathered up.

"Julian Brooks wants to use us," she said, repeating Ken's words of ten hours ago. "And there's nothing wrong with that if we can use him back. He knows we know the truth, but he also knows we'll be careful with it. We hardly have anything to back this up. Hell, I wouldn't even be surprised if he has a Christopher double stashed away in a closet just in case somebody asks too many questions."

"Oh, here's something interesting," Jeff said. "One of my sources says the UN's called an official press conference in two hours."

"No way," she breathed. Julian had told her the UN would do that, and if he'd been truthful about this, he was damned right about the merkid. *My God, people are going to love to hate this!*

"What about ORCAS's building number six? Any activity there?"

"Nothing I can really pin down. But ORCAS isn't exactly Sea World, you know. They don't have all that much going on in general. I've asked around and a couple of guys told me that as a research facility, they could very well house a merman or two."

"It's worth trying to find out what's going on there. I'm sure I can manage to get in later today if I offer some free publicity to their funding drive."

Closing her eyes, she moved her head side to side, trying to dispel the tension accumulated there since she'd checked in at the same hotel in which Julian was hiding away.

"Ha! The whole internet's ablaze with the merman story. I'm telling you, I can barely keep up with it. I've no idea what I'm going to do when it's us who get into the eye of the hurricane!"

"We have a bombshell, Jeff. Heck, we have a nuclear warhead in our hands, but we have to use it wisely. When we publish this, we'll make a powerful enemy of Julian Brooks, not to mention our credibility's at stake if he throws the ball back. We have to be airtight in our findings. Ken was very adamant about it for good reason."

"Kate?"

"Hmm?"

"Has it occurred to you that if Julian Brooks is really a merman, you've just been the first reporter in the history of mankind to have an interview with a non-human species?"

She froze. Goosebumps broke on her arms all the way to the nape of her neck. "That would be something, hmm?" she said with a nervous laugh. For the first time since Jeff had shown her that merman video ten days ago, she realized she had no idea how monumental this was.

Her phone chirped with a new e-mail notification from *concerned_citizen99*. Frowning, she read the subject. *Shooting and capture of a merman.*

She jumped in her seat. "Jeff! I have the new video!"

"Share your screen!"

She did before hitting *play*, and together, they were the first human beings to watch it.

The video had been taken on a cellphone on board a large boat, with the sun barely rising on the horizon. A man all in black and a hood signaled something further out to sea, and a second appeared with what looked to be a rifle.

Whoever was filming moved to the front of that ship, where the tail of a big fish—or a small mermaid—could be seen disappearing below the water.

"Holy Crap, did they just shoot him?" Jeff asked a moment later. By the time the six-minute video was over, she had her hand over her mouth.

"That was brutal!" Jeff exclaimed. She simply nodded.

"When—when can you publish this?" she asked with shaking fingers as she replayed the whole thing.

"As soon as Ken gives the okay. Once this hits the airways, though, we'll have a riot."

She couldn't agree more.

33

The Best Lies

This is breaking news.

If you are just tuning in, a new video has surfaced on the net courtesy of Veritas Co., depicting the capture of another merman in open sea. We advise the footage you're about to see might be disturbing to some viewers. Details are still unclear about who took the video, or why is it coming now, but experts assure us that the footage is real.

As you can see, an unnamed crew member yells to his companions to be careful before shooting at the unmistakable tail. Even with the quality of the cellphone video, you can tell it's a child-sized merman they pulled from the sea. It's uncertain if he's breathing or not.

Theories abound on the internet about the possible whereabouts of this and the earlier discovered merman, pointing to the Oceanic Research, Conservancy, and Atmospherics Society, or ORCAS as it is best known, as a possible place where they could be placed and held in captivity.

In a press conference by the UN earlier today, Spokesperson Diana Lombardi denied any knowledge of another merman being found and being detained under the protection of the United Nations. This has angered several groups clamoring for the release of all information regarding the first merman found last week.

All findings related to the first captive are being treated as classified material, but the UN Committee supervising the humane treatment of this being has reassured everyone involved that no harm is being done in the name of science or for any other reason.

Several sources have claimed the merman in this new video is already deceased and has been shipped to labs in the United States. At this hour, we cannot confirm or deny the veracity of any of these statements. Stay with us as we bring you the latest in this developing story.

* * *

"That was perfect," Matt said with approval, for the first time feeling things were moving in the right direction. Things were going to happen now. Great things.

"I still think the star of the hour is Alexander," Diana said, making the youngest merman flush scarlet at the sudden attention. "I couldn't have faked being shot like that. The way you just jumped out of the water and fell into the ocean... brilliant!"

Matt had never known Alex could turn so many shades of red so fast. *Careful there, Squid, you might even end up changing your tail's color.* He clapped his brother's back and laughed at the Squid's discomfort.

"The cameraman wasn't too shabby, either," Diana added, making Matt blush in an instant. She patted the top of his head, then went to the kitchen of their hotel suite to hunt down a cup of coffee. She was getting ready to leave for a few more press conferences, and he couldn't wait to see them.

On the couch, Julian changed the channel, where the video was being played again. It showed Alex being shot at and dragged into the boat, apparently lifeless. Shaky and blurry enough that Alex's face couldn't really be made out, but clear enough to create an uproar. It had taken them fifteen attempts to get those six minutes right, every one of them worth it.

On the TV, the news station was getting calls from viewers, the current caller stating that horrible, despicable things were being done to the little merkid in the video at ORCAS building number six.

"Was that one of us?" Diana asked, coming behind them.

"I don't think so," Drake said, standing by the door frame to his room. "It's catching fire all on its own. What do you have on the net, Alex?"

Eternally glued to his screen, the Squid whistled. "It's catching fire, all right. Our little production now has more than two million views and counting. Veritas Co. servers can barely survive the onslaught of traffic."

"Show them a kid being shot, and everyone will want your head," Diana said with approval.

"What about Kate Banes? Is she saying anything?" Julian asked, and Matt's optimism came down a notch.

"Nothing," Alex informed.

"They're strangely quiet," Drake said, exchanging looks with Julian.

"But that's good, right?" Matt asked, looking between the two adults in the room.

"Maybe..." Julian answered. "Maybe we're just delaying another storm." He changed the channel once more, and stopped to listen the news station spin on this tale.

"People have started flocking to the ORCAS facility, while calls have been flooding several news agencies, political figures, and all kinds of wildlife organizations all over the country to demand answers about the treatment of these underwater beings," the newsman said. It wasn't more than fifty people, but it was still early in the day. Their plan was working.

"Well, Drake, you wanted a big diversion," Diana said with a smile. "I don't think it can get bigger."

"People are starting to move in the right direction," Julian agreed. "But the toughest part is still to come."

"Don't worry, Dad," Matt said confidently, for the first time in ages feeling like calling Julian *Dad* again. "We won't let you down."

* * *

It was past 10:30 a.m., but Scott refused to emerge. His stomachs were grumbling rather loudly, and he was getting sleepier by the second, but he'd rather die than surrender, a fact that might actually come true if these people were growing impatient.

They won't take you out by force, Chris insisted, sounding sleepy himself. He'd been up all night, talking about everything and nothing to keep both their minds in a happier place.

Shut up, Scott said, swimming lazily from one corner to the next, always keeping an eye on the surface, waiting for the humans to return.

Sure. No problem. All I'm saying is, you will have to get out at some point, and Higgs and Andrew are the best humans you can do this with. Tell them you were kidnapped and... you know, tell them the truth.

It sounded so reasonable when Chris said it. Sure, it wasn't every day a merkid would come up to them and say, *please help me, I don't want to be dissected like a frog! Take me to the sea!*

The thought sank in after a few seconds.

Wait, would they actually take me to the sea? Scott asked, for one second feeling giddy with excitement.

I think they'll have a lot of questions first.

It was hard keeping things straight when all he wanted to do was to fall asleep, so Scott stopped in the middle of the pool, and slowly raised his head out of the water to know if they were back. The whole room was empty, but that didn't mean they didn't have eyes on him.

Come on, Scott. What's the worst that can happen?

If it so important, why don't you open your mouth and tell them they kidnapped me?

He could feel Chris chuckling, and made sure to send some dark vibes his way.

Tell them the truth, Scott. Tell them what you want, too, even if they're powerless to make it real.

Scott wasn't convinced. *How about something more personal, huh? We can say I'm your younger brother.*

Chris didn't laugh this time. He considered Scott's proposition.

I mean, Scott went on. *It will earn us sympathy, and it's less complicated than trying to explain how individuals abandon our underwater society and have children who then get orphaned and taken care of by a special Council. You know, basically spilling all our secrets.*

Chris laughed and Scott smirked, knowing he was damn right. *It does beg the question, why exactly do you keep your mouth shut?*

Because you can't tell secrets if you don't open your mouth, Chris answered with a sigh. *Matt calls it the* shut up and die *clause. Your parents never told you that?*

Scott shook his head, circling the pool and spotting at least three cameras pointing in his direction. *They were confident we were never going to be caught. Besides, do you honestly think I could keep my mouth shut? I'd rather die than have my voice silenced!*

It filled him with pride that Chris found his words true and important. Scott's parents had fled an oppressive regime under the sea, and they'd be damned if their son was going to follow vows of silence in a misguided attempt to piss off his enemies.

What did your parents do? Chris asked, his twentieth idea at keeping a conversation going. *For a living, I mean?*

Treasure hunters. They looked for sunken ships, so most of the time, they were under water.

Swimming around ship graveyards was a dangerous job, no matter how adept one was at breathing underwater.

Do you know what happened to them?

Roy Wallace happened to them, Scott said, getting to his corner and letting himself sink. He had to get out of the pool eventually, he wasn't stupid, but there was one little thing he had to figure out first: how to turn his tail back into legs.

What did he do?

My parents liked to be anonymous in their findings, so Roy was the public face of their company. They finally found the kind of treasure they'd always wanted. I think it was valued somewhere around $20m.

His scales were beautiful, and he didn't want to see them go. In all honesty, he didn't want to get out of the water at all. Maybe the humans would get a clue and let him stay.

That's a lot of money, Chris said, and Scott shook his head at that statement coming from someone who probably made that in a month's salary. *What happened?*

Roy got greedy, of course. Problem is, I don't know if he knew my parents' true origins. He came to the house with one hell of a knife, and I ran. It took me a few days but I finally pieced things together when my parents were declared lost at sea. If Roy Wallace knew what I was, I was screwed. I took Hunter as my last name and started my trip away from home. Well, anywhere but home, that's what mom used to say when she talked about running away, just in case. No ties, no regrets, she'd say. Just keep going, and keep your home in your heart, where it will always travel with you.

Scott—Chris said.

How do you turn this thing into legs, Scott asked before Chris could go all mushy on him. It had been four years now since he'd heard his mother's voice or seen his father's smile. He didn't need pity when he remembered them, he needed to be practical.

Scott, you don't have to—

How, Brooks? I don't have all day.

Okay, okay, it's easy. But before you get out, we have to get our story straight. You'll talk to Higgs and Andrew. Tell them whatever you want about your life, just add me to the details. I'll play along with whatever you say.

Scott shrugged and then imagined what life would have been like if he'd gotten a real older brother. Easier, he knew, and definitely not lonely, as things had been.

Now, follow my thoughts, Chris said, opening his mind, letting him sense Chris's experiences. *Get a feel for what you're supposed to do with your tail.*

In his mind, Scott saw Chris concentrating, imagining a straight line cutting through his tail, making it two legs, his fin becoming feet. His scales faded from vibrant blue to silver, to white, until they became skin.

Picture it, Scott. Just will your tail to be legs the same way you will your body to move. It might take a few minutes, but you'll feel the tear at the back of your tail. Don't fight it.

Taking a deep breath, Scott closed his eyes. As exhilarating and exciting his first shift had been, he had bigger problems to solve. Mainly how to get the hell out of here, which would invariably need legs and feet, and other little details— like clothes. Sighing, he let his mind go blank for a moment and then pictured his current body. He imagined the length of his tail getting smaller, the tips of his tail becoming his toes. On his sides, he willed his lateral fins to flatten themselves against his body, and when the tear at the back of his tail started, his mind rushed into it, losing his concentration.

Ouch! he exclaimed, opening his eyes and seeing his tail still there. All of it.

Don't go too fast, Chris warned. *You're doing it right, just don't rush it. Your muscles have to re-form into legs, and it takes a few minutes to get used to your new sensory inputs.*

Frustrated, Scott tried again, impatient to get this done. He went through all the steps once more, and when the separation started, kept his eyes closed and took it easy. Once he let it flow at its own pace, he felt a tingling sensation, and then cold water surrounded his old body, his legs feeling tight and itchy.

It will pass. Now, ask for help.

Getting out of the pool should have been easier, but although Scott had no problem getting out of the water and onto the edge, his legs wouldn't readily support him upright. He fell to his knees, hard, and gritted his teeth in silence. He was not going to scream.

Although he wasn't cold after basically spending twelve hours underwater, he did feel exposed by being naked. Hurriedly, he found a towel and dried himself. He had to sit down after five minutes of standing, his back protesting the abuse. Another five minutes went by before the door opened, the smell of food reaching him with such strength, he started salivating at once.

Traitor, he thought, looking at his body, and turning in time to see Andrew entering the pool area.

"We were starting to wonder how you were doing down there," Andrew said with a cordial smile, one that Scott didn't return.

"I'm Scott Hunter, and I've been kidnapped."

* * *

Drake passed the binoculars to Julian and nodded in approval. Although their eyesight was excellent underwater and good enough on the surface, long distances were as much a blurry mess as for humans. Through the lenses, though, things seemed to be shaping up nicely.

About 200 people were gathered outside ORCAS, enough for Major White to send a dozen privates to the perimeter. That meant a dozen privates who weren't watching Chris or Scott.

264

"A few hundred more and we'll move," Drake said, confident in his plan.

"I'm not sure if I should feel grateful to these people for caring about us, or just for being the best camouflage we could hope for."

"Both. There's no reason to pick one, right?" Drake said with a smirk. "But you do have a point. I wouldn't have thought humans would give a damn. One or two, sure, but a mob? In our favor? Never."

"Speaking of our favor, we'll have to deal with Veritas Co. at some point."

"Well, the cat is out of the bag—or should I say *the fish is out of the water* regarding our existence. I think they'd be thrilled if we give them a steady trickle of information about us. Help them prepare the world as a whole. Coming out without coming out, you know?"

"Maybe… I just don't like that it's my family on the line. If it were only me…"

"It's just a matter of throwing off their theory about Chris being the merman. We'll figure it out once your son's safe and sound with us again. And you know, if this fails, maybe giving *Ray* a real name and a story would be in his best interests."

Let's not go there… Julian thought, a dense black cloud forming over his thoughts.

"One thing at a time," Drake said with a knowing glance. "Diana should be done with her press conferences in about an hour, then she'll take her place as our designated pilot. Until then, let's sit tight and monitor the situation."

"I just—" Julian's response was interrupted by his phone. "Mireya?" he asked as he answered. His friend and Council colleague went straight to the point.

"Julian, the City has reached a verdict. You're not going to believe it."

34

Emergency Exit

White felt himself sinking in politics. Although the High Command was not happy with Colonel Sawyer's handling of Scott Hunter's apprehension, they were quite interested in what could be learned from the merkid. Sawyer had already painted the benefits of kidnapping the thirteen-year-old boy: from his biology to whatever they could get out of his mind, this kid was the key to understanding their enemy, even to bait it into the open.

They were missing the big picture.

Taking a turn left, he walked through the ORCAS hallways at a brisk pace. There was another group in the High Command who wanted a more silent approach, one where ensuring allies was more likely than ensuring enemies. They were the only reason White hadn't been taken out of the operation when he'd ordered Scott into the pool last night, but Sawyer had pointed out the incident as indicative of poor leadership and not playing nicely with others.

He turned a right, where two privates saluted him, and kept walking.

White was a big believer in keeping your friends close and your enemies closer. He had no solid information to guess where merfolk would fall, but he knew beyond a doubt that targeting a kid was a sure way to ruining everything.

Ten years from now—or fifty, or a hundred—people would look back on this date and judge them for the decisions taken in this place, and everything in White's gut told him to do whatever he had to do to keep Scott alive.

He entered Forest's office without knocking first.

"Sawyer's on his way to take command," he said by way of greeting. Forest was in the middle of a call, which he quickly brought to a close.

"The UN won't act on something the US government hasn't made public," the doctor said without missing a beat.

"Scott Hunter doesn't exist, Forest. The US government can't argue about losing something they never had."

"What do you propose?"

"I'm merely pointing out certain political issues. I don't know if you've noticed, but we're having a security problem right now. And this place is full of security holes. If anything were to happen, if you have any means to tell your new friends anything, you won't get a better time."

"I understand."

"Good. I'll do my damnest to hold Sawyer back. For what I've heard, he's all set to move both Ray and Scott under the disguise that there's a mob out there. The more people come, the easier it would be for him. I don't have to tell you this, Forest, but you're running out of time."

* * *

For someone his size, the kid sure knew how to eat. Andrew could watch him for hours, devouring everything and anything that crossed his path.

The best thing he could come up with for clothing had been one of his own t-shirts and some shorts, which looked six sizes bigger than Scott's lanky frame. Somehow, the kid still managed to look dignified, and Andrew would never even dare to chuckle.

"You should—" he started, and Scott froze in mid-bite, looking as if one wrong word would break their fragile trust. "—have more water. Here, let me refill it for you."

They'd moved from the pool area into the cafeteria. White had banned anyone from entering—inciting a five-minute riot from hungry people—and the same four privates who had guarded Scott the entire night guarded them again now.

True to his promise, Andrew refilled the glass of water and brought it back. All he'd gotten from the kid were a couple of evasive answers or more questions to his own, but when it was clear Scott's stomachs were empty—loud and embarrassing—Andrew had found a common ground in food. Scott was cleaning up his third hamburger while Andrew slowly chewed through his second. It wasn't a competition, after all, and he doubted he could beat the kid, anyway.

"Are you always this hungry?" Andrew asked, sipping his orange juice.

"Not like this… But I went through my first shift with an empty stomach and swam for fourteen hours. What do you think?"

Chew, chew. Sip. Chew. Glare.

268

"I'm on your side here, kid."

"It's Scott. I'm not a kid." He glared again.

"Sorry. Is there anything else I can help you with, Scott? Besides food? Do you want to sleep? Maybe take a shower?"

Thoughtful chew…

Well, that's progress.

"You would really let me sleep?"

"I could use some sleep myself. It's been twenty-six hours since I woke up yesterday, and I'm sure you haven't been having fun these past two days."

Andrew's phone chirped with a message, and he ignored it. He'd been getting constant messages for the past hour.

"There are plenty of beds around," Andrew went on, while Scott ate the final bite. He gulped the rest of the water, and then stood up with the empty glass. The privates moved as one, all ready to tackle him at the slightest provocation.

"I'm thirsty," he told everyone, but when he moved, he bumped into the table and almost fell. Andrew caught him.

"I'm fine," Scott said between gritted teeth but sat down anyway.

"Having trouble with your legs?" Andrew asked with concern.

"It'll pass. I just need to get used to them again. My equilibrium's off, that's all."

Like growing up too fast, Scott's brain had to re-adjust to new dimensions. He wondered if Ray would have trouble standing once he went back to legs. He wondered if Ray was always this hungry. The thoughts kept piling up in his mind.

"Here, let me get you the water before you make our four friends nervous."

This time, the kid's glare went directly to the soldiers, who stoically ignored it.

While he refilled it, a call came, this time from Forest.

"We're still in the cafeteria and he's still breathing, if that's what's worrying you," he told Nathan, turning to look at Scott, who had slumped in the chair and closed his eyes. From here, it was plainly clear the kid was barely keeping awake.

"There's a potential mob outside," Nathan said in all seriousness. "Major White's ordered an evacuation of all non-essential personnel. He's arranging what to do with Ray and Scott now."

269

"You can't be serious. Whatever place White chooses, it's going to be wrong for them."

"I already have the UN scouting for a place for Ray. As long as the Pentagon denies knowing about Scott, it's too risky to do anything for him. It might land him somewhere worse. We'll have to trust White on this one."

"Hell no," Andrew whispered, walking further away in the empty cafeteria. "And I'm not even talking about myself. Do you seriously think Scott is going to trust the man who shot him? They will have to knock him out to get him to follow White's orders."

"It wasn't White. Look, I'm not saying I like it, I'm saying I don't have jurisdiction over Scott. White wants to hurry the hell up before Colonel Sawyer gets here. I don't even think he's taking the mob seriously, but I don't want to risk it either—with the mob or Sawyer."

"Look, Nathan, wherever Ray goes, Scott goes. It's that simple."

"You're preaching to the choir here. In any case, be ready for an evacuation. If that crowd gets in, no one is going to be safe."

* * *

Kate's grand plan to offer some press coverage of ORCAS died a sudden death as soon as she reached the place. ORCAS building number six had turned into a media circus.

Several news stations were covering the story, not because they had any assurances that a merman—or two—were being held captive there, but because more than a thousand people and counting thought they did and were demanding answers right away.

FREE THE MERMAID! read the first message, followed by t-shirts and hand-made protest signs denouncing the government, the *savage scientists*, and the evil corporations polluting the seas. All well and interesting, except for a current of animosity palpable in the air. Everyone was waiting for something to happen—everyone including herself.

If she'd had any doubts Julian's information was true, the military guys patrolling the perimeter were all the confirmation she needed. ORCAS was not designed as a fortress, and they knew it. Too many holes, too few barriers. Some news crews had gone over the perfectly green lawn to get better angles, and as the cameras moved, so did the protesters, gaining ground by the minute.

A couple of helicopters flew low, at least one from a local station. The second, no doubt military, landed somewhere behind the building, and a few minutes later flew away.

I wonder who arrived?

On the street, more people were coming, along with police in full anti-riot armor.

"The American people have the right to know the truth!" a man with shaggy hair and shaggier intentions told the crowd over a megaphone. "If we're being invaded by creatures of the sea, we need to know the truth!"

A dozen people heckled, others just kept walking towards the entrance, while a few mingled to hear him out. She laughed. If creatures from the sea were invading them, they wouldn't go for open war; they'd infiltrate the world like Christopher Brooks had, where he would play the human game to perfection. Money and connections were a far better approach than swimming naked, attacking with seashells.

I have to find out the truth about your son, Mr. Brooks... And the truth about yourself.

* * *

The faint sound of a helicopter made Chris, Gwen, and Higgs look up at the ceiling.

What's going on? Chris asked Julian, while Higgs went through his vitals, a worried expression on his face.

We're getting ready to move, but so are the humans.

As usual, it was hard to keep anxiety a secret when Chris's heart monitor beeped it for Higgs and Gwen to know every beat.

"It's just a helicopter," Gwen said, putting her phone away. Chris bet that if she had a heart monitor, it would go neck to neck with his. Higgs was doing a better job at hiding his concern, but the truth was, all three of them were on edge.

Higgs's phone rang, and the man took the call on the corner. A minute later, he came back.

"You know, Ray," Higgs said while he placed his hand on Chris's shoulder. "Things are getting tense in here. Both Dr. Forest and Major White agree it might not be safe anymore. We might need to move you in a hurry. How about if we prepare for that, huh?"

Chris blinked. There was nothing he could do but to be wheeled out of there.

"We'll need to get a portable monitor," Gwen pointed out.

"It won't hurt to have him covered," Higgs said, "in case someone not supposed to see him crosses his path. Of course, if we have to move him out, a smaller gurney would be more practical."

The three of them turned to look at Chris's tail, the reason why his gurney was so long.

"If you roll to your side..." Gwen suggested, unsure. Chris could only bend his tail so far with the cast and his still healing wound. If he tightened into a ball by hugging his upper tail, he would gain a few more inches, but no matter how he worked this problem, at least part of his tail was going to dangle.

Unless I shift it a little... Shifting only the tip of his tail into feet was impossible since tails shifted from the base of the hip to the tip, not the other way around. But he could contract the cells on his tail, making it smaller.

He nodded to Gwen, and between Higgs and her, they managed to get him sideways. While she helped him with his lateral fins and directed him to bend slowly, Higgs went down to detach the gurney's extra half.

Dad? These people are getting serious about moving me.

That's okay, Chris. We're getting serious about it, too.

* * *

On her phone, Gwen watched terrified, seeing how the ORCAS perimeter was being invaded by curious idiots. Part of her was sure nothing was going to happen, that Major White would keep them safe, that no one was going to crash into a research facility in some misguided attempt to rescue a merman.

But part of her also knew things could go very wrong, very fast.

All non-essential personnel had evacuated already, and the empty windows on the observation deck were a sure sign of how messed up this whole day was.

"Higgs, it's just a matter of time before someone gets in," she said, while her friend and colleague covered Ray's tail with a blue fabric used to keep dolphins and other sea mammals wet. "Where's Nathan?" she asked, frustrated.

"I'm sure he has his plate full right now," Higgs answered rather bluntly. He wasn't smiling, wasn't his optimistic self. And that, more than anything, told her how wrong things could already be. "Besides, the media is playing this worse than it actually is. They always do," he added dismissively.

Like watching a tennis tournament, Ray kept looking at each of them, waiting to have his fate decided. Gwen felt her heart sink. *I'm so sorry, Ray, you shouldn't even be hearing this!* She had no idea what was going on with Scott, but she couldn't voice her concerns about that kid either. Ray didn't need that.

"Okay, what's the easiest way to get out of here?" she asked, unconsciously searching for her car keys in her pocket.

"Parking lot, basement two, where an ambulance can meet with us," Higgs said without a second thought. "We could also go for one of the research boats, but we'd need someone who knows how to pilot. And we would also need Major White's permission to clear the coast."

"If White sends his minions to help us get Ray out, I'm all for it."

"You do realize that all security is out there, trying to prevent them getting to us, right? We're going to be fine, Gwen. Ray's going to be fine. Too many people want him safe, including the mob out there."

"What about my car?" she suggested, ignoring Higgs's stupid attempt at making her feel better.

"I'm not sur—"

Whatever Higgs wanted to say, got cut short by his phone.

"It's Nathan again," he said before answering.

On his gurney, Ray looked nervous. Not scared exactly, not in the way she would be if she were in his position, but at least their patient understood they were in grave danger.

After a few exchanges, Higgs hung up. "Nathan says Colonel Sawyer has just arrived to take command from White."

"What? What the hell does that mean for us?"

"He says that—"

This time, the interruption came from the door. A man wearing black riot gear walked into the room, making the whole thing way too real. Under his protective mask, Gwen wondered if his eyes had widened at seeing Ray for the first time.

"You need to evacuate now."

"We can't just leave—" Gwen started.

"We need an ambulance—" Higgs added, swiftly covering Ray's entire body.

"You're getting a medevac, ma'am."

"A helicopter?" she asked, turning to look at Higgs who was nodding in approval. This was better than trying to get an ambulance in and out.

"The only place a helicopter can land is in the east garden," Higgs pointed out. Behind the newcomer, she could hear someone running.

"But people will be flooding that any minute now if they aren't already there," she said and turned to look at the man.

"Let us worry about that, Doctor. We have to leave now."

"What about the other doctors?" Higgs asked, putting the rails back on the gurney.

"He's the reason they're here," the man pointed at Ray's covered form. "My orders are to evacuate. All I know is that the staff is boarding a bus escorted by police. Those people out there aren't looking for a peaceful resolution."

Gwen put her hands on the cold metal, and along with the officer, they started to move Ray, picking up speed as they reached the hall. They turned left and then right, and by the time they reached the elevator, three more guards were helping them move along. Before the elevator doors closed, Higgs stepped out.

"What are you doing?!" she yelled, her heart in her throat.

"I need to find Nathan. I'll meet you wherever they're taking Ray, okay?"

"What? No! Nathan's a big guy, and—"

The elevator doors closed, and she had the insane need to hit *open* and give Higgs a piece of her mind. She would, she knew, once Ray was in a safe place.

"Where's the helicopter going to take us?" she asked the man, fears of being swallowed by a big black government hole creeping into her mind.

"I don't know, ma'am. My orders were—"

"To evacuate, I know. How are things out there?"

"Crazier by the second."

The doors opened, and it all became a blur of halls and turns until they reached the east garden. She had been expecting a military helicopter but got a standard white and orange emergency one. It didn't much matter, since she wasn't going to stay behind to face an angry mob. For all she agreed with them, she doubted they'd hear her long enough for her to claim her innocence and prove it.

A line of anti-riot operatives stood in the garden, making sure they could go straight to the helicopter. Although no rioters or news cameras were there, she could hear them, just right around the corner, clamoring for justice for the merman and for wildlife, and who knew what else.

The helicopter's rotors were still going strong when she reached the entrance, and she instinctively ducked while pushing the gurney. Under the dark blue material, Ray hadn't moved one bit. She placed her hand over his shoulder, while the guards and the officer helped get the gurney in.

Inside, a man wearing a white helmet and an orange suit—the helicopter's EMT—helped her in, and with practiced ease picked up the gurney and pulled it into the helicopter's belly. The anti-riot guy and guards got out of the way, and with one final push, the EMT closed the door faster than anyone could say *mob*.

Ray wasn't even properly secured before they were lifting into the air, and Gwen gripped the first thing she could to avoid falling on the floor, sending an evil eye to the pilot. These people were in one hell of a hurry.

Handing her a pair of headphones, the EMT signaled her to put them on, the noise getting worse by the second. He secured the rails of the gurney then uncovered Ray. He looked awfully uncomfortable on the too small gurney, and she wanted to snatch the cover from the man and put it back in its place.

"Dr. Gaston?" he asked over the headphones, looking at her instead of the merman.

"Yeah! Where are you taking him?"

"Well, we're taking him home," the man said with a smile, his hand reaching for Ray's shoulder. *Exhilarated* didn't suffice to describe Ray's look at this stranger.

"What?"

She turned to look at the back of the pilot, then at Ray, and then at the EMT, fear and hope colliding in a melting pot in her stomach. The man was giving Ray another set of headphones.

"Dr. Gaston, it's okay," he kept saying. "We really are taking him home. We're about to descend in two minutes, so we can change vehicles. A helicopter is terribly traceable."

"Gwen?" a tentative voice said in her ears, and she turned, stunned, to see Ray. His voice, raspy and weak from so much disuse, was the best sound she'd ever heard. "I'd like you to meet my father, Julian Brooks."

35

Rebel

The inevitable consequence of too much water was a bathroom trip. The Cafeteria had never been meant to hold a large contingent of people, and the three stall, one mirror bathroom was proof of that.

The guards had stayed out, while Andrew waited for Scott to finish washing his hands. The kid reached for a paper towel, then froze.

"Is everything okay?" Andrew asked, getting worried. After all, who knew if there were any lingering side-effects from the sedative, the first shift, or whatever surprises merfolk brought with them. Scott shook his head slowly, then cursed. He placed both hands on the sink, still shaking his head.

"Scott?"

"They're getting Ray out by helicopter. They're asking me how far we are."

"What? Who? How?"

"Shit," Scott said. "They can't wait on the helicopter. They're sending someone else for me. Hell, we need to get out of here." Finally, he turned to look at Andrew.

"As much as I'd love the idea, we have four friends out there waiting to get you back to the south side. And how the hell do you even know this?"

Scott sighed in frustration, and finally let Andrew in on the secret. "Telepathy."

It was Andrew's turn to freeze in place; was the kid telling the truth, or just playing with him? *Of course, what else was I expecting with these people?*

"So, wait, you're talking with… Ray?"

"Yes. Here's the thing, I'm not worried about the guards. It's—look, those people are not going to let us pass," Scott said with a certainty that left Andrew clueless.

"What people?"

"The ones outside who think they're freeing a freaking whale. Going through them is not going to work."

"I'm glad you're not worried about our guards, but even if we managed to get rid of them, we don't have to go through the protesters," Andrew said, thinking on his feet. "We can wait for this to blow over. Maybe we should get you to the pool. No one would be able to reach you there."

Scott's eyes unfocused for a few seconds, and then he frowned. "Where the hell is the east garden?"

"How am I supposed to know that?"

"That's what I said!" Scott exclaimed, then combed his hair with both hands.

It was fascinating—or fascinatingly weird—to see someone have a verbal and silent conversation at the same time. It was like having someone on the phone, except he only got snippets from this side.

Scott cursed again, in a much more colorful, extended way, apparently unhappy with whatever he was being told.

"You know, for a thirteen-year-old, you have a pretty impressive vocabulary," he praised the kid, calculating how feasible it was for him to take down the four guards.

Not feasible at all.

"Screw this! Swimming in the ocean is a better plan than stashing me in a bathroom!"

"You didn't even want to shift a tail twelve hours ago."

"Yeah, how things change, huh?"

Scott turned around, clearly intending to follow his own plan, somehow imagining the guards would magically disappear.

"You're not going to even make it to the shore, let alone the ocean," he told Scott, who cursed once more.

"This is so stupid! I'm not going to stay here for Plan B!"

"Look, kid—Scott. We'll figure out where the east garden is, how does that sound, huh?"

"Like a terrible idea," Major White said, suddenly opening the door to the bathroom. And for one glorious moment, Andrew saw himself hitting the living hell out of that man's face. "Colonel Sawyer has just taken command, and he's looking for any excuse to shoot you down."

Against all his bravado, Scott stepped back, his eyes narrowing down.

"You—you already shot me!" Scott said between clenched teeth and clenched fists. For one nanosecond, Andrew was sure Scott was going to jump and bite the man's head off, so he put himself between them.

"Okay, we all want what's best for Scott here, right?"

278

"I'm not going back to that tank," Scott said, his eyes unwavering. If merfolk could shoot killer rays through their eyes, White would be one smoking piece of meat right now.

"What's in the east garden?" White asked Andrew instead, completely ignoring the little bulldog ready to attack.

We don't even know where the east garden is, Andrew thought, slightly turning to look at Scott to make sure the kid wasn't losing it. "It just seemed a good idea to get out of the way from all the mob people."

"It's not a potential mob that should worry us. Police are already dispersing them as we speak. But Sawyer is an entirely different problem." He looked at Scott. "What happened to you was a misunderstanding."

"I'll show you misunder—" Scott said right on time for Andrew to catch him. Thin and short as he might be, the kid had strength, and it surprised Andrew how much strain it took to keep Scott on this side of the bathroom.

"I think you should leave," Andrew told White.

"I think we should *all* leave," he answered, but before he could elaborate, a strange noise interrupted; something big had fallen outside.

Frowning, White opened the door, just to find a man in full anti-riot uniform in front of him, pointing a pistol.

"It's okay, I'm Majo—"

The man shot without hesitation, and White recoiled against the stall, eyes wide.

"You shoot one of mine, I shoot one of yours," the man said, and still pointing at White, he came closer to the door. Caught in the moment, all Andrew could do was turn so Scott wouldn't be shot.

"He's a child!" Andrew shouted, his back to the stranger, but all he heard was Scott's muttered words.

"I'm not going out like that."

The shot Andrew was waiting for never came. Instead, out of the corner of his eye, he saw the man checking up on White, now sprawled in the bathroom entrance. He placed his gun in its holster after a few seconds.

"Let go," Scott said, tired, but Andrew refused.

Standing up, the man turned to look at Andrew, then sighed in the way people do when they have hard choices to make. "Mr. Summers, you have our gratitude for all you did for Ray, but I'm afraid we're running out of time to leave."

It took Andrew a couple of seconds to understand the ever-changing situation he found himself in.

"You're the one who's coming for Scott," Andrew said, feeling slightly stupid for stating the obvious.

"Yes, can you let me go now?" Scott said, and Andrew immediately released him.

"Did you just—" Andrew said, going over to White. The man might have chosen wrongly, but he didn't deserve to die. Outside, the four guards lay unconscious on the floor.

"I knocked them out. White is the only one I actually shot, with the exact same sedative he used on Scott. Call it poetic justice, if you like."

The man—or was it a merman?—unzipped something on the front of his protective gear. A black plastic bag came out, and he handed it to Scott. The kid ripped it open without enthusiasm, just to find a t-shirt and shorts, presumably his size.

"What are you planning to do?" Andrew asked, looking at the man and then at Scott. With a deep sigh, Scott displayed the front of the t-shirt: *SAVE THE MERMAID!*

Scott was going to perfectly blend with the people outside, no question about it.

"This is so demoralizing on so many levels," the kid said, while Andrew choked on his laughter, which he tried to pass as coughing.

"Hurry up!" the man said, turning to look outside, then back at them. "There's only so much time between getting Chris out and them figuring we're still here."

Chris?

Muttering unintelligible curses—because what else would Scott mutter if not curses—he rapidly changed out of Andrew's oversized clothes and put on his protester's wardrobe.

"This better work," Scott said as he turned around, presenting his wrists on his back. Without losing a beat, Scott's savior placed handcuffs that looked too big for a kid, ruffled Scott's hair, and turned him around.

"Let's put this mouth of yours to good use."

* * *

"I've just left Gwen moving Ray out to the helicopter," Higgs said, rushing into Nathan's office.

280

"You did what?" Nathan said, the cellphone pressed against his ear almost slipping from his hand.

"The evacuation," his friend said as if it was an obvious answer.

"No, no, I'm not talking to you, ma'am," he said, politely. "But it seems I'm having another crisis here. Let me call you back in two minutes." He hung up on the president of the UN Committee to give Higgs his full attention.

"What the hell are you talking about?"

Higgs recounted how they prepared for evacuation just in time to be told to leave by an officer.

"As far as I know, Ray's already airborne."

"But I didn't send for a medevac."

Nathan felt his pressure going down at realizing Sawyer or White had just taken Ray away. He reached for his phone, looking for Diana's number; he carried on speaking with Higgs. "White said the evacuation protocols were just for non-essential staff to make sure they wouldn't start babbling to cameras outside, so I thought it meant he had no desire to move Ray or Scott. I had my doubts about how much danger those protesters represented, but he's the one charged with security."

The number went straight to voicemail.

"Damn it! We can't just lose Ray!"

"Wait, Nathan, hold on. Gwen was with him."

As if it was a ray of sunlight, he called Gwen Gaston with an adrenaline rush, just to be deflated by yet another voicemail.

"She's not answering, either."

"Well, then, let's go to the source, see what White says. After all, this is a UN mission."

"Like he's going to apologize for whatever kidnapping they do…"

When the third voicemail met him, Nathan cursed. "What the hell is wrong with my phone?!"

"Easy, Nate. We'll figure this out. Ray can't have just vanished."

Storming into the room, one very red, very furious Major Sawyer practically shoved Higgs aside and went face to face with Nathan, the four soldiers escorting him choosing to stay right outside the door.

"Where are those creatures? *Where?*"

His breath was uncomfortably warm, but those words brought with them what three empty phone calls had not been able to do; they gave him hope.

"*Those creatures?*" he asked, moving slightly back.

"Don't play the fool with me, Doctor."

"I can honestly tell you I've been chained to my desk for the past twelve hours. I've just hung up on the UN Committee after a two-hour conference. I have absolutely no idea what you're talking about."

And the amazing thing was, he really did have no idea what was happening right now, except Sawyer was losing.

"I'm getting them back and you'll wish you've never set foot in this place," Sawyer practically growled. "You're not leaving until new order."

"You can't keep us here—"

"Watch me."

Sawyer stormed out the same way he'd come in, the door shutting with one loud bang. Higgs winced.

"What do you know," his friend said with a smile. "He didn't ask if I knew where Ray was."

Nathan chuckled, feeling the adrenaline leaving his body. Sitting down, he let go a long sigh. "He said *those creatures*, Higgs. He lost Scott, too."

"Well, we have two mermen, one doctor and one Major missing. D'you think Andrew knows what's going on?"

When that particular call also went to voicemail, Nathan was more than expecting it. "It seems everyone who knows something is unable to answer their phone," he said, watching the screen go black.

A breaking news notification chimed in, as so many had during the day. "Do you think they are safe?" he asked, swiping the screen to read the notice.

"I don't know. But Ms. Lombardi would be able to tell you, right?"

"If she still wants to talk to me. I might just have been used to turn the camer…" he trailed off, focusing on the article at hand. "What the hell… is that Scott?"

Intrigued, Higgs joined Nathan as he hit *play* on the news video. Met with a wall of protesters, a police officer in full anti-riot armor was dragging a teenager cursing so much the censuring beeps could barely keep up.

"As you can see," said a reporter, slightly wincing once the camera refocused on her. "A teenager boy made it into the facility. Several officers warned protesters to disperse and respect ORCAS's private property, and although the majority in here are onlookers, several activists have expressed their concern about—"

Nathan hit *pause* and rewound the video.

"Is it him?" he asked Higgs.

All Nathan had seen of Scott Hunter was a set of photographs supplied by social services, and the boy in the video was not looking at the camera, but…

"I mean, what kind of teenager doesn't wear shoes?"

"Not to mention the cursing," Higgs said, taking the phone and watching it more closely. "The guard who told us to evacuate was wearing the same armor. Could it even be the same one?"

Accessing the security files, Nathan went twenty minutes back in time to Ray's observation room, and clear enough, a man wearing the same protective gear evacuated them. Pausing the video, Nathan called to see all the cameras at once, twenty-four little squares appearing on-screen.

"What are you looking for? Higgs asked.

"For more. I mean, for more anti-riot police. They work in units, not solo."

They went back far enough to see the officer's movements, from the moment he entered ORCAS's first floor 'til the moment he left the building to carry Ray into a helicopter.

"He knew exactly where he was going," Higgs said. "The real question here is, does he play for the good team or the bad?"

"I think someone had better start answering their phones," Nathan said.

* * *

Matt kept checking the rearview mirror, the side mirror, the guy crossing the road, the woman talking over the phone. He could feel his heart accelerating each time a car passed by, just to find it wasn't them. He had parked the minivan rental some ten minutes away from ORCAS, and although the vehicle could easily accommodate ten, Matt felt claustrophobic all the same.

"Stop," the Squid said beside him, eyes glued to his computer. "They're coming. ORCAS has barely registered they've lost 'em. That gives us—sixteen minutes of advantage since Chris left, and about eight since Scott."

Eight minutes is barely a heartbeat, Matt thought with despair. Closing his eyes, he tried to reach for Chris, but he was already too far away.

"Did they make it to the boat yet?"

"Not since you asked ninety seconds ago. Look, they have already ditched the helicopter. There's no way anyone's going to pin them down in international waters."

The Squid kept typing, while Matt leaned his head back against the driver's seat. Outside, the day was perfect blue skies and sunshine, making this rescue even more daring. *We should've waited for night cover*, he thought for the millionth time.

He felt so useless; waiting was not his game. Alex was busy deleting the video evidence of their escapade as best as he could before Drake could put his hands on it, but the truth was they were hellishly vulnerable; this whole thing could still fall apart.

"Matt?" Alex said, prompting Matt's adrenaline to shoot through the roof.

"What? What's wrong?"

"Nothing, I was just thinking. When you left the house to come to Maine, you promised me that by the time this was over, I'd still have one brother, maybe even two."

Matt nodded, thinking back. That had been a lifetime ago.

"I mean, it does seem like you brought me back two brothers," Alex said.

"I think it's too early to say that," Matt answered slowly. "We don't know what he wants or what the Council will decide."

An insistent knock came on the window, scaring the hell out of Matt.

"Open the damn door!" Drake said, still donning his police disguise. Automatically, Matt reached for the master lock button and did as he was told.

The last time he'd seen Scott, he'd looked like a kid on a mission. A little wild, a little rough, but clearly under control. None of that had changed, except now he looked even wilder, rougher, and giving Drake a run for his leadership.

"What the fuck are you looking at?" Scott said as Drake closed the van's door, the four mermen free to go.

"Matt," Drake said, clearly not understanding why they weren't moving.

"Right, sorry."

Even if he wanted to speed out at 200 miles per hour, the last thing they wanted was to be stopped by real police.

"There's a backpack right beside you," Alex told Scott. "There are clothes and shoes."

Without a word, Scott found it, opened it, and spilled the contents onto the seat. Drake had moved to the row behind, and he was equally shedding his clothes in favor of a better disguise.

Stopping at the last red light before the interstate, Matt watched Scott through the rearview mirror taking off his *FREE THE MERMAID!* T-shirt, just to remain motionless at the sight of his body. Emerald scales showed up in patches across his chest, a clear indication of how stressed out the kid was.

Realizing Matt was watching in the mirror, Scott's eyes hardened. "What?" he asked, covering himself as fast as he could with a plain blue t-shirt.

284

Matt raised his arm, letting the younger boy take a look at his own red scales patching up his skin. Surprised, Scott turned to look at Alex, who showed his own yellow scales emerging on his collarbone. They were all the same, then, scared shitless on a daring double escape in plain daylight, where one false move would bring them all down. Smirking, Matt pressed the accelerator, taking the exit and leaving this nightmare behind.

"Let's get you out of here."

36

Life Expectations

The vista from Ray's room was astonishing. Gwen guessed they were somewhere in upstate New York, with green trees everywhere, and the sound of a thousand birds chirping as the sunset devoured the horizon.

It's not Ray's room, Gwen corrected herself for the 100th time. *Christopher's.*

"What are you thinking?" Chris asked, startling her. She was used to his company, not to his voice. Since the moment they'd arrived some six hours ago, they hadn't been left alone until now.

"I'm going to have a hard time calling you Christopher," she answered, smiling. She'd been afraid the journey would be jarring for him, but one look at his sheepish smile and she knew this was where he belonged. Oddly enough, it wasn't beneath the sea.

"I'm having a hard time reminding myself I can talk now, too," he confided, looking small on the king-size bed, wearing an oversized sweater. He had filled it out three weeks ago, he had joked, which meant he'd lost more weight than Higgs had estimated.

They'd removed the cast and applied a gel, and Christopher's tail was now wrapped in dark sheets of a wet material. It turned out their tails didn't do well without constant submersion, and the cast had been suffocating the tissue. She and Higgs had suspected the damage but hadn't really known the extent.

"You should've told us we were hurting you," she chastised him.

"Honestly? I didn't think I was going to live long enough to care. I didn't want to think about it," he shrugged.

She looked at his tail, at his face, at his impressive bedroom, and chuckled. "You really are a fairy tale, aren't you? Are you sure you're not some sort of prince?"

"Just a regular merman, promise," he answered, crossing his heart. "Although—"

"I knew it!"

"Julian is a member of our Council, which is the closest thing we have to royalty if you like. Would it be better if I told you I'm adopted?"

"Wait, that part is true?"

From the moment they had abandoned the medical helicopter, she'd become a guest rather than the doctor during this journey. Every thought was about their next move, evading any detection, and moving under the shadows. But Ray's care—Christopher's care—had been taken out of her own hands and given into far more capable non-human ones. That meant she'd had six hours to kill, and half of that time had been spent reading about Julian Brooks on a borrowed tablet. Her phone had been left behind in the medevac back in Maine.

"Most of what's public knowledge about our lives is true," Chris said, looking at the ceiling. "My brothers and I are adopted."

"Your brothers are also mermen?"

He nodded, his eyes lost in some memory. "I'm having trouble reminding myself I'm really out of there," he confessed, frowning.

"Hey, it's okay." Sitting beside him, she placed her hand on his shoulder. "Ray, it's real. It's just going to take time for your mind to adjust."

He looked quizzical and she closed her eyes. This *Ray-Christopher* business is going to take time, she thought.

"*Christopher*. I meant Christopher."

"Call me Chris," he said. "Christopher's so formal."

There wasn't much about Christopher Brooks in the media—unlike his father, who'd appeared in hundreds of articles. Here he was, a young man who had traveled the world, attended prestigious universities and owned a yacht bigger than Gwen's apartment. She still had to piece together the news about how he'd been "lost and found" last week, but it never seemed the right time.

"I've so little information about you, you know?" she said, thoughtful. "I told you my whole life while we were there, and now we're here."

"Ask away. Now I can talk to you, I'm never going to shut up!" he laughed, and then flinched. "Just... don't say anything funny."

"Funny? I'm dying to know everything! From the moment you arrived at my OR, I've been picturing castles under the sea and if you wanted raw fish and how the hell do you change into legs?"

He winced at the fish reference. "Hell no. I thoroughly hate seafood. And, no castles under the sea, not exactly."

"Not exactly? Now this is worth the cloak and dagger!"

288

A knock on the door interrupted them, and Julian came in. She didn't know how to act in front of this man and fleetingly wondered if it was inappropriate to be sitting on his son's bed.

"I've just talked with Drake, they're a couple of hours away," he informed his son. Gwen had been hearing about this Drake person all afternoon, surmising there were still some loose ends that this man had to tie up.

"Now, Dr. Gaston, we've several matters to discuss."

Oh. And what do you know? I'm one of those loose ends.

"There are no words to describe how thankful we all are that you helped my son. Chris trusts you a great deal, that's why we're being so open about ourselves around you."

"I didn't do this alone," she told Julian, then turned to Chris. "A lot of people were worried about you, even if you never saw them."

"We know," Julian answered. "Now, the alibi we're giving you is that we kidnapped you all the way to the Canada border. We can have you back at your home by tomorrow night if you wish to rest tonight."

"You kidnapped me? I'd rather say I stubbornly stayed by your side." That was how it had happened, anyway. Julian had told her to stay behind with the helicopter, but she'd refused. Who knew what questions any mer-doctors would have about Ray's condition?

Chris smiled.

"Okay. We released you and you stubbornly stayed. Once you were sure Ray was going to be okay, you asked us to let you go. As far as you know, we're somewhere in Canada."

"That's it? You're just—you're just going to pretend this never happened? I'm supposed to go back to my hospital and pretend nothing's changed?"

"Oh, I doubt very much your life's going to be the same, Dr. Gaston. There's a whole world out there, hungry, searching for answers. The UN Committee's going to release a joint press conference with ORCAS in two days. They'll say Ray died due to his many injuries; as far as the world is concerned, he never woke up from the coma he was found in. It saves everyone a lot of problems, including the Pentagon. No one wants to publicly explain how they lost a merman, and who's responsible."

There were too many questions, too many unknowns. "What exactly do you want me to say?"

"Everything that happened until the point Chris woke up. Become a public figure of what happened at ORCAS and they won't be able to make you disappear. You'll have Brooks Inc. legal department's resources at your disposal to weather this storm, Doctor. We won't leave you alone."

She thought about Nathan, Higgs, and Andrew. She thought about the hospital staff and about how Bill Shore had betrayed Ray by giving that conference. She thought about Christopher and Julian Brooks, people with more money than she'd ever made in a lifetime. And she thought about life before a merman landed on her hands, bleeding and unconscious.

No, life was never going to be normal again.

"Well, since it doesn't look like I'm getting my old life back, I want to know everything. And I mean *everything*."

* * *

Alex yawned as if there was no tomorrow, the screen blurring for a moment. He'd been fighting sleep for a couple of hours now, but there was so much to do, and so little time.

Sitting beside him in the minivan's middle row, Drake intently worked his way around traffic videos, deleting each appearance of their minivan through the long journey south to upstate New York. They had changed cars three times crossing interstate lines, somehow making a four-hour trip into eight hours. He bet neither of them would sleep tight until a month had passed.

Every now and then, Drake would stop typing and just take a look at the back seat, where Scott had finally fallen asleep. An AMBER alert had been issued thirty minutes after they'd escaped, one more reason to be careful on their trip home.

"How is he?" Matt asked from the driver's seat.

"Still asleep. Listen, guys, it's going to be a rough few days for both him and Chris, but it's also going to be a few rough days for you too. You're expecting to pick up where your lives left off two weeks ago, but the truth is, a lot's changed. The world knows we are real. At least two humans know who we are, and the government knows Scott's face, not to mention a way to detect us. There's a very real possibility we'll have to adapt in unexpected ways."

Alex closed his laptop and looked at Matt through the rearview mirror. Why did he feel so depressed when they should be celebrating?

"Chris is home," Matt said. "That's all that matters right now."

"Give your brother time, okay?" Drake warned, looking at Matt, then at Alex. "He's still your brother, but he might have changed... in some ways. He's going to crave normality, but don't act as if nothing's happened. If he wants to talk, listen. If he wants to talk about anything else, listen, too. With Scott, we'll have to play it as it comes. He's been used to a very different life, and we have no idea what he wants."

Drake's phone chirped with a message, and he started a text conversation important enough that he'd curse under his breath every now and then. Outside, dense woods met Alex's eyes, along with a road familiar from many summers and winters spent at the lake house. He dreaded the thought that life was over now.

He wondered how much Chris might have changed. What parts of the old Chris had been left at ORCAS that would never come back? What if he wouldn't smile anymore? What if he'd have to be living a paranoid life from now on, always looking over his shoulder?

He leaned his face on the window and watched the world passing by, hope and worry fighting for the upper hand. He must have dozed off at some point because he was startled awake by a strange feeling. Warm and welcoming and— and familiar.

Hey, Squid!

Chris! Chris! Chris! He couldn't stop saying his brother's name, getting out of the car before it even fully stopped in the garage. He didn't stop to greet his father, he didn't even wonder at the woman in the hall. He zoomed past everything and everyone, opening the door to his brother's room.

"Chris!" he yelled with a mixture of happiness and desperation, and would have pretty much jumped into his brother's arms if Julian hadn't stopped him by holding him by the waist.

"Careful!" his father chided, while Chris laughed. He laughed in the same way he always had: deep and full of life. "Don't hustle the bed, and mind the IV, okay?" Julian said, gently putting him down.

"You're here!" Alex said, panting. He hadn't known the size of the hole Chris had left when his mental presence had disappeared, and having it back left him giddy.

"Come here, little brother."

And he did. A bit awkwardly and clumsily, but he managed to get over to his brother's embrace. He wanted to tell him a thousand things, a *million* things. He wanted to thank him for not dying, for fighting through. He wanted to brag about how he'd hacked more servers in the past two weeks than he'd managed in the past two years and to tell him he was sorry for thinking Chris was going to die. Most of all, he wanted to stay here forever.

"Hey, it's okay," Chris said, with the same warmth that was all Chris.

"Don't you ever do that again!"

"Trust me Squid, never."

* * *

Matt fully parked the minivan, and slowly let go of the wheel. By the time the Squid had reached Chris on the second floor, Matt had managed to turn off the ignition, killing the headlights, the air conditioning, and the radio. He was so acutely aware of everything that he felt overloaded as if even the wrong color would shatter him.

He was a mess.

Drake closed his laptop and turned to look at Scott's sleeping form.

"We have to get him out. Maybe he'll want to eat something."

Matt watched as Drake maneuvered Scott into a sitting position and, after a few attempts of gently waking him up, had ended up carrying him into the house, all limbs, and no consciousness.

Hey, Matt... Chris said with his usual self, while Alex chattered his ear off.

Hey... Matt answered, swallowing hard. He didn't know why, but he suddenly felt like lead, like he was never going to get out of this car.

"Need any help getting things settled?" Julian asked from the front door, curious.

"I—I don't..." he trailed off, swallowed, and finally moved. "I don't think so, thanks."

Getting out of the car was the easy part. Standing up on his own was an entirely different affair.

"Hey," Julian said, walking to him and extending a hand for him to lean on. "It's okay. Your brother's here, you are here."

"Is he?" Matt asked in a strangled voice. "What if—I mean, what if I reach that room and he's not there? What if I wake up and realize nothing's changed?"

He'd been driving for eight hours knowing something was going to go wrong. Drake had needed to clean their digital prints, and Alex had helped. But all Matt had done was drive, endlessly, looking right, left, back, front, up, and

292

maybe even down. It couldn't have been that easy; maybe they were still being followed. Maybe this time, it wouldn't be just Chris but his entire family.

"Matt?" Julian said, loud, which meant he'd probably said it a few times. "It's over."

He looked at his father, unable to process those two words.

"You always believed your brother was coming home, and now he has. You always knew, and I'm so sorry I didn't see it that way in the beginning. You were right, Matthew. You were so right."

Matt wasn't sure if he reached for his father, or if his father embraced him first, but having Julian to lean on was exactly what he needed the most. In those arms, he let go of the fears, of the tension, of the doubts. He let go of the past two weeks from hell and for once, he had the crazy idea that maybe things were going to be okay.

Holding to that thought, he followed the Squid's footsteps and ran, taking the stairs two at a time, barely acknowledging Chris's doctor as he passed right beside her. The door was already open, and he saw his two brothers talking on the bed as if everything was normal again.

Chris looked at him then, his grin lighting up his face.

"Matt!"

He felt tears forming in his eyes. Chris was so thin, purple bruises on his head starting to turn yellow and green. An IV hung by his night table, and his wrapped tail—so out of place on a bed—perfectly hid the hideous cut that had made his rescue so difficult.

He saw all that, then blinked it away.

"Chris," he whispered, feeling his cheeks give away to a smile. It felt so alien, so forbidden to smile, but he couldn't stop. "Chris!" he yelled this time, running to his brother's side.

"Hey brother," Chris said as they embraced.

"I always knew you'd come home," Matt whispered. "I always knew, I always knew." He kept repeating the words, feeling tears slipping away.

"I'm so glad at least one of us knew that," Chris joked, letting him go.

Wiping his tears away, Matt smiled. And for the first time in ages, he felt happy.

* * *

Scott woke to the sound of laughter. He sat up in an instant, trying to get his bearings. He was sitting on a bed, in a dark room, and laughter was coming from somewhere nearby. Another room, maybe?

He tried to look around while his eyes got used to the darkness, enough that he could clumsily pat down a lamp until he found the switch; he was in a bedroom, all right. The left wall was made of glass, letting him see a wooded area. A clock on the far wall told him it was close to midnight. The last thing he remembered was changing cars somewhere in Vermont, arguing with Matt about French fries.

Well, we didn't get caught, he thought, looking for his shoes. He was still wearing the same clothes they'd given him after their escape, and he wished with all his heart they'd burned the *FREE THE MERMAID!* t-shirt.

Still sitting on the bed, he closed his eyes, letting his mind wander, getting a sense of how many merfolk were around. It was odd, but he felt thrilled at the thought he could sense others like himself, a sensation he'd all but forgotten after years of being alone.

Laughter came again, his mind following the trail to somewhere nearby. Matt's and Chris's minds were easy to single out, which meant the third had to be Alex's.

Further away, his mind met with two strong walls. He couldn't tell who was Drake and who was Julian—or even if they *were* Drake and Julian—but he instinctively knew these were adults' minds.

You're awake, Julian said with approval. *Maybe you'd like to join us?*

In the hall, light came from an open door on the opposite side, the origin of the laughter.

"Come on!" Matt's voice said with indignation. "You had a personal massager!"

"Masseur!" Chris and Alex corrected in unison, and Scott chose that moment to pass by unnoticed. This was their reunion, and he wasn't part of it.

The study was further away, and Julian opened the door before Scott reached it.

"Welcome," the man said, and Scott swallowed as he shook hands. He was taller than Scott had thought, and for better or worse, Scott was indebted to him.

Inside, Drake was checking something on his phone, then looked up at Scott. He felt absurdly conscious of the way he looked, what he was wearing, and the fact he couldn't go five words without cursing. He wanted to impress them all but didn't know why.

294

"How do you feel?" Julian asked as Scott took a seat on a couch.

"Fine," he answered, robotic.

"Scott," Julian asked. "How do you feel?"

Trapped. Scared. Helpless. Hungry.

"What's going to happen to me?" he asked instead. The men exchanged looks.

"We were just talking about that," Julian said. "We'll stay here until Chris can shift back into legs, maybe a bit longer. This will also give us time for your trail to cool down. It's hard to disregard an AMBER alert, and harder to get the government off your back."

"Hard, but not impossible," Drake chimed in. "A few changes here, a few changes there, and we'll get your identity replaced and your face out of their system. It's just going to require time."

"And after that?" Scott asked, looking at Julian, then at Drake. He wasn't interested in the immediate future, not really.

"We were hoping you'd choose between the three Council members who're raising children; Mireya, Aurel, and myself."

"Because you're the Council," Scott said, his heart racing. Of all the places to land, did it have to be the one his parents had warned him against the most?

"We are part of the Council, yes," Julian agreed. "It's our duty to look after you until you're twenty-eight and able to decide to live on the surface or go to the City. That's your right. But more than that, we want to welcome you as one of us. You don't have to run anymore."

"But—" Scott tried to talk, but the words got stuck in his throat. *But you're everything my parents despised.*

Standing, Drake looked down as if he could see something else. Maybe *someone* else.

"You are your parents' child," he said with approval. "They'd be so proud of you, Scott. The way you handled life, the way you've survived. Impressive. But no parent would wish their son to wander alone and in danger. Forget we are part of the Council, Scott. Forget for one second that it matters and remember you're one of us. You'd do us a great honor by staying here."

"What if I say no? Would you let me leave? Would you cage me like the City does?"

Drake chuckled and then turned to look at Julian. "What did I tell you? This kid is going to go places."

"I'm not a kid."

"Of course not," Julian said, diplomatically. "Tell you what. You don't have to decide this moment what you want to do. At the very least, stay until your name is wiped from the system. Then we can have this conversation again, see how you feel about us."

"I'll think about it," Scott said, narrowing his eyes.

"One more thing," Drake added, getting beside Julian. "Chris told us of your suspicions about your parents' disappearance, that you ran from one Roy Wallace not knowing if he knew about merfolk, but certainly he knew how to gain from their deaths. Once we've settled this crisis, we'll look into that."

"You'll bring that fucking bastard to justice?" This time, his heart slammed in his chest.

Julian and Drake winced at his chosen words.

"Yes," Drake said. "Whatever you decide, we'll take care of it."

It was one thing to understand staying with the Brooks was his best option, even against what his parents believed. But this—having things righted for his parents—this was monumental. Never in his wildest dreams had he thought it was possible.

"Promise me you'll find him," he said with clenched teeth. "Promise me he won't stay free in the world while I run from everything!"

With the most serious expression—with the tone with which he'd address an equal, not a kid—Julian came down to his level. "I promise."

And for the first time in a long time, Scott Hunter had a purpose.

37

Perspective

Each time Julian closed his eyes, he was back at the medevac, his heart racing, eyes fixed on the gurney inching its way to his arms. Each time his eyelids met, he felt so close yet so far from his son, that all he'd wanted was to jump out of that helicopter and get Chris out of harm's way.

He trembled at the memory.

Standing in the doorway, Julian watched Chris sleeping for the first time in his own bed. Gwen had counseled to leave the night lamp on in case Chris woke disoriented, and the warm light softened Chris's sharp features; he didn't look so thin, now, didn't look as if anything much was out of place.

Beside his eldest son, Matt and Alex slept, the king size bed accommodating all three. The sight reassured him all was well with the world, his three rascals back under the same roof.

Now the house had fallen silent, all there was to do was watch and plan for the future.

His perceptive ears caught sound in the kitchen below, and he turned his eyes to the clock on the wall. *Isn't it a little late for a snack?*

They're called midnight snacks for a reason, Drake answered, even if both knew it was past 2:00 a.m. already. Deciding his sons weren't going to disappear if he took his eyes off them, Julian walked down the stairs to meet his friend.

"You're sure you want to drive Gwen back tomorrow morning?" Julian asked when he opened the door. Drake was raiding the fridge for whatever food four teenage boys had left behind.

"Yes. We shouldn't leave Diana alone so long. Not if we don't want Mireya ready to hang us next time we see her."

"We need to talk about the City's decision," Julian said with a heavy heart.

"You mean, we need to talk about how we didn't give a damn about it?" Drake said, closing the fridge door with his elbow while carrying several items to the kitchen island.

When this whole thing had started, it had been reasonable to accept the Council's decision about leaving Chris's body to human curiosity. There was nothing to gain by rescuing a corpse. But once it became obvious Chris had a good chance to live, the Council was at a loss for how to solve the problem. And for the first time in a long while, they'd left the decision-making to the City, if only because this affected all surface merfolk and potentially the City itself.

It had taken the City the better part of ten days to reach an agreement—barely a blink of an eye when one thought about the enormous implications of any decision they could potentially reach—and they'd finally delivered their verdict to leave Chris with the humans.

"Their reasoning isn't exactly unfounded," Julian said. He needed to see all angles before deciding they were crazy—even if he'd already determined they were.

"Come on," Drake said, taking a sharp knife and slicing a tomato in two, then in four, eight... "They wanted Chris to stay behind as some misguided liaison between humans and merfolk. Do you honestly think if Chris had started to talk, those idiots at the Pentagon wouldn't have taken him into a black hole?"

"He barely knows anything," Julian said, opening the bread bag. Seeing so much food was only making him hungry.

"Exactly. Because he's still a minor. Who the hell was the genius who thought a minor could deal with interspecies talks?"

Julian sighed. "They probably thought it was safer since Chris couldn't tell them things he didn't know. They wanted to coach him through the talk, but..." Julian trailed off.

"No matter how you spin this, you already know the conclusion's the same; those idiots are crazy."

Julian smiled; there was no hiding this from his friend. Even Mireya had sounded dumbfounded when she'd delivered the news an hour before they executed their rescue plan.

"I'm just so glad we're here and they're three miles down there. There's a reason we left in the first place; they make bad decisions."

"They still have a point," Julian said after a moment, and Drake groaned.

"I can't believe you're still siding with them."

"Not siding, just... conceding. Now humans know we're real, and with the next migration wave so close, this would make it the right time to establish relationships."

"If we come clean with them they'll fry us up in pans and eat us alive," Drake said, his dark eyes serious. "We couldn't stop them knowing about us, but we sure don't have to make it easy for them to hunt us down."

"I'm not saying we make a grand entrance in Washington, but Chris already made allies, a UN Committee is already formed. We wouldn't have to start from scratch."

Drake sighed heavily, leaving his food and placing his hands on the table. "I know I'm going to hate myself for asking, but, what exactly do you have in mind?"

* * *

The last time Nathan had been in an interrogation was six years earlier, with an especially difficult customs officer. This had been much worse and more exhaustive, and the only reason he'd been let go right now was because the UN had intervened.

Getting out of the building in which he'd spent the last twenty-two hours was a relief. He needed a shower, a bed, decent coffee, something to eat. Not exactly in that order, but certainly all in the next hour. The sun made him squint, but he didn't miss the fact Diana Lombardi was waiting, leaning against the same rental in which she'd driven by him two days ago. She was checking her phone and hadn't realized he was watching, and he wondered if she was here to find out if he'd told them her true identity, or as part of the UN Committee.

If she thought you'd betrayed her, she wouldn't be waiting to be caught right in front of her enemies' lair.

"Nathan!" she said once he was close enough. "Sorry it took us a while, but it seems the Pentagon doesn't like to play nice when they lose."

She opened the driver's door and got in the car, expecting him to get in it too. He chuckled. He'd be an idiot if he didn't do it, but part of him still resented being left in the dark while all the action was going on.

Sighing, he realized his bath, breakfast, and bed would have to wait even longer.

"You could've told me," he said as he put on the seatbelt a minute later.

"I told you, you can't tell secrets you don't know. We didn't even tell Ray or Scott we were coming for them until we were inside ORCAS."

She started the car, and he turned to look back.

"We're not waiting for Higgs?"

She shook her head. "Lawyers took care of him and Andrew a few hours ago. You were the last to be released, so I yelled loudest for you."

"They told me you kidnapped Gwen. I didn't believe them."

"We did. I told Drake it was too risky, but he said if Gwen didn't come in the medevac, it would look suspicious. In any case, we released her three minutes later and she wouldn't go away."

He laughed absurdly loud at Gwen's antics, and with that felt the tension of the past two days draining away. "I can picture her chaining herself to Ray's gurney!" he said, still laughing.

"I bet," Diana answered, amused.

God, he felt underdressed, dirty, hungry, and too tired for coherent conversations. No wonder she was looking at him weird.

"I could've told them about you..." he pointed out, suppressing the last of his laughter, trying to get serious again.

"You could have," she said, smiling. "We kind of trusted you," she added with a wink. "But we are curious, what did you tell them?"

"Everything except about you, actually. How Drake confronted me, then let me go once he realized I wasn't the one who ordered Scott's shooting. So I came back to ORCAS to disable the cameras to prevent shooting more merfolk."

"Wise."

"Truthful. I don't want people shooting at you."

She chuckled, he didn't. "I'm serious," he said. "I don't want anyone shooting at you."

She looked at him, nodding acknowledgment.

"So Gwen's still with you?" he asked, wondering what answers she'd gotten that he wouldn't.

"No, Drake drove her back. She can tell you the story when you see her again. I'm not sure what the official version ended up being."

"How are they? I mean, Ray and Scott?"

"Adjusting, from what I've heard. But to be truthful, I've been busy with the UN. We're giving a press conference at ORCAS this afternoon."

"I know, they told me to stick to the script. Ray died of complications this morning, never woke up. Convenient."

"We thought so, too," she said, picking up speed. "Saves everyone the trouble of explaining. Plus, Ray didn't say anything, and everything you inferred from his behavior is pure conjecture."

"Like the fact he spoke English?"

"Exactly."

Nathan looked out the window, wondering how he'd gotten entangled in so many lies. White lies, black lies, green lies... whatever colors they were, they were necessary. He just needed answers—real ones, for once.

"So, what happens now?" he asked, his unshaven two-day beard scratchy and uncomfortable.

"Public opinion, of course. Conspiracy theories. Hearings. The fun part!" she said with mock enthusiasm. "The UN's denying any involvement in the second merman video, but that's not going to go away as easily."

"So it wasn't real?"

She took her time answering, turning left then stopping at a red light. "We made the video to get enough people to serve as a smoke screen."

"Ah, a real merman but not a real capture."

"You know, for a sleep-deprived mind, you're pretty sharp."

"Not really. I've no idea where we're going."

"Why? Maybe I'm kidnapping you," she teased, then sighed. "Look, this is a small payback for what you did, but it's a start."

She turned around a corner and went right into a hotel's parking lot; it was a very nice, fancy hotel, where everyone looked at Nate as if he was a homeless man intruding in their pretty world. Any fleeting ideas he might have gotten about a hotel room and a gorgeous woman alone died as fast as he saw Drake in the penthouse pantry.

"Play nice, boys," was all he received for a farewell.

Before it could get awkward, Drake shook hands with him—Drake's were cold hands as if Nate needed any more reminders he wasn't in human company.

"You trusted us when you had no reason to, Doctor," Drake said without preamble. "And you risked a great deal for a chance to sit down with us. The least we owe you is some answers."

Nathan swallowed his excitement in order to look professional, but his hungry stomach betrayed him.

"I'll call for breakfast while you take a shower," Drake added, not a trace of laughter at the interruption. So civilized. So surreal.

It was the shortest yet longest shower Nathan had ever taken. He skipped shaving in order to get a few extra minutes with Drake, and the smell of coffee seemed like overkill to his adrenaline-enhanced awareness—but he'd never say no to a coffee.

He found Drake waiting for him in the living room, breakfast ready as promised. Taking a deep breath, he sat down slowly, almost afraid of scaring away the only real source of information willing to talk. The smell of bacon and scrambled eggs threatened to send his stomach on strike if he didn't feed it, so he started to eat, a million questions zooming around his already excited mind.

"So, Nathan. What do you want to know?"

"I think the logical question to start with is what do you want?"

"It depends on who you ask. We're about 500 individuals on the surface, and each of us goes about our daily lives the same way you do. We have no great scheme other than to live. Beneath the surface, we don't even number ten thousand, and our ambitions are self-contained. We don't really care about humans in general."

"So you do live underwater."

"In a domed city. Don't get any weird ideas. We walk, we breathe air. And every once in a while, some of us decide to leave. Most go back to the City, of course, finding life on the surface too primitive and harsh. But for a few of us, this becomes home. We blend in, we learn, we live free of the strict controls of our society. With a little luck, no one will notice how cold we are or how much we love to swim."

"Primitive," Nathan repeated, thoughtfully sipping his coffee. "So your DNA isn't lying."

Drake smiled at that, pouring a cup of coffee for himself. "It's ironic, you know? If this had happened a century ago, you wouldn't have understood DNA to make the connection of our other-worldly origins. You're picking up speed, and for the first time since we arrived, we're getting interested in what humans are doing."

"Since you arrived, huh? That's gotta be an interesting story."

Drake stood up before answering, conflicted about what to say, Nathan guessed. Looking out the window to the ocean, it was hard to imagine this man wasn't really a man.

"Three thousand years ago, we came to your planet. Or rather, my ancestors came to your planet, about twelve generations ago for us. It didn't appear occupied from space, as you can imagine, and the truth is, we're good with water worlds. But finding you here gave us pause. We tried to make an alliance work for a time, but you were barely getting civilized and our leaders didn't want to interfere. In the end, we voted to leave."

302

"Strange way of leaving."

"You can't leave if your car has a flat tire. And you can't replace that flat tire if things like rubber and screws haven't been invented. So, since we couldn't leave up, we moved down, away from you. We've tried to rush you a few times during the past millennia, but it always ended in disaster, either for you or for us, and we're not that many to begin with. By the time I was born there was no interest in getting outside help, though I can't honestly say why. But, in a sense, we're not leaving yet, we're just… waiting. Waiting for you to get the right technology for us to use it."

Nathan had a vivid image of a bunch of NASA engineers dying to get their hands on whatever part of their city they could get. Flat tire or not, the things Drake knew could bring a golden age of technology for the human race.

"So, let me get this straight. You moved out of your city when we were pre-industrialized, but now we're getting interesting?"

"It started like a group of outcasts leaving a too-rigid regime," Drake explained, coming back to the couch. "But we can't be uncaring to our people, not when the answers are so close. Those of us who are up here invest in technology, we develop new materials. In fact, there are so many ways to fix our flat tires, all of them developed in the last 2000 years, but we have no way to test them. One wrong calculation, one wrong simulation, and we sink our city for real."

Drake gulped his coffee after the admission, and Nathan regrouped his ideas.

"We can't wait for you to get it right," the merman continued. "So we're helping you along this time around, without either end getting fried. In all honesty, we believe you capable of producing the parts we need in the next 100 years, maybe half that time if we give you the right push. And that, my friend, is a dangerous prospect. People in the City are restless. It's not easy to spend your entire life confined to the same golden cage. It was one thing when we knew the human world was uncaring and barbarian. Now you don't look so bad."

Nathan stopped cutting the bacon and looked at Drake.

"You're coming to the surface."

It wasn't a question, but he needed an answer all the same.

"Maybe," Drake said, uncomfortable. "Maybe not. We were told to leave Ray in your hands so a link could be established, but we didn't trust your government or your military, and quite frankly, Ray's too young for us to place this kind of responsibility on his shoulders. So we went ahead with the rescue, following our better judgment. But it doesn't mean the City doesn't want to establish some sort of communication, we just want to do it slowly, carefully, preferably without you holding one of ours hostage."

Funny how we go back to the beginning, Nathan thought as he asked the question again. "What do you want?"

"Don't dissolve your Committee, Nathan. Maybe not tomorrow, maybe not even in the next few years. But soon, we might find ourselves working together."

* * *

"In an unexpected turn of events, the UN Special Committee spokesperson and the Oceanic Research, Conservation and Atmospheric Society, ORCAS's head management, have released new information about the merman having passed away from his many injuries this morning. Details are being released on ORCAS's website, but they have both confirmed they went through every possible venue to resucita—"

Kate paused the video and narrowed her eyes. She'd been at the press conference an hour ago, and speculation was going wild.

"What I want to know, is how many people are invested in this conspiracy?" Jeff said, on the speaker.

"You can buy a lot of people when you're Julian Brooks," Kate answered. The amount of planning Julian Brooks had put into this was staggering, and she had the uncomfortable feeling she'd been one more pawn in his game.

"You can't buy this kind of commitment with the government," Ken said, her boss sounding calm and composed on her computer. "Someone screwed up royally and they're covering up."

"Well, if he died, you can't screw up worse than that," Kate pointed out. The key word here was *if* he had died, something she hoped wasn't true but had no way of proving. Yet.

"Maybe," her boss conceded. "Maybe not. Maybe they arrived at a compromise. You can buy that much with Julian Brooks' money and influence."

"But it would mean Brooks admitted his son's a merman," Kate said, visualizing her wall of truth and the connections it'd lead to.

"Hmm," her boss grunted. "Who benefits by saying the merman's dead?"

"The government doesn't have to give any more explanations as to what's being done to him," she said quickly, her mind filling with possibilities.

"No one gets access to him," Jeff chimed in. "That's going to piss a lot of people off."

"The UN loses control," Kate pointed out.

Kate sat up on the bed, now really getting into the story. "They wouldn't have anything to do with guarding a dead body."

"And most importantly," Ken said, "No one suspects Christopher Brooks if he suddenly starts giving interviews after his ordeal at sea."

"You're not buying he's dead, huh?" Kate asked, her thoughts going in the same direction.

"I'll believe it when I see the body," Ken said, laughing darkly. "The military's already classified it, and ORCAS has promised to share test results, not actual samples to do more testing. If you have nine feet of merman, that's plenty to share around with the scientific community."

"But why would the government let Christopher Brooks go?" Kate asked, thinking about Julian's steely eyes. "What kind of deal could Julian possibly do to set his son free?"

"That's the question," Ken said. "Something went down between the *powers that be*, that not only got the media looking somewhere else, it threw off whatever connections there were between Brooks and the merman."

"Where does that leave us, then?" Jeff asked.

"Exactly where we were two days ago: we know the merman's identity, we just can't prove it. Not yet, anyway." Ken's words sounded like Kate's inner voice.

If she was going to be honest, she couldn't fault Brooks for playing her, but if he thought she was going to drop this, he'd better have another thought coming.

"We'll keep looking, boss. We have our attention on the doctors and personnel who treated him, while simultaneously covering Christopher Brooks' recovery. And once the dust settles, we still have that long-term arrangement Brooks spoke about."

"He didn't exactly sign a contract," her boss warned.

"He did something better; he sent me a video. He knows we can't prove it, but also knows we can make enough noise to be a nuisance. Let's keep the story, and let's see where this goes. Sure, we lost this one, but we're already ahead of everyone else."

"I'll say we keep looking!" Jeff added.

"I think that this is going to be huge," Ken said, slowly.

Next time you move, Mr. Brooks, we'll be watching.

38

Secret Keeper

The interesting part about having Chris confined to his bed was how the entire household re-arranged itself with him at the center. Movies, games, meals, talks, were all done in Chris's room.

Julian hadn't wasted time and had claimed the corner as his new office.

With Drake and Diana taking care of the fallout of Chris's escape, and with his sons getting to know Scott and collectively healing from the ordeal, it had been time for Julian to return to his CEO's duties after a two-week absence.

The volume of e-mails claiming his attention was obscene. Urgent meetings over urgent meetings piled up, while messages claiming to be the end of the world resolved themselves in mysterious ways.

On his bed, Chris typed away as if there was no tomorrow. He'd developed an appetite for reading everything and anything the media had on the merman story, a sort of obsession Julian was starting to believe was unhealthy. Chris was not yet allowed to talk to his friends or answer messages, but that didn't mean the internet was getting boring.

Sighing, he returned to his inbox, a message from his assistant catching his attention. *Watch maker keeps calling.*

Watch maker?

The least important detail for Sarah was the most welcome of all. Kate Banes had told him Chris's watch had been examined by an expert. As he read Sarah's e-mail about one Mr. Hans who kept calling day and night to report a stolen Brooks watch, Julian's heart became lighter.

Mr. Hans insists this is stolen property and he'd like to give it to you personally. I've instructed him several times that he can just send it to your office, but he insists it's too valuable. I'm concerned about what to do, especially if this is, indeed, your property.

Why, he hadn't spoken to Mr. Hans in ten years, at least, but he was more than happy to throw a party for getting the watch without having to bargain with Ms. Banes. She was a problem for another time, he decided, and happily answered the e-mail.

"You look happy," Chris commented, closing his laptop.

"I am! We're getting your missing watch without moving a finger. The expert the reporter hired used to work for us. He's giving it back thinking Ms. Banes stole it."

"No way! Technically, it was stolen, wasn't it?"

For the past couple of days, they'd filled in the details as best as they could with Chris, trying to map out all the potential loose ends left unnoticed.

"Not anymore. Now, you should sleep. It's already past midnight."

"Dad. I've been asleep so much I could probably stay up for two weeks straight." He winced as he moved the laptop beside him. "I'm so tired of lying down."

"Well, it's only going to be for a few more weeks, then you'll get your legs back."

"I don't think I'm going to change into fins for a very long time afterward," Chris said, looking at his tail. The color was slowly improving, but they still had a long road to go. His son had been at death's door, and the irony of it all was that humans had helped him through it.

"Dad?"

"Hmm?"

"I keep thinking I'm still there. I mean, I touch, and eat, and look at you and my brothers... but I still think I'm there. When do you think that's going to stop?"

"Give yourself time," Julian said, closing his laptop as well. "I don't think you know this, but the first day you were found, everyone thought you weren't going to make it. The Council and I decided it was too risky to rescue your body, and I tried to prepare your brothers for the inevitable. I wake every night reliving that decision, thinking I still left you there to die."

"We're both screwed up, huh?" Chris said, smiling. Julian smiled back.

"We'll get over it. You're here, I'm here, and this is over. That's all that matters."

Instead of the smile he expected from Chris, his son's face became serious, sad even.

"I'm so sorry, Dad. None of this would have happened if I hadn't gone diving alone. You warned me a million times. Granted, you were talking about diving, but whoever attacked me got me because of what I did."

308

"I don't think that mattered. Every single trail Drake was able to follow has gone cold. No one has claimed beating you. Whoever attacked you wanted you dead, your tail notwithstanding. They would have killed you on board your yacht, but I guess they thought throwing you to the sea was going to make it easier. And whoever did it, they're still out there. None of us is going to be alone from now on."

He picked up his laptop and walked to his son's bedside to kiss him goodnight. He hadn't done that in years, but now it was a daily routine.

"Dad?" Chris asked one more time as Julian stood up. He looked so thin, so fragile, yet so full of life. *His son, his Chris.* "I don't think I've told you, but when I was there, when I woke up every time, knowing there was no way I could walk away, I always knew you would come. I didn't know how, or when, but I knew you were coming. I'd have gone insane without you. Thank you, Dad. I'm never going to say it enough times, but thank you."

And in the embrace that followed, Julian finally believed the nightmare was over.

* * *

The Brooks Inc. building was impressive. Like many companies in the Silicon Valley, it was wide instead of tall, with pristine landscapes, spacious offices, and people walking around wearing anything but ties.

Andrew could picture himself working there, even if he wasn't sure why he was there, to begin with. He'd gotten a call two days ago, and he'd gathered these people wanted a gym, complete with a physiotherapist. God knew, working on computers all day led to harmful postures, stressed muscles, and painful backs.

"Mr. Brooks will see you now," the secretary said, with perfect white teeth and manicured hands.

"Wait, *the* Mr. Brooks?" he gulped. She kept her smile.

"Yes. He'll see you now. One of our associates will walk you to the meeting."

If he'd known he was about to meet one of the richest men on the planet, he would have worn a freaking tie. Once upon a time, he would have told himself this was only a job interview, not a life or death situation. But the truth was, after being part of something as big as meeting Ray, life had gotten a different color, a different perspective. Things that used to scare the hell out of him weren't that big anymore. Frankly, Ray was always going to be the hardest, best challenge of his life.

At some point during the six weeks since Andrew left ORCAS for good, he'd thought keeping the whole thing secret was going to kill him. But then, he only needed to take a look at the crazies on the internet to be glad no one knew his part in the merman conspiracy.

Since the official story was that Ray died before waking, Andrew had no place in the narrative. No physiotherapist had been needed, not for a comatose merman, nor for a foul-mouthed teenager who'd never existed.

The last thing he remembered was closing his eyes as Scott's rescuer shot him with a sedative, giving him the one and only alibi to claim he hadn't actively allowed Scott's escape. Technically, he really hadn't done anything, but given the chance he'd have driven Scott out in a heartbeat.

Most days, he kept busy with patients and helping out at the rescue center, essentially going back to his life before being called by the United Nations. He often wondered if Scott had been accepted into Ray's family—or if they even had family units, or if it was more an ocean thing, complete with school fish.

He imagined Ray rolling his eyes at the idea, with Scott telling him to go to hell.

The associate guiding him through the building reminded him of Ray. That had been happening a lot, on the streets, at the grocery store, on the beach; he'd see Ray lookalikes everywhere, sometimes a couple of Higgses and a few Gwens, too. But Ray's was the face he identified the most, maybe an unconscious need to reassure himself the merman was okay.

His guide walked him through several halls until they reached the gym. As interview places go, this was one of the most common for him to visit. One day, he would have his own private gym, with a secretary, and maybe a partner. One day, but not today.

"Mr. Brooks waits for you inside. Please don't hesitate to contact the main desk for anything you need."

Contact them how, Andrew was about to ask, when he realized if he was with a Brooks, the man would have that covered.

The first thing he noticed about the gym was the glass wall. It let him see green lawns, an artificial lake complete with ducks, and bushes in the shape of animals. The gym itself was well equipped, well kept, and empty. Several posters advertising the new gym experience probably meant the space hadn't been inaugurated yet—that, or knowing the boss was around was deterrent enough to come and share it.

Standing in the far corner, a young man stood with a cane, looking outside. He was wearing shorts, a sweater that looked too big, tinted glasses, and the ever-present earbuds owned by every gym lover. He looked far too young to be *the* Mr. Brooks, especially while he moved his foot following some rhythm, lost in his own world. But then again, it wasn't like Andrew had any idea what to expect.

His professional eyes took notice of the broad back, the thin legs, and the terrible posture. *Someone is in serious need of exercise.*

"Mr. Brooks?" he asked, walking towards him. "I'm Andrew Summers," he introduced himself, and the man turned to look at him, surprised, quickly removing the earbuds and shaking hands.

What do you know? Another guy who looks like Ray.

"I'm Christopher Brooks," he said with a smile, his handshake firm and a little bit too enthusiastic. His hidden eyes didn't betray what kind of first impression Andrew had made. "I've been looking forward to meeting you for a long time," he added, letting Andrew's hand go.

"Oh. The recruiter on the phone said something about a gym position?" Andrew asked, working out that this was probably one of the boss's sons.

"Well, not exactly. I'm looking for a personal physiotherapist. I had a diving accident a few weeks ago, and you came highly recommended," Christopher said with a smile as if he found it funny somehow.

"I'm sorry to hear that. What do your doctors say?"

"We've been trying to get it right, but I'm not making any real progress."

"May I see?"

Christopher sat down, wincing. He turned around and laid face down on a bench, allowing Andrew to see where the real problem was behind his legs: twin choppy white scars marred the skin above the knees. The strange thing was, even if the muscle was still healing, the skin was remarkably smooth.

"I'm hoping by treating my legs I can have the proper use of my tail back," Christopher added off handily.

"I'm sorry, what?"

And under Andrew's eyes, he saw tiny scales starting to form around the scar, white and then silver and then blue.

He moved away so fast he almost lost his balance.

"We believe a propeller cut me somewhere not far from the shore, or I wouldn't have made it into the beach. But we have no idea how to get the muscles back into shape." Christopher Brooks kept talking as if Andrew's soul hadn't just tried to abandon his body.

"Ray?" he whispered.

Slowly, the scales became skin again, and Christopher sat up, wincing yet again. He removed his glasses and piercing blue eyes met Andrew's hazel ones.

The world stopped as all the pieces fell into their right places.

"Is this really you?" he asked, unable to move. The hair was longer, the features thinner, softer. His ears certainly were human-looking, and to tell the truth, he'd never seen Ray smiling, but there was no doubt who was sitting there—

Sitting, for crying out loud!

"It's Chris, but I don't think Gwen is going to get it right anytime soon, either."

Blinking, Andrew crashed into reality. He closed the space between them and hugged his former patient.

"Good God, you're okay!" he said, while Ray—*Chris*—laughed. After a few moments, Ray's smile diminished.

"That cast cost me dearly. I was able to shift back about two weeks ago, but I barely have any strength—in any form."

Andrew looked once more at Ray's thin legs, thinking it over. "You were always the most interesting challenge. So, what we're going to do first—"

"Andrew," Ray interrupted. "Before you accept, you should know this might not be safe for you. There are people closer to the truth than we might like. I might make you a target."

"You mean the crazy people on the internet?"

"Yeah, those, too."

Andrew smiled. "Tell you what, Ray—Chris. I keep my mouth shut, you keep yours shut, and we just concentrate on getting your strength back. And while we're at it, you have to tell me what the hell is going on, Mr. *I'm-the-son-of-the-boss*."

"Deal."

* * *

"This is Red Team. We have visual on three targets, Sir."

Jonathan White had a new mission. In the three months since they'd lost their two mermen, a lot of interest and special attention had been given to how much these beings knew about the human world, what they wanted and what threat they possessed; and most importantly, how to use them.

While it was true the burden of the escape had been shared by him and Sawyer, instead of facing a dishonorable discharge and possible jail time, White had found himself navigating in stranger waters. The investigation following the escape had been wide and thorough, every second of video and every test result scrutinized by experts in at least six fields.

Because White was already part of the classified mission, it made sense to keep him on the field rather than out of it. His insights were of national security interest, his superiors had told him. They'd also said he liked facts over emotional reactions, and facts were telling a rather complex story.

Intelligence gathered from the twelve days Ray had been at ORCAS and the fewer than twenty-four hours Scott had remained a prisoner had started to paint a broader picture of what merfolk as a community were like.

White had never forgotten the *Chris* name Scott had mentioned. Once he'd finished with all 900 hits on his original search, he'd been at a loss on how to sort them out, or even if there was anything of value to begin with. And then, the results from the listening experiment had come back: Ray understood five languages and recognized a number of classical pieces. This had given White a different angle to tackle the problem.

He'd made a profile ignoring Ray's merman status: male, between twenty-five and thirty-five, white, well educated, athletic, and who answered to Chris.

The database had shrunk to three candidates, and only one looked close enough to be Ray.

"This is Green Leader," White said from the surveillance van. "What is your status?"

"They're leaving school right on schedule, Sir."

In the three months since the world discovered their oceans weren't alone, White had gathered evidence on Christopher Brooks. The fact that he'd disappeared for close to two months before his first public appearance had proven interesting. While they had waited for the adopted son, they had scanned everyone associated with him, including his brothers and father.

"No sign of any other."

Julian Brooks had come as a surprise. Half of White's superiors overseeing this mission had wanted to immediately apprehend him. The other half had wanted to study him in his environment, and everyone knew taking on one of the richest men on the planet was going to be messy. The knee-jerk reaction was understandable, but cooler heads had prevailed, and White's new mission had been issued.

Gathering intel about the Brooks family had seemed easy in the beginning; public and legal records were scrutinized to the last detail. Even the way they avoided the tabloids and the press in general, was significant. Questions abounded on how merfolk units worked, tracking the disappearances of the young Brooks' biological parents into dead-end trails.

The more White learned about them, the more questions he had. They had constructed their lies well and kept to themselves. The Unit suspected Dr. Gwen Gaston and Andrew Summers had become part of their inner circle, but they had far more interest on seeing those bonds flourish than in cutting them loose.

Besides the Brooks, the Pentagon had been unable to find any other merfolk. Had they just arrived on the planet a few decades ago? Did they have an underwater base and were waiting?

If so, where were they?

"Thank you, Red Team. Green Team, get ready. 'Ray' must be just about to leave his therapy session."

Beyond the family, Brooks Inc. was the leader in commercial space technology and oceanographic equipment. Several military and government contracts were deeply entwined with what the merfolk company did, not to mention how far and wide it really was.

On the surface, this was a lucrative company that had diversified its assets and was prone to investing in new technologies. Digging into it, it looked like more and more technologies were focusing on propulsion systems and advancing computer power. All Brooks Inc. personnel were under surveillance because one of those scientists had to have their temperature below normal.

"Ready, Green Leader."

On the thermal monitor, White saw Julian Brooks leaving his building, talking over the phone. His cold temperature made him easy to target among the multitude of people walking around him. He was on his way to pick his son from Mr. Summers's expert hands; at least four people in the Unit were closely following Christopher's recovery.

So many questions, so little time.

One day, White would sit down with Julian Brooks, either with the intention to detain him or to discuss an agreement proposal. But for now, White watched from the shadows, learning about his potential ally—or future enemy.

314

Epilogue

Neil Thompson's life had changed in a multitude of ways since the day he'd found an unconscious merman during one of his daily walks down on the beach. For the past three months, he'd been called a liar, a hoax, a fake, an opportunistic bastard, and everything in between. And then, eventually, he'd been called a hero, an exceptional man who in the face of the fantastic—of the impossible—had done the right thing and had saved a life.

The statement was always a bittersweet moment, because ultimately, the merman had died. Half the people didn't believe that, but Neil honestly thought that was the best outcome to a creature that shouldn't exist in the first place. Merfolk were not meant for captivity, and he would never be able to sleep tight at night knowing he'd pulled that being out of the sea and placed him into a cage.

"Mr. Thompson," Julian Brooks said with an honest smile. "It's an honor to have you with us."

Of all the strange meetings, and all the celebrities he'd met in the short time since finding himself in the spotlight, getting invited to receive a special award from Julian Brooks had to be in the top five.

"Mr. Brooks, the honor is all mine," he said automatically. The man's tall frame and broad shoulders were intimidating, and Neil wondered for the tenth time why the CEO of a billionaire company had any interest in meeting with him. No press was allowed to attend this event, so he wasn't after a front page headline.

"I believe Sarah explained the protocol?" Mr. Brooks asked.

"Short speech, nice dinner, nicer watch," Neil summarized, making his host laugh.

He liked that laugh. He liked Mr. Brooks, even if he had cold hands.

"We're about to start, your seat is with my family," he indicated, and one waiter took him to where three teenage boys and a young man were discussing the finer points of free diving. The things the rich talk about, he mused, while Julian Brooks took the podium. Less than thirty people were gathered, apparently five of them being awarded this prize as well.

"It's my great honor to be here tonight with all of you. This is a special night. We usually recognize people of the scientific community with this award, people who contribute to human understanding and betterment. People who dedicate their lives to the ocean. But from time to time, we're reminded that without the human spirit, without human compassion, the best discoveries, the deepest understandings, are worth nothing. This night, ladies and gentlemen, I invite Mr. Neil Thompson to receive this award for his courage, his decision, his humanity."

Neil blushed, standing to receive the watch amidst applause.

"I know you think you didn't do much," Julian Brooks continued as he gave him the award. "But that morning, when you stopped and didn't run away, you changed the history of this planet. We might never know how far and how many people you touched that day, Mr. Thompson, but it is with my greatest pleasure, with my greatest gratitude, that we in the Brooks family thank you for helping a being in need."

End of Book I

Moments

Bonus Chapter

1.

Toys decorated the entire room, from giant teddy-bears to remote control cars, from little green soldiers to miniature roller coasters. Yet the only thing ten-year-old Christopher wanted was the coloring pencils hidden in one corner. It would always marvel Julian years later, how Chris could be the happiest with the simplest of things.

2.

When Julian reached the surface for the first time, everything was chaotic: The air was too thin, the light too bright, the land too rough. Gone was the City, with its safety, its familiarity—and its predictability. He couldn't love it more.

3.

Sometimes, the strangest part of this family wasn't that they could turn their legs into tails and their skin into scales, but the fact that against all odds, they had found each other.

4.

The first time Matt saw a kid bullying Alex, he could've scorched the earth where he stood. Needless to say, there was never a second time.

5.

In the middle of the winter, the deserted frozen lake was all theirs to explore underwater. As long as Julian didn't find out what they were doing, of course.

Find more Moments at www.mnarzuauthor.com

About the Author

M.N. Arzú (1982) was born in Guatemala City, Guatemala, and fell in love with books at age nine, when her oldest sister translated The Chronicles of Narnia for her. Those books would set her on a journey of literature and other languages that continues till this day.

She graduated as a Graphic Designer, and she now feeds her creative world with equal measures of fantasy and science fiction, always seeking adventures in other realms.

Find more about her upcoming projects and Underneath's sequel: Undercurrent – A Merfolk Myth, by visiting www.mnarzuauthor.com.

Other Works by M.N. Arzú

The Librarian – A First Contact Story

Despite the rumors, the US Government has been able to deny First Contact with an alien race for decades, but with good reason: it hasn't happened yet.

When a strange signal comes from an isolated area in the forests outside of Seattle, they find that First Contact is not going to happen with big ships and grand world-wide messages. Aliens, it turns out, like to keep their existence quiet.

Breaking a great number of rules, Seattle's resident alien has come back from a quick trip to his home planet to tell his human wife the truth about himself. Even if he has to do it behind a glass wall and with the military between them.

The Librarian is a contemporary novel set in America and dealing with first contact with an alien species unlike anything else in modern science fiction.

The details and quality of the work will blow you away and leave you wanting more.

www.mnarzuauthor.com

Made in the USA
Middletown, DE
15 July 2017